SURRENDER TO PASSION...

"We're just . . ." She sighed and ran her fingers over the edge of his ear. "Kissing. Surely that can't be harmful."

"It could be." *To your virginity,* he wanted to add, but a split second later any and all vestiges of rational thought were lost as her hands drew his head back to hers, his lips to hers.

Emma.

He couldn't get enough, taste enough, feel enough of her. The barrier of her nightdress both excited and frustrated him . . . Impatiently he fumbled with the ties on the bodice and slipped his hand inside to caress her neck, her collarbones . . . the upper swells of her breasts . . .

He needed more.

"Emma," he said urgently, pulling his hand from the opening of her nightdress and cupping her chin. "I'm on fire for you . . . I want to know every inch of your body . . . inside and out." In the silence of the darkened bedchamber, his breathing was as rapid and ragged as his desire.

"I-I can't believe I'm saying this," Emma replied breathlessly, "but I want you to know every inch of my body, Ryan. I want to . . . know . . ."

Her unfinished words hung in the air between them . . .

DIAMOND WILDFLOWER ROMANCE

A breathtaking line of searing romance novels . . . where destiny meets desire in the untamed fury of the American West.

Diamond Books by Peggy Stoks

WILD WINDS
FRONTIER HEAT

FRONTIER HEAT

PEGGY STOKS

DIAMOND BOOKS, NEW YORK

This book is a Diamond original edition,
and has never been previously published.

FRONTIER HEAT

A Diamond Book / published by arrangement with
the author

PRINTING HISTORY
Diamond edition / June 1994

All rights reserved.
Copyright © 1994 by Peggy Stoks.
This book may not be reproduced in whole or in part,
by mimeograph or any other means, without permission.
For information address: The Berkley Publishing Group,
200 Madison Avenue, New York, NY 10016.

ISBN: 0-7865-0012-3

Diamond Books are published by The Berkley Publishing Group,
200 Madison Avenue, New York, NY 10016.
DIAMOND and the "D" design
are trademarks belonging to Charter Communications, Inc.

PRINTED IN THE UNITED STATES OF AMERICA

10 9 8 7 6 5 4 3 2 1

For Jeff
My love

ACKNOWLEDGMENTS

Once again, John and Susan Gross deserve my utmost thanks for the friendliness, hospitality, and always cheerful assistance they showed me while I researched and wrote *Frontier Heat*. Without them, and without John's extraordinary knowledge of the history of the Pine Bluffs, Wyoming, area, this book could not have been written. Special thanks, also, go to Mr. Dewey Edmonds, Mr. Alfred Reher, and Mr. Tim Cooney, for a five-star tour of the Texas Trail Museum.

Western military historian, archaeologist, artist, and all-around genius James Harrell is another person to whom I owe my gratitude. I'll never forget the tour of old Fort D. A. Russell, Jim, nor any of your fascinating tidbits of history. Thank you. (P.S. You are *never* boring!)

From thanks to geniuses I lead into praise of quiet heroes. Jan Grieser is one such quiet, unsung hero; so I will briefly sing her praises and tell you that she and her son Matt taught me more about Down Syndrome than I ever learned in nursing school or in my twelve years on the job. Thank you, Jan, for your good will and cheerful words, and thank you, especially, for opening your home and your heart to me, and for sharing so many of your tender, private thoughts.

Many thanks also go to Elaine Challacombe of the University of Minnesota's Wangensteen Library, to numerous employees of the Minnesota Historical Society, to Ann Nelson of the Wyoming Historical Museum, and to Becky Lintz and Margaret Walsh of the Colorado Historical Society. Also to be thanked for their assistance are Irish-born Dr. Flora MacCafferty and wonderful proofreader, Michelle McGlade.

And to my friends and family: Once again, I couldn't have done it without all your love and support. Thank you.

Chapter One

Little lies have a way of turning into big ones, Emma Louise.

With a quick prayer of apology to her mother, gone these past five years, Emma Taylor pulled her faraway gaze from the snow-covered roof of the graceful Italianate mansion next door and studied the words she'd written. Little lies? This letter of reference from a fictitious former employer was an utter pack of them. Two full pages, the missive was, written with her left hand so that the script would appear to be from the hand of a Mr. John Gilbert, the imaginary manager of an equally imaginary lumber camp.

It was a dubious accomplishment, indeed, for someone who rarely ever bent the truth.

But at this rate she would never finish the other letter, the letter of query. In a swish of yellow silk, Emma half stood from the leather padded stool and drew down the window shade to within a few inches of the sash, blocking her view of the dreary March day. Wrinkling her brow, she began to write on the plain stationery:

> To Whom It May Concern:
>
> I am writing in response to your advertisement for a ranch cook. I have taken the liberty of enclosing a letter of reference from my former employer, Mr. John Gilbert. Mr. Gilbert, I believe, has given you the explanation of my mother's illness, which was the reason for my departure from his employ.

What else was there to say? Her well of creativity had been drawn nearly dry with the other letter. Pushing aside her feelings of uneasiness at her mendacity, she picked up the pen and added, *I would be available to start immediately*, deciding it would be best to keep her comments in this letter short and simple. After all, Mr. Gilbert had gone on and on about her skills and experience.

Twenty-five dollars a month plus room and board, the small advertisement in the back of *The Saint Paul and Minneapolis Pioneer Press* had offered. It was almost too much to hope for. She sighed deeply and set the pen in its ivory rest, thinking of how, at a rate of twenty-five dollars a month, she'd be able to save even more than two hundred dollars in a year's time—and show her brother, Michael, she could more than meet every one of the ridiculous requirements he had set for her.

Never mind that she could barely cook; she was getting desperate. This job was a long shot, but if it came her way, she rationalized, it couldn't be too terribly difficult to learn to cook beans for a bunch of Wyoming Territory cowpunchers.

There had been one other promising lead last week, an advertisement calling for LADIES TO LEARN TELEGRAPHY, but when she'd applied for the position she'd been told the thirty-five to sixty–dollar per-month salary that had been listed in the paper was paid only *after* competence was gained. That could take months, the clerk had bluntly told her.

Over the past days she'd quietly explored all feasible opportunities for employment in both St. Paul and Minneapolis, finding only unappealing prospects and impossibly low wages open to her. Taking into account everyday expenses, she wondered just how a person was supposed to be able to make a living in the world.

Well, she was determined to do it.

After experiencing months of discontent with the pleasant but boring direction in which her life seemed to be headed, she'd finally come to terms with her restless and undeniable feelings to get out into the world and make some sort of a mark for herself.

There weren't any good reasons for her to feel this way, she knew. She lived in one of the most up-and-coming areas of St. Paul with her brother, Michael, and sister-in-law, Lucille, a warm and loving couple who had taken her in after the death of her and Michael's parents. In the past five years they had seen to it that she'd had everything she needed.

Why was it, then, that she wanted so badly to open her own business?

Just a small collectibles shop in downtown St. Paul, nothing on a grand scale. She'd worked out all the business details on paper and had found an absolutely perfect location for her shop on Third Street. The only problem was financial: she wasn't eligible to use any monies from her very substantial trust fund for another two-and-a-half years.

The way her father's will had been worded, Emma was not to come into the majority of her trust until she attained the age of twenty-five or until she married. Though she knew her current beau, attorney Jon Severson, a friend and colleague of Michael's, would be more than pleased to see their relationship progress toward the matrimonial state, she also knew he would not approve of her plans for a business venture. More than that, though, her feelings for Jon were only halfhearted.

As marriage was out of the question, her only other option was to seek a partial advance on her money from Michael. It was a perfectly reasonable request, she'd thought, never predicting the wedge this idea of hers would drive into her and Michael's relationship.

"You want an advance on your money so you can open what? A *collectibles shop*?" The incredulous look on Michael's face had quickly changed to one of unwavering opposition when he'd seen she was serious. He'd plainly and unapologetically told her her idea was hogwash. Though the unpleasant scene had occurred nearly two weeks ago, she could still recall the expression on Michael's face as he'd shaken his head and said, "Sorry, little sister, but you're not going to get a dime out of me for an idea like that. What kind of nonsense is filling your head these days, anyway? You've never been one to cause trouble."

Determined to turn his "no" into a "yes," she'd calmly repeated her request, offering to show him her business plan. To that he'd waved his arm about the elaborately furnished library. "Emma, look around you," he'd said with a sigh. "Father left us well fixed. Don't you know that you have everything you could possibly want? You don't have to work. Not only that, you have the interest of one of the city's most eligible bachelors. There are many women who would give their eyeteeth to be squired about town by Jon Severson."

"I realize that, Michael, but I want to open my own shop," she'd repeated firmly, not backing down. It had been a strange feeling, openly disagreeing with someone she'd always gotten on well with. Except for a few childhood squabbles, Michael had always been her protector and champion.

Dull color had crept up Michael's neck at her continuing insistence. "You'd be a fool to throw all this away, Emma, an absolute fool." He'd thrown his arms up in the air to emphasize his point. "So put an end to your foolish talk and let Jon court you," he'd concluded with strained patience. "Forget the business idea. Get married. Have a baby or two. That's what you really need."

"I'm sorry, Michael, but what I really need to do is start my own business," she'd responded, her normally large supply of patience wearing thin as well. On and on they'd argued, and finally, out of frustration, Michael had agreed to loan her the money, adding—or bellowing out, rather, by that time—several conditions that were so ludicrous that only a fool would comply with his terms.

"Fine, I'll give you an advance," he'd shouted. Normally an even-tempered man, it was rather distressing to see his neck veins stand out like thick ropes. Lucille, who had sat quietly throughout the entire exchange, watched her husband with an alarmed expression on her face. Emma doubted Lucy had ever seen him fly into a rage.

"But if I'm going to put up some money, so are you, Emma Louise," he'd continued, making his point by stabbing his finger into the air several times. "If you're serious about wanting to get into the business world, you can go out into the real world for a year and make your own way. *One year,* you hear? These are my terms: If, at the end of a year's time, you've managed to make your way and have saved, let's say, two hundred dollars to contribute toward your business start-up, I'll loan you the rest."

"Michael!" Lucille had gasped. "She can't do that!"

"Precisely."

Outraged by her brother's stipulations, Emma had also seen the meaningful, satisfied look he'd given his wife. The bluster had gone out of him then, and he'd said simply, "These are my conditions." Holding out his hands in a conciliatory gesture, he'd shrugged his shoulders. "May I conclude that we've heard the last of the matter?"

Not if I find some way to earn a blasted two hundred dollars, Michael Robert Taylor, Emma had vowed silently. *Not by a long shot.* The smug look Michael had given Lucille caused Emma's resolve to toughen then and there— she was going to find a way to earn two hundred dollars in a year's time.

To Emma, however, whose will had continued to intensify during the days after the confrontation with her brother, the prospect of finding such employment—lawful employment, that was—was looking rather bleak. Folding the two letters and inserting them into the envelope she'd already addressed, she arose from the stool and made a slight adjustment to her bustle.

If little lies turned into big ones, she wondered, leaving

the elegantly decorated second-story suite, what did big ones turn into?

"I'm so glad to hear you've given up the idea of starting your . . . ah, business," Jon Severson casually mentioned as he guided Emma up the front walk of her home. His breath was frosty in the cool air. "Michael mentioned your plans to me a week or two ago. A shop of some sort, wasn't it? I must say that I agree with him," he went on, not giving her a chance to speak. "It would have been too much for you, my dear. Why, a lovely, sweet, petite creature like yourself dealing with the unpleasantries of the business world . . . I'm glad you've forgotten it," he concluded with a wink and a debonair smile.

"Who said I forgot it?" she asked almost querulously, stopping on the snow-packed flagstone walk. Despite the pleasant afternoon she and Jon had spent viewing a local artist's work, his unknowing reminder of her failure to find lucrative employment made her hackles rise.

"Michael said . . . well, never mind what he said." He broke off, sensing, she guessed, that he'd raised a delicate subject. Raising his eyebrows, the tall, blond, blue-eyed attorney regarded her with another brilliant, gallant smile. "Forget Michael. I'd rather talk about how beautiful you look with your cheeks flushed pink by the cold." His gloved finger playfully touched the tip of her nose. "Or how much I'm looking forward to taking you to *One of the Finest* the night after next. Or, if you're in the mood, the Boston Ideals will be in town. . . ."

Emma mentally sighed, forcing a smile in return. What *was* the matter with her? Any other woman in St. Paul would swoon from a Jon Severson smile at this close distance. With his suave, urbane manner and his Nordic good looks, he was considered the catch of the town.

"*One of the Finest* will be . . . fine," she replied limply, disentangling her arm from his. "Until Saturday, then."

He caught and held her hand. "Don't be angry, Emma." Bending his head, he placed a soft kiss upon her gloved knuckles. "Things always work out the way they are supposed to, you know." Straightening, he touched his hat. "As much as I'd like to see you inside, my dear, I've got to get back to the office. Give my regards to Lucille."

Watching until she was safely inside the door, he gave a jaunty wave and climbed back into his carriage. Stamping her boots on the thick rug, Emma peeled off her gloves and had unbuttoned just half the buttons on her coat when she spied the letter in the wide, flat brass dish atop the foyer's side table.

Knowing that Mrs. Baumann, the morning housekeeper, always put Michael's mail in the library, Emma hurriedly finished unbuttoning her coat and boots. It could be a letter from her cousin Viola in New York, she told herself, trying not to get her hopes up, but this envelope was white, not powder blue, as Viola's stationery typically was.

Stepping off the rug, she walked briskly to the side table, careful not to slip in her stocking feet on the highly polished bird's-eye maple floor. She reached the table and swallowed hard, slowly picking up the envelope bearing the return address of Pine Bluffs, Wyoming Territory. So the M. J. Montgomery to whom she had addressed the letter was a woman, she thought with surprise, seeing the name "Mrs. Maureen Montgomery" neatly written above the return address.

Her hands trembled. Had Mrs. Montgomery written to tell her yea or nay? Pushing back the glossy, chestnut brown ringlet that had escaped its comb when she'd hastily removed her hat, she was stunned to see, once she'd opened the envelope, a letter of acceptance folded neatly over a train ticket.

Excitement surged within her breast. She'd done it. She'd gotten the job. She now had a way to make two hundred dollars—no, way more than two hundred, she thought with satisfaction, quickly multiplying twelve by twenty-five. So Michael had thought the matter put to rest, had he? Well, she was going to take great delight in telling him that she intended to fulfill every one of the exigent requirements he'd thrown out. Get married and have a baby or two, indeed.

The warm, self-satisfied glow faded when she realized she wasn't even certain of how a stove worked. The wood went in through a little door on the front. . . .

"Blanche?" she called, running toward the kitchen. "Blanche, are you here? Blanche?"

"I'm right here, Emma." Blanche Faraday appeared in the pantry doorway, wiping her hands on her apron. Her benevolent lined face was smudged with flour. "What is it? My goodness, are you ill?" she asked with motherly concern. "Lucille's not back from tea at the Broders' yet, but I can send Vickie to go for her—"

"No, no, I'm not ill," Emma interrupted, allaying the kindly cook's worries for her health. Unlike the kitchen girls who came and went, Blanche had been a fixture in the household for as long as Emma could remember. In fact, she was practically family, for before working for Michael and Lucille, Blanche had cooked for their parents and had watched both Michael and Emma grow from childhood to adulthood.

A wave of nervousness assaulted Emma at the thought of all the things she needed to learn, and she realized her hands had grown sweaty. Blanche would help her, though, she knew. Blanche had always been there for her. Still, she found it necessary to take a deep breath before she spoke. "You're never going to believe this, Blanche," she announced, "but I'm going to be a cook."

At the older woman's nonplused expression, she continued. "I need you to teach me how to cook right away. I'm leaving for Wyoming Territory in less than two days' time, and I have to learn to cook by then. Not a lot, I don't think, just simple things like bread and pie and beans and stew and . . . and whatever else you think cowboys might eat." She trailed off, giving the cook an optimistic smile.

With each word of her breathless little speech Blanche's eyebrows went a fraction of an inch higher, until they had completely disappeared under her bangs. "What—cowboys? You're going where?" she asked. She squeezed her eyes tightly shut as if she hadn't heard her correctly, bringing the graying half-moons of her brows back into view again.

Emma cleared her throat. "Wyoming Territory," she repeated, lifting her chin. "I'm going to Wyoming Territory to be a cook on a cattle ranch. If you could just teach me a few things to get me started . . . please?"

"Oh, Emma," Blanche said slowly, opening her eyes and regarding her employer's younger sister with worry, sympathy, and indulgence, all at once. "What have you gone and done? You were never one for shenanigans, not you. No, no, you always stayed right in line." Raising her gaze heavenward, she spoke as if Emma wasn't there. "Did you hear that? In two days she wants to learn how to cook 'simple things like bread and pie.' "

"Making bread can't be that difficult, can it?" Emma asked, tucking the letter into her pocket and taking the cook's floury hand into her own. Pushing aside the niggling feelings of anxiety that were threatening to develop into full terror, she smiled what she hoped was her most winning smile. "After all, you do such a wonderful job of it. . . ."

"And here comes the whitewash job," Blanche began, shaking her head, allowing Emma to lead her back through the pantry and into the kitchen. "First it's your crazy business idea, and now you've got some crazy hankering to be a cook on a cattle ranch. You can't just trot off to the godforsaken West and pick up a spoon, you know, Emma. Cooking is hard, hard work." She inclined her head toward Vickie Parrin, the kitchen girl. "Tell her, Vickie."

"It ain't easy, Miss Taylor," Vickie seconded, pausing as she selected a knife with which to chop the pile of vegetables she had just finished peeling. With a weary little lift of her arm, she gestured toward the large pile of dishes in the sink. "I go home mighty tired."

"You've got to help me, Blanche," Emma entreated, ending up telling the whole of her quarrel with Michael, as well as of the outrageous letter of reference she'd written. "I have to do this now, don't you see? It's my only chance. Otherwise, I won't be able to get the money to start my business."

"Well," Blanche began doubtfully, eyeing Emma's graceful golden brown wool dress. "I do have some piecrust that I haven't rolled out yet."

"I'll change right now," she exclaimed, correctly interpreting Blanche's look. "I'll be right back. And I'll bring a piece of paper with me," she added, her warm brown eyes sparkling. "That way I can take notes as you tell me things. I must say that I'm rather nervous about all this," she confessed, "but I have confidence in your ability to teach me, Blanche." Picking up her skirts with a little skip, she turned and left the warm, good-smelling kitchen.

"She thinks she can spend a day and a half in the kitchen and turn into a cook, poof! just like that?" Neatly lining up four peeled carrots, Vickie sliced them into little rings with the sharp knife. "Did you hear her? She's goin' off to a ranch to be a cook and she expects to write everything she needs to know on *one* piece of paper?" Her tired, angular face broke into an amused smile. "I don't know about you, Miz Faraday, but I say she'd best bring the whole tablet."

At the end of the next evening an exhausted Emma lay in her bed. Tired as she was, sleep was long in coming. The dull aching in her shoulders and upper back would only become worse over the next few days, she suspected, tossing from her back to her side without finding relief from the soreness. She never would have guessed that making bread was such hard work. So much horrible kneading.

She'd picked up the rhythm of it rather quickly, however, much to Blanche's surprise. "Go ahead on, then," the cook had said, nodding her approval. "Half an hour is what I usually do. But remember, Emma—and this is important—once you start you cannot stop, else you'll have a damaged product."

Half an hour had seemed like half a century. Emma's arms had turned from lead to rubber and back to lead again during that time, but she'd been determined to succeed—and she had. Through the pain and perspiration she'd endured during that seemingly neverending period of time, she'd also felt an amazing transformation take place in the dough. It had come *alive* was the best way she could think of describing it, recalling how the sticky, gooey, heavy mass had taken on a springiness and body all its own.

Also, between yesterday afternoon and this evening, she'd filled nearly an entire tablet of paper with Mrs. Faraday's recipes and cooking hints. The woman bordered on genius, no doubt; how else could any one person know so much about household matters?

When the evening meal—the evening meal that Emma had nearly single-handedly prepared—was in the final stages of preparation, Blanche had drawn her into her arms and given her a tight hug. "I had my doubts about this whole plan—and I still do," she'd said seriously, giving Emma an extra squeeze before her tone of voice lightened, "but I'm beginning to think you're going to give these ranch folk a good run for their money. You picked up everything right off today."

Releasing her, the cook had stepped back and regarded her with a fond gaze. "But, then again, you've always been one that takes in. I guess I should have remembered that once you set your mind to something, you don't give up."

Blanche's warm words still produced a glow inside her, and she reached over to her bedside stand, running her fingers over the copy of *Buckeye Cookery and Practical Housekeeping* the experienced cook had given her. "Here, dear," Blanche had said, handing Emma her copy of the popular manual. "I got this a few years back. I have a feeling you're going to put this to much better use in the coming year than I am." Tears shone in her kind blue eyes then, and she'd promised to correspond immediately if Emma should write with further questions.

This is your last night in your own bed for a good while to come.

The thought struck her, really struck her, that she wouldn't be seeing Michael or Lucille or Jon, or Blanche, for that matter, for months and months. With as busy as she'd been today, it had been easy not to think about all the implications of her actions.

Her actions. First and foremost was the question of whether or not she could present herself as an experienced cook. Could she really pull the whole thing off? she wondered, shifting to find yet another position within the soft linens. All the arguments and dire warnings Michael had given her this evening sprang to mind. But then, that was to have been expected—she'd known he wasn't going to take the news very well.

He'd practically gone through the roof, as a matter of fact.

"Michael, do you remember giving me your word that you'd put up the money for my business if I made two hundred dollars while making my way in the world?" she'd asked while she, Michael, and Lucille had lingered at the table over fragrant cups of after-dinner coffee.

At that, Lucille's expression had faded to one of nervous apprehension; Michael's pleasant countenance had rapidly taken on the appearance of the sky before a thunderstorm. "I recall putting an end to the whole matter," he'd responded, fixing her with a stern look. "I can't believe you're back to this again after the discussion we had."

"As I recall," Emma had said stiffly, "we did not have much of a discussion. It was rather like a one-sided conversation during which you dictated and I listened. And I did listen, very carefully, to the offer you made me." She'd folded her hands carefully in her lap. "I now wish to hold you to your word."

The thunderclouds had grown darker. "Speak your piece."

Clearing her throat, she began. "I have accepted employment in the territory of Wyoming as a ranch cook in order to fulfill your requirements. I shall be sending a sum of twenty dollars to you each month," she'd proudly announced, "and at that rate, in ten months' time you shall have your two hundred dollars."

"Ranch cook—like hell." The loud, unexpected clink of cup against saucer had made both women jump. "You're not leaving this house."

"Michael!" had come the astonished voice of his wife. "Your language."

"You gave me your word," Emma had said slowly, pushing her chair back. "Blanche has been teaching me to cook. And for your information, it was I who prepared the meal you just proclaimed delicious."

"You, a cook? Even if you . . . you . . ." He'd shaken his head in disbelief. "You can't go running off to Wyoming Territory," he'd spoken, his voice gaining volume with each successive word. "I won't permit you to do something so foolish—so damned *dangerous,* Emma. How could you even think of leaving Minnesota? For heaven's sake, you used to be afraid to leave the house while we were growing up!"

"Well, that was because—" she'd begun defensively.

"If you think that boy next door used to terrorize you," he'd said harshly, "what do you think a bunch of rough-talking cowboys are going to do? Did you even think of that?" He'd run his hands through his hair before planting them, palms down, on the table. "You're not going anywhere, sister, and that's final."

"I am leaving for Wyoming tomorrow. A deal is a deal." Though she was angry, her words had been deliberate and evenly spaced. Tantrums just weren't her way. In fact, Michael's close-mindedness had only caused her determination to become more dogged.

Her brother had closed his eyes for a long moment and had sighed deeply, struggling to gain control of his emotions. "I am truly impressed at your quick grasp of the kitchen arts," he'd finally said in a careful tone, opening his eyes, "but one day in the kitchen does not a cook make." His brown gaze had regarded her beseechingly then, and with more than a little confusion. "Why are you causing so much trouble, Emma? Please tell me what's really troubling you, and I'll try to understand."

"Nothing is troubling me except your refusal to truly listen to what I am saying," she'd said with exasperation. "I want to open my own business," she'd repeated, "and I'm willing to work very hard for the opportunity to do so."

Lucille, who had until that time wisely stayed out of the whole matter, inclined her head slightly in Emma's direction before fixing her husband with a weighty stare. "She's serious, Michael," she'd spoken slowly. "And you did give your word."

His brows had drawn together, and he'd spoken to his wife without any of the customary politeness for which he was known. "Stay out of this, Lucy."

"No, I won't," Lucille had shot back. "For as long as I've known you, you've said that a man of integrity stands by his word. Well, that's what I thought I married—a man of integrity." Now drawn fully into the conflict, Lucille had arisen from her chair and walked around the table. Planting her hands on her hips, she'd added, "Until today, that is."

At that, Michael had gotten up from the table and stalked off to the library. Lucille had remained standing, shaking her head at his departure. Walking over to Emma, she'd given her a little hug. "I can't say that I'm not more than a little frightened for you, honey," she'd said candidly, "but I'll work on smoothing things over." Her hazel eyes had flashed. "I hope you succeed, Emma. I really do. St. Paul needs a good collectibles shop," she'd concluded with an encouraging smile.

The two women had heard Michael telephone Jon Severson, telling Jon he must come over immediately. "You've got to talk some sense into Emma," he'd said, his voice carrying clearly from the next room. "Yes, it's that business idea of hers again. She's gone completely daft."

But Jon, arriving within a half-hour of Michael's call, hadn't been able to dissuade her from her course either. Lucille had continued to argue steadfastly in her favor, making Emma wonder if there wasn't a bit of insurrection locked behind the mild outward manner of her sister-in-law.

In the end, Jon had folded his arms across his chest, giving a knowing nod to his colleague, and had wished Emma the best on her brief trip West.

Michael had immediately picked up on his friend's cue. Mirroring Jon's practiced courtroom gesture, he'd also folded his arms across his chest. "A week, you figure?" he'd asked, nodding.

"Two days," Jon had replied, sotto voce.

At that, Emma and Lucille had exchanged exasperated glances.

"Well, Emma, as you seem determined to do this thing, you may do it," Michael had said patronizingly. "I will keep my end of the bargain. And when your, ah, employment has run its course, your home and family will be here waiting for you. . . ."

Michael's voice faded from Emma's mind as she changed position in the bed once more. Letting out her breath in a deep sigh, she felt tiredness hum throughout her body. Her thoughts continued to run at a rapid pace, however, not allowing her fatigued body to find sleep. Nervous as she was about pulling off her ruse, a spark of excitement also burned deep inside her.

The dark outline of the small trunk she had packed was visible in the unlit chamber. She'd selected several of her oldest and plainest dresses, following Blanche's advice to make certain her skirts were "nothing fancy" and "just a hair on the short side." She'd also laid out an unassuming travel dress and pair of boots to wear on the train tomorrow.

Beneath *Buckeye Cookery* sat the tablet of paper she'd nearly filled with Blanche's recipes, cooking hints, and "plain old directions" for running a kitchen. *Was it possible to memorize all that on a train ride from St. Paul to Pine Bluffs?* she wondered. She'd begun reading the cookbook this afternoon and had gotten nearly to the end of the section entitled "Breadmaking." There were only another three hundred and some-odd pages to go.

With thoughts of bread sponges and potato yeast, and the merits of second-risings versus third-risings running through her mind, Emma closed her eyes and tried to find sleep.

Chapter Two

"The good Lord willin', Ginny, m' love, our new cook'll be here later today," Maureen Montgomery commented to her daughter-in-law as she stood in front of the wood stove and shook first salt, then pepper, into an enormous bubbling pot of stew. Though she'd married an Englishman and had lived in the States for nearly thirty years, the lilt of the widow's Irish homeland was still evident in her speech.

Her dark blue calico dress hung gracefully from her small frame; around her waist was tied a red-and-white-checked apron. Setting the seasoning on the worktable behind her, Maureen picked up a long-handled spoon and gave the contents of the iron pot a stir. "An' may I be the first t' say," she added, a tired smile gracing her softly freckled face, "that she cannot get here a moment too soon."

"Amen to that," Ginny Montgomery replied with an answering, good-natured grin, laying out plates and bowls for the nine ranch hands who would soon be coming in for their noontime meal. "Do you suppose we can talk her into starting tonight?" Ginny thought of the last cook, a surly young man who had been of an extremely undependable nature.

The jackass hadn't even lasted three months, she thought with dissatisfaction, borrowing a pet cuss word of her husband's. After weeks of bad food and an even worse attitude, he'd up and left one day without giving any sort of notice. Consequently, she and Maureen had been sharing the ranch's kitchen duties for nearly a month now.

Like Maureen, Ginny was garbed in plain, unadorned work clothing. Instead of hanging gracefully, though, the iron-gray calico of her bodice clung to her slightly plump form, causing stress, in areas, on the row of buttons up the center of the dress. Above the garment's high-necked collar her cheeks were flushed from the heat of the kitchen, adding fresh pink color to a complexion that was normally as fresh and smooth as pure cream.

Setting the last of the dishes on the well-oiled wooden table, Ginny held up her chapped, reddened hands. "I believe I've had my hands in enough dishwater of late to set the entire Territory afloat."

"Aye. You an' me both."

"It's a good thing Edward didn't marry me for my soft, lily-white . . ." Ginny's words trailed off, and she peered past her hands. "My goodness," she remarked jocosely, picking up the plate and scratching at an area with her short thumbnail. "Why is it so hard to get good help nowadays?" Wiping at the spot with her apron, she shrugged and returned the plate to the table.

"I don't know, but 'tis indeed," came Maureen's somewhat muffled voice. Bent over as she checked the biscuits in the oven, she missed the humor in her daughter-in-law's question. Straightening, she closed the oven door and turned to Ginny. "This time I advertised from Minneapolis to Denver, an' I found me a good, sturdy woman from Minnesota who used to cook for a loggin' camp."

"A logging camp . . . well, she should be good, then," Ginny said with an encouraging nod. Her lips curved mischievously. "She probably has the shoulders of an ox."

"Well, I cannot attest to the size of her shoulders, but accordin' to the woman's letter of reference, she was quite a cook, indeed." Clearing the gravy from the long-handled spoon by tapping it smartly on the rim of the cast-iron pot, Maureen laid down the implement and reached for a hot pad. "Them biscuits are smellin' about done, don't you think?"

"You're asking me?" Adding two bowls of butter and a pitcher of honey to the table, Ginny shook her head and gave her husband's mother a helpless, comical look. "You know what kind of cook I am."

Watching her mother-in-law's deft, tireless movements in the kitchen, some of Ginny's lightheartedness fled. Maureen simply worked too hard for a woman approaching her fiftieth year. Ginny gave her all the help she could, for she loved kindhearted Maureen as she did her own mother.

Edward's father, Andrew Montgomery, had died a month after Ginny had married Edward, leaving Maureen one of the largest, most successful cattle ranches in the area—and an expensive silver mine that had yet to produce ore of any value. Whereas most women would have shrank from such enormous responsibilities, the new widow had bravely faced them. Without so much as a backward glance, she'd left the social life of Cheyenne behind, rolled up her sleeves, and gone to work.

Putting Edward in charge of the mining operations, Maureen had taken over as the ranch's top "man," quickly earning the respect of her employees and fellow cattlemen with her gentle ways and shrewd management. Not for the first time, Ginny tried to imagine what kind of strength and determination it must take to walk in Maureen Montgomery's shoes.

"I sent Ryan off to meet Miss Taylor at the train," Maureen commented, sliding the biscuits from the baking sheet into a towel-lined basket. She sighed deeply and turned to Ginny, sadness evident on her face. "I wish I knew what was troublin' that boy's heart. Me oldest boy, he is, an' I know him no better than a stranger."

"He's always been the type to keep to himself, hasn't he?"

Ginny got on well with Edward's four sisters and his younger brother Joey, but she barely knew Ryan

Montgomery. The raven-haired army captain—*ex*–army captain, she reminded herself—had returned to the ranch just a week ago after resigning his commission. Though he lived here, he wasn't really here, she'd observed in the past days, wondering why Ryan chose to distance himself, both physically and emotionally, from his family.

Edward had told her that against their father's wishes Ryan had pursued a career in the military, rarely returning home since he'd left for West Point nine years ago. Even after graduating and being stationed at nearby Fort D. A Russell in Cheyenne, his visits home were no more frequent.

Ginny thought of the first time she'd met Ryan, at her and Edward's wedding nearly two summers ago. She'd been struck immediately by the resemblance between the two brothers, but she'd also quickly seen their differences. Both were dark-haired and dark-eyed, bearing a strong resemblance to their father, but while Edward was quick to smile and tell a joke, Ryan was aloof and detached. His eyes, too, were empty and sad, unlike the merry brown eyes of his brother.

"Edward heard there was a suicide at the fort last month," Ginny said thoughtfully. "An officer. Maybe it was someone Ryan knew." Pausing while setting the spoons and forks around the table, her sandy-brown brows drew together in concern.

"There's no tellin'," Maureen replied softly, removing two pans of plum cobbler from the warming oven. "With him there's just no tellin'."

"Why do you suppose this cook wants to come all the way from Minnesota?" the younger woman asked after a long pause, considerately trying to draw Maureen's thoughts toward a less troubled topic. "It surely can't be for the weather."

"No, daughter, I'd be guessin' it ain't for the Wyomin' weather," the widow declared in a lighter tone of voice. "The letter o' reference said she had to quit the loggers last year an' tend to her dyin' ma. I take it now that the poor woman's passed on."

"Who's passed on?" Edward Montgomery stepped into the large kitchen and gave his wife a kiss on the cheek. "And did he leave me any money? Hey, Ma," he greeted his mother, inhaling deeply. "It sure smells good in here. How long before we eat? I'm mighty hungry after the hard morning I put in." Though his tone was light, small wrinkles of worry fanned out at the corners of his deep brown eyes.

"Edward James Montgomery," Maureen said, shaking her head and regarding her second-born with fondness. Motherly concern took over as she studied his appearance. "You're lookin' a wee bit peaked this mornin', me son. Are you feelin' poorly?"

"Aw, I'm fine, Ma." He brushed off her worry. "Just a wee bit tired after doing the books, is all." Flashing her an engaging grin, he imitated her brogue to a tee.

"A truly taxing affair, I'm sure," Ginny teased, earning herself a gentle tug on the shining, sandy-brown plait that lay neatly down the center of her back. Looking adoringly into her husband's eyes, she also noticed the faint stress etched on his lean features.

"Ryan?" came the far-off voice of eighteen-year-old Joey Montgomery.

"Ryan's gone to fetch the new cook, m' dear," Maureen called brightly. "He'll be back later this afternoon."

"Oh" was the boy's disappointed reply from farther off in the house.

Again Ginny watched the sadness flicker on her mother-in-law's face. Since he'd moved back home, Ryan had barely given a minute's attention to the younger brother who worshipped him so. Joey's dejection was obvious to all—to all except his hero, that was.

"I'll talk to Ryan, Ma," Edward said, also noticing Maureen's pensive expression. "I don't know what's the matter with him, but the way he's been ignoring Joey just isn't right."

"No, 'tisn't," Maureen replied with heaviness in her normally lilting voice. Pausing while arranging pieces of golden-topped cobbler on a large plate, her blue eyes shimmered with unshed tears. " 'Tisn't right at all."

*   *   *

The rocky bluffs for which Pine Bluffs had been named rose sharply from the flat prairie. Extending southward for sixty miles, the ridge of yellow-gray sandstone hills attained heights, in some places, of three hundred feet. The stunted pines that had once abundantly covered the hills and lent their appellation to the town, however, had disappeared beneath the axes of the railroaders in 1867, their wood becoming ties for the westward-bound Union Pacific railroad. There was no longer a tree of any sort to be seen in any direction.

Ryan Montgomery stood on the wooden Union Pacific platform and waited for the late afternoon train to arrive, a chilly northwesterly wind biting at his face. His gaze flicked first over the side tracks and great cattle yards, empty at this time of year, then down the town's barren main street. Entirely unimpressive, he thought emotionlessly, for one of the largest cattle shipping centers in the country.

The area where Pine Bluffs stood had once been a vast Indian hunting area. The clear, plentiful waters of Lodgepole Creek that had once attracted the Arapahoe, Kiowa, Cheyenne, Ute, Blackfeet, and Sioux, among many other Indian tribes, had also attracted Texas Trail drivers and their miles-long herds in more recent years.

Not only was Pine Bluffs an important watering place along the Texas Trail, but the town's population swelled to bursting each autumn as vast herds of cattle were driven in for shipment to the eastern markets. Ryan supposed it was entirely possible that Pine Bluffs was, as some cattlemen claimed, the largest cattle shipping point in the world.

And here comes the shipment of one Minnesota cook. The far-off sound of an approaching train drew his attention, and he vaguely wondered why his mother had hired a cook from so far away. It didn't make much sense to him, but he thought she must have her reasons. She and Edward seemed to have the ranch business well in hand.

Though Edward had been interested in the family business since his adolescent years, Ryan had never cared to be a part of its operation. What he'd thought had been the glamour and heroism of military life had appealed to him instead, and he'd set off for West Point, a young man of eighteen, just after his father had received one of the first homestead grants in Laramie County.

During the summer of 1875, Andrew Montgomery had moved his family from their modest-sized ranch in central Nebraska to the wide sweeping grasslands south of Pine Bluffs. An intense, commanding personality, the Montgomery patriarch had quickly increased the size of his beef herds, thereby establishing one of the largest cattle companies in the Territory and becoming one of the area's leading stockmen in the process.

He'd also expected to pass his empire on to his eldest son. It didn't matter to Andrew whether the son wanted to be a rancher or not, Ryan remembered with bitterness, thinking of the harsh words that had passed between the two of them when he'd told his father he wanted a career in the military.

If only the old man hadn't been such a pig-headed, dictatorial son of a bitch. . . .

Reflecting on his own stubbornness, Ryan thought of how it had become more and more easy, over the years, to pretend the estrangement didn't matter. But it did. Pain twisted deep in a secret place in his heart as he thought of the peace he and his father had never made, realizing, ironically, that all the things Andrew Montgomery had told him about a career in the army had been true after all. It had certainly taken Jim Hopper's best years.

Taken them and used them . . . hell, the army took your friend's life, plain and simple.

"Excuse me?" came the softly cultured voice of a young woman, breaking into the black silence of his thoughts. The train had arrived a few minutes earlier with squealing brakes and a great roar of smoke and steam, but he'd barely noticed. The sole Pine Bluffs passenger had already disembarked. The petite woman stood on the platform like a lost soul, her heart-shaped face clearly showing her uncertainty. "Sir?"

"Ryan Montgomery," he said curtly, touching his hat.

This was the new cook? Doubtfully he eyed the expensive cut of the woman's black repped silk cloak, also taking note of the fashionable hat perched atop a mass of nutmeg-colored hair. "You're Emma Taylor?"

The woman nodded rapidly. "I am. I'm here to—"

"I know why you're here."

As soon as he said the words he doubted them. His skill at quickly sizing people up had become second nature over the years, and there was something about this frightened young woman that just didn't wash. Even as dusty and fatigued as she looked, it was obvious to see she was well-bred. She came from money, he'd guess. Attractive as she was, with her pert nose and melting brown eyes, he'd also guess she'd been involved in a scandal of some sort and was fleeing her home . . . an affair with a married man, maybe.

Why should you care? he asked himself, blunting his curiosity. *As long as she can cook, her business is no business of yours.* With a sigh he bent over to pick up her trunk.

Scared to death didn't even begin to describe how Emma felt. Though she'd read *Buckeye Cookery* from cover to cover—three times—on the way to Pine Bluffs, meticulously studying the tablet of Blanche's instructions as well, she was certain she'd made a terrible mistake in accepting the position.

You can't cook, Emma Louise, a voice inside her head screamed as she watched the tall man in the buffalo coat bend down and easily lift her trunk to his shoulder. *You can't cook, you have no business trying to cook, and you've wasted a good woman's money on a train ticket with your ridiculousness. Just tell this Mr. Montgomery you've made a terrible mistake, find a place to stay the night, and, God willing, you'll be home by the end of the week.*

But she could scarcely tell the man anything, for he was already halfway down the platform steps with her trunk. A team of horses, hitched to an unassuming farm wagon, sat obediently next to the platform in the slushy, wide track of the town's main street. Turning and giving her an impatient "come on, lady" look from beneath the broad brim of his hat, the man stepped onto the street and set her trunk in the back of the rig.

Emma clutched her leather satchel more closely and walked slowly to the steps, feeling as low and empty as she could ever remember feeling. She certainly hadn't expected any sort of royal treatment upon her arrival, but after spending two long uncomfortable days traveling second-class was a pleasant greeting and a bit of hospitality too much to ask for? Mr. Montgomery's dark eyes had quickly examined and dismissed her. . . . *Had she already done something to offend the man?* she wondered, feeling hurt and confused by his unwelcoming mien.

"We've got a drive ahead of us," he said impatiently, climbing aboard the wagon. His arm stretched toward her. "Are you coming or not?" With the collar of his great buffalo coat drawn up around his neck and the brim of his hat pulled low, only the center of his face was visible.

The train's bell clanged harshly behind her, and the door of the car she'd just exited was pulled shut with a bang. *Too late to back out now.* The sounds that had become so much a part of her life in the past few days now rubbed rawly on her ears, and she shivered slightly in the chilly late-afternoon air, realizing she didn't feel too badly, after all, about leaving the soot and cramped discomfort behind. *Think of your business, Emma. You can do this.*

"I'm coming," she answered bravely, lifting her skirts to clear the slushy steps. Accepting Ryan Montgomery's brusquely proffered hand, she barely had time to seat herself before he called out, "Gidd'ap," and shook the reins. Gaining her balance on the rough wooden seat as the wagon moved down Pine Bluffs' main track, Emma looked about her and wondered if this treeless spot on the prairie could truly be called a town.

She'd visited some of the smaller towns around St. Paul—Osseo, Anoka, and Shakopee, among others—but they'd *looked* like small towns. They had trees, shops, businesses, and homes—not to mention people. Surely there had to be more to Pine Bluffs than side tracks and sprawling cattle pens, the combination railroad depot and telegraph office, and a few forlorn-looking buildings.

Sneaking a glance at the forbidding profile of the man beside her, Emma thought the better of asking. "You don't have as much snow as we do in St. Paul," she commented, feeling as though she should say something.

He shrugged, keeping his gaze on the reins.

Emma swallowed, wondering what it was about this man that made her feel so nervous—more nervous, even, than she'd been on the train. There was also something about his face that drew her attention. She couldn't see his eyes, but she covertly studied what she could see of his features, observing that his nose was proud and aquiline. The planes and angles of the side of his face were equally strong; the line of a high cheekbone disappeared beneath the brim of his hat. His lips were full and smooth, the lower one, in particular, and she found herself wondering what his mouth would look like if he smiled.

As friendly as he is, you'll probably never know.

The wagon hit a jarring rut that caused her teeth to snap together sharply, but the expression of the man beside her didn't change. Adjusting her aching posterior on the hard seat, Emma tried to imagine his lips curved into a smile. *What kind of smile would he have?* she wondered. Would the faint line on the side of his mouth deepen into a groove? For that matter, what would make him smile?

Disturbed by the amount of attention her thoughts seemed to be giving Ryan Montgomery's mouth, her nervousness increased. "How far is it to the ranch?" she asked, trying a question that would at least require a spoken response to fill up a little of the silence between them.

"A ways."

Swallowing, Emma attempted a polite smile. "And do you have a great many cows?"

"Yeah." Pushing his hat a little higher on his head, he turned and regarded her with eyes so dark and intense they seemed almost black—and almost as if they could see through a person.

"Oh . . . well, that's good," she remarked weakly, feeling extremely uncomfortable under his scrutiny. She wanted to ask more about the ranch, learn what kind of place she'd be working at, but his penetrating eyes and curt manner discouraged her from asking. A chill ran through her that had nothing to do with the cold, and she dropped her gaze from his eyes to his full mouth. *What was he thinking?* she wondered. Did he suspect she was a fraud? Fresh nervousness rolled in the pit of her stomach.

After a long moment he pulled the brim of his hat back down and turned his attention back to his driving. Letting out a deep breath she didn't even know she was holding, Emma huddled beneath her cape and stared at the winter-weary grassland. *It's not even going to take a year to save the money you need,* she told herself, trying to bolster her spirits. *Maybe you can be home by Christmas.*

Already uncertain and uneasy, it didn't take long for Emma to feel lonely, as well, with only the company of her thoughts. Turning her head to look at the high bluffs beyond the other side of the wagon, her glance briefly lit on Ryan Montgomery's face. Though it had been obvious he didn't want to talk about the ranch, maybe another topic would interest him, something broader. Talking always made her feel better, particularly when she was upset about something. She cleared her throat. "What do you think of President Arthur?" she asked, thinking of all the time Michael and Jon devoted to discussing politics.

"Not much." This time his head didn't turn.

The pattern of their conversation remained much the same until they arrived at the ranch. Dusk had fallen by that time, and Emma was heartened to see welcoming yellow light spilling out the windows of the two-story frame structure. It looked like a comfortable homey place. Maybe it wouldn't be so bad here after all, she thought, wondering what kind of woman Mrs. Maureen Montgomery was.

During the long ride, she'd learned from her laconic companion that the ranch presently employed "eight or nine" cowhands. She also learned a little about the Montgomery family, discovering that Ryan was Mrs. Montgomery's oldest son, and that the widow had been managing the large ranch since the summer before last. The thought that the older woman was operating her own business didn't escape Emma; in fact, it gave her heart.

"We're here." Ryan's elbow bumped hers as he pulled on the reins and called *whoa* to the horses. In an agile movement he stepped down from the wagon. "Go up there and knock on the door," he said, pointing to the front veranda. "I'll bring your trunk in the back way."

His grip was tight and impersonal as he assisted her down from the wagon. Making no response to her thanks, he climbed back up to his seat and shook the reins. The wagon creaked as the horses eagerly stepped out, impatient, no doubt, for their supper and their warm stalls.

Emma stood alone in the near darkness. The wind quickly carried off the sounds of the team and wagon, bringing to her ears the faint, far-off bawling of cattle. Accustomed to the sights and sounds of a busy city, she was struck by the silence here, a silence broken only by the wind. Turning to face the direction from which they'd come, she thought that she'd never seen a space so empty and vast. The sound of a door opening made her turn back to the house.

"Hello?" a voice called. "Hello, is there someone there?" A small, kindly faced woman appeared in the doorway a moment later, holding a kerosene lantern aloft. "Why, goodness, come on in from the cold an' warm yourself. You'll be catchin' yer death standin' out there."

The middle-aged woman's smile and compassionate tone were almost Emma's undoing. Gripping the satchel containing *Buckeye Cookery* and the precious tablet of Blanche's cooking instructions, Emma blinked back the burning in her eyes and gratefully ascended the wooden steps toward the warmth and light.

"Did that Ryan just go an' drop you here?" the woman asked, concern intensifying the unmistakable Irish brogue as she stepped onto the porch and peered out into the darkness. "I do not know what to do with that boy," she said softly, sighing. Extending her free hand toward the satchel, a smile again graced her even features. "I'll be takin' that, dear. I'm Maureen Montgomery, an' I take it you're to be our new cook—Emma Taylor, am I right?"

Emma smiled hesitantly and nodded. "I'm pleased to meet you, Mrs. Montgomery," she said, allowing herself to be relieved of the satchel and drawn into the house. "Thank you." The thought of having deceived such a kind woman caused her to feel a sudden terrible guilt.

What have you done, Emma Louise?

Setting the lamp on a table, Maureen closed the door and called out, "Ginny, our new cook has just blown in with the wind. Fetch us that pot of tea, dear, will you now? The wee girl is near frozen to the bone."

Already having formed an opinion of what a Wyoming Territory ranch house would be like, Emma was surprised at the interior of the Montgomery home. The wide hallway in which she and Mrs. Montgomery stood opened into attractively furnished rooms on either side. Above the hallway's richly colored waist-high wainscoting, a fashionable floral-stripe wallpaper of turquoise and off-white covered the walls. Ahead of where they stood, a carpeted set of stairs, beginning just beyond the doorway to the right, rose from the glossy, dark-stained entryway floor; the same wallpaper and waist-high wainscoting that graced the walls of the first-floor hallway also followed the angle of the stairs' ascent.

"Here now, let's get you out of those and in by the fire." Giving Emma another friendly smile, Maureen set the satchel along the wall and assisted her with removing her outer garments. "There, now, that's better," she said, hanging the hat and black cloak on the many-hooked coat stand and leading her into the drawing room doorway to the left. "Welcome to our home, dear," she said, indicating that Emma should take a seat in the basswood chair in the grouping near the wood stove. "We're glad to have you here, we are, indeed. We've been without a cook for near a month now."

Nervousness and apprehension pounded in Emma's breast as she perched on the edge of the broad-seated chair. Though she felt the stove's heat against her face, she doubted she would feel warm and relaxed ever again in her life. "I-I'm glad to be here," she replied. Glancing around the room, she was again surprised by the touches of fashion and finery she saw, as well as by the sight of an ornate piano of some dark wood sitting at the opposite end of the room.

"Hello, Miss Taylor," another, younger voice greeted her. Balancing a tray containing a teapot, spoons, cups, and saucers, a slightly chubby woman in her early twenties entered the doorway at the rear of the room. "Or is it

Missus?" The woman smiled, her honest gray-green eyes regarding Emma out of a sweet round face.

"It's 'Miss,' but you can call me Emma." Despite her nervousness, Emma found herself smiling back at the younger woman.

"It's good to meet you, Emma," the woman replied, setting the tray down on the round table in the center of the room. "I'm Ginny. Edward's wife—" She broke off with a quick, questioning glance at Maureen. "You probably haven't even gotten that far yet, have you?"

"Well, I'll save you the introduction. I'm Edward," said a tall, dark-haired man as he walked into the room and flashed a grin her way. "Second son of Maureen and younger brother of Ryan, in case you haven't gotten the family lowdown yet, but what I really am is all hers," he added in a loud whisper, jerking his thumb at Ginny. " 'Til death do us part, you know."

Ginny's eyes rolled heavenward at her husband's words, but the dimples that creased her cheeks gave Emma the idea that she wasn't the least bit angry. Emma accepted a steaming cup of tea and another friendly smile from Ginny, wondering how Ryan could possibly be related to Edward. They shared the same proud nose and bold cheekbones, she decided, making another observation of Edward's features, but unlike Ryan's closed face, his brother's was open and full of expression.

At the moment his gaze tenderly followed the form of his wife.

"Thank you, dear," Maureen said to Ginny, accepting her tea.

The next few minutes were spent in pleasant conversation with Maureen, Edward, and Ginny, and Emma felt her nervousness begin to diminish. Why, it was almost as if she were sitting down to tea with old friends, she thought curiously, rather than meeting her employer for the first time. Even Edward pulled up a chair and joined them in a cup of tea.

Emma had rehearsed several answers to possible questions about her past "employment," but to her surprise no questions of the sort were forthcoming. They talked, instead, about the ranch and life in the West, and a little about the Montgomery family.

"Ryan and Edward are my two oldest boys, as you already know," Maureen said fondly, smiling at her second-born. "An' Moira and Irene are my next two. They're off an' married, the both of 'em, an' they're livin' in Cheyenne with homes of their own. The wee ones, Ruthie an' Colleen, are livin' in town, as well. They're goin' to school, but you'll be meetin' 'em when the term is finished. I've another lad, too, Emma," she said with a gentle, poignant smile, "but I need to—"

A door closed farther off in the house, causing Maureen to pause. Emma turned her head toward the door at the rear of the room, hearing male voices approach. One of them was Ryan's, she knew, but the other was thin-sounding, flat, and hard to understand, belonging to someone she had not yet met.

"Wyan here . . . Wyan come," the voice said loudly, oddly.

Abnormally.

Loud, shuffling footsteps sounded in the back hallway. "My Wyan c-come. Wyan here."

The quality of the voice suddenly turned a key inside Emma's mind, unlocking memory after terrifying memory. A quaking began in her chest as the old panic filled her, and she felt the blood drain from her face all at once. Looking at the faces of the people around her, she saw nothing amiss in their expressions; somehow, that terrified her all the more.

She couldn't breathe.

"My Wyan," the voice said slowly with both pride and delight as its owner shuffled into the room, followed by the tall man who had driven her from the train station. "Wyan brudder. My brudder . . . here."

"Yes, Joey, he's finally here," Maureen said patiently, giving her youngest son a tender smile as he came into view. "You were waitin' the whole day for him, weren't you, m' love?"

"Who lady?"

The youth stared at Emma, cocking his head to one side, his mouth hanging slack. Clean, neat clothing covered his round-shouldered frame, and in his left hand he carried a slightly grimy handkerchief. Small ears, with the tops folded over, were exposed by the short cut of his dark brown hair. His neck, also, appeared shorter than normal.

Dread and horror ran through Emma as she stared at the youth standing in front of Ryan. Taking in the young man's upward slanted eyes beneath his broad flat forehead, Emma instinctively shrank back in her chair.

No, it can't be, she thought, *not another one.*

Chapter Three

"Who lady?" the youth repeated, sounding as if he'd said *who-eighty*. He cocked his head the other way and licked his lips several times with his thick tongue.

"Emma, this is my other son, Joey." Maureen's gentle voice barely penetrated the fog of Emma's fear. "An' Joey, dear, this nice lady is t' be our new cook. Miss Emma Taylor's her name. Can you tell her hello?"

"Hah-low." Joey looked at her curiously for a moment longer before turning to Ryan and smiling. The smile faded then as he began to look around the room, shaking the hand in which he held the handkerchief.

Emma couldn't respond. Even if she'd had the words, there was no wetness in her mouth with which to form them. Her gaze slid from Joey to Maureen to Ryan—oh, God, the tall dark man looked more forbidding than ever—and then to the carpet. She studied the rug's intricate pattern without really seeing it, trying desperately to compose herself. The room was silent save the snapping of wood in the stove, and she knew they all must be staring at her.

She couldn't help her silence, though; she simply couldn't speak. She was lost remembering the years of her childhood, remembering the long frightening days when another such boy—the Mantle Monster, he'd been called—

had roamed the backyard of the house next door. Treated no better than an animal by his family, the boy—*had he even had a name?* she wondered abstractly—had been turned out-of-doors from spring until fall, to shuffle and ramble about the fenced lot as he would.

The strange noises, yelps, and grunts that issued from the other side of the fence were not usually terribly loud or disturbing, but whenever Emma ventured outside, the boy erupted into wild howls, screams, and squeals. His pudgy brown arms would reach through the slats of the fence for her, his fingers reaching, clawing. . . .

"Emma, dear, I know it's a bit of a shock—" Maureen began gently.

"Don't make excuses for her" came Ryan's tight, angry voice. "It's obvious she's no different than anyone else."

"Now, Ryan—" Edward said, but Ryan's next words cut him off.

"I realize you've been rendered speechless, Miss Taylor." Ryan spoke with such censure that Emma was forced to slowly raise her head and look at him. "But you'd better listen to what I have to say."

Having been curious to see the whole of his face during the ride from the Pine Bluff depot, she was now dismayed—nay, intimidated—by the full effect of Ryan Montgomery's visage. Penetrating black eyes glittered at her from beneath thick slashes of equally black brows. He was approximately the same age as Jon Severson, she quickly estimated, but so much more . . . seasoned.

And so dark.

Hair so thick and dark it appeared blue-black crowned his hatless head. His jaw was square, every bit as proud as his nose, and the angles beneath his strong cheekbones were shadowed dramatically by the room's lamplight. Displeasure narrowed his finely sculptured mouth, the mouth that had so captivated her attention during the long ride to the ranch.

"I see that your ears, at least, are working." Sarcasm mixed and flowed with the disapproval in his deep voice. "I'll make it fast and simple, lady, in terms you can understand in that little piece of fluff you call a brain." He raised a finger and stabbed it toward her. "If you do not adjust your narrow attitude about my brother—in damned short order— you will not have employment in this household. Period."

Emma felt color flood her face as she looked from Ryan's furious countenance to Joey's puzzled expression, then to the rest of the Montgomerys. "I-I'm so very sorry," she stammered, feeling her eyes fill with tears. "I didn't mean to . . . Honestly, I didn't mean anything. . . . It's just that there was this . . . this other b-boy . . ."

"There, now, dear," Maureen soothed, "it's quite all right. You don' have t' go explainin' yourself. You're a sweet girl, I can see it." She patted Emma's arm and glanced at her eldest son. "You'll forgive Ryan for jumpin' all over you, won't you now, Emma? Me Ryan's always been a mite too overprotective of Joey."

"Oh, for Christ's sake." Ryan made an impatient, disgusted sound and stalked from the room. Unable to help herself, Emma watched his broad-shouldered form fill the doorway and disappear. What had she ever done to make him hate her so? A tear spilled from one eye and ran down her cheek.

"Wyan go?" Joey's expression was crestfallen. "No . . . Where my Wyan?"

Farther off in the house a door slammed. Joey's round shoulders rounded even more as he lowered his head and blinked hard several times. The handkerchief fluttered wildly as the shaking movement of his left hand became more pronounced.

"Ryan's probably gone out to check the horses, Joseph," Edward said with false cheerfulness. "You know how he likes his horses." He rose from his chair and put his arm about his brother's hunched shoulders. "How about me and you go on out to the kitchen and see what kind of goodies we can find?"

"No food. Want Wyan." A stubborn edge crept into the voice, and the handkerchief shook more furiously.

"I know you do, Joey," Edward said patiently. "And he'll probably be back in a short while. If you don't want anything to eat, then, why don't you show me your paintings from this afternoon? I don't believe I've seen them yet."

"Aye, that sounds like a fine idea," Maureen seconded. "Ryan'll be in t' say good night to you, m' love, have no doubt."

"Want Wyan," Joey repeated once again, but the movements of his hand stilled, and he allowed his brother to lead him from the sitting room. Over his shoulder, Edward offered Emma a smile and an encouraging nod.

"Joey still hasn't let go of Ryan's handkerchief, has he?" Ginny observed quietly. She looked at Maureen and shook her head. "I thought he might not be so attached to it now that Ryan's come home, but it appears he's not going to give it up."

"Aye, Joey's been carryin' somethin' of Ryan's around for years." The older woman paused thoughtfully. "An' if it brings him some measure of comfort to carry a handkerchief or sock or such, I cannot tell him to stop."

"Speaking of Ryan, I do believe that's the most I've heard him say since I've known him," Ginny commented. "Although poor Emma had to suffer for it." Her wide gray-green eyes regarded Emma with concern.

"Aye, she did at that. Here," Maureen said kindly, standing and offering Emma a clean, neatly pressed handkerchief. "Dry your tears an' think no more of this unpleasantness. Ryan was meanin' only to protect his brother, but he did not go about it well. I'm hopin' it's in your heart to forgive his tearin' temper. He's been home from the army but a week, an' his moods have been naught but the blackest o' black."

Emma nodded and gratefully accepted the cloth. Dabbing at her eyes and cheeks, she willed the embarrassing flow of tears to stop.

"Did you say you once knew a boy like Joey?" Ginny asked as she rose from her chair and carried her teacup and saucer back to the tray.

Emma nodded again.

"Before I met Edward's family," Ginny said, "I never knew anyone with . . . with . . . like Joey," she finished lamely.

"Aye, an' there's a large part of the problem," Maureen said sadly. "What to call him?" Her voice dropped. "He's a boy, he is, but he's called mongoloid by some and idiot by others." Her eyes flashed with maternal outrage. "I absolutely cannot abide those vile terms. An' then there's the other names we've heard, like freak, an' cretin, an' monster, an' mooncalf, an' moron, an' half-wit . . . I could go on an' on." Her expression softened into a tender smile. "But I'll tell you something, an' I'm tellin' you true: I would not trade my sweet innocent Joey for all the riches in the world. He's brought a measure o' joy into our lives that we would never have known."

Emma's tears were gone, and she listened intently to her employer's plain talk. Most surprising of all was that there was no shame or embarrassment in Maureen's voice when she spoke of Joey—only love and pride.

Once again, Emma thought of her childhood, and of the Mantle family that had lived next door. There were other, older Mantle children, she recalled, but she could not remember a time when she'd seen any of them spend time with the boy in the backyard.

No one had ever spent any time with the Mantle Monster.

Sometimes Emma used to peek at him from her second story bedroom window, being careful to keep herself hidden behind the curtain. One thing she remembered was that he'd been fed once a day, like a dog. In the evening the Mantles' kitchen girl would carry out a bowl of scraps and set them on the porch, pause a minute, shaking her head, and return inside. The raggedly dressed boy always waited until the girl returned indoors, then he'd shuffle over to the porch with that peculiar walk of his, hunker down, and begin to eat from the bowl. At sundown he used to curl up beneath a small oak tree, or beneath the back porch, with only a filthy blanket to protect him from the elements.

And in the winter . . . Emma had heard whispers saying that the boy was kept in the cellar the whole winter long. Then one spring—was it the year she was twelve or thirteen?—he simply hadn't come out.

And she'd been so relieved.

How could it be that things in the Montgomery family were so different? Emma wondered, looking into Maureen's kind hazel eyes. In the short time she'd been here, Emma had seen that Joey had a valued place in this family. The older woman had been serious when she'd said she wouldn't trade her son for all the riches in the world. *How can that be?* Emma wondered. *What kind of joy could a . . . a boy like that have possibly brought into their lives?*

"Well, Ginny, me dear," Maureen said, clasping her hands together and smoothly changing the topic. "Shall we be showin' our new cook about the place?"

Emma took that as her cue to rise from her chair. Following Maureen's example, she placed her teacup and saucer on the tray. Her tentative smile froze on her lips, however, at Maureen's next words.

"I'm supposin', though, Emma, that with the experience you have, you won't need a great deal of help to be gettin' started here. Your letter o' reference was quite impressive, indeed." Maureen picked up the lamp and began walking toward the doorway at the rear of the room.

"Maureen told me how you used to cook for thirty-five men each day," Ginny said with awe, shaking her head. "How did you do it? For the past month Maureen and I have been cooking for only a third of that number, and I'm about as worn out as a wet dishrag."

"Oh, I-I was . . . it was—"

The plump young woman's giggle saved Emma from having to finish her reply. "We sure didn't expect you to be a little bit of a mite, though," she confessed with another giggle, bringing her hand to her mouth in a fetching manner. "Why, in my mind I had you pictured as a big tough woman, complete with a hairy mustache and shoulders like an ox."

"Virginia!" came Maureen's laughing reproof.

The nervousness and insecurity Emma had felt while traveling to the Montgomery ranch was back, worse than ever, as she followed the two women through the dining room that lay beyond the sitting room. Even the stinging hurt of Ryan Montgomery's harsh words and disapproving manner faded in the face of her fear.

It's all over now, Emma, a voice inside her spoke. *They're going to sniff out your lies in no time at all,*

*and you'll be back on a train to St. Paul quicker than
a flock of snowbirds can scatter. Or maybe they already
know you for the fraud you are, and they're just waiting
for you to admit it.*

With her thoughts racing pell-mell through her head,
Emma found it difficult to focus on what Maureen and
Ginny were saying. She numbly followed them to the far
end of the dining room, then through a swinging door that
opened into a large pass-through pantry.

Maureen paused in the pantry, setting the lamp she carried on the small wooden table in the center of the room.
"Come on in, Emma . . . that's it." She gestured broadly
with her arm. "Come right on in the pantry, here. You
can see for yourself that you'll find just about everthin'
you could possibly want or need in here."

Emma looked around, feeling overwhelmed by the
dizzying array of cookware and foodstuff before her.
For heaven's sake, she thought with stunned amazement,
there's enough food here to feed an entire army. A single
tall window, adorned by cheerful blue-and-white plaid curtains, was the only thing, besides the two doors, that broke
the room's efficient arrangement of floor-to-ceiling shelves
and drawers and cupboards.

You can't do this, the voice spoke again. *You're in over
your head.*

"Well, on to the kitchen," Maureen said, picking up the
lamp and pushing open the far swinging door. "We got the
evenin' meal an' the dishes all taken care of tonight, Emma,
so you can start fresh in the mornin'."

"Maureen set the bread sponge while I was doing dishes,"
Ginny added, holding the door open for her. "It's in the
crock by the stove. We put some beans to soak, too." She
shrugged. "We didn't know for sure what you liked to cook,
but with the men at this ranch, you'll be safe with beans."

"Thank you," Emma murmured, with a last glance
around the now-shadowed pantry. Feeling as if she were
in a dream, she moved into the kitchen. The dream quickly
turned to a nightmare, however, as an enormous black
cookstove caught her eye. Heaven help her, this metal
monstrosity seemed at least twice as big as the stove

Blanche had taught her to operate.

You can figure it out, Emma. The voice spoke sternly this time. *Because if you don't, you'll be sent home in disgrace. Do you want that to happen? Michael and Jon will both say, "I told you so"—Jon's betting you'll last only two days, remember?—and you'll be no closer to starting your business than you were two weeks ago.*

The mental picture of the men's sage nods and knowing smiles did more than anything to help Emma tamp down her trepidation. *The business, think of the business.* She walked farther into the kitchen with a sure step, trying desperately to exude self-confidence. Her nose caught the faint aroma of pleasant cooking odors lingering in the air, and, as she drew close to the stove, she could feel its gentle warmth.

That's the way, the voice inside her head congratulated. *See? It doesn't bite. So what if the iron beast has six cooking lids instead of four? A big strong experienced lumberjack cookwoman such as yourself would be glad for the extra cooking space.*

She nodded and forced herself to look about the room. The kitchen was quite modern, she noticed, complete with an icebox, an indoor hand pump, and a sink with a drain. Sturdy wooden shelves near the stove held several cast-iron spider frying pans, roasters, cooking pans, and two large coffeepots.

The food preparation area was situated between two eating areas, she noticed, the smaller of the two being just a nook in the kitchen. The larger area lay beyond a wide doorway at the rear of the kitchen. It was really quite large, Emma realized, for it comfortably accommodated an enormous wooden plank table, benches, and a large sideboard.

"We call that the 'back kitchen' or just the 'backroom,' " Maureen explained, following Emma's curious gaze. "Although what it really is is a dinin' room for our help." She carried the lamp to the doorway of the large dining area. "The ranch hands take their meals in here. That way we don't have to run two kitchens—or have two cooks. Me Andrew, God rest his soul, set it up that way when we added onto the house a few years back," she added, pointing to the rear wall of the cowboys' dining area. "See? There's another door back there—an' a washstand, too, just for them, so they're not bringin' their dirt an' grime into the house." She nodded. "I must admit to likin' this way o' doin' things. Meals are nothin' fancy here, much like at your loggin' camp, I expect. We—the family, I mean— often take our meals with the hands, too." She lowered her voice slightly. "It helps in me managin' of the place to know what's goin' on from day to day."

Emma nodded her understanding, not able to help herself from making comparisons between Maureen Montgomery and the fifty-year-old "Texas Cattle Queen" she'd recently read about in the newspaper. Apparently Maureen Montgomery managed her ranch in much the same way that the widowed Mrs. Rogers, of the Corpus Christi area, ran her late husband's ranch—in a plain, no-frills, but very successful manner.

Emma remembered the respect and admiration she'd felt for the Texas woman when she had read the news item. Then, on another page of the very same paper, there had been an item about a Canadian woman who had moved to New York and was making a successful living as an artist. In a low moment, before Maureen's letter had come, it was almost as if an invisible force had drawn Emma's eyes to those two particular articles, to give her the strength to keep believing in her dream of opening her collectibles shop.

"Emma?" Maureen asked, breaking into her thoughts. "I cannot believe I've forgotten me manners. Do you want a bite o' supper? It just occurred to me that you probably haven't eaten a thing since the noon meal."

Despite Emma's protestations that she was fine, Maureen bustled about the kitchen and fixed a cold plate of delicious-looking biscuits, ham, and cheese. "Let's sit over here," the older woman said, gesturing to the small table.

With all that had gone on during the day, Emma would never have believed she could eat a bite. But she surprised herself by finishing every morsel on her plate while Ginny and Maureen spent the next half an hour explaining the usual ranch and kitchen routines. Emma listened carefully to what they said, trying to calculate how many times she would need to multiply Blanche's recipes to make enough food to feed eleven or twelve hungry people at each meal.

Edward's and Joey's voices could occasionally be heard from another area of the house. Each time Emma heard Joey's peculiar voice, she felt unnerved. She also felt ashamed and embarrassed about her reaction to him, however, especially after Maureen had been so frank in speaking of her son's affliction, and of her feelings for him.

The next time she saw Joey, Emma pledged, she'd make a special effort to smile and tell him hello. Curious as he was, he apparently did have the ability to say a few things. She tried to remember anything enlightening she'd read about idiocy, but nothing immediately came to mind. Well, she could at least follow the lead the Montgomery family had set, for after all, it wasn't as if she was going to have a whole lot to do with the boy; she'd been hired as a cook, not as Joey's tutor or caretaker.

What kind of feelings did Joey have? she wondered in an abstract way. Though she'd always been too frightened of the Mantle boy to think of him as a person, much less a person with feelings, she was certain she'd seen a sadness about Joey when Ryan had stormed from the room. . . .

Thinking of Ryan Montgomery, Emma swallowed. She wondered what, besides her unfortunate reaction to Joey, she could possibly have done to antagonize him so. Or maybe it was that military men just acted that way, she speculated. Unsmiling and harsh and severe. . . .

"I'm guessin' we've told you enough for one night," Maureen said, interrupting Emma's thoughts. "Your room is just off the kitchen, down the hallway there." She pointed to the entryway on the other side of the kitchen. "First door on the left. 'Tisn't much, but it's neat an' clean. Did you bring a clock?"

Emma nodded.

"Good, then. You'll be wantin' to set it for four-thirty or so. And if you wouldn't be mindin'," Maureen added with a weary, apologetic smile, "me an' Ginny are lookin' forward to sleepin' in a wee bit in the mornin'. It's been a long month."

It had been a long month since Jim Hopper's death, Ryan Montgomery thought darkly, standing alone in the main barn and watching a new foal nuzzle its mother. The mare whickered and bent her neck lovingly toward her offspring, and it struck Ryan that the special bond he and Hopper had shared—the deep respect and affection cavalry officers have for their horseflesh—was gone forever.

Because Hopper was gone forever.

Ryan sighed and looked about the barn. It was in excellent order, just as the entire ranch seemed to be. The mare whickered again, drawing Ryan's gaze back to the pair, and he felt a moment of outrage that life should continue to march blithely along while his best friend lay dead in his grave.

Would this pain never dull itself? he wondered. During the first few weeks after Hopper's death—*Hopper's suicide,* his subconscious hissed—it had been easy to numbly push the grief aside and focus instead on counting each day until his resignation became official.

Damn you, Hopper, for taking the chicken-shit way out.

Forty-one years old, Captain James B. Hopper had been a thousand and forty-one times more deserving of the rank of major than Anthony Julson, the politically connected little brown-noser who had been commissioned in Hopper's place. Ryan had been stunned to hear that Hopper had been passed over for promotion again, for, as rumor had it, his mentor had been first in line for the commission.

The military was in decline, however, and promotions were few and far between. Also, the factors of who a man knew and how well he was connected took precedence over the much more mundane qualifications of, say, his leadership qualities or service record. In the past three years both he and Hopper had become increasingly disillusioned with the army. In fact, they'd had several evening discussions, over bitters, about just that and about returning to civilian life.

Jesus, God, and all the saints, Hopper, what was the matter with just giving your resignation to the post commander?

Ryan had turned in his resignation the night Hopper had . . . died. For three weeks, the thought of getting out of the army and putting military life behind him had been the whole of his existence, his focus, his reason for going on. Or was it merely his reason for not focusing on the fact that his friend had . . .

Closing his eyes, Ryan remembered the first time he'd met Hopper. It had been in '79, just before the Ute uprising at White River Agency in Colorado. Fresh from West Point, Ryan had been a green first lieutenant stationed at Fort Steele—a damned dirty trick for a young man who thought Wyoming Territory wasn't big enough for both he and his father.

For some reason Hopper had taken a liking to him, an angry youth with a chip on his shoulder. "You Andrew Montgomery's boy?" the captain had asked with a friendly smile after they'd been introduced. "Don't know him, but I've heard of him," he'd responded to Ryan's abrupt answering nod. "Guess we all have. Prob'ly eat his beef, too." He'd clapped his hand on Ryan's shoulder then. "I can't imagine as he'd want a military career for you, not with that big place of his by Pine Bluffs, but welcome to Fort Steele anyhow."

Holding in common many opinions and philosophies, the two men had fallen into a fast friendship, one that became firmly cemented after the vicious battle with the Ute along the Milk Creek branch of the Yampa River. They'd both been transferred to Cheyenne's Fort D. A. Russell not long after that, and in the ensuing months and years they had enjoyed countless evening card games and glasses of bitters. And when Andrew Montgomery had died suddenly of a heart attack last year, not long after Ryan had attained the rank of captain and before any progress had been made at father and son putting their differences aside, Jim Hopper had been there with a listening ear and his brand of quiet understanding.

If someone put a gun to his head—*nice thought, Montgomery,* he caustically reproached himself—he couldn't say for sure what it was he was going to do with his life now that he was on the outside. He didn't know. In the week he'd been home, he'd tried to lose himself in all kinds of odd jobs and pursuits, but Jim Hopper's death dogged him . . . pursued him . . . haunted him.

It wasn't as if he'd never seen death before—during the battle with the Ute he'd seen plenty of dying and death. Red men. White men. Black men. Men he knew. Men he didn't know. But Hopper's death was different, and not only because he had known Hopper.

It was different because it was his friend, and because he remembered vivid things about that night, things like the smell of gunpowder in Hopper's room . . . and things like the sight of the sentries carrying the blanket-wrapped body from the officers' quarters in the dead of the night, out into a swirling snowstorm.

So now you're out, Montgomery. Now what?

Home no longer felt like home. Sure, his family was here, but if he thought about it, this Wyoming ranch had never felt like home. Home to him was the Nebraska farm the Montgomerys had left several years ago. He'd never really lived at this new ranch . . . he'd only been a visitor.

He felt like a visitor, too, an out-of-place visitor.

Ryan walked to the barn door and stared at the ranch house. Warm lamplight shone from several windows of his family's dwelling. He knew he should go in and apologize for losing his temper. He owed his mother that much. He knew he should also spend some time with Joey, but he just couldn't bring himself to do either thing. So he just stood half in, half out of the barn. Staring. Thinking.

He couldn't help his reaction when the new cook had frozen in horror at the sight of Joey. The froth-headed little thing. She'd jabbered like a jay the whole way home from the train station, but she couldn't even give his brother a simple hello. What kind of person was she? Thoughtless, ignorant, or both?

Not ignorant, he decided, remembering some of the topics she'd tried to draw him out with during the ride to the ranch. She possessed an education, of that he was certain. It also solidified his first impression of her: the girl was probably fleeing some sort of romantic entanglement.

He cursed to himself as her image appeared in his mind. The bit of fluff also possessed nutmeg brown ringlets, a heart-shaped face, and a dainty waist he knew his hands could span, although he couldn't imagine why he should be thinking of any of that.

Damn it, though, she'd made him mad. Thinking of her, he still felt the same gut-gripping wrath he'd felt when she'd looked at Joey like he was some kind of . . . monster. Then she couldn't even look at him. What was the matter with her? Didn't she realize Joey had feelings?

What about you, Montgomery? a voice inside him questioned. *Don't* you *know Joey has feelings? You've barely given him two minutes of your time since you've been home. You know he'd like nothing better than to just be near you, yet you keep pushing him away.*

Guilt piled atop Ryan's anger and grief, further paralyzing him, and he stood staring at the house and at the black night beyond for a very long time.

Chapter Four

Morning came too soon for Emma—if a person could say four and a half hours after midnight *was* morning.

Though she'd been dead tired last evening, it had been difficult to fall asleep with all that weighed and whirled in her mind. The Montgomerys had apparently gone to bed right after she'd turned in, for she'd heard several sets of footsteps on the stairs as she undressed and slipped under the covers. She never did hear Ryan come in, but she'd heard the murmurs of Edward's and Ginny's voices—apparently their room was above hers—for quite a long time. They'd talked about the ranch, about Joey, about Ryan . . . and about her.

Ginny talked more than her husband, but Emma could only hear snatches of the young woman's side of the conversation. "She looks so delicate . . . too bad about Joey . . . I can't help it, Edward, Ryan scares me . . . She seems very sweet" were some of the things that drifted down from the upper story to where Emma lay.

"She talks like she's had learning," Edward added, then the murmurs had deepened into the same soft secret sounds Emma sometimes used to hear from Michael and Lucille's bedchamber. Whispers. Quiet rhythmic squeaking. An occasional muffled moan.

Although Emma knew what went on between married people, she didn't understand exactly *why* it went on. Nor did she understand the peculiar feelings inside her—feelings that originated in unmentionable areas of her person—as she had tried not to listen to the hushed sounds of love-making in the room above her.

No such feelings were present this morning, however. Standing in the Montgomerys' large kitchen, Emma decided the only thing she felt was a knot of fear in her gut. That, plus tiredness, she amended. Though she'd splashed cold water on her face, she could barely keep her eyes open.

Setting down *Buckeye Cookery,* the recipe tablet, and the lamp she'd carried from her room, she walked to the window and peered outside. The Montgomery women had mentioned the ranch hands would already have been up working an hour or more by the time they came in to take their morning meal. *Did all people in the West rise this early?* she wondered, rubbing her eyes. The eastern sky was barely light.

The clouds had cleared overnight, though, she noticed, for she could also see stars winking and shining overhead. Maybe a bright sunny day would be just the thing she needed to start things off on the right foot.

Emma shook her head and stepped away from the window, thinking about all she had to do in the next hour. Ginny and Maureen had told her the cowboys would be in for their breakfast between five-thirty and six. Well, she thought with fresh fear—and a little less sleepiness— the first order of business was to get the iron brute fired up. For the first time she became aware of the kitchen's chilliness.

Half an hour later she had the stove's water reservoir filled and had a fire—of sorts—going. At least she *hoped* the fire was going. She'd followed all the directions Blanche had given her—she'd cleared the ashes from the banked fire, then opened both the draft and damper wide, at the same time making sure the oven damper was open and the check draft was closed—but her first three starts had gone out without catching. *For heaven's sake,* she thought with more than a little irritation, *who would have ever thought*

*a person needed an advanced education to light a simple
cookstove fire?*

Hearing the growing crackles from inside the firebox, she
sighed in relief. The tinder had finally caught. She removed
the front cooking lid and added more wood to the little fire
below, giving thought, at the same time, to what her first
meal would be. Blanche had recommended she stay with
simple things until she knew her way around the kitchen a
little better.

A good suggestion, she thought, pumping water to fill
the two coffeepots. Fried ham and griddle cakes should be
simple enough, while at the same time being hearty fare for
hungry working men.

After removing a large ham from the icebox and cutting
several thick slices—two per person ought to be plenty,
she decided, she flipped through *Buckeye Cookery* until
she found the one recipe for batter cakes that didn't require
an overnight sponge. Why did so many of them call for
overnight sponges? she wondered. Blanche had told her all
about bread sponges, about why it was necessary to start
a flour and liquid and yeast mixture the night before, but
she hadn't said anything about griddle cake sponges.

This particular recipe called for one quart each of flour
and sour milk, three eggs, a tablespoon of butter, and two
teaspoons of soda. How many cakes would that make?
Emma wondered, trying to figure how much batter might
be used for each cake. Of course, it all depended on what
size one made them, but it seemed as though this recipe
would make at least . . . thirty or forty.

Would that be enough to feed eleven people, though?
she wondered uneasily. It probably would, she decided,
but better to double the amounts and err on the side of
making too much food this first meal, rather than to have
not enough to serve the men.

Serve the men.

She suddenly remembered she had to set the table, too.
The eastern sky had grown lighter; the men would be in
soon. "Mix the griddle cakes, set the table," she spoke
aloud to herself at the same time the fire gave a great
crackle and pop. *The fire!* From the noises coming from

inside the firebox, it sounded as if her little blaze had turned into an inferno.

Lost in her worries about griddle cakes, she'd forgotten all about the fire. She remembered what Blanche had told her about adjusting the drafts and dampers once the fire was established, to provide the proper flow of air to produce a *steady* fire. Flipping open her tablet to the pages on cookstove operation, Blanche's underlined words jumped off the page.

"There's no quicker way to ruin a good stove than to let it get red hot."

Oh, dear, Emma thought with alarm. Although the stove's color was still black, she had no doubt the T and cooking lids over the firebox would soon begin to glow if she allowed the flames to continue roaring away. Using the diagram she'd drawn of Michael and Lucille's cookstove, as well as the elaborate instructions Blanche had given her, she adjusted the draft and dampers to slow the fire.

There. Now the fire was . . . smoking up the kitchen.

Coughing and choking on the acrid fumes, Emma opened the chimney damper a bit more, remembering what Blanche had also told her about each stove having its own personality. "It takes you a while to learn a stove's quirks," she'd said. "Different days make for different fires, too, so just be patient and keep fiddling with things, and soon you'll come to understand what your stove wants you to do with it."

This new adjustment seemed to take care of the smoke, she observed, wiping the tears from her eyes. She walked to the outside door and opened it wide, waving the worst of the smoke out into the early morning air with a dishrag.

All right, now, she congratulated herself, coughing one last time, *the fire is going and the ham is sliced. You're off to a fine start, Emma Louise—Blanche would be proud. All you have left to do is start the coffee, mix the batter, set the table, and begin to cook.*

Indeed, things seemed to go much more smoothly now that the fire was burning properly. She mixed ground coffee beans with eggs, just as Blanche had showed her, then tied the mixture into two small muslin sacks, put one sack into each water-filled coffeepot, and finally set the heavy pots on the stove.

Humming a little, she found the necessary ingredients for the griddle cakes and mixed a double recipe of the batter—not quite whipping the egg whites to a stiff froth—but then, who, besides her, was there to say otherwise? As she set two heavy spiders on the stove to heat for the ham, she was satisfied to see a little steam curling upward from the coffeepots.

The large cast-iron griddle straddled the two remaining cook spaces, and she gave a little prayer of thanks that the stove had six cooking lids, rather than four. Quickly greasing the spiders and the griddle, she hurried over to set the table while they heated.

Dawn was breaking. Out the window of the back dining room, Emma could see a large barn and several fenced corrals, as well as a few men on horseback. It had to be at least five-thirty, she estimated, haphazardly slapping down two bowls each of butter and brown sugar, as well as the tin dishes and utensils from the sideboard, before running back to the stove.

The grease was hot, just beginning to smoke, and with a spatula Emma spread it evenly over the cooking surfaces. A few minutes later she had eight fine-looking griddle cakes browning, and several slices of ham sizzling away. The coffee was boiling now—*let it go five or ten minutes once it boils,* she remembered Blanche saying, and Emma thought things were coming together nicely.

The first set of griddle cakes turned out a little dark on one side, but she placed them, light side up, on a towel-covered plate, covered them with another towel, and set the plate into the warming oven. The ham cooked up faster than the griddle cakes, the two spiders being on the burners directly over the fire, but Emma quickly learned when to turn each item from one side to the other, then to make the transfer from cooking surface to warming oven.

"Good morning, Miss Taylor."

Emma jumped at Edward's voice. With the noise of the frying ham and boiling coffee, she hadn't heard him come in the kitchen.

"I didn't mean to scare you," he said, reaching into the warming oven and snitching a slice of ham. "Sure smells good," he added with a grin. "Do you suppose that coffee's done yet?"

Remembering the sounds she'd heard from his and Ginny's room last night, Emma felt a little flustered as she looked into his kind, handsome face. "It should be, just about," she said, seeing that this new batch of griddle cakes was ready to be turned. She flipped them over, seeing that the ham was also ready to turn. How on earth was she going to pour him a cup of coffee when both her hands were already overly occupied?

"The men should be in pretty quick," he commented, seeing her predicament and helping himself to a hot pad. Taking one of the pots from the stove, he poured himself a mug of the steaming brew. "You haven't seen Ryan yet this morning, have you?" he asked, returning the pot to the stove.

A wave of mortification deepened the pink in Emma's cheeks, she was sure, more than the heat of the stove and her other discomfiture already had. She'd been too busy during the past hour to think about her unfortunate reaction to Joey last evening, but Edward's question caused her shame and embarrassment to come flooding back.

"I feel like I should apologize for him," Edward added, surprising Emma into turning all the way around and looking at him. He gave her a gentle smile, one much like Maureen's. "Because I have a feeling he's not going to do it himself. Don't worry about your job, either, Miss Taylor. Ryan doesn't have anything to do with running the ranch—he never has," he added with a little shake of his head. "And neither Ma nor I is going to send you packing just because of last night. You'll soon come to know Joey—and not be frightened," he added with another smile. "I'm sure things are going to work out just—"

"Howdy!" a deep, unfamiliar voice greeted from the back dining area. "Hey, Montgomery," another voice said.

"Mornin', Webber," Edward replied. "Owens, Ferguson, Lorenzo," he added, nodding, as he stepped over to the doorway of the back kitchen. "Our new cook got in last night," he said, gesturing toward Emma. "Her name's Miss Emma Taylor, and she came all the way from St. Paul. She used to cook for a lumber camp up in northern Minnesota."

Emma heard several male voices greet her, and she turned and flashed a polite smile toward the four men who stood bunched up in the entryway, all craning their necks to get a look at her.

Arms and elbows bumped and collided as four hats were immediately doffed. Jockeying for position in the doorway that was wide enough to comfortably accommodate only two men standing side by side, the cowhands called out their welcomes and their names amidst cries of "Hey, watch it," and "Come on, I was here first."

"Good morning. Pleased to meet you." Emma lifted her spatula in greeting and turned back to the griddle cakes, smiling a little at the comical picture they made. The last of the ham was frying, and there was only a little more batter left in the bottom of the bowl.

"Here come the rest of 'em," she heard Edward say, just as a door slammed and more voices filled the backroom. "I'll take the coffee over while you finish up," he said, reaching over her shoulder with a hot pad.

Good timing, she thought with relief. The food was nearly done.

A few minutes later she pulled the hot pans from the stovetop, removed the food-laden plates from the warming oven, set them on the worktable, and straightened her apron. She was a thoroughly unpresentable floury greasy mess, she knew, but there was nothing she could do about it now. The men were waiting for their breakfast.

A steady buzz of male conversation came from the backroom, and Emma realized a long moment of nervous self-consciousness at the thought of having to walk in there and serve all those strange men. She'd never before served anyone in her life. What if she didn't do it right? Worse yet, what if she did it wrong and they were upset with her . . . or made fun of her?

Come on, Emma, she told herself, *you've already cooked the blessed meal. Serving it can't be that difficult.*

Taking a deep breath, she carried the plate of fried ham across the kitchen and into the back dining room. Several men—eight or nine?—were seated around the large table. All conversation stopped when she entered the room, and all the men hurried to rise from their benches, causing a loud scraping racket on the wooden floor.

"Oh . . . my," she said, overwhelmed by so many hardy cowboys trying to capture her attention and tell her good morning. "Please . . . Thank you . . . Really, you don't have to—"

"This here's Miss Emma Taylor," Edward said loudly from the other side of the table, giving her a reassuring smile. "For those of you who just came in, Miss Taylor's the new cook from St. Paul. Used to cook for loggers, you know."

The word "loggers" rolled around the room as the men nodded their heads in approval and reseated themselves.

"Let me take the ham for you, Miss Taylor," said one of the men she'd first seen in the doorway. He had a chubby, boyish face and short carrot-colored hair. "Remember me, ma'am? I'm Zachariah Ferguson, but you can call me Zach."

"You can call me whatever you like," said the man next to him as Zach took the hot plate of meat from Emma's hands and quickly set it on the table. The speaker was a weathered-looking man Emma hadn't yet met, somewhere in his thirties, she guessed, with blue eyes that looked like they were always laughing. "Yep, Webber's the name, but you can call me whatever you like, ma'am," he repeated with a grin. "Just don't call me . . ." He paused artfully.

"Late for dinner," several long-suffering voices finished for him, in unison.

"Webber, that one's so old that it's beginnin' to limp," a bearded blond man called from across the table.

"Limp?" queried the man who had been introduced as Lorenzo. "Hell, that one's so old it needs a cane."

Emma couldn't help but smile at the men's banter.

"That ham sure looks good, ma'am," Ferguson commented longingly. "Do you s'pose . . . ?"

"Please go ahead and get started." Her smile brightened at the warm reception she'd gotten. "I'll go get the griddle cakes."

A buzz of conversation broke out when she left the room, quieting into polite nods and friendly shy smiles when she returned with a plate of griddle cakes in each hand. Helpful hands relieved her of the heavy platters, and she watched as the serving dishes made their way around the table.

"Ma'am?" a young man of seventeen or eighteen inquired from the other end of the table. "Ma'am, we're ready for some more ham now." He held up the empty plate and smiled disarmingly.

More ham?

The nervous knot twisted in Emma's stomach. "I . . . ah . . . figured on two slices apiece," she said cautiously, looking around the table and seeing, to her horror, that about half the plates contained no ham.

"Two slices of ha—"

Ferguson's incredulous voice ended in a soft grunt as the elbow of the man on the far side of him, the man that had introduced himself as Paul McDermott, landed in his ribs. "This breakfast sure looks good, ma'am," McDermott said with a nod, pulling five griddle cakes off a platter and reaching for the butter.

Five at once? Lord in heaven, there aren't going to be enough of those, either.

McDermott passed the platter on to the next man, who paused a moment, looking at the others waiting for the cakes. Carefully counting the cakes remaining on the plate, he glanced again at the remaining men and took three cakes. The same thing was occurring on the other side of the table, too, Emma noticed, much to her dismay. Murmurs of "looks good" and "good breakfast" echoed around the room as, suddenly, the men seemed to be very busy buttering and sprinkling brown sugar on their griddle cakes. The slices of ham, too, were counted and redistributed evenly.

You didn't make enough food, Emma Louise.

Twisting her apron, she dumbly stood and watched the food disappear. "I-I can go make some more—" she began.

"Oh, no, ma'am," McDermott hastened to say. "Don't go to the bother. This'll do me just fine."

"Yeah, me too, Miss Taylor," the blond man said, bobbing his head. "I wasn't none too hungry this mornin'. Prob'ly none of us was."

As the rest of the men smiled and hastened to assure her they had plenty to eat, the door opened and Ryan walked in. He removed his coat and hat and hung them with the others on the row of pegs near the door. "What's for breakfast?" he asked curtly, his gaze flicking over the table and landing on her.

He was dressed in leather chaps and a well-fitting blue-and-gray plaid flannel shirt that emphasized his wide shoulders. Freshly shaven, his face bore a striking resemblance to Edward's, but austerity, not easy friendliness, emanated from his countenance. As his dark eyes bored into hers, Emma felt the color rise in her cheeks, and she dropped her gaze.

A long awkward silence ensued, then Edward spoke up. "It *was* griddle cakes and ham, brother, but you missed it."

"Yeah, sorry, Captain," Ferguson said as he scraped the last of the butter and melted brown sugar from his plate with his knife. "Miss Taylor's food was so good we ate it all up already." He licked his knife and scraped the plate again, though there was nothing left to scrape.

The same scraping noises came from several other plates as several heads nodded in agreement, and Emma wished she could fall through the floor. If she doubled—or even tripled—the amount of food she'd prepared this morning, she doubted it still would have been enough to satisfy these cowhands.

"I suppose the coffee's gone, too?" Ryan's deep voice was sardonic.

"Yeah, I think we 'bout knocked the pot off, Captain," McDermott said.

"No, there's another pot in the stove," Emma said quickly, glad for a reason to leave the room. "Let me go get it."

By the time she fished the muslin bag of grounds from the pot, burning her fingers a little in the process, she could hear that several of the men had arisen from the table and

were putting on their outdoor gear. Edward walked through
the kitchen and disappeared into the pantry, nodding and
giving her a good-natured smile as he passed. Carefully
holding the hot pot away from her body, she walked back
toward the back dining room.

" . . . sure is purty," one voice said as she neared the
entryway, causing her to stop and listen.

"Yeah, who needs food?" another agreed. "Them kinda
looks can fill a man up by just bein' in the same room
with her."

"That, or make him more hungry."

Soft laughter.

"Her cookin' ain't bad," Ferguson proclaimed. They
added in a thoughtful tone, "Musta bin that that loggin'
camp was tight on money. She prob'ly jus' got used to
stretchin' everything out."

"Yeah, the coffee was a little thin," Lorenzo agreed.

Amusement was easy to hear in Webber's voice. "Ain't
none of you ever heard that the prettier a gal is, the worse
coffee she makes?"

More laughter.

Oh, dear Lord, they were laughing at her.

"Hey, Montgomery, you plannin' on workin' that bronc
again today?" Webber asked, changing the subject.

The coffeepot grew hotter and heavier beneath the hot
pads, but Emma didn't have the courage to walk into the
room just yet. Not while the men's grins at her ineptitude
still undoubtedly played about their lips. Shifting her grip
on the pot to ease the strain on her arms and shoulders, she
swallowed hard, listening to Webber try to draw Ryan into
conversation.

"I dunno who got the best of who yesterday, but that paint
you was breakin' was showin' his belly like he was damned
proud of it."

Still no response from Ryan.

"Say, you was cavalry, wasn't ya, Cap'n?" a younger
voice asked.

"Was."

Ginny had been right—Ryan Montgomery barely talked
to anyone. Emma supposed she should feel flattered that

he'd deigned to say so much to her last evening. Though it was obvious Webber had given up on further conversation with Ryan, the owner of the young voice wasn't daunted by the crisp reply he'd gotten.

"I heard you was one of Major Thornburgh's men," the youth went on. "You know, back in '79?" He paused for a moment, during which the sound of rustling coats and hats quieted dramatically. "I heard you was there when them Ute ambushed his troops by Red Canyon, an' that Thornburgh got shot off his horse right when he was fixin' to parley with—"

McDermott cleared his throat. "Time's a wastin', Eaton. Here's your hat." The hinges of the backdoor squeaked, and the sound of bootsteps and rustling outer clothing resumed. "See you later, Montgomery . . . Bye, Captain . . . So long, Miss Taylor . . ."

The pot of coffee had grown so heavy that Emma was sure her arms had each lengthened by several inches. She had to set it down. "So long," she called weakly, stepping around the corner just as the last few men exited the room.

Ryan was seated at the table, toying with an empty coffee cup, his expression looking, if possible, more forbidding than before. He glanced up at her and thrust his cup forward.

Asking him about army battles apparently wasn't the way to get on his good side, Emma concluded. But did he even have a good side? she wondered. A happy side? A light side? Carefully pouring steaming coffee into his cup, she realized she felt terribly jittery being alone in the same room with him—more jittery than she'd felt yesterday during the ride from the train depot, when she'd been unable to see his entire face or form. There was just something about him. . . .

This is ridiculous, Emma, she told herself, setting down the pot onto one of the hot pads. *There's no reason to be frightened of him. He's just a man, albeit an ill-tempered one. Remember what Mama used to say about spreading a little kindness?*

She cleared her throat, summoning her mettle. "Can I make you some breakfast, Mr. Montgomery?" she asked politely, beginning to stack plates. "Oh . . . I'm sorry," she added, as an afterthought, "I'm not quite certain of military protocol. Should I be addressing you as Captain?"

The black gaze flicked upward. "I resigned my commission," he said abruptly, pushing the bench from the table. He stood and reached for his coat and hat, dismissing her with one last black glance. "Think I'll skip breakfast." Donning his outdoor dress, he picked up his coffee and departed.

Well, of all the uncivil, discourteous . . . He didn't even answer my question.

Stacking the rest of the plates, Emma carried them to the kitchen. She was beginning to feel a little less hurt and flustered—and a little more irritated—with Ryan Montgomery's manners. Or lack thereof.

What a boor he was.

Catching sight of him out the window, she watched his long legs eat up the ground as he strode toward the barn. She felt a small pang of guilt, though, when she realized he hadn't had anything to eat. And he wasn't the only hungry man; none of the other cowboys had full stomachs, either.

She noticed a group of men congregated at the nearest corral fence. *Was that Edward standing among them?* she wondered, trying to make out the profile of the dark-haired, hatless man standing amidst the tight huddle of cowboys. It was indeed Edward, she decided, but how on earth had he gotten outdoors?

Probably through the front door, if it's any of your business at all, she answered herself as she stepped away from the window. With all the work she had to do this morning, she didn't have any time to waste on wondering who went where. There were dishes to wash, beans to start, bread to make—and yet another meal to prepare.

She was just about to go back for another load of dishes when she saw one of the cowboys slap Edward on the back, then break from the group. In one of the cowboy's hands was a large hunk of . . . *bread*?

It *had* to be bread, Emma thought with stupefaction, stepping back to the window. Nearly half a loaf. She watched the man—Ferguson, she guessed—bring the mass to his mouth and take a bite. Where had he gotten *bread*?

She had her answer a moment later when she saw, from the opening in the knot of men Ferguson's departure had created, other men breaking off large chunks from the loaves Edward held in his arms. Dear Lord, she'd left the cowhands so hungry that Edward had to sneak dry bread out to them.

And worse than that, there was no breakfast for Ryan . . . or for Maureen or Ginny or Joey, either, she realized. Some fine ex-logging camp cook she was. She only hoped she caught on to things quickly, before the Montgomerys ran her out of the Territory on a rail.

What an awful morning it had been, Emma thought. Truly, truly awful. Watching the men disburse, leaving Edward to chew on his own chunk of bread, she thought dispiritedly that things couldn't get much worse.

Chapter Five

Things that morning didn't get worse, but neither did they get much easier.

In fact, Emma thought wearily as she kneaded an enormous mass of bread dough, things hadn't gotten any easier at all since she'd arrived at the Montgomery ranch. After the past three days of cooking, cleaning, kneading, chopping, peeling, and washing dishes, dishes, and more dishes, she was so tired she could barely see straight.

Thinking of Blanche as she worked the dough, Emma wondered how things were going back in St. Paul. She'd been meaning to write, to tell Blanche and Michael and Lucille she'd safely arrived at Pine Bluffs, but she simply hadn't had the time. She rose well before sunrise, and it was well after sunset by the time the bread sponge was set and the last of the pots and pans were scrubbed. By then, she could barely keep her eyes open long enough to undress and fall into bed.

Thinking of the sheer amount of food she'd cooked and served since she'd been here, Emma shook her head. Three days of food for these cowhands was probably enough to feed the Taylor household for half a year. She was lucky she hadn't realized what she was getting herself into by taking this position—if she had, she never would have attempted such an . . . such an *arduous* occupation.

But she was committed now. There was no other way to raise the money she needed to open her business, so consequently she had no choice in the matter—not if she was going to succeed, that was.

And she was determined to succeed at this—if only to thumb her nose at Michael and Jon.

She paused a moment and brushed a brunette ringlet from her forehead with the back of her flour-encrusted wrist. Dratted hair. Why would it never stay where she put it? And, as long as she was asking herself rhetorical questions, when was this bread kneading going to get any easier?

She lifted her shoulders up and down a few times, trying to loosen her aching muscles. *Only another five or ten minutes to go*, she told herself, feeling her heart pound rapidly within her breast. A trickle of sweat rolled down her spine. *You can do it, Emma. Come on, think of all those pies you have to have ready for the noon meal.*

She knew the quality of her food was nowhere near the caliber of Blanche's tasty fare. Whereas Blanche's preparations were always perfectly simmered, baked, broiled, or browned, the components of Emma's meals, during her first days on the job, had ranged from underdone to overdone to occasionally just right. Thankfully, though, she hadn't made any further gross quantity estimations, as she had for that first, awful, embarrassing breakfast.

Blanche would have quite a chuckle over that calamity, Emma suspected, feeling the magical change in the dough's texture beginning to take place under her hands. It was at this point in the seemingly interminable kneading process, the point at which the dough was transformed from a soft mushy mass into a springy supple substance, that Emma became heartened.

It meant the end of the kneading.

"Thank you . . . thank you . . . thank you," she said aloud, in time with her motions. A little of her gladness evaporated when she looked up from the worktable and saw the pile of breakfast dishes waiting to be done.

"Hah-low?"

Emma jumped at the sound of Joey Montgomery's voice. Turning her head, she saw he'd come into the kitchen through the pantry door. Dressed in blue woolen pants and a blue striped shirt that was half tucked in, half hanging out, he regarded her with a quizzical expression on his broad face. He cocked his head to the side and licked his lips, screwing up his face a little as he looked at her. The ever-present handkerchief was in his left hand; his right hand came up to scratch his nose.

"Hello, Joey," she said, doing her best to give him a pleasant smile. Though none of the old panicky feelings rose inside her, she still found it disconcerting to look upon his irregular features. *What is he doing in here again?* she wondered uneasily. Beginning yesterday he'd made several trips to the doorway to look at her shyly, staying only a minute or two each time.

Be patient with him, she told herself, *he's just at loose ends because of Ginny and Maureen being in Cheyenne.*

The two women had left yesterday to spend a few days with Maureen's youngest daughters, Ruthie and Colleen. Judging by the way Maureen talked about her girls, Emma could tell she missed her daughters dreadfully. She also learned that the Montgomerys owned a house in town, and that before Andrew Montgomery died the family used to spend a lot of their time in Cheyenne.

Now, during the school year, the youngest girls lived away from their mother with an attendant.

"Wouldn' you like a nice visit to town, Joey?" the petite Irishwoman had asked during the noon meal yesterday, trying to talk her son into accompanying her and Ginny. "Think of how your poor wee sisters are missin' you."

"No town," he'd said to each of his mother's attempts to attract him into going, his brows drawing together. "Not go. Joey stay . . . Wyan."

After several such exchanges, with Maureen showing not so much as one bit of impatience with Joey as he stubbornly maintained that he was going to remain at the ranch with his Ryan, Edward had interrupted.

"If he wants to stay so bad, he can stay, Ma. I don't mind keeping an eye on him if Ryan's too . . . ah . . . busy these next few days," he'd said, glancing at his older brother's empty spot and the untouched table setting next to him.

After an obvious moment of indecision, Maureen had said Joey might stay. The younger boy's face had creased with joy, and he'd pattered on and on about Ryan, his "peshal brudder." Emma remembered wondering what on earth was so special about Ryan Montgomery. Her first impression of the man . . . and second, and third, and fourth, for that matter, had been less than favorable.

Joey's first solo trip to the kitchen had come a few hours later, after the women had departed, while Edward was occupied with his books. Ryan, who had disappeared somewhere on horseback early that morning, still hadn't returned. Emma had had a start when she turned to see the lonely lad peeking at her from behind the swinging pantry door.

Nervously she called out a greeting, but Joey had quickly backed up and let the door close. Since then, he'd turned up in the doorway again and again. His watchfulness unnerved Emma, but, feeling as though she needed to atone for her unfortunate reaction the first time she'd met him, she continued smiling and giving him a pleasant greeting each time she saw him.

Resting her aching arms a moment, Emma glanced again over her shoulder. Joey was still there, staring at her. The handkerchief shook fitfully in his left hand. *Why does he do that?* she wondered with irritable uneasiness. She nodded her head and forced another smile, aware that his visits were growing in both frequency and duration.

Just ignore him and maybe he'll go away, a not-so-nice voice inside her spoke. She turned back to the dough and attacked it with sudden vigor, feeling both disturbed and ashamed by her thoughts, but not knowing what she should do or say around someone such as . . . well, someone like . . .

"Am-ma," he said, pronouncing her name in a flat, two-part manner. "Taw . . . thelf."

"Taw thelf?" She turned and looked at him as she repeated his articulation. What on earth did that mean? Though Joey's family members usually understood his indistinct speech, Emma was often left wondering what he had said. This instance was no exception.

Taw thelf? What could that possibly mean? Taut self? Taught self? Either was correct, she realized uncomfortably, wondering if the boy possessed some kind of uncanny intuition.

"Am-ma . . . taw . . . thelf," he repeated, his face breaking into a grin as he tucked the handkerchief into his breast pocket with great care, raised his arms, and began to mimic her kneading motions.

Oh, wonderful. He could tell she'd only just taught herself to make bread by the way she kneaded it? *If your incompetence is obvious to Joey, imagine what the rest of the Montgomerys must be thinking of you. It's amazing they haven't fired you—*

"Am-ma taw thelf . . . Am-ma thay, 'thankyouthankyou-thankyou,' " he further mimicked, running the words together. His pudgy arms continued to knead the air as he walked closer to the worktable. "Why Am-ma thay 'thankyouthankyouthankyou?' " His smile faded, and he tilted his head to the side inquisitively.

"Oh—I know what you mean!" Understanding burst through Emma's uncomfortable confusion, bringing with it a tingle of achievement. "Joey, did you just ask me why I was talking to myself—why I was saying 'thank you'. while I was kneading the bread?"

He nodded vigorously, dropping his arms and shuffling over to stand near her. Though he was a few inches taller than she, his droop-shouldered, chubby body type made the two of them seem about even in height. He also smelled clean, of soap, Emma was surprised to note; no unpleasant body odors lingered about him.

Making a quick study of his features at this close range, she decided he did resemble his brothers. Although Joey's face was a different shape . . . his cheeks wide and flat . . . his nose smaller . . . his eyes slanted, with no eyelids, it appeared, until he blinked . . . he had much of the Montgomery look about him. The likeness was blurred, but it was definitely there. His eyes, too, were very much like Edward's, a warm shade of brown, with thick dark lashes.

Though Joey was studying her appearance every bit as openly as she had his, Emma forgot about her uneasiness. The warm glow of satisfaction from interpreting his words was still with her, and she watched carefully as he licked his lips five or six times and prepared to speak again.

"Am-ma taw . . . taw-k-k-k," he said, making great effort to pronounce the plosive consonant. He closed his eyes tight, opened them, licked his lips several more times, and scratched his nose with great concentration. "Am-ma tawk thelf," he repeated proudly, nodding his head affirmatively. His lips curved upward then, transforming his flat features into those of a grinning image of Buddha. "Am-ma c-cwazy?"

"Emma . . . crazy? . . . Are you asking me if I'm crazy because I talk to myself?" she inquired with surprise, seeing Joey's smile broaden at her quick grasp of his words.

Good heavens, she thought, it wasn't possible that he was . . . *joking* with her, was he? Watching his upward-tilted eyes crinkle even more, nearly disappearing in a face so broad and jolly, Emma was helpless to prevent the answering grin that lit across her own features.

"Yah!" He laughed out loud, a raspy, guttural sound. "Am-ma cwazy. Tawk to bwead."

Wonderment dawned over her, and she giggled out loud. "You're absolutely correct," she said. "Emma is *very* crazy. Only I wasn't talking *to* the bread," she explained, still chuckling. She raised her hands and brought them down on the dough with a *smack.* "I was just so tired of kneading this stuff that I was saying 'thank you' because I was almost done."

"Am-ma done now?" His expression was hopeful.

"With the bread, I am, and I've also got the soup started for the noon meal." She made a face and pointed at the dirty dishes. "But I still have those to do, and pies to make, and—"

"Joey wash," he interrupted. "Joey can."

"Oh, no, no," she said in a rush. "That wouldn't be right. This is my job, not yours."

"Joey wash." There was a determined edge in his voice. "Me help."

"It's very kind of you to offer, Joey, really, but I can't let you—"

He placed his hands over his ears and looked at the floor. "Me no hear Am-ma. No, no, no, no." He shook his head, and Emma swore she saw the corners of his mouth twitch. "Am-ma hear Joey?"

"Yes, Emma hears Joey," she said gently, another grin tugging at her lips. The scoundrel. How could she say no to him?

As if sensing she was about to yield to his wishes, Joey let his plump hands slide from his ears to his jaw. His face thus framed, he titled his head and raised a pair of beseeching chocolate brown eyes. "Wash? Pwease? Ed-wer brudder work. Wyan brudder gone." He sighed deeply.

"Oh. . . ." What could she say? It was incredibly improper of her to even think of putting her employer's mentally impaired son to work. Wasn't it? What would Maureen say? But then again, it seemed as though he truly had nothing else to do at the moment. "Are you certain you wouldn't rather just watch me do the dishes?" she asked hesitantly. "You don't want to get your hands all wet, do you?"

The dark eyebrows drew together. "Me wash."

And he did, washing every last dish with slow dogged determination. He also dried them carefully, one by one, and put them away, stubbornly shaking his head each time Emma asked if she could help. She was impressed by his tenacity, and even further impressed by the fact that he knew the proper place for each dish and cup bowl and plate and spoon.

While Joey progressed with the dishes, Emma set the bread to rise, then mixed and rolled out several piecrusts, just as Blanche had taught her to do. A few mishaps occurred during the rolling . . . and also when she transferred the pastry to the pie tins, but nothing so terrible that couldn't be fixed with damp fingers and some gentle stretching. Joey talked a little about Ryan while they worked, but with each of them concentrating on their respective chores, conversation was minimal.

When the sixth pastry lay in its baking receptacle, looking nearly every bit as imperfect and wrinkled and patched together as the other five, Emma carefully trimmed around the edges of the pastries with a knife, leaving an inch of overlap. Moistening her fingers again, she began fluting the edges. Or maybe *trying* to flute the edges was a better description of what she was doing. Without Blanche's helping hands to guide her, the edges didn't really look fluted at all. They just looked sort of . . . lumpy and uneven, just like the edges of her pies had looked yesterday.

At the speed with which the cowboys ate, however, Emma doubted the pie would remain on any given man's plate long enough for him to take notice of how the edge was fashioned. Though all of them seemed to have voracious appetites, she'd come to notice that Ferguson and Webber, especially, could really pack away the food.

Joey carried a heavy spider over to the shelf near the stove, pausing to study her handiwork.

"Do you like cranberry pie?" she asked with a smile.

"Pies," he said after a long moment, as if he only just recognized what they were.

Terrific, she thought, watching him lift the spider to the shelf. *You're some cook, Emma, if he had to think that long to decide whether or not these were pies.* Nodding in Joey's direction, she consulted Blanche's cranberry pie recipe and multiplied two and a half cups of cranberries by six. It meant she needed . . . *fifteen cups* of chopped cranberries? Was that right? Lord, she'd never get used to these quantities. "Well, I'll get these in the oven and I can start chopping the cranberries," she said with false cheer, trying to decide which pot would be large enough to simmer all that filling. "Would you mind getting me a bowl to—"

"No, no, no, no, Am-ma," Joey said, shaking his head, just as she reached for the oven latch. "Em-tee pie."

She smiled at his concern. "I know this is empty pie right now, Joey," she explained, having come a long way in understanding his speech in just the little time they'd spent together. "But this recipe calls for the filling to be cooked separately, on top of the stove. I'll put the filling in the pie after each is cooked. Don't worry," she added, seeing that his doubtful expression did not change one bit with her explanation. "It will be good pie. My old . . . well, someone I used to know made this pie quite frequently." With a hot pad she lifted up on the oven latch and pulled the door open.

"No, no, no, no. No cook. Am-ma nopoke pie." Joey's voice was insistent. "Shut. Shut."

"What?" The heated air from the oven caused her hair to flutter around her face as she hesitated. She closed the oven and turned, seeing that Joey looked very upset. "Nopoke pie? What do you mean?"

"Nopoke pie," he repeated, shaking his head. "No, no, no, no. Myma poke pie."

"Nopoke pie? Myma poke pie?" Emma said the words over and over in her mind, trying to make sense out of what he was saying. He watched her closely, expectantly, while she thought, his face falling when she finally shrugged helplessly and shook her head. "Joey, I'm sorry . . . I don't understand what kind of pie you're talking about."

"No kind." He shook his head vigorously. "No poke . . . Am-ma get f-f-fat pie." He filled his cheeks with air to make his point. "Joey help." He walked a few steps and turned, holding up a warning finger. "Joey help Am-ma . . . No cook, Am-ma."

"But I . . . Joey, I have to get these—"

"Am-ma wait." The stubborn edge crept back into his voice, and he frowned. "Wait."

Emma sighed as she watched Joey carefully select a fork from the drawer, nod, and return to the worktable. Just as she was wondering what he was going to do with the fork, the meaning of "nopoke" hit her. She'd forgotten to prick the pie crusts! She remembered Blanche telling her that unless empty pastry shells were pricked many, many times, they puffed up like blow-fish when they were baked. Fat pie—*of course!* It hadn't mattered yesterday when she'd made the dried apple and raisin pies, because the filling had been baked within the crusts.

How could she have forgotten to write down that important fact? she wondered, running her finger down the notebook page of her handwriting. She now remembered Blanche warning her of the consequences of not pricking the pastry

just as clearly as she remembered the experienced cook
telling her what a mess she'd have in the oven if she
didn't cut steam vents in the top crust of a two-crust pie.
Thank goodness for Joey. What an embarrassing disaster
he'd averted for her. "I forgot to poke the pie, didn't I?"
she asked humbly. "That's what you were telling me."

Joey looked at her gravely and nodded several times,
extending the fork toward her.

"Thank you for reminding me," she said, taking the fork
and offering him a grateful smile. "Whatever would I have
done without your help? These pies would have certainly
been ruined if you hadn't spoken up."

Emma's heart was warmed from top to bottom by the
slow, shy smile he gave her in return. A sudden passion
rose in her breast as she thought of the list of horrible
names Maureen had recited the other night. Moron, monster, mooncalf, mongoloid idiot . . . Had Joey ever heard
any of them? Though he was somewhat . . . impaired, he
certainly wasn't stupid.

And if Joey had heard any of those things, she further
speculated, did he know what they meant? He had to at least
know he was different from other people. Looking into his
innocent brown eyes, Emma felt an upsurge of anguish for
him. He hadn't asked to be born this way. She stabbed at
one of the piecrusts with the fork, not understanding how
people could be so cruel—or was it just thoughtless?—not
to take the time to look past . . .

Guilt flashed all through her as she thought of the Mantle
boy. The Mantle Monster. The way the boy's family had
treated him had been abominable, but, then, no one else in
the St. Paul neighborhood had acted in any better manner.
All the grown-ups on the street had tried to pretend the
boy didn't exist . . . while their sons taunted him and their
daughters ran shrieking from him. . . .

"Am-ma nice." Joey lifted his eyebrows and nodded
several times. "Nice pies."

"You know what, Joey?" she asked, suddenly remembering something Blanche used to do for her and Michael. "I
think we deserve a treat for all the hard work we've done
this morning, don't you?"

A half hour later the thick sweet cranberry concoction was simmering on the stove, the pie crusts were baked, and Emma and Joey were seated at the small table in the nook of the kitchen, nibbling at the piping hot pieces of sugar-and-cinnamon covered pastry they'd made. Golden April sunlight spilled into the warm, good-smelling room, and for the first time in days, Emma felt truly relaxed.

"G-good cooker, Am-ma," Joey complimented her, taking a drink of milk from his glass. A mustache of white now joined the crumbles of pastry, sugar, and cinnamon above his mouth, spreading out wide as he smiled. "Nice."

"This is nice, isn't it?" Emma swallowed a mouthful of crust and took a deep drink from her own glass. The contrast between hot pastry and cool milk was divine, reminding Emma of her childhood, and of many such pleasant visits to Blanche's kitchen. "We should probably save some for Edwa—"

"Wyan!" Joey interrupted excitedly as the kitchen door opened and Ryan walked in. The youth pushed back his chair and scrambled to his feet. "Come eat, Wyan. Am-ma nice. Am-ma good cooking lady. Am-ma make pie—" He glanced at her quickly and smiled before hurrying over and taking Ryan's hand. "Me help crust. Come eat . . . Crust good."

The dark preoccupied expression on Ryan Montgomery's face changed to one of irritation, and Emma noticed that the large man pulled his hand free of Joey's grasp. Undaunted, Joey clasped his hands together and moved to stand in front of his brother, continuing to chatter away about Am-ma and pies and cooking.

Ryan listened for only a few seconds before uttering a tight, "Not now, Joey," and moving to step around his brother. Emma noticed that his boots and riding gear were soiled with dirt and mud and . . . more. The pungency of the barnyard aroma assailed her nostrils just then, causing her to wrinkle her nose a little and set down her pastry. What on earth had he been doing? Mucking out the stables?

With a glowering glance in her direction, Ryan strode across the kitchen and disappeared down the hallway. Joey's word stream trailed off, and he stared after his brother with a woebegone expression, his hands still clasped before him. Slowly he separated them, and his chubby fingers began working to remove the handkerchief from his breast pocket.

Emma's appetite had fled as quickly as had the light atmosphere of the kitchen. She cleared her throat, which suddenly felt thick. "Would you like to come back over and sit with me, Joey?" she asked, wanting to give him comfort but not knowing how. Rising from her chair, she held out her hand in invitation. "We haven't even finished our pastry yet."

Joey did not reply, but continued to stare down the hallway, his fingers working busily at the cloth in his pocket. Little by little the handkerchief was freed, and he gave a great ragged sigh when it was once again secure in his left hand. The shaking movements of his arm were subtle at first, growing more pronounced as his head and shoulders drooped forward.

Emma let her arm fall, sensing there was nothing she could do, at this moment, to ease the pain of Joey's rejection. She cleared the few dishes from the table and stirred the cranberry mixture, alternating between feelings of great sadness for Joey and feelings of great rage for his brother. As far as she was concerned, the Montgomerys would be better off if Ryan just went back to the army.

"Ow—ouch!" Not giving her full attention to her stirring, she had inadvertently laid her inner wrist on the edge of the hot cast-iron pot. The sudden searing pain made her suck in her breath sharply, and she nearly let the spoon drop all the way into the bubbling pie filling.

A moment later Joey was at her side. "Am-ma hurted?" he asked with concern. "Am-ma sayed 'ouch.' "

"Oh, I just . . . no, I'm fine, Joey," she said, knowing her voice sounded strained. "But if it's not too much trouble, could you get me a cool cloth?" She set the spoon on the rest and tried to smile through the waves of pain.

His brown eyes remained fixed on her for a long moment. "Am-ma c-c-cwy?"

"Oh, no, I'm not going to cry. I just burned myself a little," she said, holding up her wrist to show him the mark.

She took a few steps and checked the soup's progress, wincing when she lifted the lid and a cloud of steam rose past her wrist. "It's nothing to worry about, Joey," she added, "it just smarts a little, is all."

"Joey help Am-ma."

"Thank you, Joey, that's really very kind of you, but—"

"No, no, no, no! Joey help Am-ma!"

"Really, Joey, I'm all right . . ." Emma let her words trail off as the youth hurried from the kitchen just as fast as his thick legs would carry him.

The grimy handkerchief lay on the floor near the table, fluttering a little as the pantry door swung back and forth in decreasing arcs. Emma was surprised that Joey had dropped his most precious possession, for she was beginning to understand the strength of his attachment to the square of linen.

Trying to ignore the pain in her wrist, she walked over and retrieved the handkerchief from the floor, folded it neatly, and set it on the table. Just then, Joey burst back through the pantry door with a little pot in his hands. His shirt had come completely untucked in his great haste, and he was breathing hard.

"My ma . . . medda . . . medda . . . medda . . . *here*!" he said, thrusting the jar toward her, looking as if he were about to explode.

"Oh, my goodness," she said, accepting the small container from him. "Are you trying to tell me that this is some kind of medicine for my burn?"

Still breathing hard, Joey nodded rapidly. "My ma salve . . . good . . . help."

"This is your mother's salve?"

He nodded again, rubbing his nose at the same time.

"Well, I must thank you for bringing it to me so quickly," she commended, touched by his thoughtfulness. "What would I have done without you this morning, I wonder? First you saved the pies, and now you saved my burned arm!"

The slow shy smile again turned up the corners of his lips, and he self-consciously brought his hand up over his eyes. "Not save Am-ma. Jus' help . . . I-I wike Am-ma."

"I like you, too, Joey," Emma replied softly, smiling in return. "And you really did save the pies."

His smile bloomed into one of happiness, and he brought his hand down.

"Maybe you should put this on for me," she said, opening the salve and holding it out to him. She shrugged helplessly. "This burn's on my right wrist, you see, and I'm not very good at trying to do things with my left hand."

The smile faded to a look of solemn responsibility as he took the salve and indicated that she should sit at the table. Once she was seated, she lay her hand on the table, palm up, exposing the angry red mark on her wrist. Making a sympathetic noise in the back of his throat, Joey carefully dipped his index finger into the pot. As he applied the unguent to the burn with a deliberate but surprisingly light touch, Emma was surprised to feel that the salve immediately cut the pain.

"H-help, Am-ma?"

"It doesn't even hurt anymore," she said, flexing her wrist. Looking up into his concerned face, she gave him a reassuring smile. "See? It's as good as new."

Ryan Montgomery stood on the other side of the kitchen, scowling at the sight of his brother smiling and bending over the ringlet-haired cook. He'd come back down the hallway, intending to tell Joey he was sorry he'd brushed him off a short time ago, but it didn't appear that his brother was feeling too bad at the moment. He watched as the cook lifted her arm into the air and waggled her fist around a few times, causing Joey to burst into laughter.

Ryan worked the fingers of his left hand, wondering if he'd splinted his wrist tightly enough. He was pretty sure no bones were broken, but the joint ached like hell from the spill he'd just taken in the corral.

He'd busted a few ponies since he'd been home, but none like the salty five-year-old buckskin he'd tried to tame this morning. McDermott had labeled the buckskin an outlaw—a horse that couldn't be broken—and Ryan was beginning to wonder if the foreman might be right. After a couple of sweaty, grueling, and brutal hours for both man and horse, the pony had, if possible, even more fight left in him than before they'd started.

Ryan had gotten as far as getting the frenzied buckskin bridled and hobbled and saddled. He'd also managed to swing himself astride the bucking beast . . . once. But before he could get his far leg hooked in the stirrup, the horse had twisted and jerked and thrown him backward.

Landing on all fours with his arms behind him, Ryan had managed to absorb most of the shock of the fall in his limbs, but his left wrist had suffered greatly. The sprain hadn't been helped any by Joey yanking and tugging on his hand, either, he thought rancorously, immediately feeling ashamed for the harshness of his thoughts. Joey couldn't possibly have known he was coming in to bind his wrist . . . or even that he'd injured himself.

He would have if you'd told him, a voice inside his head pointed out. *What was so damned difficult about opening your mouth and telling him what you were doing?*

Ryan hated the blackness that choked his soul, but his intellect was powerless against the force of the dismal feelings inside him. Since Hopper's death he'd retreated into himself, spurning everyone and everything he'd ever held dear. He could barely bring himself to speak a civil word, and now, as a result of his behavior, nearly everyone skittered around him as if he were something despicable. He hadn't missed the aversion and loathing on even the cook's face when he'd walked in from outdoors, either.

The young woman's clear laughter joined that of Joey's then, pulling Ryan's attention back to the pair. She'd certainly gotten over her terror of his brother in a hurry, he thought unkindly, watching her extend her hands to Joey so that he might help her rise from the chair. What was her coquette's game now? Did she find it challenging—or perhaps amusing—to add his brother to her collection of adoring males?

She had certainly cultivated a crop of them in the short time she'd been here. Webber, Ferguson, Owens, Lorenzo, Eaton . . . even McDermott. He'd thought they were all worthy of his respect, but he was beginning to wonder if their heads were filled with rocks.

Into the dining room they trooped, three times a day, to smile and nod at the cook—and to shovel down mouthful after mouthful of terrible food. Hell, they even asked for seconds and thirds. Compliments on Miss Emma Taylor's dee-licious cooking flew thick and fast around the table while they ate, causing the curly-haired woman's cheeks to tint a delicate shade of pink, and her uncertain expression to give way to an occasional sweet smile.

Ryan had barely had an appetite since he'd returned home, but it hadn't taken him more than a few bites of Miss Taylor's cooking to realize how awful it was. He couldn't understand why none of the men bad-mouthed Miss Emma Taylor, or why no one threatened to quit and sign on at a ranch with a decent cook. Even well out of earshot of the young woman, they continued to champion her.

Yesterday morning near the barn Ryan had heard Owens say to Webber, "Her cookin's comin' right along, ain't it? Them eggs she made actually wasn't too bad."

"Yeah, I s'pose she might turn out," Webber had allowed, nodding. His blue eyes twinkled as he adjusted his hat. "She does give a fella a reason to comb his hair in the mornin', don't she?"

"She sure does," Eaton interjected, coming around the corner with a wistful grin on his lips. "And she's nice, too. It's prob'ly jus' gonna take her a little while to change over from lumberjack cookin' to cowboy cookin', is all."

"Yep, I think you're right," Owens agreed. "Give her another week or two, an' I think she's gonna settle in an' be a damned fine cook. Jus' lookit how much better it's got since yesterday."

Webber cinched his chaps more tightly, then pulled on his leather work gloves. "Yeah, at first I was thinkin' that them lumberjacks were prob'ly walkin' around as skinny as bed slats, thankin' their lucky stars that Miss Curly quit an' came out West, but, then, hell, I realized that them poor bastards don't git to look at her no more, neither." His weathered face creased into a smile. "Yeah, she's startin' to catch on. It'll prob'ly be rocky for a while, but look at it this way—if her grub ain't killed us yet, it prob'ly ain't goin' to."

The conversation faded from Ryan's mind as he watched Joey assist the cook to her feet, his young face practically glowing. *Oh, God. Not him, too.* The abject feelings inside Ryan intensified as he watched the fetching young woman give his brother a brilliant smile. *What was it about her that turned men into fools?* he wondered, scrutinizing her appearance and wanting to find fault with everything about her.

In the first place, she couldn't cook worth a darn. She was small, he observed, too small, really, to be working in a kitchen. And if she had *ever* worked in a lumber camp, he'd eat his hat. He stuck by his original assessment that she was not of the working class.

As she gently removed her hands from his brother's grip and turned to the table, Ryan let his gaze run over the shape of her lean shoulders and back and waist. Nothing to complain about there, he observed, except that she had no meat on her bones. The front of her form got equal attention from him as she turned back to Joey and offered him a folded square of white.

Wait a minute . . . was that Joey's special handkerchief? Ryan forgot all about his visual inspection of the cook's trim form, seeing only that she was holding Joey's handkerchief. How the hell had she gotten ahold of that? Joey never let anyone hold his special item.

The throbbing in Ryan's cloth-wrapped wrist was worse now, and he squeezed it tightly with the fingers of his other hand, feeling a strong urge to get out of the house and back outdoors.

Joey could let the cook hold his handkerchief all he wanted; the cook could bat her pretty eyelashes all she wanted; he would just go back out to the corral and teach the buckskin a lesson it would never forget.

Chapter Six

After a string of mild but cloudy, dreary days, Emma was inordinately pleased to see large patches of bright blue sky peek through the clouds. With a fresh burst of optimism, she pulled the last four loaves of bread from the oven and set them to cool alongside the twelve fragrant golden brown loaves that already sat cooling on the worktable.

There. The bread was done . . . for another day or two.

For some reason the thought of making that much bread, all over again, didn't weary her as it usually did. Amazing what a little sunshine could do for a person's spirit. She looked around the kitchen as she removed her apron, her glance settling on the black hands of the clock. Only a quarter past three? How could it be that the last of the noon dishes was done, all the bread was baked, and her suppertime preparations were already well underway—with so much time to spare before supper?

Could it be that she was finally getting organized?

Her lips curved into a musing smile as she stepped out the back door to enjoy an unexpected few minutes of fresh air and sunshine. With Maureen and Ginny gone, things had been very quiet around the ranch house. Too quiet. She found herself missing the women's friendly companionship, and now that the weather was nice, Joey spent a good deal of time out in the fresh air. Though Edward was cordial and chatty, his work frequently took him outdoors; lately he appeared in the kitchen with the other men only to take his meals. The other remaining Montgomery—Ryan—showed himself even less frequently, and he was hardly wont to say more than a half dozen words through an entire meal, if he spoke even that much. While clearing dishes from the table one day, Emma heard Ferguson pronounce under his breath that Maureen Montgomery's eldest son was "as closemouthed as a tree full of owls."

The call of a red-tailed hawk broke into her thoughts, drawing her attention from Ryan Montgomery to the beauty of the springtime day. It had to be at least sixty-five degrees, she thought, stepping out into the yard and looking around. Despite the dreariness of the past days, the temperature had remained mild enough for the remainder of the snow to melt. Fleetingly she wondered if the snow back home was all gone, as well.

"Hey, Miss Taylor," Lorenzo called from a nearby corral, touching his hat. "Sure is a purty day, ain't it?"

"It is indeed," she remarked, walking over toward the neat whitewashed fencing. "It must be a nice kind of day for you to be outside working."

"The best, ma'am," he agreed, smiling broadly as she approached. "Say, if you've finally found yourself with a spare minute or two, I have to attend to a few chores just a ways west of here." Bashfully he lowered his head. "Ahh . . . if you've got a little time on your hands, ma'am, I'd be honored to have you ride along with me. It's real purty country around here. If you give me a minute, I can saddle you up a mare that's 'bout as gentle as a little bunny rabbit—"

"Oh, thank you, Mr. Lorenzo," she interrupted, flattered at his kind offer, "but I'm afraid I must decline. I don't . . . ride, you see. I never seemed to get the knack of it." Recalling her disastrous experiences with riding lessons during her growing years, she shivered with distaste. "Horses just don't like me very much. They never . . . they never do what they're supposed to do when I get on."

Lorenzo grinned and raised his head, his dark eyes glowing with amusement. "You wouldn't happen to be scared of horses, would you, ma'am? You know, a horse can sense a nervous rider a mile off."

"I suppose I am a little frightened. They're so big . . . and I'm not."

Lorenzo made a knowing sound in the back of his throat. "That can easily be remedied, ma'am. Any of us here'd be happy to show you just how easy ridin' can be."

Like Ryan Montgomery? For some unknown reason, the ex–army captain's handsome face appeared in her mind. Was it because she frequently caught glimpses of him from the kitchen window on the back of a wildly bucking horse in the far corral . . . or was it because she knew how truly *un*happy he would be to show her how to ride?

"Your offer is extremely kind, Mr. Lorenzo," she said, fingering a knotted area on the fence and at the same time hoping he wouldn't press the riding issue, "but what I'd really like to do this afternoon is take a short walk about the grounds. It seems as if I've been cooped up in that kitchen ever since I got here."

"You have, at that." Lorenzo nodded and thoughtfully scratched the side of his face. " 'Cept there ain't much for 'grounds' here, ma'am; only up around the house." He pointed toward the north. "Come to think of it, there's a nice little crick that comes off the river up that way. You can't miss it. Jus' start walkin', an pretty soon you'll see a stand of cottonwood. It ain't too far, an' you shouldn't have any problems gettin' there an' back."

After thanking the good-natured cowhand for his suggestion, she returned to the house for a bonnet, deciding to forego an outer wrap. Lorenzo was mounting a roan gelding as she began walking in the direction he had suggested. He smiled and gave her a friendly wave as he rode past her, politely offering her one last chance for a "professional ridin' lesson."

Emma just as politely declined his offer and wished him a good afternoon. The roan's hoofbeats soon faded from hearing, leaving only the sound of the wind in her ears. Steadily she walked northward, noticing how different this land was from that of her home city.

Whereas St. Paul was extremely hilly and, in many areas, wooded, the plains of Wyoming Territory were flat, with scant tree cover. Well, maybe this Wyoming land wasn't perfectly flat, she amended, taking in the gentle dips and swells of the grassland. She tried to imagine the prairie cloaked in waving green grasses—a blanket of endless, rolling green as far as the eye could see. It was a great stretch of the imagination, to be sure, for yellow-brown winter grasses and spiky clumps of yucca presently covered the land as far as the eye could see, but the promise, the scent, of spring rode on the breeze that caressed Emma's face. Closing her eyes, she stopped on a small rise and pictured the prairie dotted with the abundant wildflowers Ginny had told her about.

At this moment, she could almost pretend as if she didn't have a care in the world. With a beautiful picture in her mind, and her body warmed by sunshine and exercise, it seemed as if her problems back in St. Paul were a million miles away. Even the thought of preparing, serving, and cleaning up one more meal yet this day didn't burden her spirit. Perhaps she ought to make time for a walk every afternoon.

Opening her eyes, she looked about her. Above her. The sky was different here, too, she realized. Very different. She'd vaguely noticed how immense it had seemed during her ride out to the ranch with Ryan Montgomery, and during the past frantic days of toil she hadn't had time to do much more than catch fleeting glimpses of the outdoors every now and again from the kitchen window. But now, today, she fully realized just how enormous the heavens above this winter-barren grassland appeared. Just standing here beneath its vastness had a way of making her realize how very large the world was . . . and how very small a part of it she was.

The Montgomery spread was large, too, she thought, turning and taking in the far-off ranch house, outbuildings, and neat lines of whitewashed fences. Impressive, even. Andrew Montgomery had obviously executed the plans for his cattle empire with great care and pride.

Turning back to the north, Emma spied a grove of trees in the distance. They had to be the cottonwoods Lorenzo had spoken of—there simply weren't any other trees in sight. Starting off toward the trees—and, hopefully, the creek—at a brisk pace, she once again imagined this strange, rugged Wyoming land garbed in the tender green beauty of early summer.

She heard the creek before she saw it. The sound of its rushing waters mingled sweetly with the song of the warm wind and the cheerful call of the meadowlark, and she thought it was entirely possible that a springtime day in Wyoming Territory could rival a springtime day in Minnesota. A large bird—an eagle?—was perched high in the tallest cottonwood, and Emma craned her neck upward, enchanted, trying to get a better look at the bird as she moved toward the little brook and the stand of trees.

A sudden, surprised cry left her throat as she lost her balance and hit the damp ground in a heavy, ungainly heap. Instinctively she'd broken her fall, as best she could, with her hands and her right elbow, landing midway between her backside and her right side. Her heart was pounding madly, her elbow and palms were uncomfortably encrusted with moist dirt and gravel, but, thankfully, other than that, nothing else seemed to cause her discomfort.

Until she tried moving.

A sharp twinge shot through her right knee as she tried to push herself to her feet, and with shock she belatedly realized that her right foot and lower leg had disappeared down some sort of hole . . . and were stuck fast. Gently at first, then with increasing effort, she tried to free her leg from the cavity in the ground, but her shoe seemed to be turned outward and wedged tight inside . . . inside what? Alarm coursed through her when she realized her foot was most likely trapped inside some sort of animal burrow.

What if the animal was at home?

The image of a furry, angry creature gnawing on her foot caused her to redouble her efforts to free herself. If the diameter of this tunnel was such as to accommodate her entire lower leg, this hollow could certainly be nothing so paltry as a mere gopher hole. *What other burrowing animals lived out here on the prairie?* she wondered with alarm. Big ones—and ones with very sharp teeth, she imagined, realizing that her leg simply wasn't going to come out of the hole. And, as tightly as her shoelaces were tied, there was no chance of her slipping her foot from her shoe.

She was stuck.

Panic threatened to bubble up inside her, but she firmly quelled her fears. *Come on, Emma Louise,* she told herself sharply, *this predicament is nothing compared to the challenges you've undergone—and conquered—in the past several days.* She remembered that Lorenzo knew exactly where she was, and if she didn't return by dinnertime, he'd be out to retrieve her. She ought to be thanking her lucky stars that her leg wasn't broken.

The thought of one or more of the Montgomery cowhands having to pull her out of the ground—like a cow from a boghole—was humiliating, however, and she resolved to free herself before the situation could come to that. The idea of thick ropes and hearty male laughter was almost worse than the thought of a rabid animal chewing off her foot. Seeing nothing nearby with which to dig, she released a long sigh and began to work at the tough prairie sod with the only instruments at hand.

Her fingers.

On the opposite bank of the creek, Ryan Montgomery sat astride a tall black horse, not quite believing the sight he took in from between the leafless branches of the grove of cottonwoods. If he wasn't mistaken, the curly haired ranch cook sat on her haunches on the wet ground . . . *digging?*

Uninterested yet somehow intrigued, he watched her ceaseless toil for a good quarter hour before letting out his breath with an exasperated sound and guiding the horse down to ford what he knew was a shallow bend in the spring-swollen stream.

His curiosity had gotten the better of him.

What in the world was the cook doing out here? he wondered, continuing to be puzzled by her curious movements. And why on earth was she digging at the ground . . . *with her bare hands?* Her sleeves were rolled up way past her elbows in an unladylike fashion, her skirt was askew, her arms were caked with dirt, and what appeared to be a discarded bonnet lay on the ground beside her. She sat awkwardly, too, unevenly, hunched over as she labored.

The black snorted when he reached and scrambled up the opposite bank of the creek, the sharp sound causing Emma's head to snap up and her digging movements to suddenly cease. Quickly she arranged her skirt modestly about her and made a futile attempt to brush off her bodice. The picture of her heart-shaped countenance, smeared with nearly as much dirt as her arms, would have been comical had it not been for the grim, distressed expression she wore. Their gazes locked, and as he neared her he became even more puzzled.

What was she doing out here?

"Have you lost something, Miss Taylor?" he asked curtly, stopping the black approximately five feet from where she sat. Her normally neat person was nearly covered with dirt, and her nutmeg-brown ringlets stood out in wild disarray—truly, this Emma Taylor was a far cry from the plainly dressed but impeccably neat young woman who inhabited his mother's kitchen.

"I . . . ah . . . seem to have lost my foot," she admitted after a long moment, dropping her gaze. The volume of her softly cultured voice faded as she spoke, and an embarrassed, crooked expression played on her face. "I wasn't paying attention to where I was walking, and I stepped into some sort of hole. My foot is wedged down there somehow, and I can't get it out." Briefly raising her gaze to him once more, she shrugged. "You don't happen to have a shovel handy, do you?"

Ryan cursed to himself and dismounted the black.

Women.

"Are you hurt?" he was compelled to ask as he walked over toward her and knelt next to the small crater she'd managed to dig through the tough sod, realizing she could have a serious sprain, or even a broken ankle.

"No, my leg's just getting cold from being down there." She attempted a tremulous smile and held out her filthy hands before her. "I've been trying to dig myself out, but as you can see, it's been rather slow going."

At this close range, even through the dirt, it was impossible to ignore the fact that Emma Taylor was one hundred percent woman. Perhaps it was the riotous mass of glossy curls that framed her heart-shaped face . . . or the sight of her dirt-smeared, sunburned nose . . . or perhaps it was the unmistakable scent of her womanly fragrance that drifted from her and filled his nostrils. It didn't much matter. As much as he'd tried not to think of her winsome face and trim form as he lay in his bunk at night, as much as he'd tried to tell himself that he wasn't aware of her as a woman . . . he was.

Very much so.

Biting off a sharp oath at that realization, he loosed his blade from the sheath that hung from his belt.

"You aren't planning on amputating, are you?" A nervous smile lit her grimy yet still-lovely features.

"No, Miss Taylor, I'm not planning on amputating," he responded more sardonically than he'd intended. Would it be easier to look at her . . . or not look at her? Not look at her, he decided. "If you would be so kind as to pull your skirt back out of the way, I'll slice through the sod and free your foot."

"Oh." Cautiously she pulled the edge of her skirt back a small amount, being careful not to expose any portion of her lower limbs. "Thank you."

The knife cut into the sod with a grainy hiss that made Ryan want to cuss for the detrimental wear this abuse was causing his keen blade. Applying both his hands to the task of sawing through the dense web of roots that grew beneath the ground's surface, he winced as soreness lanced through his left wrist, for his sprain hadn't quite healed yet.

"Is something the matter, Mr. Montgomery?"

Without glancing up at her, he shook his head and continued his work, making a V-shaped cut in the ground just beyond where her lower leg disappeared into the ground . . . or at least where he assumed her lower leg disappeared into the ground. With the way she was guarding the edge of her skirt, he could only guess.

"This is really very kind of you, Mr. Montgomery. I'm quite sorry to trouble you . . . I was out taking a walk because it was such a beautiful afternoon. Were you out taking a ride for the same reason?"

Making only noncommittal grunts in response to the cook's chatty conversation as he worked, Ryan tried not to think about her legs . . . or any part of her. Finally the sod was cut to his satisfaction, and with more than a little effort he rolled it toward him, exposing the brown dirt below. It was a simple matter then to scoop the remaining dirt out of the way, thereby exposing her earth-covered though shapely lower leg. A final cut with the knife dispatched the thick root that held fast her foot. "There," he announced. "You should be able to get up now." Wiping his knife on his chaps, he resheathed it in its case, brushed himself off, and stood.

"I can't thank you enough, Mr. Montgomery," she said sincerely, her breath catching on his name.

Glancing down at her, he saw a flicker of discomfort cross her face as she eased her foot from the ground. *The least you could do is help her up, Montgomery,* he told himself, watching her slow movements. "Are you certain you're not injured?" he asked harshly, feeling a wave of unfamiliar tenderness course through him.

"No . . . I believe I'm just a little stiff from being in this position."

The brave smile intended to reassure him was his undoing. "Here," he said grudgingly, bending over and reaching for her hands. "Let me help you up."

Emma Taylor was even lighter than she appeared, he discovered, so very delicate. So feminine. A part of him that hadn't flared to life in . . . in how long? . . . blazed painfully inside him, making him think of all sorts of wild things that could never be. At this moment, not even the logical, rational part of his intellect could block the burst of attraction, the explosion of pure feeling, that threatened to set him afire.

An awkward moment passed while he held onto her hands slightly longer than necessary, lost in his imaginings. Gently she extricated her fingers from his grasp, and if not for the sun- and wind-pinkened tint of her cheeks, he would have sworn that she blushed.

"I'll give you a ride back to the ranch," he offered, strangely unwilling to part from her. "Your foot . . ."

"Oh, no, I couldn't impose upon you any further," she demurred, dropping her gaze downward. "Not after all you've already done." She took an experimental few steps. "There's no damage to my foot. My leg is just feeling a little cramped from being in such an awkward position . . . it's probably good for me to walk on it. Goodness," she exclaimed, looking from her clothing to his. "I've caused you to become nearly every bit as dirty as I am." Self-consciously she brushed her hands over her blouse and skirt. "I'm sorry . . . I must look a fright."

"On the contrary," he responded gallantly, the words slipping from his lips before he could stop them. "You look . . ." He hesitated, his words trailing off as he wondered what it was he'd been about to say. Beautiful? Exquisite? Charming? Entirely kissable? Any of them was true.

This time, he was certain of her blush. Was it possible that she found him attractive, as well?

"I look as though I need a dip in the creek," she said drolly, finishing his sentence for him.

Ryan had to close his eyes against the titillating picture her words conjured in his mind.

"Thank you again for your assistance, Mr. Montgomery," she said sweetly. "I'd best be going now . . . I have to be getting back to my supper preparations. By the way," she asked, "what sort of animal burrow do you suppose I stepped into?"

He opened his eyes and allowed them to feast over her petite, womanly form briefly before he glanced at the ground where her foot had been trapped. "Hard to tell now, but badger, I'd say."

"Do they bite?" The concern on her face was genuine.

He nodded.

"Oh." The smile on her face was sickly. "Well, I'd best mind my wool gathering and pay attention to where I step from now on, then, hadn't I?"

Good advice for you, too, Montgomery, he silently warned himself, not able to help the flood of expectancy that coursed through him at the thought of sitting at her dinner table tonight.

"Hello, Emma," Ginny greeted, holding open the pantry doorway. She and Maureen had been back from Cheyenne for a week, during which Ginny had paid several friendly calls upon Emma. "Oh, hello to you, too, Joey," she added. "Are you helping Emma with the dishes again?"

"Uh-huh . . . I help Am-ma," Joey replied, polishing a knife with his towel.

"Would you two mind some company?" Ginny stepped into the kitchen and sighed. "I know I was just in here for the noon meal, but I can't seem to find anything to do right now."

"Come on in, Ginny," Emma invited, looking up from the huge bowl of batter she stirred. "I'm just mixing up some layer cake . . . or should I say some layer *cakes*?" she added with a smile, shrugging her shoulders. "Three of them ought to be enough, don't you think?"

"Good cake," Joey interjected authoritatively. "Am-ma make f-for me. Am-ma find choc-lit. Good cake with choc-lit."

"Chocolate's your favorite, isn't it, Joey?" Ginny commented distractedly, walking over to the worktable. She sighed again.

"Is something the matter?" Emma asked, taking note of Ginny's downcast appearance. In the short time she'd known her, Emma had never before seen the gay sparkle missing from the young woman's gray-green eyes. Letting the spoon rest against the edge of the bowl, Emma wiped her hands on her apron. "Can I make you a cup of tea?"

"Oh, no, don't trouble yourself. You look very busy." She sighed a third time.

Despite Ginny's protestations, Emma reached for the tea tin and measured four teaspoons of black leaves into a clean pot. Over them she poured a quart of steaming water from the large kettle on the back stove, her nose twitching a little at the tea's fruity aroma. After setting the pot aside to infuse, she turned back to Ginny and smiled warmly. "There. See? It was no trouble at all."

"Thank you, Emma. You're very kind."

"Am-ma nice cooking wady." Joey gestured toward Emma with a handful of dripping spoons. "Am-ma 'peshal . . . pwetty . . . nice . . . Make Joey choc-lit cake."

Emma returned to the worktable and resumed her stirring, flashing Joey an amused look over her shoulder. "You're not looking forward to this cake at all, are you?" She tapped the open copy of *Buckeye Cookery* with her finger. "You know, Joey, there's a recipe here for caramel cake that looks pretty good, too. Maybe we should make that instead."

"No choc-lit?" Shock caused both his jaw and the dish towel to drop. "N-no choc-lit? Am-ma not my 'peshal friend?"

Ginny held up the container of Baker's chocolate, a pensive smile curving her lips. "Don't worry, Joey. I think she's just teasing you."

"Oh," he said loudly, bringing up his forearm to cover his eyes. "Am-ma tease." He smiled and let his arm fall. "Me know Am-ma tease. F-foolish Am-ma."

"So I'm 'foolish Emma' now, am I?"

He nodded, still grinning.

"Well, I suppose that's at least an improvement over 'crazy Emma.' "

"No, no, no, no. Am-ma cwazy . . . t-t-too." Joey chuckled to himself and picked up the dish towel. "Tawk, tawk, tawk to bwead." Carefully setting the cloth aside, he reached for a clean towel hanging on the rack near the sink.

Instead of taking part in their banter like she usually did, Ginny was silent. Her smile had faded, and she set down the chocolate and swirled her finger in a pile of spilled flour. She didn't look ill, Emma decided, but there was something definitely troubling her.

"What's Edward doing this afternoon?" Emma asked cautiously, wondering if the couple had had words. Come to think of it, for the past several nights she hadn't heard anything but whispers coming from the room above her. Not that she *tried* listening to the couple, a little voice in her head hastened to say. Hearing them was just rather unavoidable, given the location of her small bedchamber.

"Oh, Edward's holed up with his books again." Sad gray-green eyes swung up to meet Emma's concerned gaze. "I swear, Emma, for the past two weeks he's done nothing but eat, sleep, and frown over his books and receipts. Some days it feels like I don't even have a husband any . . . oh, never mind," she broke off. "I'm just a little lonely, I guess. Maureen went out on the range with McDermott again, too, so I don't have any company."

"She's been out there a lot lately."

"She likes to keep up on what's going on with the stock. And now that the weather's getting nicer, she'll be out with the men a lot more. She was last year, anyway." Ginny shook her head. "I don't know how she does it all. She gave up so much when her husband died, yet she never complains about anything."

Emma was puzzled. "What did she give up?"

"An *easier* life, I suppose, is the best way of putting it. Did you know that she owns a lovely house in Cheyenne?"

"I'd heard—" Emma began, nodding.

"The family used to spend quite a lot of time in town," Ginny broke in. "Most ranchers around these parts have town houses. And now, here Maureen is out on the ranch while she pays a hired woman to stay with Ruthie and Colleen in that big beautiful house. It just kills her to be separated from the younger girls," she confided. "Colleen, most of all. She'll be twelve this year, but Maureen still thinks of her as her baby. It's a little different with Moira and Irene because they're both married, but you should have seen poor Maureen when we had to say good-bye to everyone and come back to the ranch. It nearly broke her heart."

Emma was silent as she evenly distributed the batter into six buttered and floured cake tins. Joey, too, was quiet as he finished the utensils and started on the coffee mugs. "Poor Maureen" was right, Emma thought, feeling doubly guilty for her original deceit in falsifying her credentials. With all Maureen Montgomery's responsibilities and burdens, the last thing she needed in her life was a cook who didn't know how to cook. Not that Emma wasn't learning . . .

but surely the widow had to have guessed she wasn't the experienced cook she had represented herself to be.

With her apron Emma lifted the oven latch and set the tins on the wire racks, three on the upper rack, three on the lower, thinking of how patient Maureen, Ginny, Edward, and all the ranch hands had been with her as she settled into her new position. Their kindness made her feel more ashamed of her duplicity, but it also made her endeavor to work as hard as she possibly could to learn the kitchen arts.

"And then there's Ryan," Ginny said in a low voice, looking troubled. "Maureen's about at her wits' end with the way he's been acting around here."

Emma's attention was captured by the mention of the dark man's name, her feelings rising as hot and fast as the heat that escaped from the oven. Using more force than she intended, she closed the heavy black door with a bang, thinking that in her entire life she'd never felt more ambivalent about a man than she did about Ryan Montgomery. If she had to admit it, she felt a strange pull of attraction for the ex-army captain, yet she'd never met a man with such an aura of darkness about him. She thought about all the wonderful things Joey had told her about him, wondering if they could be true.

Emma had listened to Joey talk about his "'peshal brudder" for days, not believing that the attentive and fun-loving older brother he described was the same man that appeared at the table for only about half the meals she prepared. Sometimes Joey spoke fondly of Ryan; at other times, sadness and bewilderment seemed to overwhelm him. Emma couldn't help but liken Joey's loss to a death, for it seemed as though the youth had truly lost his favorite brother. Her heart ached for him, and she did what she could to ease his unhappiness.

He seemed to enjoy spending time with her in the warm kitchen, helping with dishes and other odd jobs. Together they passed many enjoyable hours together, she cooking and he directing her efforts, and Emma had come to realize that she very much enjoyed his company. His sweet innocence had charmed her, and each one of his smiles gladdened her heart and gave her fresh determination to continue her toil.

"That Ryan makes me so angry I could just spit," Ginny whispered, breaking into Emma's thoughts. "But he scares me, too. Isn't that a perfectly dreadful thing to say about my husband's brother?"

Emma glanced over her shoulder, seeing that Joey was still diligently drying the mugs. "I don't think it's dreadful at all," she replied in an equally hushed voice, thinking of Ryan Montgomery's piercing eyes and large imposing form. "Most of the time I walk around wishing someone would horsewhip him for the shameful way he's treating . . ." Not wanting to say Joey's name aloud, she gestured in his direction with her elbow. She took a deep breath and slowly released it. "But then I see him, and it's another matter entirely. All he has to do is look in my direction with those black eyes of his—"

"I know what you mean!" Ginny whispered. "There's just something about his eyes, isn't there?"

Mutual understanding flowed between the women as Emma poured two cups of tea. Joey made a face and stuck out his tongue when Emma asked if he wanted a cup, so the two women took their tea and walked to the small table.

Once they were seated, Ginny glanced nervously around the room before moistening her lips and leaning toward Emma. "You've heard that Ryan's a war hero, haven't you?"

"No." For some reason, a tight shiver shimmied down Emma's spine at that revelation. Ryan Montgomery a war hero? What did that mean, exactly? What had he done? And in which war? She tried to recall the questions Eaton had asked Ryan the first morning she was here, but she couldn't remember anything except the mention Eaton had made of the Ute Indians and of a Major Thornton or Thornburn, or some such name.

"Did you ever hear of a man named Nathan Meeker?" Ginny asked, toying with the handle of her cup.

Emma shook her head. "I don't recall his name right offhand."

"He was the Indian agent in charge of the White River Agency—just south of Rawlins, in Colorado, you know—in the late seventies. From what Edward told me, Meeker was supposed to teach the Ute how to farm."

Joey cleared his throat and began to sing to himself as he continued drying dishes.

"The Ute didn't want to farm, though," Ginny continued, sitting back a little in her chair, "and things went from bad to worse when Agent Meeker decided to teach them a lesson by plowing up their pony racetrack."

"Oh, dear."

" 'Oh, dear' is right—the Ute revolted. Some refer to the battle as the Meeker Massacre, but others call it the Thornburgh Massacre after Major Thornburgh, because the major's troops were the first to respond." Ginny picked up her tea and blew on it before taking a sip. "Ryan was one of Major Thornburgh's men," she said quietly. She set down her cup, her gray-green eyes looking directly into Emma's, and once again her voice dropped to a whisper. "When the troops got to Milk Creek, they were ambushed by the Ute. Major Thornburgh was killed almost immediately."

Ambushed by Indians.

Emma's mouth had grown dry at this unexpected account of Ryan Montgomery's past, and she took a sip of tea, her mind suddenly bursting with questions. A rich chocolate baking aroma was beginning to fill the kitchen, but she barely noticed. "Was he wounded?" she asked, certain that Ginny was going to tell her of some awful injury that continued to plague him.

A reason, at least, for the way he acted.

Ginny shook her head. "No, I don't think he was hurt."

"But why is he . . . the way he is, then?"

"I don't know, exactly. One thing I do know, though, is that there were bitter feelings between him and Andrew until the day Andrew died. Mr. Montgomery didn't want a military career for Ryan, you see. He wanted both Ryan and Edward to be involved in running the ranch."

"Oh." Emma paused for a long moment, nonplused. "Well, what happened after the ambush?" she asked, anxious to hear more about the Ute uprising and Ryan's involvement in the battle.

Ginny's eyes grew round. "Edward told me that several men were killed right off, but that the remaining troops managed to defend themselves while they dug trenches. The Ute even tried burning the soldiers out by setting fire to the brush along the river."

Another shiver ran through Emma at the grisly thought of being burned alive.

"No one in the family has ever heard any of this from Ryan," Ginny explained. "But Edward told me Andrew used to hear things because he had beef contracts with some of the forts around here. He also said how proud his father was of Ryan when Andrew learned Ryan had distinguished himself with his bravery during the three days it took for reinforcements to arrive at Milk Creek." She took another sip of tea. "Edward figures Ryan's actions had a lot to do with him being promoted from first lieutenant to captain at such a young age."

If Ryan Montgomery was such a hero, why did he resign his commission? And if Andrew Montgomery was so proud of his son, why was there unresolved bitterness between them until the day he died?

"N-not happy tawking," Joey said from across the kitchen. "Not, not happy. My fawder not happy. Wyan not happy."

Emma realized she'd forgotten about Joey's presence. Looking toward the sink, she saw he had finished the dishes. "No, your brother certainly doesn't seem very happy most of the time, does he?" she said sympathetically.

Joey shook his head vigorously and walked toward them. "Wyan tell Joey no like kill Yoots. No like army. Joey wemember. S-s-sad Wyan . . . mad Wyan. He says gubberment not f-f-fair Yoots. Cheat, cheat, cheat, cheat."

"Ryan said the government cheated the Utes?" Ginny gave Emma a quizzical look before turning her head to look at Joey and asking, "When did he tell you that?"

Joey's expression faded. "Long t-t-time." He shrugged his shoulders and licked his lips several times. "Me get dry shirt. All w-wet," he said, first pointing to the large dark spot over his waist area, then walking from the kitchen.

"Well, it's nice to know that Ryan at least *used* to talk to Joey," Ginny commented. "I was beginning to believe Edward and Maureen had lied to me about all the special attention Ryan used to give him." With a last sip, she finished her tea. "Maureen says Ryan even taught Joey his letters and his ciphers. Joey can do simple reading, you know."

"He reads?" Emma whispered, taken by surprise. "I mean, I know he isn't anywhere near stupid, but—"

"You should see some of Joey's paintings," Ginny interrupted. "I bet he'd show you if you asked him." She smiled then, the first genuine smile Emma had seen cross her lips all day. "Although lately Joey seems to prefer doing dishes to painting. He really likes you, Emma."

"I like him, too."

Ginny's smile faded. "Your kindness is helping Joey through a very rough spot in his life. Ryan just seems to have decided that he doesn't want a family anymore." She rubbed the bridge of her nose with her fingertip, once more looking troubled. "Edward says that since Ryan left the army, he hasn't once asked how the ranch is doing."

"It seems as though Ryan hates everyone and everything." Emma let out her breath in a delicate snort. "Me, especially." She tried not to think of the mysterious, flustered way he'd made her feel at the creek that day. It certainly hadn't seemed as if he'd hated her that day. In fact, it had almost seemed as if . . .

Ginny's voice interrupted her thoughts.

"Don't feel singled out, Emma. I've been married to Edward for coming up on two years, and I don't think Ryan and I have shared more than a half dozen sentences during that whole time." Ginny leaned her head forward, sliding her fingertip from the bridge of her nose to the center of her forehead. "Edward says Ryan doesn't talk to him anymore, either. All he's been doing is breaking horses, did you know that? I've watched him a few times . . . it's amazing he hasn't broken any bones yet." She sighed deeply. "I wonder what Ryan would say if he knew about the mine . . ."

"The mine?"

"Yes, the silver mine. It's so expensive, and it still hasn't produced any decent ore, you know." Worried eyes looked beseechingly at Emma. "Oh, dear, I probably shouldn't have said anything. Edward would skin me alive."

"I doubt that," Emma responded, thinking of the warm look that was present in Edward Montgomery's eyes whenever he gazed at his wife. "But I'm a little confused. Are you saying that you own a silver mine *and* a ranch?"

Ginny nodded. "Edward's father bought into a silver mine over in the Medicine Bow range just before he died. He was sure there was a fortune to be made." She sighed. "Edward's been managing the mine since then . . . and he says we've nearly *spent* a fortune on it, instead."

The gray-green eyes filled with tears, and Emma intuitively knew that Ginny was getting to what was really bothering her.

"I've never seen him this worried about anything, Emma," Ginny went on. "He says he's figured and refigured, but if the mine doesn't start producing some higher grade ore soon, there might not be enough money to meet the payrolls."

Pay*rolls?* Emma swallowed nervously. Did Ginny mean the ranch payroll as well as the mine payroll?

"I'm sorry, Emma, I shouldn't have said anything, but you're so nice . . . and this is such a burden to carry around. Maureen doesn't have any idea how bad it's gotten—" A tear spilled from one of her eyes. "I'm sorry," she apologized once again, reaching into her sleeve and bringing out a dainty handkerchief. Dabbing at her eyes, she continued. "Edward feels like such a failure . . . and I don't know how to make him feel any better. I-I tell him that I'm proud he's doing the very best he can, but I can't seem to console him." She sniffed, and fresh tears filled her eyes. "He's so torn. Half of him wants to close the mine and just cut our losses before the ranch gets dragged down any further, but the other half keeps reminding him of how much the mine meant to his father . . . and what hope and excitement Andrew had for it."

Before the ranch gets dragged down any further? Realizing that Ginny had indeed been talking about the ranch payroll, Emma's mind began to race as quickly as her pulse. *If the Montgomerys run out of money, Emma Louise, you aren't going to be paid. They might even have to let you go. . . . And if you can't keep working and earning money, you're not going to get your advance from Michael. . . .*

"Thank you for making tea and sitting down with me, Emma. You're such a good listener." Ginny made another dab at her eyes and attempted to smile. "It's been very nice having you here . . . and you've been so good for Joey. You'll never know what that means to Maureen." Shyly she looked down at the table before lifting her gaze to Emma. "I also hope that we might become friends."

"I'd like that," Emma responded sincerely, trying at the same time to force the string of awful possibilities out of her mind. Tears prickled in her eyes as she thought of how she'd stood up to Michael and Jon, left home, and taken this grueling position . . . all because she wanted to open her own business. Dear Lord, it just wasn't fair that she'd come this far only to fail now.

"Well, I'll get out of here and let you get back to work," Ginny said, pushing back her chair and rising.

"Yes . . . I should check on the cakes . . . I need to get the corned beef going." Emma's speech was disjointed.

"Thank you again for the tea, Emma."

"You're welcome." Emma turned up her lips, certain her smile must be as hollow as the feeling in her breast. "Try not to worry," she said with false reassurance, realizing she was speaking as much to herself as she was to Ginny. "I'm sure things are going to be just fine."

Chapter Seven

The unmistakable report of a .45 Colt revolver echoed through Ryan Montgomery's dreams, jerking him from the thin sleep into which he'd fallen. Disorienting darkness pressed all around him, allowing the horror of the nightmare to linger on in his mind.

Easy, Montgomery. You're not in the officers' quarters, you're in the bunkhouse at the ranch.

Heart pounding, every muscle in his body tensed for action, Ryan ran his hand over his face and through his hair, realizing that his long underwear and the cot beneath him were wet with sweat. Across the room, someone snorted and changed position, and Ryan envied the man for his peaceful slumber. He allowed his arm to fall back at his side and willed his galloping heart to slow. Dear God, how many more nights had to pass before these dreams stopped coming?

How many more nights was he destined to hear the report of the .45 that had snuffed out his friend's life?

As it had this night, the sound had pulled him from his slumber that stormy February night at Fort Russell. Silence had followed the pistol shot, silence broken only by the soft sounds of snow swirling against his window, and in those first hushed moments after he'd awakened, he told himself he must have been dreaming. Ever since the battle with the Ute, he'd often had . . . violent dreams.

But then the shouting had begun, and a heavy fist had beat on the front door of the bachelor officers' quarters, waking him all the way, and it was then he'd known the shot hadn't been any dream at all. In an instant he'd been out of bed, running across the sitting area and down the opposite hallway of the bachelor officers' quarters toward Hopper's rooms.

He remembered the crack of dirty light shining from beneath Hopper's rough pine door, remembered the dread that had risen within him as he'd laid his hand on the cold brass knob.

Suddenly feeling chilled, Ryan pulled the wool blanket up around his neck. Though he was in the midst of several sleeping men, he felt alone. His gaze flicked around the blackness of the bunkhouse as the sequence of events that had begun in his dreams continued to surge forward with all the force of a speeding locomotive. . . .

"Open up!" The fist against the door was insistent, as was the voice of Willard Penlay, sergeant of the guard. *"Open this door! Hopper, Montgomery, what the hell is going on in there?"*

Ryan clutched the blanket and tried to swallow, trying desperately to think of something else—the damnable buckskin he still hadn't been able to break . . . his family . . . his hated engineering professor at West Point . . . the winsome face of the curly haired cook . . . anything at all—but he was powerless to stop the hurtling train of his thoughts.

Slowly, he turned the brass knob and pushed. Nothing was out of place in Hopper's room . . . nothing within his view, that was. With the door partly open, he could see only to his left and straight ahead. By the room's kerosene lamplight, the hands of Hopper's wall clock read one-fifteen.

He also remembered that Hopper's elaborately tooled liquor case remained atop the chest of drawers directly across from where he stood, looking just as it had when he'd left an hour earlier. In fact, their two empty glasses still stood next to the case. A soft crackle and the sound of settling wood had come from the potbellied stove.

Though it was April, not February, and the weather mild, not stormy, Ryan heard, in his mind, the whistling of the wind as it blew harder, trying to push its way through the BOQ's board-and-batten construction. His nostrils twitched at the sulfurous smell of black gunpowder in the air, and a sick churning began in his stomach.

Instinctively he'd known what he was going to find when he pushed the door open wider. *No, Hopper!* a voice inside him had cried. *Why? Oh, Jesus, God, and all the saints, why?*

Just as it had that night, a feeling of unreality gripped him—not unlike the strange sense of being-there-but-not-really-being-there that descended during battle.

A hinge had wailed its mournful protest as he'd given Hopper's door a final decisive push, and then Hopper's legs had come into view . . . and then his torso . . . his head. Or, rather, what was left of his head.

Words Hopper had once uttered to him years ago flashed through his mind: *If you're ever serious about doing yourself in, Montgomery, take the muzzle in your mouth just like you're a babe suckin' on your mama's teat. Don't mess around. Do it fast and do it quick.*

Hopper hadn't messed around; he'd died instantly. Seated in his easy chair, just as he'd been when Ryan had turned in for the night, Hopper was comfortably dressed in long johns, trousers, and galluses. A dressing gown was tied loosely over his garments; royal-blue carpet slippers encased his feet. Trails and spatters of blood drizzled downward from his thrown-back head, staining his clothing and the Colt that had fallen back into his lap.

The ceiling and wall behind the chair were unspeakable.

Ryan pushed his fists over his eyes, trying to force from his mind's eye the next vision, a sight even more horrible than the last.

But he couldn't stop it from coming.

Something had gleamed on the arm of Hopper's chair, capturing his attention. Carefully making his way across the room, he'd stopped two feet from the chair and thrown his head to the side in a painful grimace when he'd realized what had caught and reflected the light.

A tooth.

For some reason, the sight of Jim Hopper's tooth lying on the arm of the chair continued to strike Ryan as the worst thing of all, worse, even, than the smell of death, the gore, the blood. The piece of bone that had once been a part of his friend's smile was a symbol of more than a broken body. It stood for a good man's broken spirit . . . and broken dreams.

"Oh, hell," had come Penlay's voice from near the door. "Look at what Hopper's gone and done." Shock and grief made the sergeant's voice sound thick. "The rest of you go on and wait out there," he ordered to the curious throng crowding the doorway.

"It's a'cause of Major Julson bein' here, ain't it?" a young voice asked over the sound of several men's hushed voices and the noisy scuffling of several sets of boots on the wooden floor.

Penlay had removed his snow-covered hat and walked over to Ryan. Shaking his head, the sergeant chose not to answer the lad.

"Come on, Montgomery," Penlay said, extending an arm toward him. "Let's wait out in the other room. He don't need us staring at him. Torbinson," he said, turning toward the sentinel with irritation in his voice, "do I have to spell it out for you? We'll be needing the surgeon and the officer of the day."

"Yes, sir," the sentinel replied, turning on his heel, only too glad to leave.

Ryan remembered the grim expression on Penlay's face . . . remembered hearing the word *suicide* ripple through the group of men in the hallway and sitting area.

Penlay's arm dropped. "Was it Julson?" the sergeant asked, his voice low.

"I suppose," Ryan answered, listening to the wind.

Was it Julson? he continued to wonder, or was Julson's promotion merely the final, unbearable link in Hopper's chain of career disappointments?

The silence between the two men had stretched out, then Penlay's breath had escaped him in a deep sigh. "You want a few moments alone with him?" For all of the sergeant's gruffness, he was an unusually perceptive man. At Ryan's curt answering nod, Penlay inclined his head and walked stiffly out of the room, pulling the door closed behind him.

A shiver ran through Ryan's body now as coldness continued to seep into his bones, just as it had as he'd stood before Hopper in his stocking feet, and he brought his fists down from his eyes and crossed his arms tightly over his chest. He remembered how his throat had grown thick as he'd tried to keep his gaze focused on the blue carpet slippers, away from the gleaming tooth on the arm of the chair.

Staring up at the black bunkhouse ceiling, his throat grew thick again. He'd failed his friend. That evening, during their conversation about the army's present state of affairs, he'd heard the bitterness in Hopper's voice, the hopelessness. Why hadn't he really listened?

Because you wanted out as bad as he did.

Throwing the blanket aside, Ryan swung himself to a sitting position and reached for his shirt. There would be no more sleep this night. Like a galloping horse's hoofbeats, his heart still pounded madly within his chest, and every muscle and nerve in his body was strained to its limit. He had to get up, get out of here, get outdoors and clear his head.

It didn't seem to matter where he bunked down, in a guest room in the house or out here with the other men; there was no escaping the smothering horror of the dream-that-wasn't-really-a-dream. He finished dressing as quietly as he could, pulled on his coat and gloves, and let himself outdoors.

The moon was faint, but he could see well enough to make his way over to the corral fence. His boots crunched on the rough soil as cool night air caressed his face, and, slowly, as he walked along the fence, the intensity of his nightmare began to fade. He ran his gloved hand loosely along the second-from-top board of the wide-planked enclosure, absently noticing that his sprained wrist no longer gave him pain.

What are you going to do, break horses for the rest of your life, Montgomery? he asked himself, realizing that after years of structured military life—years of constantly being told where to go, what to do, and when to do it— he no longer had any direction. As a West Point graduate, it wasn't as if he didn't have any options . . . and, too, there was the money he'd been sending home to invest in the ranch.

The ranch.

He sighed as he remembered the year the family had moved from Nebraska to Wyoming Territory, the year his father had sat his two oldest sons down and told them how he planned to build a vast cattle empire—and what their roles were going to be in his cattle kingdom. Edward had listened eagerly, but Ryan had been a youth of eighteen then, bursting with the desire to break free of his family and be part of what he then perceived to be the glamorous military.

At first the strong-willed patriarch had patiently argued with his son, telling him that there was no glamour in the military, only discipline and hard work. *And if hard work is all you're after, son,* he'd said, strong white teeth flashing in his commanding face, *why don't you just stay here? At least you'll have the pleasure of shaping the destiny of the West as a free man, not as the slave of another.*

But Ryan, as all-knowing as any other young man of eighteen years, had insisted that his father didn't know what he was talking about, and that furthermore, no man, not even his father, was going to tell him what he could or could not do with his life. Then, just for spite, he'd scurrilously told his father how selfish he'd been to uproot his family from their comfortable Nebraska home just to chase some flimsy dream of being the next Charles Goodnight.

Words between them had quickly grown bitter. Maureen had cried and pleaded for peace as irate threats and ultimatums had flown back and forth between father and eldest son, but in the end, Ryan had left his family and gone to New York, certain that Andrew Montgomery was wrong about everything.

And now his father was dead . . . and, as it had turned out, he hadn't been so stupid after all. Not only had Andrew Montgomery succeeded in building his great cattle empire, but he'd also been correct about life in a governmental military system riddled with injustices.

Ryan stopped walking and leaned on the fence, staring at the dark outline of the ranch house. There were no longer any chances to rebuild bridges with the proud man who had shaped this cattle kingdom . . . the same man who had shaped his childhood, his life.

With emptiness, Ryan realized how far from his family he had fallen. The rest of the Montgomerys had banded more tightly together since Andrew's death, leaving him feeling as if he were a stranger standing outside a glass house, looking in. It was also obvious that Maureen and Edward had developed an especially close relationship since they'd begun comanaging the ranch, a competent, efficient relationship from which Ryan felt very much apart.

A light appeared in one of the first-story windows of the house. The cook was up, he surmised, watching a petite form move around the kitchen. That meant it wouldn't be long before the men in the bunkhouse were up, and the two cowboys out on night watch came back for some sleep. Though it was still dark, it wouldn't surprise him if Joey would soon join Miss Taylor, or "Miss Curly," as the men had taken to calling her; the lad was nearly inseparable from his "Am-ma."

Ever since that day at the creek, he hadn't been able to put his thoughts about—his longings for—the St. Paul woman from his head. She lingered there, in both his conscious and subconscious thought, doing naught but befuddling his mind. Sometimes, in the dark, he allowed himself to wonder what would happen if he were to court her . . . woo her . . . and even beyond that, love her, but then the gate on his fantasies came crashing down. She'd never shown the slightest interest in him.

He started to walk again, seeing the first indication of light in the eastern sky. Coming back to the ranch hadn't been a good idea, he realized. He simply wasn't needed—

or wanted—here. Besides, his presence just seemed to make everyone uncomfortable.

Reaching the end of the corral, he turned and faced the awakening sky, thinking that perhaps it was time to move on.

Emma cleared the ashes from the banked fire in the cookstove as she tried to clear the sleep from her head. *At least dawn was coming a little earlier each morning,* she thought, *looking out the window and seeing a first faint tint of light in the eastern sky.*

The past week had passed in a haze of uneasiness, ever since Ginny had mentioned the Montgomerys' financial problems. Now, each time Emma saw Ginny, though Ginny hadn't said anything further about her worries, Emma couldn't help but fear for the safety of her job.

Cut our losses before the ranch gets dragged down any further . . .

Just how far "down" had Ginny meant the ranch was already? Had she meant that the cash flow was so far depleted that *this* month's payrolls might not be met? The weather had turned warm, and the last of the snow had disappeared, but the beauty of the lengthening springtime days was lost on Emma as the end of her first month on the job approached and two questions ran over and over through her mind.

Would she be paid?

Or not?

Each time she told herself not to worry, that Ginny had probably exaggerated things a bit, Emma would see Edward. She had only to glance at Maureen Montgomery's second-born to see the worry that clouded his warm brown eyes, and she wondered how she could not have noticed his misery before.

It was ironic that now that she had begun to settle more comfortably into her role as cook, she had to worry about losing her job for a reason other than failing to perform adequately. Perhaps ironic wasn't the right word, Emma considered. . . . Maybe *unfair* was a better choice of terms. The thought of being let go—after daring and risking so much, and working so hard to learn so many kitchen skills—made her want to weep.

Her cooking had finally progressed to an adequate state, she estimated, for the loud false compliments the cowboys had initially hastened to heap upon her had given way to just occasional, but more genuine, praise. In the past weeks her breads had become lighter and more finely textured, the edges of her pies were now plainly but neatly scalloped, her coffee had improved to consistent strength, neither too strong nor too weak, and she finally felt as if she'd caught on to the vagaries of the cookstove.

The men now fondly addressed her as "Miss Curly"—or just plain "Curly"—instead of "Miss Taylor," after Ferguson had announced one day while chewing on a piece of her surprisingly well-made pound cake, that "any biscuit shooter worth her salt needs a nickname." Though "Miss Curly" wouldn't have been her first choice of nicknames, Emma remembered how inordinately pleased she'd been at Ferguson's words.

Was Owens in danger of losing his job, too? What about young Eaton with his disarming smile? Or carrot-topped Zach Ferguson? As the two youngest men . . . boys, really, Eaton and Owens were probably in the most danger of being let go.

Having gotten the fire going nicely and the bacon sliced, Emma set to peeling and slicing several pounds of potatoes. As she worked, she again contemplated seeking new employment. But every time she entertained the possibility of finding another job, she remembered the difficulty and duplicity that had been involved in getting this one.

She never wanted to go through anything so awful again, not after she was just starting to feel somewhat comfortable in her position here. Besides that, she really liked the Montgomerys—all except ill-natured Ryan Montgomery, that was, but she had gotten rather good lately at trying to ignore him.

Except when she was bumping into him.

With a flush of embarrassment, she recalled the evening, a few days ago, that she'd come around the corner and run smack-dab into him with a pitcher of hot gravy. Her forehead hit his chest at the same time the pitcher hit his waist, and the thick sauce—with hardly a lump!—had spilled down the front of both of them.

She'd been mortified, but fortunately neither she nor Ryan had been badly burned. And to their credit, none of the men had laughed. As the cowhands had suddenly busied themselves eating their gravyless mashed potatoes and fried salt pork, both Ginny and Maureen had jumped up from the table to help clean up the mess.

Emma had tried to apologize to Ryan, but the grooves of displeasure on either side of his mouth had deepened as she spoke, and his dark eyes had glared furiously at her before he'd walked out of the dining room without a word.

It was after incidents such as this that Emma was amazed she still had a job.

But she did, and as long as she had this job she continued to get closer, hour by hour and day by day, to realizing her dream of opening her collectibles shop.

Well, she decided, slicing potatoes into a large bowl, if the Montgomerys—excluding Ryan, of course—could be friendly and loyal to her despite her shortcomings, she would stick by them as well. She would just have to hope and pray that their financial situation would work itself out.

"I hired a new cook today, Edward. He'll be startin' the day after tomorrow."

A new cook?

Maureen Montgomery's words struck terror into Emma's breast, and she paused in the dim hallway outside her small bedchamber, shock running all through her body. After a long exhausting day of cooking, she had been looking forward to turning in. Though it was a lovely spring evening, she had declined the opportunity to accompany Ginny and Joey on a sunset kite-flying expedition about the ranch grounds, only wanting to wash up and get some sleep.

Instead, it appeared she was going to be fired.

Prickles of sweat broke out under her arms, and her stomach felt as if she'd swallowed a lead ball. She knew she wasn't the world's best cook, but she had certainly improved by leaps and bounds during the past weeks . . . hadn't she? She'd tried just as hard as she possibly could.

Fired! Dear heavens. What was she going to do now? Already she could hear, "I told you so" after "I told you so" coming from Michael's lips—and Jon's, too. Lord in heaven, there was just no other way she could earn two hundred dollars in a year's time. She also knew it was wrong for her to be eavesdropping on the conversation Maureen and Edward were having just down the hall in Edward's office, but her legs wouldn't move.

"You . . . you hired a new cook, Ma?" It was small consolation to Emma that Edward sounded just as stunned as she felt.

"I did, indeed," Maureen replied. "Would you be rememberin' that fellow Mueller that ran the chuck wagon here two summers ago?"

"Well, yes, but—"

"Well, he stopped by this afternoon lookin' for work, an' I snapped him up."

"You snapped him up? But why, Ma? I thought we had decided to hang on to Miss Emma."

Move, Emma, just go into your room and shut the door. You don't want to listen to any of this. Her hand curled tightly around the doorknob and made to push the door open, but another part of her stopped the movement, *needing* to hear Maureen's reply, no matter how awful it might be.

"Goodness, Edward, you should see the expression on your face. I can see you're misunderstandin' me already."

You said you hired a new cook, Maureen . . . what was there to misunderstand? Emma silently answered for Edward. Tears began to fill her eyes, and silently she reached for the handkerchief in her pocket.

"I didn't hire Mr. Mueller in *place* of Emma," Maureen went on. "I hired him for doin' the outdoor cookin' this spring an' summer. No, no, Emma's a dear girl, an' we'll keep her on, too, jus' like we agreed. I was just thinkin' that she was a mite too frail to send out with the chuck wagon." Her voice softened. "Besides that, she's so good with Joey, an' she's made him thrive as he hasn't done in . . . in I don't know how long. It would be a shame to separate them for weeks an' weeks."

I'm not getting fired! Relief made Emma nearly sag against the door, and she dabbed at her eyes with her handkerchief. *You should be ashamed of yourself for eavesdropping, Emma Louise,* her inner voice berated. *Your mother taught you better than that.* Quietly she again made a move to open the door to her bedchamber, but Edward's next words made her freeze.

"Ma," he said in a choked sounding voice. "I-I've got to tell you something."

The lead ball in the pit of Emma's stomach dropped lower.

"Edward James Montgomery! What on earth is troublin' you?" came Maureen's concerned reply. "I know I haven't been around the house much the past several days . . . are you ill? Oh, Lord, is Ginny feelin' poorly?"

"No . . . no, that's not it at all. I—" Emma clearly heard the deep shaky breath Edward took. "I'm so ashamed, Ma."

"Ashamed? Ashamed of what?"

Instinctively Emma knew what Edward was going to say. Dark and fast, dread burst forth within her, the same dread she'd been carrying around all week.

"We're nearly out of cash, Ma," he blurted forth. "I don't know how we're going to pay the new cook, the cook we already have . . . or anyone else, for that matter."

Maureen's voice was faint. "W-we're out of cash?"

"Yeah." Edward's voice broke. "I didn't want to worry you about it, but I-I've gone over and over and *over* the books, and I just don't know what to do anymore. I've tried to make this mine work, Ma, I really have . . . I know how important it was to Da—" His voice abruptly stopped as he blew his nose, but he sounded no better when he continued. "It's still not producing anything," he whispered in a strangled manner. "I'm sorry, Ma, I-I'm just a failure as a manager."

"I'll not be listenin' to such nonsense, Edward," Maureen said briskly. "You're not any kind of failure. 'Twas your father's heavy investin' in the mine that began the snowball rollin'. Ah, lad," she continued more gently, "you cannot help what does or does not lie below the surface of the mountains any more than you can be controllin' the clouds or the wind. And are you forgettin' the cattle, son? God forbid any misfortune, they'll be turnin' a handsome profit in the fall."

"But . . . we can't make it till then, Ma. Oh, God, it kills me to say this . . . but we're going to have to borrow until the cattle are sold. I-I don't know how we're going to hold up our heads—"

Sadness was evident in Maureen's voice as she interrupted her son. "If we're needin' a little money to tide us over, son, we'll go to the bank, then . . . although your father's probably rollin' in his grave as we speak." She sighed. "Well, it's not as if askin' for a loan is the end of the world. I'll just go—"

"No, Ma! After all you've gone through since Father died, I won't put you through the shame of having to ask for money. I'll do it—I insist."

Emma heard another long sigh. "Aye . . . I think I'll let you, at that. Thank you, son. Goodness, it's gotten dark in here," the Montgomery matriarch commented, changing the subject. Emma heard the rustle of her skirts. "Let me get this lamp lit before you're goin' blind over your papers."

Indeed, it had grown nearly black in the hallway where Emma stood. At Maureen's movements, Emma silently turned the knob and stepped into her bedchamber, lest she be discovered. *The Montgomerys needed a loan.*

Hands shaking, Emma undressed in the dark, a crazy scheme blooming in her mind. Though she could still faintly hear the murmurs of Maureen's and Edward's voices, she no longer tried to listen to what they were saying. Like a lightning bolt, the shocking idea had struck her with unbelievable force.

It was perfect, so perfect.

As she crawled under the covers, Emma wondered if all the mixing and kneading and standing over a hot stove had somehow unhinged her mental faculties, for what she was contemplating went far beyond daring. She let her

head fall back against the pillow and stared up at the
black ceiling, the scheme growing and taking shape in
her mind.

It would work, she decided, her heart hammering within
her chest as once more she thought the plan through, from
beginning to end. It would work for everyone. But could
she dare to do such a thing?

Did she dare?

Morning dawned clear and beautiful, but Emma was too
preoccupied to notice. The idea that had sprouted in her
mind last night hadn't left her alone, and as she cooked
and served breakfast, she rehearsed, over and over, what
she was going to say to Ginny this morning.

"Am-ma not tawk," Joey commented from his usual
place at the sink. "Am-ma s-sick?"

"No, Joey," she replied with a sigh, working the huge
pile of bread dough with strong sure strokes. Too sticky.
She lifted one side of the dough and sprinkled some flour
underneath, making sure her hands were liberally covered
with the stuff before she commenced kneading again.

"How c-come no tawk, Am-ma?" Joey chuckled to himself. "Bread no tawk to Am-ma today?"

"No, it's decided to just be difficult instead," she said,
shaking her head and sprinkling more flour on the dough.
Looking up, she saw that Joey stared at her with concern.
"I'm sorry I'm not very good company this morning," she
said, forcing a smile. "I've a lot on my mind."

"Am-ma good company for Joey . . . C-curly Am-ma my
crazy 'peshal friend." Joey chuckled again as he dried a
plate. "Make Joey happy forever an' ever."

Only till autumn. Her inner voice was hollow as it spoke.
At the thought of never seeing Joey again, Emma felt a great
rush of sadness, and a lump rose in her throat as she took in
his round, dear face. "You make Emma very happy, too,
Joey," she spoke sincerely. "Curly Emma likes being your
crazy special friend."

They continued their work in silence, until finally the
bread dough was smooth and springy and had been set
aside to rise, and all the dishes were done.

Time to find Ginny.

"Joey, do you know what Ginny was going to do after breakfast?" she asked, setting a cloth over the bowl of dough and walking over to stand next to him. "I need to talk to her."

Joey scratched his nose, screwed his face up in concentration, and reached into his breast pocket for the blue satin hair ribbon he'd shyly asked her for one day last week. Reverently running his fingers over the length of smooth glossy fabric, he carefully placed it in his left hand and shook his head negatively several times.

"Oh . . . well, I suppose I can find her myself."

Joey nodded. "Am-ma no-talk . . . care if Joey p-p-paint?"

"Oh, no, Joey, please," she said with relief. She took off her apron and smoothed her skirt. "Go ahead and paint."

"Paint g-good pick-cher for Am-ma," he said, still nodding. "G-good breakfast," he complimented before he turned and walked from the kitchen, the blue satin band fluttering in his hand as he moved. A minute later, she heard his footsteps on the stairs.

Emma found a long-faced Ginny in the drawing room, bent over an embroidery hoop. Taking a deep breath and squaring her shoulders, Emma entered the room. "Am I disturbing you, Ginny?" she asked, grateful that her skirt hid her shaking knees.

"Not at all," Ginny replied. "I'm just stitching. Edward's over in his office there," she added, gesturing with her head toward the room on the other side of the spacious foyer. Her expression was troubled as she sighed and pushed her needle through the cloth in her hoop.

Emma glanced nervously in the direction of the wide doorway, wondering if she should approach both Ginny and Edward with her idea.

No, talk to Ginny first, her subconscious spoke.

"Is something the matter, Emma? You look kind of funny."

"W-would you like to go for a walk with me, Ginny?"

A few minutes later their hats and capes were in place, and the two women were outdoors. Though the morning air was still on the chilly side, bright sunshine warmed their faces. A light breeze, scented with the freshness of the awakening earth, ruffled their garments, while overhead, the sky glistened brilliant blue from horizon to horizon.

Emma's eyes followed the neat lines of the whitewashed fences enclosing the ranch's various corrals and pastures as she walked along with Ginny in thoughtful silence. How could she begin to present such an outrageous idea to her new friend? She caught sight of Ryan Montgomery's commanding form in a far corral, and what little bit of the composure she possessed was nearly scattered.

Don't look at him right now, her inner voice spoke. *Just take one thing at a time. Talk to Ginny.*

But how could she even speak? Her heart felt as if it were in her mouth.

"I can see that something's troubling you, Emma," Ginny said, taking her hand. "I have to tell you that I'm not much good for anything myself today, but I'll help you in any way I can."

"I-I have something to confess," Emma began, slowing her pace. Gathering her courage, she looked into Ginny's sweet concerned face. "I eavesdropped on Edward and Maureen last night," she admitted, hurriedly adding, "but I didn't mean to. I mean, I was coming down the hallway . . . and I just heard them talking," she finished lamely, still feeling terribly ashamed at her actions.

Gloom crept over Ginny's features. "I assume you know about the money, then." At Emma's nod, she shrugged her shoulders. "Well, don't feel bad for listening . . . I told you the ranch was in trouble a week ago. You don't have to worry about your job, though," she added. "Edward's going into Denver to get a loan. That should be far enough away from here so no one will—" She dissolved into tears. "Oh, Emma . . . it's just killing him to have to borrow money. He's such a proud man. He feels like he's let everyone down . . ."

Tell her your idea, Emma's inner voice urged as Ginny wept. *Look how miserable she is! . . . You can help her . . . and Edward and Maureen . . . and the ranch!*

Emma's attention was drawn to the corral by a sudden wild and angry neighing, and a shiver swept through her body as she saw that Ryan Montgomery had lassoed a reddish-yellow horse. The buckskin bucked and jerked furiously as the broad-shouldered man struggled to wind the rope around the snubbing post in the center of the corral. Emma held her breath as the rope was secured, then she gasped as the horse dropped its head and hooves and charged the one who had thus ensnared him.

As Ryan nimbly moved out of the way, she let out her breath in relief and tried to swallow, realizing she had no moisture in her mouth with which to do so. Stars above, what the ex–army captain was doing in the corral was so . . . dangerous, so violent.

Was that what lay beneath his brooding façade . . . danger and violence? Was that why he had been distinguished for his bravery during the battle with the Ute?

Don't think about it, Emma Louise. You won't have that much to do with him . . . not really.

Next to her, Ginny delicately blew her nose. "Goodness, I didn't mean to burst into tears," she said, her voice thick with emotion. Fresh moisture formed in her gray-green eyes. "I just feel so bad for Edward . . ."

"Ginny?" Emma began hesitantly. "I've been thinking about something . . ."

Ten minutes later Ginny stood in wide-eyed astonishment, her tears gone. Clapping her hand over her forehead, she exclaimed, "I can't believe what you just told me. You really took this job and came out to Wyoming Territory knowing nothing of cooking?"

Emma nodded, nervously chewing her lip. Her heart thumped in her chest so loudly that she was certain Ginny could hear it.

"Well, I can't say we didn't notice that your cooking wasn't . . . well, never mind about that!" Ginny dropped her hand and shook her head in wonder. "I can't believe this, Emma! You're rich—well, you're *going* to be, anyway. You must want to open your shop very badly to have done all this."

"I do," she answered quietly.

"Well, what you've suggested certainly is ... shocking. I-I just don't know what to say ... but ... it really *would* work, wouldn't it? I think Edward would ... well, I don't know, but I think he'd ..." Ginny clapped her hands to her cheeks. "Oh, heavens, did you say your brother is an attorney?"

Emma nodded once again.

"Do you think he'd find some way to ... well, I mean ... is this somehow *illegal*?"

Emma had wondered the same thing while lying awake last night. "I gave the matter a great deal of thought," she answered slowly, "and I don't think what I'm proposing is unlawful. It's dishonest, I'll admit, but ... but it's a way to help you—and me—at the same time. Michael," she paused, sighing deeply, "will just have to accept it, just as he's going to have to accept the fact that I *will* be opening my shop—a little ahead of schedule." With a flush of irritation Emma remembered her brother's initial reaction to her business proposition. "Do you know what he said to me when I showed him my business plan and asked him for an advance on my trust fund?" she asked.

"What?"

"He said, 'Get married and have a baby or two,' like there's something the matter with me for wanting to do something a little different with my life."

"But why not marry that one fellow that was courting you? You said he—"

"Marry Jon?" Emma snorted in an unladylike fashion. "He's every bit as stuffy as Michael. Sure, I'd get my trust fund, but he'd never let me *use* it—especially for something like opening a shop in St. Paul! He'd want to invest it—" She pulled a face before brushing an errant nutmeg-colored curl from her forehead. "Besides, Mrs. Jon Severson would never be allowed to do something so unseemly as *work*."

"So you want to marry Ryan instead?"

Both women glanced over to the corral, where the tall man struggled to throw a saddle blanket over the back of the cross-hobbled but still belligerent buckskin, and another shiver scooted down Emma's spine as she scrutinized the movements of the rugged man. *Did* she want to marry Ryan?

"Well . . . no," Emma began, visibly flinching as Ryan hefted a heavy-looking saddle up atop the blanket and fought to tighten the cinch. "N-not really."

Chapter
Eight

"But I don't have any other choices," Emma continued, speaking too quickly, she knew. "Edward's already taken, and Joey's . . . well, I could never involve Joey in anything like this." Gesturing toward Ryan with the back of her hand, she added, "And it's not as if Ryan's *really* going to be my husband . . . we'll just slip off somewhere and go through the ceremony. Then with the proper documents I gain access to my trust fund and loan Edward enough money to keep the ranch operating until you sell your cattle in the fall—"

"And we don't have to go to the bank for a loan!" Ginny finished, the bloom fast returning to her cheeks. "We just pay you back when the cattle are sold!" She cocked her head to the side, studying Emma for a long moment. "For having such a sweet face, you really are devious, Emma Taylor. You're not going to have to cook for a whole year then, either, are you?"

Emma shook her head as an apprehensive but audacious smile curved her lips. "No, I'm not. After the annulment this autumn, I'll be going back to St. Paul to open my collectibles shop. There's nothing in my father's will that says I have to give back the money if my marriage is subsequently . . ." She cleared her throat. "Dissolved."

"Gosh, Emma, did you ever think that you could have temporarily married *anyone* and gotten your money?"

"No, I didn't . . . but I guess I could have, at that," she responded in a bemused manner, realizing that, until recently, she never would have dared to even *think* of such a thing. It was as if, by taking Michael's "dare," such that it was, she'd begun thinking of—and doing—one outrageous thing after another.

"What are you going to tell your brother?" Ginny asked, interrupting her thoughts. "He sounds as if he could be a little . . . well, I don't want to say anything unkind about him, but he sounds a little *difficult.*"

A sudden sting of waspishness made Emma's voice sharp. "Ever since I asked him for an advance on my trust fund to start my business, 'difficult' is a word I'd definitely use to describe Michael." Almost immediately, she was pricked by a sharp twinge of conscience for having presented her brother as some kind of unreasonable monster. "But he's really not a bad person," she hastened to assure Ginny. "His ethics and values are very . . . conservative, is all."

A strong gust of wind tugged at Ginny's hat. "So he'll just accept your marriage and hand over the money, then?"

"If I tell him I've fallen head-over-heels in love, he'll have to." A nervous pounding began in her breast when she thought about marriage—and being in love—with Ryan Montgomery. What *were* her true motives in suggesting such an arrangement? she asked herself, relieved not to have to give the matter any deeper thought when Ginny spoke again.

"Head-over-heels in love . . . with *Ryan*?" Ginny glanced dubiously at the corral, where her husband's older brother was swinging himself up onto the buckskin's back. She gave a delicate little shudder. "What's there to love about him?" At that, her expression became contrite. "Oh, dear, that wasn't very kind of me, was it? I'm sure there must be something to love about him. After all, Maureen thinks he's . . . Oh, my goodness, Maureen! What are we going to tell Maureen? She would never go for an arrangement like this, not in a million years."

"I agree that this whole scheme does get a little tricky," Emma replied. "But think of it as a double lie: I make Michael believe that I'm marrying Ryan because I love him, yet here at the ranch we keep the marriage a secret so Maureen doesn't find out. Nothing will have to change, you see, and no one needs to know Ryan and I have wed except me, you, Edward, and Ryan."

"What about when you get the marriage annulled? What will Michael say then?"

"I . . . don't know," Emma said with a deep sigh. Indeed, she had no idea what she would tell Michael in the autumn. "I suppose I'll think of something. Of late, I seem to be excelling at dishonesty and deceit." In an attempt to push her pensiveness aside, she clapped her hands briskly and lifted her chin. "Well, Virginia Montgomery, if you care to follow me into my newest transgression, I have two questions for you."

Ginny nodded several times before a conspiratorial smile spread across her face. "I'll follow you, Emma. What you've proposed is perfectly wicked . . . but it's also *perfect!* Oh—" she broke off, seeing what Emma knew was a still-weighty expression on her face. "What are your questions?"

"First of all, Ginny, how do we get Ryan to marry me? What's Edward going to say about all this? Will he even agree to—"

"Leave Edward to me," Ginny said, nodding sagely. "I'm sure I can make him see reason." She pursed her lips. "As for Ryan . . . well, maybe we can just leave Ryan to Edward. . . ." Her voice trailed off as the prospective groom attempted to force the bucking animal to submit to his will.

Emma's attention, too, was drawn by the wild, powerful sight of man and beast locked in a struggle for control. Could she really marry this man? She didn't even know him. . . .

You don't have to know him, Emma Louise. All you have to do with him is stand in front of a preacher and say a few words, then he can go back to his horses, and you can go back to the kitchen. . . . And if anything else were to happen, well . . .

"Emma? Did you hear me? I asked if that was both questions."

"Oh, I'm sorry," Emma replied distractedly, her eyes still on Ryan Montgomery's commanding form. "No, I still have one more question for you," she said, turning to Ginny and pasting a counterfeit smile on her lips.

"Would you like to be my matron of honor?"

Emma's nerves were tightly strung for the remainder of the day, and when Ginny's whisper and soft rapping came at her bedchamber door at half-past ten, Emma was out of bed in an instant. A wide crack of light entered the room as the door was pushed open a few inches.

"Emma," came Ginny's voice, a little louder now. "Emma, are you awake? May I come in?"

"Come in," Emma whispered in reply, hastily pulling a wrapper over her nightdress. The whole day through, she'd had second thoughts . . . and third thoughts . . . about the scheme she'd proposed to Ginny. Michael's reaction, most of all, was what terrified her—even more than being joined, in name only, with Ryan Montgomery. She had received a long chatty letter from Lucille last week, but between her sister-in-law's flowing lines of script and carefully chosen words, Emma had clearly read of Michael's continuing displeasure with her and her actions.

A hasty wedding between Emma and a man he had never met would likely send Michael right over the edge.

But on the other hand, there was the incentive of gaining access to her funds much more quickly than she had ever dreamed. After the annulment, she would be free to open her business, live independently—and do whatever else she wished. Even if Jon Severson never wanted another thing to do with her, she was pretty sure Michael would come around eventually . . . given enough time.

Nervously Emma regarded Ginny, who had come into the bedchamber still dressed as she had been during the day. The plump young woman's face was over-illuminated by the lantern's glare, making her expression hard to read. Did defeat sit on her features, she wondered, or was it uncertainty . . . or even despondency?

"Have you talked to Edward yet?" Emma quickly asked as she tied the sash around her waist. Her words gained speed as one possible outcome after another ran through her mind. "You have, haven't you? Oh, Ginny, what did he say? Goodness, I knew it. Your husband's ready to throw me out on my ear, isn't he?"

"No, no, slow down. He's not ready to throw you out on your ear—on the contrary!" A small guilty smile curved Ginny's lips, giving her a puckish expression. "He grabbed ahold of your idea like a drowning man would a life rope. First off, I loosened him up with a few kisses and a few whiskeys before I broached the subject . . ." Her words trailed off as she set the lantern on the small dresser and stepped away from it. Out of range of the flame's immediate glare, the shading of her face returned to normal, and she frowned as she tilted her head to the side. "Although I must admit it seemed the whiskey did more for putting him in an amenable mood than my kisses—"

"Oh, Ginny, what did he say?" Hope rose in Emma's breast, and she impatiently interrupted her friend.

"He said—" Ginny quietly pushed the door closed and walked over close to Emma. "He said he wants to do it." A grin broke out on her face, and, in a whisper, she excitedly chattered on. "You should have seen his face, Emma. At first he didn't believe what I was telling him, but when he realized I was serious, he started grinning and waving his arms around like . . . like I don't know what! I haven't seen him so happy in I don't know how long. He'd like to talk to you now, if you don't—oh, dear! You haven't changed your mind, have you, Emma?" It was Ginny's turn for a moment of anxiousness, and she caught her lower lip between her teeth. "I mean, if you've changed your mind it's *okay*, but—"

"I haven't changed my mind," Emma reassured her. "But I've been wondering how Edward is going to talk Ryan into marrying me, and when—and where—this so-called marriage is going to take place."

"I can answer the last two questions: You're getting married tomorrow in Denver. As for how Edward's going to talk Ryan into it, I don't know." Ginny hugged her arms to her chest. "I don't think I want to know, either. All he said is that he's going to go out to the bunkhouse to talk to Ryan, and that you and I should be ready to leave early in the morning. . . ."

Ginny's voice faded from Emma's ears as she mentally staggered at her friend's words. *Married tomorrow . . . in Denver?* Things were moving along a lot more quickly than she had ever anticipated. *How can you and Ryan possibly be married tomorrow in Denver? It's just not possible! What's Maureen going to think if the four of us take off for Denver in the morning? And who's going to do the cooking. . . .*

"Emma, did you hear me?"

"Um . . . no. I'm sorry, Ginny. My mind is racing in a hundred different directions at once, and it . . . it just seems like everything is happening so quickly."

"It is, I'll agree," Ginny responded sympathetically. "But I'll be right there with you, Emma. If you'd still like me to be your matron of honor, that is," she shyly added.

"Gin?" A light tapping came at the door, followed by Edward's loud whisper. "Gin, are you still in here?"

Quickly, Ginny moved to open the door. "Shh!" she scolded as she ushered her husband into the small room. "Keep your voice down."

The first thing Emma noticed about Edward was that the worry that had clouded his features during the past weeks had fallen away. Before her stood a tall, dark, vital, energetic, albeit slightly drunken man, and self-consciously she folded her arms across her chest, her nose prickling at his whiskey-scented exhalations.

"Emma Taylor!" he whispered noisily, pointing directly toward her, his already potent expression intensifying even more.

Nervously she moistened her lips. "Yes?"

"Emma Taylor," he repeated just as ominously. His face broke into a wide easy smile then, and he appeared to sway slightly. "Emma Taylor, I could just kiss your pretty little face!"

"Edward! Shame on you!" Ginny remonstrated, her outraged expression softening as she realized her husband had no intention of carrying out his declaration. Affectionately wrapping her arms around Edward's waist, she looked up into his face and sighed. "I'll never know how I ended up marrying such a rascal."

" 'Cause you like me to kiss *your* pretty little face, that's why," he replied, running his finger down the bridge of his wife's pert nose before encircling her shoulders with his arms. "And don't think I wasn't paying attention to your smooches before you started with the whiskey," he murmured, his voice carrying clearly to Emma though he bent his head close to Ginny's. "It seems I have been remiss lately—"

Just as Emma grew so uncomfortable that she wished she could disappear, Ginny wriggled free of Edward's embrace and cleared her throat. "Now, Edward, we've a lifetime for kisses. Right now, we've got to talk."

"Indeed we do," he replied, straightening his shirt and smoothing a hand over his hair. His expression grew sober. "Before we go any further, Emma, I need to hear with my own ears that the offer you made Ginny was serious."

"It was," she replied, drawing a deep breath. "But I don't know how we're going to get Ryan to—"

"Don't worry about Ryan," Edward interrupted. "I believe I can . . . ah, persuade him to go along with things." Stepping forward, he extended his hand to Emma. "From what Ginny told me, I realize that both of us will ultimately benefit from this arrangement. In case you have any concerns about being permanently parted from your funds, however, I want to reassure you that your loan to the Montmac Ranch will be repaid in full when our cattle go to market."

Slowly Emma extended her right hand toward Edward's. "Then you have yourself a deal, Mr. Montgomery," she said as Edward's warm palm closed over her ice-cold fingers. Looking into his face, Emma was struck by the similarities—and differences—between the two eldest Montgomery sons.

"What are you going to say to Ryan?" Ginny asked anxiously. "And your mother?"

"Don't worry, ladies," Edward spoke reassuringly. "Just be packed and ready to leave in the morning, and leave the rest to me."

Ryan was awakened by a rough hand shaking his shoulder. *Was this some new manifestation of his nightmare?* he wondered. Had Hopper now taken to visiting him from the grave? Groggy and disoriented, Ryan didn't know what time it was, what day it was, nor could he recall for certain whether or not he'd had the dream yet this night.

"Ryan!" a familiar voice whispered in his ear, and the shaking grew rougher. "Damn it all, Ryan, you haven't gotten any easier to wake since we were kids. Wake up now. We need to talk."

"Take your friggin' talkin' somewhere else," came Ferguson's cross voice.

"Yeah, an' take that light with you," Lorenzo groggily added. "Come on, Montgomery, we already don't git enough sleep the way it is."

"Sorry for waking you all," Ryan heard his brother reply, "but as long as you're up, is Archie Mueller bedded down in here with you tonight?"

"Right here," a deep voice grumbled from the far side of the room. "Whaddaya want?"

"I know my ma told you to start loading the chuck wagon tomorrow, but there's been a slight change of plans. You'll be cooking at the house for the next few days, until it's time to start roundup."

"Yeah, whatever. Now jus' git outa here an' let us sleep, will ya?"

"I'll be gone just as soon as my brother here gets himself out of bed. Come on, Ryan," Edward said in a grim tone, giving his shoulder another rough shake.

"Just what the hell is going on?" Ryan asked, pushing Edward's hand away and throwing his arm over his eyes to block the glare of the lantern. "Have you taken leave of your senses?" Flinging the blanket to the end of the cot, he wondered if he was destined to ever have an uninterrupted night of sleep again in his life. As he swung his legs to the floor and sat up, the unmistakable odor of liquor reached him, and he realized that Edward had been drinking.

"There had better be a good reason for you coming in here like this," Ryan warned in a low voice, "because if there's not . . ." His voice trailed off as he considered that there very well may be a good reason for Edward drinking . . . and waking him. "Is it Joey?" he asked, quickly pulling on his pants and boots and following Edward out the door. "Is he sick?"

Having not taken the time to grab his coat, the cool night air immediately raised a chill on Ryan's arms. "Has he got pneumonia again? . . . Or . . . Oh, God." His legs stopped moving as a horrible thought struck him.

"It's Ma, isn't it?"

Ahead of him, Edward, too, stopped walking. Raising the lantern aloft, his younger brother turned to him with a grim expression. Overhead, the faint glow of the quarter moon was obscured by a layer of wispy clouds, and the shadows cast by the lantern gave the yard outside the bunkhouse a sepulchral look. "It's Ma," Edward gravely intoned, causing the bottom to drop out of Ryan's stomach.

"Ma . . ." Ryan suddenly found it difficult to speak. He swallowed hard. "Ma? Is she . . ."

"No, she's not dead." The sudden edge in Edward's voice was as sharp as a freshly stropped razor. He closed the distance between them in a few angry strides. "But it's nice to know you'd care one way or the other if she was," he sneered.

Matching irritation rose inside Ryan at being duped in such a manner. "Then what's going—"

"Keep your voice down," Edward interrupted in a furious whisper as he started toward the barn. "Come in here, and I'll tell you exactly what's going on with Ma and our 'family' business," he said, pointing at the large dark structure. "Unless you'd like to continue to keep to yourself. Oh, excuse me," he added disparagingly, "maybe I should say, 'continue to keep your head in the sand.' "

Continue to keep your head in the sand! Ryan followed Edward into the barn, prepared to tear his younger brother's head off for his meddling, righteous arrogance. Who did he think he was to talk to him in that manner? Perhaps the time to leave the ranch was now, he thought, kicking the barn door closed behind him.

That's it, Montgomery, his inner voice advised. *You don't need this kind of shit. . . . Just yank your cash out of the ranch and be on your way.*

Instead, a scant few minutes later, he was reeling with quiet shock as Edward told him, point-blank, about the floundering silver mine and the ranch's cash-flow problems. If what his brother was telling him was true, then all the money he'd sent home was gone, eaten up by mine machinery and miners' wages.

While trying to digest that piece of information, Ryan was further astounded to hear of Edward's proposed "solution" to the problem. At first he wasn't certain he'd correctly heard his brother—Edward was saying that if Ryan cared anything about the ranch, or poor Ma ever being able to hold her head up without shame, then he'd *marry . . . Miss Taylor?*

"The cook," Edward said impatiently, "you know, the young woman from St. Paul that you picked up from the train station—"

"I *know* who Emma Taylor is," Ryan exclaimed in exasperation, an image of the attractive young woman springing into his mind as he spoke. "But what—"

"She's loaded, Ryan," Edward interrupted, holding up his hands. "Just hear me out on this," he added, letting his hands drop back down. Quickly Edward told him of the conditions attached to Emma's trust fund and of the circumstances that had led her to take the job on the ranch.

"So what you're saying is that I'm just supposed to blithely marry some spoiled little rich girl and save the day?"

"Don't you think it's about time you did something for this family?" Edward asked accusingly. "For years now, you've held yourself so far apart from us that we don't know who or what you are anymore. You don't even know us anymore; not me, not Ma, not Joey, and sure as hell not any of our sisters. Can you tell me when the last time was, besides an hour or two at Christmas—or your brief appearance at Da's funeral—that you've spent time with *any* of us? We're your family, for God's sake—and a loving one at that!" Edward paused for breath, a dark flush suffusing his features.

Ryan opened his mouth to disagree, to say *something,* but curiously he was speechless. *Miss Taylor wanted to marry him?*

"You know Joey has always worshipped the ground you walk on," Edward began again in a low tight voice, this time going for the jugular, "yet you keep pushing him away. Ma, too. She's worried sick about you, Ryan, not that she doesn't already have enough to worry about. She works her fingers to the bone here on the ranch to keep the family business going, but where she *really* wants to be is in Cheyenne with Ruthie and Colleen. She's afraid her babies are going to end up as much strangers as . . . well, as you."

Quick pain flashed through Ryan's heart at his brother's critical words.

"You just don't have any idea how hard Da's death was on her, do you?" Edward continued, emotion now evident in his voice. "Or how much she took on when he died. All I'm asking, Ryan, is that you help out the family . . . help poor Ma. If you had any idea of what going to the bank for a loan would do to her, you wouldn't . . ." Edward broke off for a long moment, and when he spoke again, his voice was choked. "Going to the bank for money would just kill her. Think of it—everyone laughing and talking and sniggering behind their hands . . ."

Wounded and to a degree benumbed, Ryan involuntarily flinched when Edward clapped a warm hand on his shoulder. He felt his brother's warm brown eyes searching his face.

"I'm sorry to spring this on you like I did," Edward said in a more gentle manner, "but we need your help. Marrying Miss Taylor is simply a business arrangement, Ryan, a mutually beneficial business arrangement. It's not like you . . . well, not like you *really* have to be married to her or anything. All she needs is your name and a certificate of marriage to get ahold of her money. Then, four or five months down the line we pay her back, you two get an annulment, and she's back off to St. Paul to open her . . . her store, or whatever it is she wants to open."

"And you think Ma's just going to go along with this?" Ryan's voice sounded hollow in his ears.

"No, Ma would never go for anything like this," Edward concurred, dropping his hand from Ryan's shoulder. Stepping back, he took a deep breath. "That's why we have to get her away from here until things are settled. See, when you and I are done talking, I'm going to go wake her up and tell her I've made a terrible mistake in the books—that we really do have enough money to meet expenses until fall." He cleared his throat and looked meaningfully at Ryan. "Imagine her additional happiness at learning that you now want to be a part of ranch operations. . . . Ryan and Edward at the helm, so to speak, just like Da always wanted."

"So I not only marry the cook, I also have to—"

"You don't have to work the ranch, Ryan," Edward added in an uncertain tone. "I know that's probably asking too much of you. I'll just find some way to manage both the mine and the ranch. . . . Maybe I can ask McDermott to . . ." His voice trailed off. "Well, anyway, first things first. I'll tell Ma to pack for her and Joey, and they can stay in town with Ruthie and Colleen until the end of the school term. . . ."

Ryan listened numbly as Edward outlined the rest of his plan: that the four of them, Ryan, Miss Taylor, Edward, and Ginny, would accompany Maureen and Joey to Cheyenne in the morning, ostensibly for a day trip of shopping. Then, once Maureen and Joey were safely off to the town house, the four of them would take the southbound Union Pacific to Denver.

"Denver is far enough from here so no one will find out about your marriage," Edward continued earnestly. "Miss Taylor can also conduct her financial transactions by wire from there, so that none of the snooping eyes and ears of Cheyenne will catch wind of your joining." Edward rubbed his hands together animatedly. "Emma's plan is perfect, Ryan. It can't fail. She's agreed to continue working through the summer so as not to spark any suspicion, and then in the fall she'll simply give notice and move back to St. Paul."

Though Ryan could think of a hundred good reasons why not to involve himself in such duplicity, Edward had conducted a powerful assault on long-dormant emotions. *For years now, you've held yourself so far apart from us that we don't know who or what you are anymore. . . . We're your family, for God's sake. . . . Help poor Ma. . . . Think of it—everyone laughing and talking and sniggering behind their hands. . . .*

Miss Taylor wanted to marry him only because he was a convenient means for her to get her hands on her inheritance that much sooner, not because she had any feelings for him. If the situation weren't so pathetic, he could almost throw back his head and laugh at the irony of it all.

Guilt and confusion mixed together inside Ryan as his brother stood silently before him, waiting for an answer. Farther off in the barn, a horse snorted and moved restlessly, its slumber disturbed by their voices. Inhaling deeply of the earthy smells of hay and animals, Ryan looked overhead—as if the solution to this problem were to be found in reading crisscrossed beams and timbers—and a sudden absurd urge struck him. *Turn around and run, Montgomery,* it said. *Turn around and run until you can't run anymore.*

"Do I have your answer, Ryan?" A hopeful, expectant look lit Edward's features. "There's really nothing more to this for you than having to make a trip to Denver tomorrow. . . ."

An empty sigh escaped Ryan's chest as he focused instead on the lantern that Edward had hung from a sturdy hook inside the barn. The answer to this dilemma hadn't come to him while looking overhead; perhaps it was to be found in the flickering flame. . . .

"Ryan?"

Tearing his gaze from the lamp, Ryan unwillingly met the proud but pleading expression in his brother's eyes. "All right, I'll do it," he heard himself say in a faint voice. "I don't like it one bit, but I'll do it."

Chapter
Nine

A glorious sunrise unfolded over the plains as the west-bound Union Pacific train approached the Pine Bluffs depot. The sound of cheerful morning birdsong was obliterated by the roaring and chugging of the powerful black iron horse, and Emma watched as dark smoke billowed upward from its wide smokestack and stained the flawless sky.

"Whoo-woo," Joey mimicked the train whistle. "Whoo-woo-woo!" Standing between Maureen and Emma on the wooden platform, he glanced between them, grinning wide-ly. "Whoo-woo!" he shouted, placing his hands over his ears. "Twain . . . loud!"

Maureen smiled indulgently at her son, her answering words becoming lost in the roaring racket. Emma watched as the older woman's glance traveled to Ryan, who was helping Owens tie a pair of saddle horses to the back of the Montgomerys' carriage. While the three women and Joey had made the journey to the depot by carriage, Ryan, Edward, and Owens had ridden ahead of the conveyance on horseback.

Emma watched Maureen's expression lighten even more as she studied her eldest son. Though Emma had always considered the widow quite an attractive woman, she couldn't help but be amazed at the overnight transformation in the

petite Irishwoman. Her softly freckled face was fresher and
more animated than Emma could ever remember seeing, and
during the carriage ride, the mother of seven had chattered on
like a schoolgirl about how excited she was to be going back
to Cheyenne. Her happiness at rejoining her two youngest
daughters was painfully obvious, as was her joy at Ryan
"wantin' to be a part of things now." Emma didn't know
for sure what Edward had said to his mother last night, but
it seemed that he had indeed taken care of everything, just
as he had promised.

A delicious breakfast had been ready and waiting when
Emma had arisen this morning, prepared by a skinny, griz-
zled, pan-rattling man who brusquely introduced himself as
Mueller. Two trunks and a valise sat in the hallway near
the staircase, and Maureen and Joey were already up and
dressed in travel clothing.

"How nice it is you're makin' the day trip to town with
the other kids, Emma," Maureen had warmly told her. "I
know Ginny'll be pleased to have your company."

Not knowing for sure what to say, Emma had politely
smiled and murmured that she was looking forward to
seeing Cheyenne.

"Edward told me he talked to you about why we hired
Mueller, so there's no need to be frettin' about your job. . . .
Oh, so much has happened since last night that I simply
cannot concentrate this mornin'. I'm so confounded excited
about spendin' the rest of the school term in town with
my girls!" Maureen gushed, a brilliant smile suffusing her
features. "An' that Ryan! I cannot believe he's actually takin'
over for me, bless his heart. . . . And Edward! Discoverin'
them accountin' mistakes in the books last night. . . . Well,
I guess the good Lord's got his own schedule for answerin'
all kinds o' prayers."

"I guess Ryan finally decided it was time to be a part of
things." Edward smiled and directed a meaningful glance
in Emma's direction as he and Ginny entered the kitchen.
Walking over to stand before his mother, he splayed his
hand over his chest and earnestly added, "I know I already
told you this last night, Ma, but it was really touching the
way Ryan told me how much it bothers him to see you

working so hard. And then he asked what he could do to help out. . . ." He shrugged and looked around at the four of them, his gaze settling once again on his mother's joyous face. "I don't know what to make of it, Ma, but I couldn't be more pleased to be working with him after all these years. It's like all of a sudden he had a . . . a change of heart or something."

At that, Ginny glanced at Emma and surreptitiously rolled her eyes heavenward. Affixing a bright expression on her round face, Ginny added, "So, to celebrate, as long as spring roundup hasn't started yet, we thought we'd accompany you and Joey to Cheyenne and spend a couple of hours in town."

"An' Ryan's goin' along, too?" Maureen asked dubiously.

"Wyan brudder . . . come with?" Joey's lower jaw dropped as he put down his fork and placed his hands atop his head. "No, no, no, no. Not be-*leeve*!"

Edward nodded emphatically. "Believe it, Joey. He's coming. He told me last night how much he wants to come with us. In fact, I bet he was up before all the other men in the bunkhouse, and that he's getting ready to come right now." Turning to Maureen, he inclined his head. "He probably wants to go over to Fort Russell and say hello to some of his old army cronies."

Forking up a bite of hash, Maureen shook her head in wonderment. "It's a miracle, Edward me boy, an absolute miracle. . . ."

"Am-ma come . . . Shy-ann?" Joey asked, suddenly looking concerned. "Want my Am-ma."

"Aye, m' love, Emma will be comin' with us to Cheyenne this mornin'," Maureen answered cautiously. "But I must tell you, dear, that she won't be stayin' in town with us. She has to come back to the ranch an' cook for Ginny an' your brothers. Mr. Mueller's got to get the chuck wagon ready an' go out on roundup, and we've already got us a woman at the town house who cooks an' cleans."

"Want Am-ma." The concerned expression became one of obstinacy.

"Joey, it's not as if you're never going to see Emma again," Edward reasoned. "You and Ma and Colleen and Ruthie will be coming back to the ranch when the girls are done with school. It's not that long till then."

"An' you know, Joseph," Maureen quickly interjected, "your sisters were terribly disappointed when you did not come with me last time. Colleen, especially, was wishin' you'd have come. She's got a grand kite, you see, but she could not get it off the ground. Ruthie an' Ginny tried to help her, but . . ." The auburn-haired woman allowed her voice to trail off.

"K-kuh-kite?"

"You're really good at flying kites, Joey," Ginny said in a genuine tone. "Gosh, I don't know how you can get them up as high as you do."

Seriously, Joey nodded several times. "I good." As he picked up his fork and stirred his hash around his plate, his indecision was clearly apparent. Finally he sighed. "Co-ween need Joey. Am-ma need Joey. Who do d-d-dishes?"

"With the men out on roundup, I'm not going to have very many dishes," Emma replied. "I'll be lonely for you, but I'll be brave and manage until you come back," she replied, adding in a confidential tone, "because it sounds as if your sister is in much greater need of you right now than I am. See, I can wash a few dishes, but she's in a terrible fix—she can't fly her kite at all."

Screwing up his face as he mulled over Emma's logic, Joey finally nodded in agreement. "Help Co-ween," he announced, eliciting quiet sighs of relief from all of them.

Emma pulled her thoughts back to the present as the noisy locomotive entered the station. Despite her trepidation at what lay ahead of her today, she managed a small smile at Edward and Ginny, who had finished their business at the ticket window and were approaching. Next to her, Joey continued his imitations of a train whistle.

It took a little more than an hour to get to Cheyenne by train, Edward had quietly told her this morning as he loaded his mother's trunks on top of the carriage. "Then from Cheyenne, it's another four and a half, five hours to Denver," he'd said. "And if all goes on schedule," he'd added, arching one eyebrow and giving her an unfathomable look, "by nightfall your name will be Emma Montgomery."

Emma Montgomery.

By chance, Emma's glance met that of the tall man who would, this very day, lend her the use of his name. His dark gaze penetrated deeply and he lifted his eyebrows in an expressive gesture that meant . . . what? What was he thinking?

Emma shivered and clutched her satchel more tightly to her body, wondering what Edward could possibly have said to Ryan to make him go along with this. Knowing what little she did of the heroic army officer, Emma was certain he was not the kind of man who could be forced to do . . . anything he did not want to do.

Maybe she didn't want to know *what* Edward had said to him.

As the conductor hollered, "Boa-oard!" in a deep musical basso, a sudden quivering began in Emma's stomach. Up until now, she'd almost been able to make herself believe that she and Ginny really were about to embark on a day of shopping and girl talk. *You're not going shopping, Emma Louise, you're going to be married today— married to a man you do not know, in the presence of two persons you only barely know, in a city you have never been to. . . .*

"Am-ma," Joey shouted over the din of the railway depot, causing Emma to tear her gaze away from the tall imposing man who, later today, she would swear before God to love, honor, and obey for the rest of her life.

"Sit by Joey?"

Emma nodded as she prepared to board the train, telling herself that God surely understood that she was trying to help the Montgomerys as much as she was helping herself. She was happy to have the means to assist them in their hour of need, for after all, they were such nice people.

Right, Emma, her conscience whispered, *if your motives are so pure, then why do you feel you're doing something wrong?* And why did she get a flustered, tingly feeling every time she thought of Ryan Montgomery?

Ryan and Edward boarded the train after Joey and the women, and as Emma made her way to her seat, she wondered if Ryan's dark eyes were still on her. It was a terribly unnerving feeling to know that he was walking behind her, thinking . . .

What was Ryan thinking? she wondered. What was going on inside his head? Was he thinking about the wedding, feeling as uneasy as she about the deceit and trickery involved in pulling off this scheme? Or was he a risk-taker like Edward, a man who subscribed to the philosophy of the end justifying the means? Or was there something else entirely that was motivating him?

Emma was willing to bet any amount of money that Edward Montgomery had lied through his teeth this morning, that Ryan hadn't had any kind of "change of heart" or whatever kind of twaddle it was that he'd told his mother. Furthermore, she didn't believe that self-alienating Ryan Montgomery was ever going to be part of his family's ranch operations.

Nonetheless, she'd been impressed by Edward's storytelling abilities this morning . . . or perhaps it was his *acting* abilities, she thought wryly.

If Maureen believed Edward—and it appeared that she had—it was so much the better for all of them, and for their plans. Emma couldn't help but fret, however, that if Ryan didn't make an effort to be just a bit more . . . *social,* Maureen was bound to become suspicious. Wasn't she?

Maybe not, she decided, hearing the widow chatter excitedly ahead of her in the aisle. Or maybe, unbeknownst to her, Ryan had already talked to his mother this morning.

Thinking of the day she'd arrived in Pine Bluffs, Emma remembered how intimidated she'd been by the man in the buffalo coat. And his boorishness wasn't limited to only her; he treated the ranch employees and his family, too, in the same wretched manner. During all the weeks she'd known him, Emma had been certain he was full of mean-spiritedness and barely leashed violence.

But this morning, despite his baleful expression, it seemed there had been something different about him. A kind of blankness in his Cimmerian eyes, perhaps. . . .

"You two must be plannin' quite a day o' shoppin'," Maureen commented as they took their seats. She pointed first at Emma's generous-sized leather satchel, then at the large carpet bag in Ginny's hands. The younger women's eyes met nervously, and Emma prayed that Maureen would not discover that the bags each contained a few essential items for an overnight stay. "I may be exaggeratin' just a wee bit," Maureen went on, "but it seems as though you could fit about half o' Cheyenne in them two bags, there."

"Oh, you know me," Ginny said with a guilty smile as she set the bag quite close to her feet. "I'm always prepared to carry home anything I might find."

Emma, too, curved her mouth into what she hoped was a smile and wrapped her arms more securely around her satchel as she situated herself more comfortably in her seat. She was relieved to see that Edward and Ryan had taken seats farther down the aisle. From where she sat, all she could see of the two men were the backs of their dark heads. Since the six of them were the only passengers at this stop, the doors were closed, and the train was soon on its way.

Egbert was the next stop, then Burns. This train was evidently not an express, Emma thought wearily, recalling the long days she'd spent traveling to Pine Bluffs. Now, as then, her eyes burned with tiredness, and out of nowhere she thought of her comfortable bed back in St. Paul. How wonderful it would be to curl up in her big fluffy bed, in her big, beautifully decorated room, and sleep until she was no longer tired.

Watching winter-dead grassland whiz by outside the window, Emma wondered if what she was doing really was so worthwhile. Maybe Michael and Jon had known what they were talking about, she thought, for no matter how she looked at things, the truth was that she'd traded an easy, pampered existence for one of hard work, sore muscles, and exhaustion.

Come September or October, you're going to be mighty glad you did all this, a bolstering voice from somewhere inside her spoke. *Don't let yourself get discouraged. You're just tired right now. Remember, every day that passes brings you closer to the day your shop opens.*

Across the aisle from her, Ginny and Maureen made small talk, but Joey, seated on her right side, had been curiously quiet since the train departed the Pine Bluffs station. After one passenger departed and two got on at the Burns depot, his warm pudgy fingers reached over and awkwardly tapped the back of her hands.

"Am-ma miss Joey?"

"Oh, yes, indeed I will," Emma answered truthfully, shifting her satchel toward the left side of the seat and taking Joey's hand in her right.

"Joey help Co-ween sister," he said earnestly, as if he were trying to apologize for leaving her. "Co-ween need k-kite help."

"I understand, Joey," she said, giving his hand a gentle squeeze. "It's very important for you to help your younger sisters. They're very lucky, you know, to have such a talented and helpful older brother such as yourself."

"Oh-hhh . . . I not." Pulling his hand from hers, he covered his eyes in embarrassment and shook his head.

"You're not what . . . talented and helpful?" Tugging lightly at his left wrist, Emma was pleased to see Joey's lips twitch. She tugged again, and the twitch became a grin. "Come on, Joseph Montgomery, admit it; you're the most talented and helpful young man I know."

The grin grew wider, and his hands fell away from his face. "I g-good," he admitted, nodding several times. "Joey good brudder." His expression faded then, and he folded his hands in his lap.

"Joey?" Emma asked, sensing that something was still troubling him.

Lowering his head, Joey alternately licked and pursed his lips several times. "Make 'peshal w-w-wish," he finally admitted.

"A special wish?"

He nodded, and with slow deliberate movements he reached inside his coat. After what seemed like an eternity to Emma, he extracted a messily folded sheet of paper and handed it to her.

"What's this?"

"Paint p-pick-cher for Am-ma," he said with a downcast expression.

"You did? How nice."

"W-wish pick-cher." His head drooped even farther forward.

"You . . . you painted me a picture of your wish?" Emma asked, hesitantly taking the paper.

Joey glanced shyly at her, then looked quickly away, and suddenly Emma felt as if she were on uncertain ground with him. She'd seen his pain and sadness before, particularly when he talked of Ryan, but the way he was acting right now was much . . . different. Carefully she unfolded the paper, not knowing what to expect.

Wide blue and yellow streaks of watercolor boldly crisscrossed the top of the page, while at the bottom left corner was a large untidy brown square. Several roundish blobs, of various colors, were scattered about the remaining lower half of the page in a random manner. A thick stripe of green separated the blobs from the blue and yellow streaks, but, oddly, one blob sat at the top of the page in the blue and yellow area, well outside of the green boundary.

Emma wasn't certain what Joey's painting was supposed to be, but aside from the distracting brown mess on the bottom left-hand side, she decided the colors and overall composition were pleasing to the eye. It also appeared that Joey had taken pains to carefully rinse his brush when he switched from one pigment to another, for the painting's colors were bright and true, not at all muddied.

"W-wanch."

"Wanch?" Looking up at Joey, Emma saw that he studied her face. "Wanch . . . oh, *ranch*!" she exclaimed, pointing at the brown figure. "This is your ranch, isn't it?"

Joey nodded, a pleased smile splitting his lips.

"And these are your cattle, aren't they!" she exclaimed, pointing at one of the colorful blobs. "Does this one give violet-colored milk?"

Joey's smile faded. Pursing his lips, he did not reply.

"Oh, dear, they're not cattle, are they?" Emma murmured, trying desperately to imagine what significance the blobs possessed. If they weren't cattle, could they possibly be . . . horses? *Come on, Emma*, her inner voice charged, *use your imagination. He's looking at you like he expects you to know what these things are.*

"I-ween," he said impatiently.

"I wean? Like a calf or a foal?"

His tone was offended. "No, no, no, no! Not calf-foal! I-ween *sister*."

"You wean your sister? No, that can't be it," she muttered to herself. "Oh," she exclaimed in a flash of comprehension. "That's *Irene*, your sister Irene, isn't it?"

Joey nodded. "I-ween sister. An' Co-ween sister, an' Mor-ra sister, an' Roo-fee sister," he further expanded, pointing to a different blob as he spoke each of his sisters' names. Delicately he touched a blob of vermilion on the lower portion of the page before running his finger up the page to stroke the blob at the top right corner. "My ma . . . my mudder," he said softly, "an' fadder. Fadder dead."

"You must still think of your father a great deal," Emma said sensitively, as her index finger met Joey's. "You painted him up here in this beautifully colored sky—in heaven, am I right?" At his nod, she continued. "But I see that you kept him close to your family." She allowed her finger to drift across the upper edge of the paper. "Did you know that my father's in heaven, too? Maybe over here somewhere," she added softly, letting her finger stop at an intersection of blue and yellow sky.

"Fadder d-dead?"

"Yes, both my mother and father are dead." Emma felt her throat grow thick as she spoke. "And I miss them terribly. What helps me feel better, though, is knowing that heaven is a wonderful place, and that one day I'll be with them again." Tears prickled the corners of her eyes, but she blinked them away and strove for a lighter tone of voice. "You've painted a lovely picture of your ranch and your family, Joey," she complimented, pointing to the figures he had not yet named. "These other . . . er, people must be you and your brothers, right? You and Edward and . . ." Her words trailed off, and she quickly counted the number of figures on the page. "Oh, look here, you've made one too many."

"No . . . Not." Joey shook his head and slowly moved his finger to a pink figure he had not yet named. "'Peshal w-wish . . . best wish."

"That's right, this is your wish picture, isn't it?"

"Yeah," Joey spoke as the train slowed again. " 'Peshal wish."

"Hillsdale," the conductor called out. "Hiillss-dale."

Glancing around the compartment, Emma saw that a few people were preparing to depart. How many more stops to Cheyenne . . . and how many between Cheyenne and Denver? Her attention jumped from Joey's painting to her impending exchange of nuptials with his older brother.

How on earth were her nerves supposed to tolerate a long day of stop-and-go travel *and marriage* to Ryan Montgomery?

Her heart nearly stopped in her chest when, a moment later, her glance was drawn to the front of the car—to the gazes of both Montgomery men. Seeing that she had noticed their attention, Edward flashed her an encouraging smile and turned around. Ryan, though, didn't immediately move, and for a long moment Emma's gaze locked with his. Lord help her, she didn't want to stare at him . . . but she couldn't seem to make herself look elsewhere.

Even across the distance his eyes seemed black, so very black. Then, without any warning, he abruptly turned his head, leaving her feeling shaken and weary and winded all at once. Taking a deep breath, Emma tried to calm the agitated feelings inside her. Why had he been looking at her like that? Had he been thinking of their marriage? Assessing her appearance? Oh, dear, did he somehow find her unattractive . . . or offensive . . . or even repulsive?

Don't waste your time on such foolish considerations, Emma Louise. He may think you're as ugly as a three-headed goat, but it matters little, because physical attributes do not enter this equation at all. Your marriage is to be nothing more than a business arrangement.

Despite the sternness of her intellect, Emma couldn't control the fluttering of her heart as she contemplated what kind of woman might spark Ryan Montgomery's interest.

Did he even have romantic interests? she wondered, continuing to stare at the back of his glossy dark head.

The ex–army captain was a strong man. Emma recalled his work with the untamed horses, and also, oddly, she remembered how hard his chest had been against her forehead as she'd come around the corner with the gravy and collided with him the other night. She also remembered wondering afterward, as she changed her clothes, if his breast was made of flesh and blood. It had seemed as firm and impenetrable as . . . chiseled stone.

Was the heart that lay beneath also made of granite?

The quality of Ryan Montgomery's heart is no concern of yours, Emma Louise. Five months from now, all he—and his solid thorax—will be is a memory.

"Am-ma?" Joey tapped the paper in her hand, pulling her thoughts from the physical properties of his brother. Once again he pointed to the pink figure on the page.

"Oh, sorry, Joey." Emma cleared her throat and swallowed. "You were telling me about your special wish picture. Let's see, is this one you?"

"No, no, no, no. That Am-ma!"

"Me?" Surprise made her utterance end in a squeak. "What am I doing in your family picture?"

"W-w-wuh—" Appearing nervous, Joey stopped himself. Licking his lips several times, he looked pleadingly into her eyes. "W-wish Am-ma sister," he finally whispered, pulling his hand from the paper and dropping his gaze. " 'Peshal wish . . . b-best wish."

"Oh, my . . ." was all Emma could say, touched more deeply by Joey's heartfelt admission than anything she could ever remember. The train had come to a complete stop, and the doors had opened, but neither she nor Joey noticed the few disembarking passengers. "What a special wish, indeed," she managed to say through the thickness in her throat as she smoothed her hand over the picture. "I think it would be wonderful to be your sister, but . . ."

Slanted nut-brown eyes looked at her questioningly.

She sighed. "But you know I can't be." Slowly she let her hand fall away from the picture and reached for his hand. "Could we settle for being friends instead? I can't think of anyone I'd rather have as my best friend."

"Joey b-best . . . fwiend?" His slanted eyes grew round with astonishment and pleasure before he clapped his hands over them and bent forward.

"Indeed you are, Joseph Montgomery. I can't think of another person alive who has taught me more about friendship than you." Gently she stroked the back of his arm, fully realizing what richness he had added to her life.

"Best fwiend!" A smile a mile wide broke across Joey's face as he popped up and clapped his hands together in excitement, and it was at that moment that Emma realized, with a flood of regret, that later today, on paper, she *would* be Joey's sister . . . and that he would never know.

Chapter Ten

The early morning breeze outside the Cheyenne Union Pacific depot held a promise of the day's coming warmth, but Ryan Montgomery did not notice its mildness against his face as he stepped from the train. Though he'd snatched forty winks between the stops of Archer and Cheyenne, the only thing he'd gained from his slumber was a dull and groggy head.

He supposed he should be grateful that Edward had shut up long enough to allow him at least *some* sleep. During the first portion of the journey, all Edward had done was talk about the ranch, talk about the mine, and, mostly, talk about what a wonderful person Emma Taylor was.

"And if a man's got to be temporarily married to anyone, Ryan . . . well, let's just say that Miss Taylor's muzzle doesn't exactly belong in a hackamore," Edward had commented as the train slowed for the Hillsdale depot. "I mean, I like my women with a little more . . . er, you know, with a little *more,* like Ginny, but Emma is real pretty in her own right. Clever mind, too," he'd added, nodding. "I admire that in a woman."

"And I suppose all her money has nothing to do with what you most 'admire' about her." Ryan couldn't help but snap, trying, at the same time, to fight the sensual images his mind had painted of the lovely St. Paul woman. Lewd pictures . . . erotic pictures.

"Just look at her," Edward invited, craning his neck toward the rear of the car, "sitting back there with Joey. She's so patient with him . . . and he adores her, you know."

As the conductor announced Hillsdale, Ryan also turned his head. Miss Taylor was indeed seated next to Joey, he saw, and furthermore, their heads were bent so close together—over a paper?—that her nutmeg-brown ringlets had to be brushing the side of his brother's face.

Did her hair have the same delicious fragrance as it had the night she'd run into him with the gravy? he wondered. Granted, the smell of salt pork gravy—not to mention its hot sting against his abdomen—were what he most remembered about the incident, but he also recalled her warm, sweet, womanly perfume, and what it had done to his insides.

The St. Paul woman must have somehow sensed his and Edward's stares, for she slowly raised her head from what she and Joey were studying and looked directly at them. Just like the day Ryan had picked her up at the Pine Bluffs depot, her sweet, heart-shaped face wore an uncertain expression.

What lay behind those soft brown eyes? he wondered, not able to help the cynical part of himself from asking if perhaps Emma Taylor was nothing more than a spoiled, self-centered opportunist who was only out to take advantage of another misfortune.

And speaking of misfortune, how had the ranch gotten into such an awful financial predicament? Ryan broke contact with Miss Taylor's timorous gaze and turned his head back around, thinking about all that Edward had told him last night. Being the eldest son of proud, hardworking Maureen Montgomery, Ryan knew Edward had not exaggerated when he'd told him how devastated their mother would be if she were forced to take a loan to meet the payroll. Edward was also correct about Ryan distancing himself from his family and from the family business.

But was pulling one over on Ma and using Miss Taylor's money really the best solution to the problem?

There seemed to be little choice in the matter at this point, however. Ma had apparently fallen for whatever smooth line of malarkey Edward had given her about how he'd made a mistake in the books, and now the wheels were already well in motion.

Speaking of Edward, how had he gotten so far ahead? Ryan scanned the crowd of passengers that thronged the wooden platform, but he didn't see any of the members of their little traveling party.

"Over here, Ryan! We're over here." Edward's furiously waving arm was visible beneath the tall white letters that spelled CHEYENNE on the side of the wooden depot building.

Ryan nodded and slowly made his way through the crowd feeling sluggish, numb, insensate. Everything . . . anything . . . nothing was just too much to think about right now. If he could only get a little more sleep . . .

"Tell him to step a little livelier, Edward," he heard his mother call as he neared them. "I want t' tell him a proper goodbye before me an' Joey have t' leave. If I can hire a carriage straight away, we can be t' the house before the girls leave for school."

"Don't worry, Ma, Ryan's almost here," Edward said with a laugh. "You can't see him 'cause you're only ankle high to a grasshopper."

"If you're thinkin' you're too old for a lickin'—"

Ryan didn't hear the end of his mother's good-natured threat due to the conductor's loud announcement of the next several westward destinations. Stepping around a fat farmer in overalls and a pair of sprucely dressed young men, Ryan was upon his family.

You mean your family and the family cook, a part of his brain corrected as he took in the sight of the petite, curly haired woman who stood hand in hand with his youngest brother. *Emma Taylor isn't family.*

She's going to be your wife later today, Montgomery, another area of his mind informed him. *Family doesn't get much closer than that.*

"Ah, here's me boy," Maureen said, interrupting Ryan's thoughts. A wide smile lit her face, and she stood with her hands clasped before her. "Come here, Ryan Andrew, an' let your mother give you a big kiss. Oh, I cannot thank you enough for takin' over at the ranch an' allowin' me to finish out the term with the girls here in town."

"Think I'll see to getting you a carriage, Ma," Edward said as Ryan dutifully bent over and brushed a kiss on his mother's cheek. "I'll be back shortly."

Ryan was surprised at the strength in his mother's hands as she placed her palms on either side of his face and held his head near hers for a long moment. "It's been a long time since I've said the words, Ryan," she whispered, "but they're always in me heart. I love you, son. Past, present, an' future, me darlin'. I've got more love for you in this old Irish heart than you'll ever know."

"I love you, too, Ma," Ryan automatically whispered in return, feeling a spasm of contrition at neglecting his relationship with this woman.

"Well, how 'bout a smile, then?" Maureen asked, releasing him and gazing adoringly up into his face.

Smile, Montgomery, Ryan told himself as he straightened his back and stretched to his full height, wondering at the same time how long it had been since he'd really, truly smiled. Probably long enough so that he'd forgotten how, he thought, attempting to affix a pleasant expression to features that felt as dry and lifeless as wood.

"Aye, 'tis such a handsome lad you are," Maureen said softly, with a faraway look in her hazel eyes. "Tall an' dark an' proud jus' like your father." She cleared her throat. "Edward says you've got business at the fort today," she said in a more normal tone. "Do you . . . do you think you'll be all day over there?"

"I do believe Edward has got the day planned for all of us," Ginny interrupted, moving a few steps closer to them. "He mentioned that he has some things he needs to do this morning while Emma and I are shopping and Ryan is at Fort Russell. I know he wanted to be on the train back to Pine Bluffs no later than early afternoon, too. . . ."

Emma watched her friend smoothly steer Maureen away from inviting them all over to the Montgomery town house. Ginny and Edward were certainly cut from the same cloth,

Emma thought, amazed at the ease with which the lies rolled off of Ginny's tongue.

"Will you be seein' some of your old friends, then, Ryan?" Maureen asked, looking at her eldest son with loving eyes.

Emma was disappointed to see Ryan's smile fade as he nodded, for his face had softened and looked . . . well, nice for a moment. Very nice.

Very *handsome* actually.

Emma swallowed and directed her glance toward the train, her heart thumping rapidly in her chest. *What's the matter with you, Emma Louise? So Ryan Montgomery looks as handsome as sin when he smiles . . . so what?*

Edward came back around the corner then, announcing that the livery stable hands were already hitching a team of horses to the carriage he'd hired. A flurry of goodbyes ensued while Maureen picked up her valise and Ryan and Edward each hoisted a trunk.

Ginny watched the four Montgomerys disappear around the corner of the board-and-batten depot. "Well, now that Maureen and Joey are safely out of our way," she said brightly, "things can only get easier from here on out." As the crowd at the depot had thinned considerably, Emma clearly heard her future sister-in-law's long sigh. "Oh, Emma, do you think Maureen suspects anything?" the good-natured young woman asked, her glib manner slipping away almost visibly.

"No, I don't think she does," Emma replied slowly, thinking of the joy with which the Montgomery matriarch had embraced her eldest son. She shifted her grip on the leather satchel that contained a bare minimum of toiletries, a few essential articles of underclothing, and a clean shirtwaist.

Her *wedding* shirtwaist, she thought wryly, not understanding why it had been so important to her this morning— if her union with Ryan Montgomery was to be nothing more than a business arrangement—to take along a clean shirtwaist in which to be married.

"I only hope Maureen never finds out about this," Ginny said heavily, allowing one of her shoulders to lean against the depot. "Because I don't know if she'd ever forgive us if she did."

"She's not going to find out." Emma laid a reassuring hand on Ginny's arm, recognizing that her normally cheerful friend was in need of some bolstering. "And besides that," she added with a nonchalance she did not feel, "Maureen will be so busy in Cheyenne with her four girls that she won't have any idea that we'll have temporarily slipped her an extra daughter."

At four o'clock that afternoon Emma stood in her skirt and corset in her third-floor room of Denver's New Markham Hotel. The journey from Cheyenne to Denver had been tense and long and boring all at the same time, Emma reflected as she squeezed excess water from her washcloth, thinking of how quickly even the breathtaking view of the snow-capped Rockies had grown monotonous. At least she and Ginny had managed to doze for a few hours on the train.

"We'd better hurry, Emma. Edward said he'd be back for us by four-thirty, and it's getting pretty close to that now." Ginny's optimistic spirit had been restored with a little sleep, but her voice sounded strange. Muffled.

"I'm almost done." Emma turned from the basin and saw that her friend had nearly bent herself in half to brush her hair. *How could someone so plump bend over like that?* she wondered, watching Ginny make a few more sweeps through her hair from top to bottom, roots to ends.

"That's good," Ginny replied in the same muffled tone, for, in that position, she was speaking directly into her skirt. "You know, though, Emma, I don't understand why Edward seems to know so many people here in Denver. He said he knew of someone he was sure would perform the wedding ceremony this afternoon, and then he mentioned an acquaintance he just happened to have in banking." Without straightening, Ginny tossed the brush onto the bed, deftly plaited the lustrous sandy-brown mass, and twisted the braid into a neat coiffure.

Her creamy complexion was flushed bright pink when she raised her head and looked at Emma. "Now where did

I put those pins? Oh, here they are," she said, stepping over to the dresser. "You think you know all about a person when you marry him—you know, things like what books he reads, what he likes to do, who he knows, things like that—but . . . well, I guess you just can't know everything, can you?"

Emma shook her head, thinking of how little she knew about the man who, in less than an hour's time, would be her husband. The thought of being married to Ryan Montgomery sent a shiver of apprehension coursing through her, but along with that came a shiver of something else. Something dangerous. Something exciting.

"Gosh, I really like the smell of your perfume, Emma," Ginny complimented, securing one last hairpin in place. "What kind is it?"

"I'm not sure what's in it, but it is nice, isn't it? Sweet, but not too sweet. Michael and Lucille gave it to me for my birthday last year." Emma restopped the small flacon and held it out to Ginny. Her fingers trembled. "Would you like some?"

"Oh . . . may I?" Ginny dabbed perfume at her wrists and throat, then briefly closed her eyes with pleasure as she inhaled the fragrance on her right wrist. "Mmm. You know, Emma," she commented matter-of-factly, opening her eyes, "your perfume and your underthings give you away."

"Pardon me?"

"Your perfume and your underthings give away your true background. I bet this perfume cost your brother a fortune. And your chemise—it's China silk, isn't it?"

"Well—"

"Well, nothing. You probably have closets and racks and drawers full of beautiful clothing back home, don't you?" Not allowing any time for Emma to reply, Ginny sighed and continued on. "It must be hard for you to wear plain clothing after being accustomed to such fine things." A mischievous dimple appeared on one of her round cheeks. "You know, Emma, our cowboys would be baying at the moon if they knew all this silk and lace lay beneath those plain work dresses you wear."

"Ginny! I don't think—"

"Oh, I'm just teasing." With a regretful smile, Ginny set the flacon of perfume on the dresser. "What's it like to be rich, Emma? I mean, it's not that we're exactly poor or anything. . . ." Her expression faded to a half grin, half grimace. "Well, come to think of it, we Montgomerys are rather on the poor side right now, aren't we?"

Emma paused while buttoning her clean shirtwaist. "I guess I don't think about it much," she began musingly, "and I certainly don't walk around classifying people as 'poor' or 'rich.' " She let out her breath in a deep sigh. "Michael takes that to mean that I have no idea of the value of money. That's what he seemed most upset about when we had that terrible fight about me wanting to open my collectibles shop. He told me I'd be throwing Father's money away. . . ." She felt her mouth curve into a frown as an arrow of anger shot through her. "No, what he said was worse than that. He said I'd be *foolish* to throw—"

Edward's knock at the door interrupted Emma. "Ginny? Emma? Are you ready to go?"

"We'll be right there, Edward." Ginny's plump bosom heaved as she took in a deep breath and slowly let it out. Honest gray-green eyes searched Emma's face. "Are you still sure about wanting to marry Ryan?" she asked softly. "Because if you're not . . ."

"I'm sure." The flush of Emma's ire made her words sharp.

"Well, I'll go out and wait with the men, then, and let you finish dressing. See you in a few minutes." With a subdued expression, Ginny let herself out of the room.

Emma finished buttoning her shirtwaist with a sense of finality. The details of her plan that she had glibly glossed over—the unpleasant, frightening details, such as actually standing before a man of God with Ryan Montgomery . . . and notifying Michael of her marriage and arranging for a large sum of money to be transferred west—now needed to be faced, and she was prepared to face them.

In fact, compared to what Michael's reaction was likely to be, the aura of danger surrounding Ryan Montgomery suddenly seemed as gentle as the twilight of a summer night. Running a smoothing hand over her shirtwaist and making a quick check of her appearance in the glass, she reached for her jacket.

In fact, she thought, recalling more and more of the things Michael and Jon had said to her, *she was going to walk right out of this room and marry Ryan Montgomery without so much as a qualm.*

"Come in, all of you, come in," the slender, just-beginning-to-gray minister greeted the four of them, throwing open the front door of the unassuming parsonage. "Would your driver like to come in as well?" he asked loudly, peering past them to the street.

"No, thanks," hollered the adolescent in the driver's seat of the rented carriage. "I'll just wait here, if you don't mind." For good measure he shook his head in an unmistakable fashion and slouched back in the seat.

"As you wish, young man," the minister conceded, pulling his gaze from the street. "Edward Montgomery," he went on, a broad smile breaking over his bearded face, "after all these years, I can't believe how you just turned up this afternoon. And I can't get over how you've *grown* up! You must be another three or four inches taller than you were the last time I saw you."

The minister's gaze shifted to Ginny. "And this must be your lovely wife." As he extended his hand, the crinkles around his eyes became more pronounced. "It's quite a pleasure to meet you, Mrs. Montgomery. I trust you've been successful in reforming this young rapscallion into a virtuous and upright citizen of Wyoming Territory. He used to be quite a prankster, he did, with his big brown eyes and his ability to tell one outrageous fib after another."

Ginny had already accepted the minister's proffered hand and was murmuring her pleasure at meeting him, too, when her mouth suddenly opened into an "O," and she swung her head to look at her husband. "Edward!" she said in a shocked whisper. "Surely this isn't the minister your family told me about. You actually put mice into this man's—"

Edward cleared his throat and flashed an uncomfortable grin. "It appears you've come quite a way since those circuit-riding days, Mr. Kessler," he declared, cutting off his wife and at the same time changing the subject. "From the size of your church, I would guess your congregation is quite large."

"It is large," Mr. Kessler agreed, "but in my opinion—as well as that of the Good Shepherd's"—he gazed upward—"even a large congregation is never large enough. There is always room for more of His flock within our walls." At that, his expression grew serious. "And speaking of His flock, I meant to tell you how sorry I was to read in the newspaper of your father's passing. I was so surprised to see you when you were here just a little while ago that it slipped my mind. Andrew must be gone . . . what, a year now?"

"Going on two," Edward replied.

"And your mother?"

"She's well. Being widowed is difficult for her, I think, but she keeps herself busy by running the ranch."

"Andrew Montgomery is missed by many, I'm sure," Mr. Kessler said, nodding. "He was quite a man."

After a respectful pause, during which Emma sneaked a glance at the stone-faced man standing next to her, Mr. Kessler ushered them into the front hallway of the house and closed the door. With a long stride he walked to the end of the hall and called to his wife. "Mary, they're here."

"I'll be right there," a female voice trilled from farther off in the house.

"She's preparing some refreshments for after the ceremony," the reverend explained with a wink and an indulgent smile. "Let's go into the parlor and be seated," he invited, indicating with a broad gesture of his arm that they follow him. "I'd like a chance to become acquainted with this quiet young couple I'm going to be marrying this afternoon."

Ginny turned and flashed Emma an encouraging smile as they moved into the parlor. The room was small but very clean, Emma noticed, its furnishings wholly unpretentious. The faint smell of linseed oil hung in the air, and not a speck of dust was to be seen anywhere. Snowy eyelet curtains graced the windows, and a plain wooden cross on the wall above the sofa was the only thing that adorned the room's whitewashed walls.

Mr. Kessler indicated that she and Ryan should sit together on the horsehair sofa, while he and Ginny and Edward took their seats in individual chairs. To Emma's surprise, Ryan politely waited for her to be seated before taking his own seat—leaving a distance of several inches between them. His dark glance flicked over her as he joined her on the sofa making her wonder once more what thoughts were running through his head.

Her own mood had changed at least twenty-five times today; at the present moment, she was back to being scared witless. The silent ride from the hotel to Mr. Kessler's parsonage had tied her nerves into knots.

Apprehensively she turned her head and glanced at the cross on the wall behind her, then at the imposing profile of the man seated next to her. His glance was now directed at some unknown point before him, and his features were fixed with a blank expression. The bold lines of his jaw and cheekbone appeared to be set in stone as well.

"It's good to have you here, Miss Taylor," Mr. Kessler said kindly from his seat, breaking her surreptitious examination of her soon-to-be husband. "Edward told me you came all the way from St. Paul to work for them."

"Yes . . . I did," Emma replied, wondering just how much Edward had told Mr. Kessler about this situation. Surely he hadn't told the minister that this marriage was taking place solely for the purpose of allowing money to exchange hands. A man of God, in good conscience, could not condone such a union.

"And Ryan," Mr. Kessler continued warmly. "What a pleasure it is to finally meet the man for whose continued health and safety I once said so many prayers. Though you were away from your family and never able to be present at our humble country worship, your father made certain that you were never forgotten."

From the corner of her eye, Emma saw Ryan's head incline slightly.

"It was good of you to see us on such short notice," Edward said. "We appreciate your willingness to . . .

ah, help us out, so to speak."

"Well, in situations . . ." Mr. Kessler nodded and softly cleared his throat, "of this nature, it is generally best to set things to rights as quickly as possible."

Situations . . . of this nature? Situations of *what* nature? Emma wanted to scream, her mouth growing dry at the minister's implication. *Oh, Lord, Edward, you didn't . . . please tell me you didn't tell him—*

"Edward told me of the reason for your haste," Reverend Kessler said directly to Emma, his eyes searching her face with patience and gentleness, "so, sister, I will speak plainly. I know of the new life that will soon stir within your womb—"

Emma's and Ryan's heads swung toward each other, their eyes locking in horror.

" . . . but before I ask God to join you to the man beside you," the minister continued, politely waiting until he once again had her dumbfounded attention, "I also need to hear, from your own lips, of the love for Ryan Montgomery that stirs within your heart."

"I-I, ah . . ." Having looked from Ryan to Mr. Kessler to the folds of her skirt, Emma could only stammer in mortification. She was aware, too, of the sudden tension in Ryan's body as, beneath the fabric of his black woolen trousers, a ridge of hard thigh muscle appeared.

For a full five seconds no one spoke, then Ginny's voice broke the silence in an astounded tone. "Edward! You told the minister—"

"I had to tell him of the babe," Edward quickly spoke. "It was the only way Ryan and Emma could be married on such short notice." His voice was earnest and regretful . . . and completely believable. Emma felt a sense of doom growing within her as she raised her head and looked into Edward's apologetic brown eyes.

"But, Edward, you didn't have to—" Ginny began again.

"No, no, Mrs. Montgomery, I'm afraid I must stop you," Mr. Kessler interrupted. "I realize this must be quite embarrassing for you, as well as for the young couple," he added sensitively, gesturing toward Emma and Ryan. His voice was passionate when he spoke again, however, and Emma imagined that the minister's talent at the pulpit must be formidable. "But, dear woman, I cannot allow you to indict your husband for being perfectly candid with me. The Edward Montgomery who came to my door today is a far cry from the prevaricating youth I once knew. Indeed, your husband's righteousness speaks greatly of his maturity and integrity."

"Good afternoon, everyone," a cheery voice chirped. "I'm so sorry not to have met you at the door, but I was just finishing up some things in the kitchen." A bird-thin woman exuding restless energy greeted them from the doorway. Her hair was coffee-colored and was pulled back in a severe style, but the kindness that shone from her face made her appear anything but harsh. "I'm Mary Kessler," she said, smiling graciously and nodding at each of them in turn. "And you must be the Montgomerys. Well, all, but one of you is a Montgomery—" She looked back and forth between Ginny and Emma in an expectant manner. "But that's a situation that's to be quickly remedied, I understand."

"Miss Taylor is seated on the couch next to her fiancé, Ryan Montgomery," Mr. Kessler clarified, making the remainder of the introductions as his wife stepped into the room and to his side. Garbed in a conservatively styled dress of dove gray, Mrs. Kessler moved with quick little steps that made Emma think of the movements of a chickadee.

"Well, why don't we get on with things?" Mrs. Kessler suggested after an awkward few minutes filled with long pauses and stilted conversation, during which even Edward's silver tongue faltered noticeably. Once again the minister's wife smiled graciously at everyone before walking briskly to the small table in the corner of the room to retrieve a heavy-looking black Bible. "Here you are," she said brightly as she placed the book in her husband's hands. "The sooner you marry this handsome couple, the sooner we can get to our refreshments. I baked a little cake in honor of your wedding," she explained to Ryan and Emma, "but I must apologize in advance for its plainness."

"You're far too kind, Mrs. Kessler," Emma managed to reply, wondering how on earth she would be able to get anything down her parched throat. "And I'm certain your cake is going to be delicious."

Mother was right, Emma Louise, her inner voice upbraided as she attempted to execute an appreciative smile in Mrs. Kessler's direction. *Little lies turn into big lies, and it only gets worse from there. Look at what good and decent people you're involving in your chicanery.*

The fact that good-hearted Mrs. Kessler had been so thoughtful as to bake them a wedding cake—for what was truly a mockery of a wedding—made Emma feel almost worse than being thought of as . . . well . . . expecting. Too, at any moment, she expected Ryan to snap, to call off the wedding and storm from the Kesslers' home. The muscles in his legs hadn't lost any of their tension since Mr. Kessler had spoken of the babe that would soon stir in her womb.

As the minister asked them all to please stand, Emma was sure it was going to be the moment Ryan walked out. She held her breath as he stretched himself to his full height, a height several inches above her own, but curiously he didn't say a word.

Dare she take Ryan's continuing silence as a sign that he still intended to go through with the wedding, then? Emma sneaked a peek at his impassive profile, nearly jumping out of her skin when Mr. Kessler asked the two of them to join hands.

"Come, now, Mr. Montgomery, surely by this time you know where you might find Miss Taylor's hand." A bubble of laughter was audible in Mrs. Kessler's high, birdlike voice. "It's natural to have a case of the nerves right now, but trust me, it'll all be over in a few minutes, and you'll feel ever so much better."

Something like an electric shock went through Emma when Ryan's large warm hand first bumped against hers, then loosely took her fingers in his own. Her whole arm tingled at the contact of his right hand against her left, and she felt the skin on the entire left side of her body raise into gooseflesh.

"And there you are," Mrs. Kessler announced, fairly beaming. "They're all ready for you."

"Not so fast, Mother," the minister spoke, a slight frown creasing his forehead. "I have not yet heard either one of these young people declare their feelings for the other, nor have I checked to make certain they have their license."

"I've got the license right here." Edward stepped forward with a piece of paper. "We saw the clerk whose name you suggested to me, and we didn't have a bit of trouble."

Despite the warmth of the day and the heat of the fingers around her own, Emma felt her hands grow colder and clammier by the second. Ryan probably thought he was about to marry some kind of reptile, she thought disjointedly, belatedly realizing that she hadn't taken into consideration the possibility that the ex–army captain already thought less of her than he did of a serpent.

"Well, Miss Taylor, Mr. Montgomery," Mr. Kessler addressed them solemnly, "is each of you certain that the love you share is strong enough to endure for a lifetime of joys and sorrows?"

"Yes," Emma whispered as she dropped her gaze to the floor in shame, feeling as though she was now drawn too deeply into the web of her lies to make any other answer than one of affirmation.

Her course was unalterably set.

"Oh, Carl, for pity's sake, just marry the poor dears," Mrs. Kessler said sympathetically, clasping her hands together over her breast. "They're standing here before you. Doesn't that say something about their feelings for one another?" She made a *tsking* sound in the back of her throat and directed a meaningful glance toward her husband. "I do seem to recall a certain gentleman, some years back, who was so nervous when *he* stood before the preacher, that he forgot to—"

"Very well, Mother, enough said," Mr. Kessler interrupted his wife, a half smile curving his lips. "We will proceed."

A scant ten minutes later, Emma and Ryan were married. The ceremony had been conducted in a brief but traditional manner, Emma numbly supposed, with she and Ryan each making the responses that were required of them. Thanks to ever-thinking Edward, who had stepped forward at the proper moment with a gold wedding band that looked suspiciously like Ginny's, Emma now wore a loose symbol of Ryan's love and fidelity around the third finger of her left hand.

Loose as it was, though, the circlet of metal felt strange, confining. And now, listening to the fervency in Mr. Kessler's voice as he concluded the ceremony with an Apache wedding benediction, an overwhelming sense of wrongdoing broke through her numbness, filling her mind and body and soul with the utmost sense of contrition.

"Now you will feel no rain," the minister spoke as he closed both his eyes and his Bible, raising one hand high into the air, "for each of you will be shelter for the other. Now you will feel no cold, for each of you will be warmth to the other."

After placing the ring on her finger, Ryan's warm fingers had unconsciously remained around her own. Even so, the iciness of Emma's fingers had not diminished one bit. Though there was nothing in her mouth to swallow, her Adam's apple reflexively worked up and down as she looked at the devout expression on Mr. Kessler's face.

Beyond the minister, late afternoon sunshine radiantly lit the parlor's west windows. Some of its brilliance freely spilled forth into the room, between the upper and lower valances of the simple white curtains, but much of the brightness was captured and highlighted by the starched eyelet fabric, making Emma think of a painting she had once seen—a painting in which the dazzling white robes of Christ had been lit in the very same manner.

Emma glanced quickly at Ginny, and saw mirrored on her sister-in-law's face the same expression of disgrace that she was certain was on her own. *Please forgive me, God,* she implored as Mr. Kessler continued.

"Now there is no more loneliness. Now you are two persons, but there is only one life before you." The minister's slender long fingers clenched into a fist, and dramatically he pulled his arm toward his chest and opened his eyes. Beside her husband, Mrs. Kessler gave a little hiccuping sigh and dabbed at her eyes with a handkerchief. "Go now to your dwelling to enter into the days of your life together," the minister concluded sonorously, looking back and forth between Emma and Ryan. "May your days be good and long upon the earth, and may the peace of God go with you always."

"Ohh," Mrs. Kessler said with a sigh and a final dab at her eyes, "that was so beautiful. Congratulations, my dears."

Abruptly Ryan released his grasp of Emma's fingers. At the same time the heel of her hand heavily thunked against her thigh, she was certain she heard a soft, seething exhalation from the man beside her, and she had the sudden feeling that, like an overstoked steam engine, he was about to blow. Perhaps it would be best to forgo the cake and make a hasty retreat, she thought with a swift bolt of panic.

"Indeed, the union of a man and woman in love is always a beautiful thing," Mr. Kessler agreed with his wife. As Emma self-consciously clasped her hands before her, she heard both Ginny and Edward murmur their assent. Edward stepped forward then and extended the marriage document toward the minister.

"Carl!" Mrs. Kessler exclaimed. "You can't sign that yet—you forgot to ask the groom to kiss the bride!"

"So I did," the kind-faced minister replied, first accepting the paper that Edward had offered him, then bestowing an appreciative smile upon his wife. "Thank you for reminding me of my oversight, Mother. Whatever would I do without you?" His brows went up as he turned toward Ryan and Emma and dangled the paper in his hand. "Well, you heard the missus . . ."

"That's right, Ryan," Edward chimed in, "you've got to kiss the bride." Emma wasn't sure, but she thought she heard a suppressed chuckle in his voice.

So not only did she have to marry Ryan Montgomery . . . she had to *kiss* him, too?

Apparently Ryan was leaving the initiation of the kiss to her. The silence in the little room stretched out uncomfortably until finally Emma knew she had no alternative but to offer her lips to the man. As stiffly as if her head and neck were made of lead, she turned to face her new husband, lifting her gaze upward from his broad chest at the very last moment.

She was nearly knocked off her feet by the churning power of his gaze. *I'm sorry,* she tried to communicate to him with her expression, but all she saw within the depths of his dark eyes was a simmering mixture of anger, frustration, and . . . what else? Was there something else there? For how long their gazes remain thus locked, Emma was not certain; it could have been a second or it could have been an hour.

Then, ever so slowly, his head bent toward hers.

Chapter Eleven

The touch of Ryan's sculptured lips against her own felt hot and cold all at once, and Emma neared hysteria as his dark gaze continued to entrap her own. Stars above, was it some kind of instinct that made his index finger come up beneath her chin and take control of the angle of her face?

There was a spark burning inside Ryan Montgomery's soul, something vital, something alive, and something much more complex than the passel of disagreeable emotions that had been revealed to her at first glance. She saw it; she felt it, and as his lips pressed briefly against hers, Emma was also aware that the spark was nearly smothered by the presence of something else—something tortured, something tormented. . . .

Agony.

Where the word came from Emma did not know; she only knew, at such intimate proximity to the man, that it was so. *Jon Severson has never given you a kiss with this much feeling,* she thought absurdly, feeling her hands and knees tremble, her pulse pound in her ears. A crimson blush spread upward, from her chest to her forehead, as Ryan's lips left hers and she became aware of the great interest with which the other persons in the room looked upon her.

"Well, now, that was lovely," Mrs. Kessler beamed, effusively taking Emma's hands into her own. "I wonder if I might ask, while my husband signs the marriage certificate, if you and your new husband might indulge me in my newest hobby? Oh, my, yes!" she exclaimed longingly, releasing Emma's hands and bobbing over toward the windows. "The light is absolutely perfect in here right now."

"What she wants to ask you," Mr. Kessler clarified, smiling indulgently at his wife over his shoulder, "is if she can take your photograph. Since I got her a little magazine camera for her last birthday, she seems single-mindedly determined to photograph the entire world, person by person."

"Oh, Carl, really," Mrs. Kessler demurred, "I'm not that bad."

"Whatever you say, dear," the minister responded with a chuckle, turning back to Ryan and Emma. "Seriously, if you wouldn't mind," he said to them, lifting his eyebrows, "it would give my wife great pleasure to capture your happiness on film."

Capture their *happiness* on film?

"Well," Emma began hesitantly, feeling, in truth, quite shaken by the kiss she and Ryan had just shared. There had been many emotions in that kiss, but she doubted that happiness was one of them.

"Oh, come on, you two," Edward urged, "it's only a photograph. Ginny and I had several taken on our wedding day."

Later, as they repasted on cake and iced lemonade in the parlor, Emma was certain it had been nothing short of a miracle that had allowed the ebullient Mrs. Kessler to tamely lead Ryan to a simple straight-backed chair in front of the windows.

The minister's wife had flitted off then, quickly returning with a compact, efficient-looking black camera mounted on a tripod. After directing Emma to stand next to Ryan, she set up her camera and fussed and frowned and made several slight adjustments to their positions before she was finally satisfied that everything was just so.

During this time, Emma was uncomfortably aware of the waves of silent anger that emanated from the big man seated next to her. In fact, she could actually *feel* the heat that emanated from him. *Why is he going along with all this?* she couldn't help but wonder, the hair on her arms prickling reflexively as the feeling came back to her that Ryan Montgomery was a man whose emotions were in danger of exploding. The impression did not diminish as the photos were taken, not even after Mrs. Kessler had put her camera away and served generous slices of the wedding cake she had baked.

Ryan remained seated in the chair near the window while the rest of them drifted back to the other side of the parlor. A curt "no thanks" to Mrs. Kessler's offer of refreshment was the only thing he contributed to the polite conversation that ensued, and all Emma could think of was that they had to get him out of the Kesslers' home, the sooner the better.

Perhaps Edward was also aware that he had pushed his luck as far as it could possibly be pushed—that the storm brewing inside his brother was nigh onto bursting—for he made short work of his cake and quickly drained his lemonade. "I wish we had more time to visit," he said, making a show of checking the timepiece in his vest pocket, "but we've really got to be going."

"My goodness, it is getting late, isn't it?" Ginny seconded, leaning over her husband's arm and looking at his watch.

"Oh, and it's been such a pleasure having you here," Mrs. Kessler said disappointedly.

"We've got another long day of travel ahead of us tomorrow," Edward explained apologetically, "and Emma seems to tire much more easily of late."

"Of course," Mrs. Kessler said, bustling about collecting their plates and glasses on the tray on which she'd served the cake. "We understand."

It wasn't until the farewells had been made and the four young Montgomerys were in the carriage on their way back to the grand hotel on the corner of Seventeenth and Lawrence streets, that the first driving pellets of the tempest inside Ryan were loosed.

"Honestly, Ryan," Edward said, breaking the uncomfortable, ominous silence inside the carriage, "the least you could have done was eat a piece of Mrs. Kessler's cake. The good woman obviously went to a great deal of trouble for us."

"Oh, I see," Ryan said sarcastically. "And is there anything else you might have me do today, Edward? . . . Perhaps *getting married* wasn't quite enough." The heavy dark sheath that had cloaked Ryan's spirit since Jim Hopper's suicide— no, really, it had begun years before that, he realized with a flash of comprehension—was rapidly lifting. And it wasn't just anger that he was feeling at this moment—for meanness and blind anger were things he *had* been able to feel. First and foremost he felt a sense of . . . betrayal.

How could they have? he asked himself as the feeling built inside him. *How could they have—Edward, especially—taken advantage of his vulnerable emotional state to manipulate him into this . . . this . . .* He couldn't even think of a term vile enough to describe what he thought of this whole affair. The things Edward had said to him last night in the barn filtered back through his mind, one by one, increasing his outrage.

His gaze swung to the gold band on Emma Taylor's finger.

Her name isn't Emma Taylor anymore, Montgomery, a voice inside him mocked. *You've been such a mindless boob that you actually allowed yourself to be hornswoggled into marrying this woman. For money.*

"Don't you think you should give Virginia back her ring?" he asked aloud, fixing a corrosive stare at the extremely attractive brunette woman who sat across from him. "Or were you planning on wearing it all night?"

"Oh!" Color flooded Emma's delicate features as she hurried to remove the ring from her finger. "Goodness, I'm sorry for keeping this so long," she apologized to Ginny. "I . . . I forgot I had it on," she finished lamely.

"Now, Ryan," Edward began in a placating manner, "there's no reason for you to speak to Emma in that tone of voice. She's not—"

"I'll speak to Emma in any manner I choose," Ryan interrupted in a clear but dangerous tone. "She's *my wife* now, Edward, or have you already forgotten, in your eagerness to get your hands on her money, about the wedding ceremony that just took place?"

"Now, Ryan, this arrangement is strictly business," Edward shot back, dull red color rising in his cheeks. "And it's not as if Emma's money is for any personal gain—it's for the ranch . . . and for Ma," he finished emotionally.

"Touchingly done, brother, but your pretty prose isn't going to cut shit with me anymore." A feeling of vitality coursed through Ryan, or more, perhaps, a feeling of coming together after having been fragmented into so many pieces for so long a time. Gone, at last, were the everpresent and bone-weary feelings of fatigue, the numb sluggishness; instead, his blood fairly sang within the vessels and muscles and compartments of his body.

As did the righteous outrage.

"You're a liar, Edward," Ryan continued, the volume of his voice rising with every word he spoke. Briefly he looked at the opposite seat, at Ginny and Emma, before turning back to his brother. "You're all liars! Just how long did you expect me to be your trick monkey? Go here," he mimicked, "sign this paper, marry this woman . . . and yet you have the gall to sit there and tell me you did this *all for Ma?*"

"But . . . I did—"

"But nothing! No matter how you try to twist and turn things, you'll never convince me that you managed to execute this elaborate scheme for the benefit of anyone other than Edward Montgomery. You forget that I covered your lies—and your ass—plenty when we were kids. I *know* how your mind operates, Edward, and I know you're looking to slide out of your problems the easiest way possible." While Ryan paused for breath and a modicum of composure, the lingering echoes of his angry voice resounded within the small confines of the carriage. "And while we're talking about lies and asses and operating," he said in an equally angry but slightly more restrained fashion, having come to a quick decision, "I'm going to cover your ass one more time, brother."

"What do you mean?"

"I'm going to turn one of your many lies into truth. As of this minute, I'm in on ranch operations, and starting now a few things are going to be done *my* way."

"Y-you're . . . what?" Edward sounded angry and incredulous all at once.

"You heard me. As of this very minute, I will be assisting you in the management of the ranch. Or, rather, once I finish a full audit of the books, perhaps I will permit you to assist *me*." Ryan shrugged in what he knew was a hard-hearted manner. "And then again, perhaps not. You've taken one hell of a company, Edward, and run it into the ground by making poor decisions."

"And where have you been while I've had to make these poor decisions all by myself?" Edward shouted defensively. "What gives you the right—"

"The mine will be the first thing to go," Ryan averred, allowing his glance to flick over to Emma. "And I think I've done enough to earn the right." Ignoring Edward's loud protests, he continued to fix the lovely but treacherous St. Paul woman in his sights. "You just may well be the second thing to go, sweetheart," he warranted, "so don't get too comfortable with your new marital status." His eyes narrowed, and his feelings of indignity increased as he thought of Emma's tender relationship with Joey, her cordial relationship with his mother. "Perhaps you can explain something to me, *Mrs. Montgomery*," he went on caustically. "Are all little rich girls as selfish as you are? Do you all think that you can use others to get what you want, without a thought to what consequences you may wreak in another's life . . . or is it simply that you are a particularly shallow and spoiled little rich girl?"

Not able to prevent herself from taking Ryan's anger personally, Emma lashed out with a verbal offensive of her own. "Well, at least selfish is better than self-absorbed! I swear, you're nothing but a brooding, sulking waste of a man who can't see beyond the end of his own nose." Grabbing a quick breath, Emma continued her harangue in a different vein. "You know, I heard some claptrap about you being distinguished for your bravery in the army, Mr. Montgomery, that you were supposed to have been some kind of *hero*." Deliberately she allowed sarcasm to drip from the word, her show of asperity causing the remainder of her pent-up anger and frustration for this man to follow its lead and come tumbling forth. "Some kind of hero, indeed. Do you want to know what I really think of you?"

"Oh, dear. I think you've told him quite enough already," Ginny interceded, coughing nervously and laying her hand across Emma's arm. "How about if we ask the driver to stop the carriage, Emma, and we'll just walk the last few blocks to the hotel?"

"Absolutely not!" Emma shook off Ginny's arm. At the same time she lifted her hand and pointed her index finger accusingly at the dark man who was seated across from her in the suddenly sweltering carriage, feeling and hearing a nearly audible *click* as their gazes locked. "I'll tell you just what I think of heroes, Ryan Montgomery," she repeated recklessly. "If you ever *were* one, you are now definitely a has-been."

Though the anger Emma had felt for Michael had heretofore been the most intense emotion she had ever experienced, the depth and strength of her feelings for Ryan Montgomery far surpassed that. Ginny's presence was forgotten, as was Edward's, as Emma continued her verbal onslaught against the man who aroused such vibrant passion inside her.

"True heroes don't stop being men of great courage and daring once they walk off the battlefield, Captain," she articulated, feeling every nerve inside her body hum with the force of her feelings. "True heroes are regarded for their outstanding qualities in all areas of their lives, and exist as ideals and models for the rest of mankind. *True heroes*, Captain Montgomery, don't run and hide from adversity, nor do they wall themselves off from their grieving mothers and lonely little brothers."

The carriage slowed, then came to a stop, as Emma finished speaking. "New Markham Hotel," the young driver called, breaking the taut silence in the vehicle's interior. For a long moment no one moved, then Emma deliberately broke contact with Ryan's glittering black gaze and laid her fingers on the shiny handle of the door. She was physically weak from the energy her words and feelings had cost her, as well as from the enormous amount of strength it had taken to keep her gaze locked with that of the large man.

"And you know something really ironic?" she asked as she unlatched the door, turning her head for one last brief glance at the object of her outburst.

"To Joey, you're still a hero."

With that, Emma exited the carriage with the assistance of the startled driver, wanting only to seek her bed and curl up in a ball, and pretend that everything that had happened today was really a bad dream.

"You gonna sit there drinkin' them bitters all night, honey, or you gonna come dance a little dance with Fancy?"

Ryan blearily looked up from his glass to inspect the pretty but heavily painted young woman who stood before him, arms akimbo. Glossy brown curls spilled over her bare shoulders and settled beguilingly on the plump swells of her creamy breasts—breasts that appeared to have their upper limits defined by the prominences of the young woman's collarbones. *How did these hurdy-gurdy girls get them to stand so proudly?* Ryan wondered abstractly as his gaze traveled downward, taking in the shameless cut of the woman's sapphire-colored silk dress and her tiny waist. Were there special pads built into their dresses?

"It's all me, honey-bun, in case you're wonderin'," the girl said with a laugh as the band struck up another lively tune. "They don't call me Fancy for nothin', you know." In an agile yet practiced move, she lifted her skirt and threw a well-formed leg over the back of the empty chair across from Ryan. Framing her face in her hands, she leaned forward and spoke as intimately as was possible over the din of the music and the whoops and hollers of the merrymakers. "My, but you're a big strong one, honey. An' good-lookin' as all git-out, too." She batted her lashes and leaned forward even farther. "You know, I don't think I ever seen you in here before. You from around here?"

Ryan lifted his glass and took another swallow of the acrid, biting liquor. How many hours had it been since he'd had the carriage driver take him somewhere—anywhere— away from the New Markham Hotel?

And away from the pampered little rich girl with soft lips and melting brown eyes and vitriolic words of heroes.

"No, I'm not from around here," Ryan drunkenly replied to the young lady as she continued to smile at him in a suggestive but friendly manner, and as he stared at the soft mass of chestnut ringlets that were close enough to reach out and touch, all of the terrible, *truthful* things Emma had said to him in the carriage wormed their way, once more, through his besotted brain. He took another swallow of the bitters. "No, I'm a goddamn hero from up north," he said out loud. "And don't you dare call me a has-been," he admonished the young woman, pulling his gaze from her brown curls to the imperious finger that he hadn't realized he'd been pointing toward her.

"A has-been?" Fancy purred, her eyebrows raising. In a smooth motion, she slid her voluptuous body all the way into the chair. "My, oh, my, honey," she said with a *tsk*, "if there's anything Fancy knows, it's men. And Fancy can jus' *tell* that some woman went an' done a job on you, big boy. You wanna tell me about it?" Bending her arms and placing her elbows on the table, Fancy leaned forward and rested her chin on her hands. Shiny brown ringlets cascaded forward over her shoulders and arms.

"No. Go away. Your hair is curly."

Fancy giggled out loud as she casually flicked her hair back over her shoulders. "So she's got curly dark hair, does she?" After a moment, her satisfied expression faded. "What's her name, honey?" she asked gently, at the same time placing one of her hands over his to prevent him from lifting the glass to his lips once more.

"No, no, no, no; you don't understand," he slurred. "She's my wife now, but only because of the money." The dreadful wedding scene inside Reverend Kessler's parlor played itself through his head once more. "There's no way you would even believe any of it, anyway, so jus' lemme alone."

"Honey, I think it's safe to say that there ain't much Fancy ain't heard." Her smile faded as she glanced over her shoulder. "Look, mister, I'm gettin' paid to keep your glass filled to the brim—among other things," she said earnestly, "but I been watchin' you for quite a few hours now, an' I can tell you ain't like most of the regulars in here. I can tell you're different . . . an' I can tell you're really hurtin'. Now why don't you jus' tell Fancy all about this curly haired girl that's gone an' given you some reason to toss down them awful bitters like there's no tomorrow?" There was a genuine offer of assistance in her dark-fringed blue eyes as she added, "If nothin' else, maybe I can help you sort things out some."

Ryan shook off the young woman's hand and raised the glass to his lips. It was laughable, really, that some soft-hearted Denver whore thought she could help him sort out the mixed-up, muddled mess that his life had become. And besides that, this Nancy or Fancy, or whatever she was calling herself, had things all wrong. He didn't have any feelings for Emma other than . . . plain old lust.

Did he?

As he held up his empty glass and signaled a passing barmaid for another refill, a crazy sudden picture flashed in his mind, a picture of Emma leaning seductively forward and moistening her lips. "Talk to me, honey," she whispered, tucking an errant nutmeg ringlet behind her ear. "I want you to open that magnificent mouth of yours and—"

He blinked.

"Just talk to me," Fancy was saying. "It ain't that hard once you get started."

Ryan closed his eyes hard and opened them, seeing only a lush-featured young dancehall girl before him who, in truth, didn't look anything at all like the woman he had been railroaded into marrying. His refill came then, and he shut his eyes and swallowed half the contents of the glass. *This one's for you, Hopper,* he said in his mind, nostalgically recalling his friend's predilection for both bitters and large-busted women.

If this Fancy woman was anything, she was certainly persistent, Ryan thought, sensing that despite his closed eyes and advanced state of drunkenness, she hadn't yet removed herself from where she had settled what was undoubtedly a delicious little bottom. As he opened his eyes he saw he was correct, but once again, for just a split second, Emma's face blurred with that of Fancy's.

Saints alive, was he so drunk that he was hallucinating? Things were getting hazier and fuzzier by the second, and not just because the air was thick with noise and music and cigar smoke. "I need another drink," he announced to no one in particular, feeling certain that something funny was happening to him. Something damned funny.

Thunk.

Fancy winced as the big man fell forward, his forehead solidly striking the wooden table. Slowly his head listed to one side, then lay still. *Damn,* she swore to herself, her hands hadn't been quite quick enough to break the man's fall. Well, if he hadn't completely passed out, he'd certainly *knocked* himself out the rest of the way. He was liable to have himself quite a bruise on his forehead.

What a handsome man he was, she thought with longing—and more than a little disappointment—as she reached out and stroked a thick strand of his glossy dark hair. She'd never even learned his name. Whoever the curly haired woman in his life was, she was undoubtedly one lucky lady to have a lover like this at her disposal.

"Well, Fancy, it looks like he was sure impressed with you!" Fancy couldn't help but smile at her coworker Eve's facetious comment and amused laughter. "He's out, huh? What a shame," Eve went on. "We don't get his kind in here just any old day."

"Yeah, tell me about it."

"I came to warn you, too, Fancy, not to sit there too long," Eve warned. "Johnson knows you ain't upstairs right now, and he's been wonderin' where you're at."

"Where is he?"

"At the far faro table."

"Okay," Fancy said with a regretful sigh, pushing her chair back and taking her feet. "If that old son of a bitch is already askin' where I am, that means he's gonna start canvassing the room in another couple minutes looking for me."

"Just thought I'd warn you." With a commiserating smile, redheaded Eve was off.

"Well, I can see that you've got some pretty powerful feelings for the curly haired woman in your life, honey, but I didn't quite understand that 'hero' business," Fancy said out loud, gently settling the man's head in what she deemed was a much more comfortable position. He didn't need to suffer the discomfort of a crick in his neck in addition to a hangover and what was sure to be a bruised forehead for his night of overindulgence. Regretfully she trailed her hand over the powerful bunch of muscles at his shoulder.

"I'll tell you one thing, though, honey," she added as she broke contact with the big man and made a slight adjustment to her bodice. "You sure as hell ain't no has-been."

"Emma? Emma, wake up. A return wire from your brother just came!"

Emma groaned as Ginny hesitantly tapped her shoulder. "I'm awake," she croaked, not believing that after all the tossing and turning she'd done last evening, she'd actually fallen asleep.

As she opened her eyes, she saw that a fully dressed Ginny had already pulled open the room's heavy drapes to reveal a gray and dreary sky. *What time was it?* Emma wondered, taking in the sight of a newspaper that appeared to have been well read, the neatly arranged plate of pastries on the table, and the half empty carafe of coffee. Ginny must have been up for hours.

"It's a little before ten," Ginny answered Emma's unasked question. Kind gray-green eyes looked sympathetically into her own. "I knew how much trouble you had drifting off last night, so I tried to let you sleep as late as possible."

"I kept you awake, didn't I?"

"No, I think my guilty conscience kept me awake," Ginny replied as she sat on the edge of the big double bed. Her sweet round face appeared extremely troubled, and she sighed deeply. "I'm worried about Ryan, Emma. He didn't come back to the hotel last night, and Edward still hasn't seen or heard from him yet this morning."

"Maybe he just checked into another room."

"No, Edward already looked into that possibility."

"Well, maybe he used an assumed name, or maybe he's in a nearby hotel." Though righteous anger still bubbled up when Emma thought of Ryan Montgomery and all the insulting things he'd said to her in the carriage yesterday, she couldn't stop a little part of her from catching ahold of some of Ginny's concern and wondering if anything unfortunate had befallen him.

"We thought of that," Ginny said, sighing again, "and Edward's going to check a few other establishments on his way back from the recorder's office. You know, we're into things too deeply to back out now, Emma. That's why Edward's going ahead and filing your marriage, but I have to say that I think we went too far with Ryan. We really, truly did."

Ginny rose and began to pace between the table and the bed. "I feel so awful! All those things that Ryan said yesterday . . . he accused us of using him as our trick monkey, do you remember?"

"I . . . remember." Guiltily Emma studied the weave of the bed's thick coverlet, thinking of all the other things he had said.

And how his lips had felt against hers.

"He was right, you know. We did use him. Oh, Emma, we were so wrong. How could we ever have assumed that Ryan didn't have any feelings?"

"Well, given the way he'd been acting, I think it was only natural to—"

"Oh, gosh!" Ginny interrupted, suddenly extending the small sealed envelope that she'd been carrying in her hand. "I almost forgot! Here's your telegram."

Emma's already nervous stomach rumbled out loud as she accepted the envelope. *What was Michael's response?* she wondered, suddenly feeling very glad that she was hundreds of miles away from the eruption that surely occurred in St. Paul when Michael received word of her marriage.

During a subdued and very strained dinner in the hotel dining room last evening, she and Ginny and Edward had put forth a great deal of effort into carefully wording Emma's message to her brother. Then, after dinner, Edward had taken care of dispatching the telegraph while Emma had collapsed in her bed and fitfully tried to sleep.

No matter how a person looked at it, there just wasn't any good way to sugarcoat the fact that she'd married a man her overly protective brother had never even met.

Michael was going to kill her.

Her fingers shook as she tore open the envelope and read the brief message, and her stomach contracted into a tight ball of panic. Sudden sweat broke out under her arms and between her shoulder blades; she couldn't breathe.

"What does it say, Emma?" Ginny asked. "Is it as bad as you thought?"

"It's worse," Emma tonelessly replied, handing the paper over for Ginny to read. "Michael told me not to move until he gets here."

Chapter Twelve

The remainder of the morning passed, then the afternoon, with no word from Ryan. Emma took a small bite of her orange pie, thinking that if the atmosphere at last evening's dinner table had been tense and subdued, the mood tonight was downright dreary and depressing.

"Where do you suppose Ryan disappeared to?" Edward asked for perhaps the fifth time since they'd been seated at their table in the sumptuously appointed dining room of the New Markham. He shook his head as he took a bite of his pie, then set down his fork. "I checked for a man fitting Ryan's description at the front desks of the Lindell Hotel, the American House, and the Grand Central," he said with his mouth full of orange fluff. He swallowed, and his voice was once again clear when he spoke. "But he wasn't at any of those places."

"Denver's a big city, Edward," Ginny gently reasoned with her husband. "There are lots of places Ryan could be."

"That's what I'm worried about." Deep furrows creased Edward's forehead. "With the frame of mind he was in yesterday afternoon, I can only pray that he stayed on the decent side of town."

"This whole thing is my fault," Emma said miserably as the delicately tart flavor of the pie turned sour on her tongue. "I was just so afraid that I was going to lose my job and be sent home without a way to earn my two hundred dollars that I came up with this stupid marriage idea." She smiled without humor. "And look where my brilliant scheme has gotten us. Ryan's missing, Michael's madder than a hornet and already on his way out here . . ." She broke off, suddenly thinking of something none of them had yet considered. "You don't suppose Ryan went back to the ranch, do you?"

"God only knows," Edward said slowly, leaning his head forward and massaging his temples with his second and third fingers. "I gave up trying to second-guess what goes on inside my brother's head years ago."

"Don't blame yourself for everything, Emma." Ginny also laid down her fork, leaving the greater portion of her pie uneaten. "If anyone's at fault, it's me and Edward for going along with things. And I feel just awful about leaving you all alone here in Denver," she added, changing the subject. "Are you sure we can't—"

"No, I think it would be best if you went back to the ranch and I met Michael alone," Emma interrupted her temporary sister-in-law. "He's liable to be quite . . . unpleasant."

"You don't think he'll . . . Well, I don't mean to insult the man, but . . . But you don't think he'll do anything to *hurt* you, do you?" Edward asked awkwardly. "Because if there's even a remote possibility that you're in any sort of danger, Emma, Ginny and I won't leave you here alone. McDermott can handle things at the ranch for a couple more days."

"No, no, Michael's not like that," Emma quickly reassured both Edward and Ginny. "He'll be furious, no doubt, but I tell you true when I say he's never once raised a hand to me. As a matter of fact, I can't recall that he's ever raised his *voice* to me, not until I talked to him about wanting to open my collectibles shop, anyway."

"What do you think he's going to say about your marriage if you can't even produce a husband for him?" Edward's dark eyes were grave in the dim light of the dining room.

"I've got two more days to worry about that before Michael gets here," Emma replied. "And if Ryan doesn't turn up . . . well, with the way I've been lying lately, I'm sure I'll come up with something good."

"You've still got the name of the banker I gave you, don't you?" Edward asked.

Emma nodded.

"Jefferson Heaney is one heck of a nice fellow. After I went to the recorder's office this morning, I stopped to see him and apprised him of all the . . . ah, particulars of our situation. Jeff'll be keeping an eye out for you, and he's assured me that he'll handle our financial matters with the utmost discretion. If you have any problems, Emma . . . or if you have second thoughts and simply want to change your mind about the loan," Edward offered straightforwardly, "just send a wire to Pine Bluffs, and a town boy will bring it out to the ranch."

"I don't think I'll change my mind, Edward, but thanks for leaving the door open." Emma managed a small smile at her brother-in-law. "As soon as I square things with Michael I'll arrange to have the money transferred, then I'll return to the ranch."

"How much longer until our train leaves, Edward?" Ginny asked.

Edward checked his watch. "Another hour or so. The Number Four leaves the Denver station at nine-fifty." The dark-haired man curved his lips into a lame smile and covered his wife's hand with his own. "We ought to arrive in Pine Bluffs by . . . oh, well, dear, let's just say we'll be back home for breakfast."

The hours and days Emma spent all alone in the strange city dreading Michael's arrival were the most nerve-wracking she had ever endured—far worse than the days she had spent on the train from St. Paul to Pine Bluffs. A soft rain pattered against the window of her small but comfortable hotel room as she glanced at the small alarm clock on the night table for the tenth time in as many minutes. Five minutes to two. Michael ought to be here any minute now. A fresh burst of panic rolled through her as she recalled the wire he'd sent her from Omaha yesterday, informing her that he would arrive at the New Markham at two o'clock the following afternoon.

Adding to her nearly feverish state of mind was the fact that Ryan had not yet made any attempt to contact her. He hadn't turned up at the ranch, either, for she had received a second wire yesterday, one from Edward, saying that no one in the Pine Bluffs area had seen or heard from his older brother since before their departure.

Where could Ryan have gone?

Over and over Emma's mind replayed the dreadful and demeaning things she'd said to Ryan in the carriage. Though a small part of her secretly affirmed that the words she'd spoken were the truth—that the things she had said to him needed to be said—what Emma mostly felt was shame for her outburst. She had never, ever spoken to *anyone* the way she had spoken to Ryan Montgomery.

In fact, she'd never before felt such antagonism for another living person.

Why, then, she asked herself, if she so despised this man she had married, was she so concerned about what had become of him? Why did his face keep appearing in her mind? Why did she remember, time and time again, the unmistakable raw agony she'd seen in his dark eyes? And why did her fingers still tingle when she thought of the contact their hands had made? Emma swallowed hard as she stared at her work-worn digits. Slowly she brought her right hand up to her mouth and pressed her fingers against her lips.

And why, oh why, did her lips still tingle when she thought of the kiss she and Ryan had shared? She was still at a loss to put into words the incredible amount of *feeling* the touch of his eyes and lips had wrought inside her.

"Emma Louise!"

Emma jumped at the sound of Michael's voice and imperious knock at the door. With unwilling limbs and a pounding heart she arose from the chair and unlocked the door, having to jump back out of the way as Michael Taylor turned the knob and pushed his way into the room without waiting for an invitation.

He appeared to be nearly apoplectic.

"Well, well, well, if it isn't the little newlywed," he spoke scathingly as he stood before her, his eyes scouring her appearance. Droplets of moisture clung to his hat and coat, but he made no motion to remove either article. "Where's your husband?" he demanded roughly.

"He's . . . out." Though the day's humidity was high, there wasn't so much as a trace of moisture inside Emma's mouth.

"What do you mean, *'he's out'*?"

"Well, he just—"

"Never mind!" he roared. "I'd as soon rip his head off as meet him! Do you realize what you have gone and done, Emma Louise? *Do you fully comprehend that you have married some man you've known for only one month?*" In an angry motion Michael ripped his hat from his head and threw it on the table, sending a fine spray of moisture into the air. "You've gone daft—no!—you've been corrupted! First it's your business idea, then it's your stubborn insistence to hold me to my word by any senseless means you can find, and now . . . now you've allowed some man to . . ." With obvious effort Michael bit off his words. "This Montgomery character is only after your money, Emma," he went on, angrily blowing out his breath. "Have you become so blinded that you can't even see the truth for what it is?"

"No, that's not true," Emma cried, knowing she must hold fast to the elaborate web of lies she had spun. "Not at all! Ryan and I are in love."

"Love?" Michael asked incredulously. "I don't believe that rubbish for one minute, little sister. Particularly since you asked for such a tremendous amount of money to be transferred to Denver. So help me," he muttered furiously, "I knew letting you go to Wyoming Territory was all wrong. I just knew it in my—"

"You've got to listen to me, Michael," Emma interrupted. "I have . . . *we* have good reason for needing the money . . . you've got to believe me. Besides that, Ryan really loves me."

"You don't even know what love is, Emma," Michael said with a sneer. "For God's sake, back home you had true love right under your own nose and you were too stubborn—or too foolish—to realize it." He took a deep breath and slowly blew it out from between gritted teeth, at the same time extending his arms in appeal.

"Just come home with me," he pleaded, his chestnut-colored eyes beseeching her with the depth of his feelings. "Come to your senses and come home with me right now. I haven't told Jon anything about this . . . this newest mess you've gotten yourself into, so it won't be that difficult for you to patch things up with him—he misses you terribly. In fact, if you come home with me and let me take care of annulling your marriage, Jon will never have to know any of this. He still wants to marry you, Emma."

"You don't understand, Michael. I don't want to marry Jon," Emma maintained, taking a step backward. A suffocating, stifling feeling came over her as she thought of the tall Nordic attorney. "I *can't* marry Jon—I'm already married! And as Ryan Montgomery's wife, I have responsibilities, obligations—"

Michael's hands curled into angry fists as he cut off her words. "What the hell kind of obligations do you have as this man's wife that you need such an exorbitant amount of money to fulfill them? No matter what sweetness and sunshine this fortune hunter has pumped you full of, the ugly truth of the matter is that he's *bilking* you, Emma—he's bilking us!—out of Father's hard-earned money." He paused then, as if struck by a revelation, and his angry expression slowly turned to one of dismay . . . and disappointment. "You're in on this whole scheme, aren't you, Emma?"

"I-I . . . t-there's no scheme," Emma stammered, shaken to the core by Michael's perceptiveness. "Ryan and I got married because we love each—"

"Save it, little sister. I can see the answer written all over your guilty face." He stepped over to the table and reached for his hat. "You make me sick," he spat, fresh anger spewing forth as he jammed his hat back on his head and turned toward the door. "You just couldn't wait to get ahold of your money, could you?"

"No, Michael, that's not tr—" Bitter tears stung her eyes.

"I'll arrange to have your entire trust fund transferred to the bank you specified in your first wire to me." He cut her off in a clipped tone, speaking with his back still toward her. "You're married now. It's legally yours."

"I don't need all of it, Michael, I only need—"

"Your trust fund is yours to do with what you will, Emma Louise," he reiterated, still speaking to the door. "In fact," he added, reaching for the knob, "your *life* is yours to do with what you will." He opened the door, then paused. "Before I leave, I will need to see legal proof of your marriage," he said, turning back toward her but keeping his eyes carefully averted from her.

"Don't be like this, Michael," Emma pleaded, hot tears freely spilling from her eyes. "Oh, Michael, please don't—"

"Let me see the marriage certificate!"

"It's right here." With shaking, fumbling fingers and a breaking heart, Emma turned and reached for the certificate she had placed on the dresser.

"I see you wasted no time in recording your marriage," he said as he briefly perused the document she extended toward him. "May I also presume that you consummated your great 'love' for each other in an equally precipitate manner?" With that vicious barb, he once again turned his back on her.

"It's a good thing you have a husband, Emma Montgomery," he said in a terrible tone of voice as he stepped through the doorway, "because you no longer have any other family to call your own. I wash my hands of you."

Ryan Montgomery rode the passenger elevator of the New Markham Hotel with a fresh sense of determination to make the best of the wretched situation in which he and his family were hopelessly involved. After giving matters a great deal of thought over the past few days—after *first* sobering up from the terrible bender he'd gone on on his wedding night—he had made the difficult decision to stay married, on paper, to Emma Taylor over the summer. Telling Ma the truth about everything at this point would only hurt her, he'd decided, and for no good purpose.

He'd also searched his soul and had come to the realization that he really *did* want to be part of ranch operations. He needed a home, a place to belong, and most of all, a sense of purpose. Pulling the ranch out of the financial quagmire Edward had allowed it to slip into filled him with that sense of purpose, as well as, perhaps, if he had to admit it, the hope of somehow canceling his debt with his father.

Absently he rubbed his fingers over the painful lump on his forehead. Though the swelling had gone down greatly in the past few days, he'd awoken with quite a goose egg, not to mention quite a hangover, the morning after he'd swilled bitters like cheap beer.

He didn't have any idea how he had gotten the bruise; in fact, he didn't have any memories from the evening at all, except for downing one glass of booze after another. Then nothing. He had no idea, either, how he'd ended up in a bed in a cheap flophouse across the street from the saloon. What was truly incredible was that he awoke with his wallet—still containing money—in his pocket. Surely God had been watching over him.

For the better part of two days he'd been accursedly ill from the poisonous amount of alcohol he'd consumed, but today it finally felt as if all the toxins in his system had been purged. He was thinner, he knew, but at least his body was inhabitable once again. Now all that was left to do was to continue to work at making his mind a healthy place.

Something funny had happened this morning when he'd gone to settle up at the front desk. The smelly, aging clerk had moved his cigar over to one side of his mouth and said, "You don't owe nothin'. Fancy took care of your tab." He'd tried asking the clerk who Fancy was, but the old man just readjusted his cigar, clammed up, and motioned for him to get lost.

Then, after visiting a barber with a shower and taking his noon meal today at a small saloon on the seamier side of town, he'd been on his way to the train station when a strange notion had compelled him to go back to the New

Markham one last time—just for the hell of it—to make sure Edward wasn't still sitting there waiting for him to return.

It was no great surprise to learn from the New Markham's front clerk that Edward was no longer a registered guest of the hotel. Ryan thanked the man and was nearly out the door when the clerk called, "Wait, sir, we have a Mrs. R. Montgomery in three-fifteen. Might that be a relation?"

Mrs. R. Montgomery? Ryan stopped full in his tracks. *Mrs. R. Montgomery?* What was Emma still doing in Denver? "Three-fifteen?" he said, turning and heading toward the elevator without waiting for a response.

"Here we are, sir. Third floor," the elevator operator announced, bringing Ryan's thoughts back to the present. Impatiently he waited for the young man to set the brake. Through the closed elevator doors the sound of an angry man's voice carried to the two of them, as did a woman's faroff, anguished cry of *"Michael!"*

"Lovers' quarrel," the operator said, shaking his head as he made to open the doors. "You wouldn't believe the half of what goes on round here some days—and just about every night, t' tell you the truth."

Ryan nodded but made no reply, his thoughts instead being on Emma and on any possible reason she could have for remaining in Denver. As he stepped into the hallway, a furious-looking man clad in a dark hat and coat brushed roughly by him, nearly knocking him off balance. "First floor," the man snarled to the operator as he entered the car, not bothering to look back over his shoulder to see who he'd run into, much less to apologize.

"Yes, sir," the operator responded smartly, poking his head all the way out the door to look both ways for any additional passengers in the corridor. Seeing none, he shrugged his shoulders and gave Ryan a commiserating smile as if to say, "See what I mean?"

What an idiot, Ryan thought, dismissing the encounter and starting off down the hall. The sound of a woman weeping carried clearly to him, and he absently wondered what had transpired between her and her ill-mannered lover, for the woman cried as if her heart were broken.

Three-oh-nine, three-eleven. Ryan judged that the crying woman's room must be very close to Emma's, for the sound of weeping grew louder with each successive step he made down the corridor. *Three-thirteen.* Looking ahead to the next door, three-fifteen, Ryan saw that it was ajar.

No, his mind rejected. *That can't possibly be Emma crying like that . . . can it?*

When he stopped in front of three-fifteen, he no longer had any doubt as to the identity of the weeping woman— it *was* Emma. Though her voice was raw with pain, he recognized its distinctive quality as he laid a heavy hand on the knob of three-fifteen.

Now what, Montgomery? You've never been any good with crying ladies. He hesitated as the voice inside him grew demanding, angry. *Just what the hell is going on here, anyway? And who was that man—some lover from her past?* Glancing down the hallway in the direction of the elevator, he was of a sudden mind to retrace his steps and go after the rude son of a bitch in the black hat and—

"N-now what am I g-going to do?"

Emma's heartrending plea and subsequent burst of fresh anguish froze him with indecision. Damn it all, anyway. This whole situation was getting odder and more uncomfortable by the minute, and Emma's woeful sobs weren't helping matters—or his peace of mind—one little bit.

"Emma?" Ryan made his voice deliberately brisk as he pushed open the door.

"Michael?" From her crumpled position on the floor, Emma glanced up with such sadness and longing that Ryan couldn't help but be moved. "Ohh . . . it's you. . . ." Emma's voice trailed off as she dropped her head. Her shining nutmeg-colored ringlets, as well as her small shoulders, shook with the force of the sobs she now tried to disguise. "Please go away," she managed to say through her tears, her voice sounding thick and muffled.

Go away? He'd like nothing more than to go away—as far away as possible from this room, as far away as possible from this tear-stained woman who wept as though she had lost anything and everything she had ever held dear.

But he couldn't seem to make himself move.

For some reason, Emma's tears affected him as nothing else had for . . . as long as he could remember. Ryan could see that her present grief was genuine, and he was filled with an overwhelming urge to impart some sort of comfort to her, even if her pain was caused by the rejection of another.

His eyes traveled over her crumpled, petite form, then around the tastefully furnished hotel room. As raindrops continued to patter steadily against the window, Ryan realized that it bothered him—very much—that all of the effervescence had gone out of Emma. He also thought, with more than a little admiration, that the lovely young Minnesota woman had ventured far and dared much to follow her dreams of opening her own business.

He also had to admit to himself, albeit rather grudgingly, that for being raised in the lap of luxury and undoubtedly having led a life of ease, Emma was as unpretentious and hardworking as any other ranch employee. In fact, she had probably been working even harder than the other employees, in a manner of speaking, because she had been working to *learn* her duties as well as to execute them.

And not once had he ever heard her complain. He probably owed her an apology for all the things he'd said to her in anger. She'd truly wanted to help his family.

Ryan stared down at his hands, not realizing, until this second, that he'd been tensely clenching them together. He turned and softly closed the door behind him. Walking over to where Emma lay on the rug, he knelt before her. "Let me help you up," he said as gently as he knew how, staring into the mass of silky brown curls atop her head.

"I . . . no . . . g-go away." Though her weeping seemed to be on the wane, there was no strength in her command.

"You don't really want me to go away and leave you . . . like that other man did, do you?" Ryan realized he was bidding for information in a shameful fashion, but something inside him burned to know the identity of the man who'd been in this room with the woman he'd married. Almost as an afterthought he glanced at the bed . . . and was inordinately pleased to see that it was neatly made. "Let me help you," he began again, awkwardly extending his hand—but halting its motion just short of a delicately rounded shoulder.

In truth, he didn't quite dare touch this woman. Why? He didn't understand. She was no bigger than a minute. He could easily lift her into his arms and lay her on the bed and . . . *and then what, Montgomery?* a voice inside him asked. *Make love to her? It's not as if you're actually married.*

"That other man was my brother," Emma whispered, interrupting his thoughts as she wearily lifted her head to look at him. "He said . . ." She took a deep, shaking breath before continuing. "He said he washed his hands of me."

Something in Ryan's heart twisted painfully as their eyes met, as he took in her swollen, tear-stained face. "He washed his hands of you, did he?" he said with what he knew was a poor rendering of a sympathetic smile. For a long moment he studied every feature of the heart-shaped face before him. "Well, Miss Curly," he said with a sigh, "you went and fixed things so *I* can't wash my hands of you, not till autumn, anyway." He dropped his hand lower, toward the elbow she was using to prop herself up with, and his smile faded as he continued to stare into a pair of melting brown eyes that spilled over with such great sadness. "Why don't you at least let me help you up off the floor?" he asked gently. "I won't hurt you, Emma. I promise."

The hesitant touch of Ryan's fingers against Emma's upper arm made a shiver ripple through her entire body. His kindness, too, was completely befuddling to her already distraught senses, for she had never imagined in a thousand years that she'd see Ryan Montgomery's expression so soft, so yielding. . . .

Befuddlement turned to shock, however, when in a bold and decisive movement Ryan effortlessly scooped her up from the carpet and carried her the few steps to the bed. The brand of two hard-muscled arms burned briefly against her, one across her upper back, and the other first at the back of her thighs, then sliding to the area just behind her knees, leaving her senses reeling from the heady combination of raw male strength, a genuinely compassionate act, and the musky scent of shaving lotion that clung to what appeared, at such close range, to be a freshly shaven face.

As he laid her on the bed, his head bent toward hers, his lips stopping just a fraction of an inch from her own. She read a wanting in his eyes, a hunger, and deep inside her she felt an answering need of her own.

A second later, however, the spell was over and Emma was lying alone on the bed, watching a suddenly stiff-backed Ryan walk away from her, toward the window. As she struggled to sit up, Emma realized her body still burned where the big man's arms had touched her. And that wasn't the worst of it. Her mouth was dry, her tongue was most certainly tied into hopeless knots, and her heart thrummed forcefully in her chest as she studied the powerful form of the man she had married, once again finding herself very aware of him. . . .

As a man.

What was he thinking right now? she wondered, her gaze running over the broad set of shoulders that had just supported her weight as effortlessly as if she'd been a feather. Were his thoughts as scrambled as hers? Is that why he'd broken eye contact with her and was now staring, with his back toward her, out the window at the gray Denver afternoon?

Emma let go of the marriage certificate that she'd forgotten she'd been clutching in her left hand and dabbed at her eyes with a corner of the slate-blue bedspread. Just what was Ryan feeling at this moment? Had the brief encounter produced . . . well, *feelings* in him, too?

And what does it matter to you what type of feelings Ryan Montgomery is having, Emma Louise? her inner voice spoke sharply. *Your marriage can only be a business arrangement, nothing more.*

"As I mentioned, I've decided to remain married to you for the summer," Ryan said as if he were reading her thoughts. His form appeared rigid as he continued to face the drizzly Denver panorama. "I'll be honest. I don't like the arrangement much, but with things being what they presently are, I don't see a better alternative than to go along with the scheme you and Edward and Ginny cooked up." He sighed deeply and half turned to face her. "That is, if you're still planning on going back to the ranch."

If she was still planning on going back to the ranch? Where else did she have to go now? As Michael had closed the doors of his home—as well as his heart—to her, there was simply no other place for her to go than the Montgomery ranch. Besides that, she had made a deal with Edward and Ginny; she'd given her word that she would silently loan them the money *and* continue to work as their cook over the summer, so as not to arouse Maureen's suspicions.

Emma nearly broke into fresh tears when she thought of Joey, and of the carefully folded painting in her satchel, for the thought of never again seeing her young friend filled her with unbearable melancholy. With absolute certainty, she realized what she'd told Joey on the train had been true: he *had* taught her more about friendship—and honesty and love and acceptance—than anyone else on earth.

It was good that he would never know of her brief marriage to his beloved "Wyan," Emma reflected with more than a little shame. Given all the lies and deceit in which she was presently involved, she was not worthy of being called Joey's sister.

"Am I to take it that you're not coming back to the ranch, then?" Ryan's businesslike tone broke into her thoughts.

"N-no . . . I mean, yes, I'm coming back."

"Have all the necessary financial transactions been completed?"

"No." Emma bit her tongue to keep from adding *sir* to her reply, as Ryan's last two questions had been issued in the manner befitting an . . . an army captain. Dropping her gaze from her temporary husband's virile profile, Emma felt a crushing tiredness descend upon her. "I need to go see a Mr. Jefferson—"

"Jeff Heaney?"

"Y-yes, that's who Edward told me to go see," Emma said slowly. "He said Mr. Heaney would take care of everything. . . ." Much to her horror, she heard her voice break, felt fresh tears begin in her eyes. "But I-I just don't know if I can pull myself together enough to go meet anyone this afternoon."

A wry half smile twisted Ryan's lips. "I agree, wife, that your appearance would distress poor Jefferson. He would undoubtedly conclude that you were forced into this arrangement . . . but we know better than that, don't we?" With his last words, the old sarcasm was back in his voice, and in a rough motion, he turned the rest of the way around to face the bed.

Gone was every last vestige of the kind stranger who had, just a few minutes before, offered her his comfort, and Emma didn't know which Ryan Montgomery frightened her more, this Ryan Montgomery with the angry dark eyes, or the Ryan Montgomery with the soft expression and gaze as rich and velvety as dark chocolate.

"I'll go square things at the bank," he said brusquely, "wire Edward, and make arrangements for us to return to Pine Bluffs tomorrow morning. I suggest you get yourself . . ."—Ryan paused, clearing his throat as his eyes flicked over her—"put back together by doing whatever it is you women do to make yourselves look presentable. You'll be back to your duties tomorrow evening." With that, he departed, closing the door with a sharp click.

"Oh, why did I ever think any of my ideas were good ones?" Emma moaned out loud as she stared at the door, allowing the hot tears to spill from her eyes. She felt so alone. Not only had she alienated her only brother and, more than likely, ruined any chance of Jon Severson ever wanting to marry her, but also she now had a husband who fairly despised her, a hot summer of cooking ahead of her, and, worst of all, an obligation to live out the enormous pack of lies she had concocted.

Mother was right, Emma Louise, her inner voice further chastised her. *Little lies only lead to bigger ones . . . and look where all your lying has gotten you now.*

Chapter Thirteen

After a fitful night of sleep, Emma was not any better prepared for the journey back to Pine Bluffs than she had been the previous afternoon. And it wasn't solely her misery over Michael's harsh words that had kept her from slipping into deep slumber last evening; intertwined were her thoroughly confusing feelings for Ryan Montgomery.

Over and over through the night, against her will, she remembered the feel of Ryan's strong arms against her body . . . the sound of his breathing in her ears . . . and the musky scent of his shaving lotion in her nostrils as he'd carried her from the floor to the bed. He'd been about to kiss her, she was certain of it.

With a great effort of will, Emma pulled her thoughts back to the present. The object of her thoughts sat alongside her in the first-class area of the northbound Union Pacific train that chugged steadily toward Cheyenne. Since coming to her room to fetch her this morning, he'd been nothing but distant and detached. After tersely informing her that he'd taken care of the banking matters—adding that he'd missed meeting her brother by just a few minutes—he'd picked up her satchel and led the way to the lobby. Just like that.

No smiles, no softness, no tenderness.

In truth, however, Emma found that Ryan's remote manner made it much easier for her to firmly set her mind on her goals: making it through a summer's worth of cooking, then, after the Montgomerys sold their cattle, pursuing her dream of being a small business owner. Regretfully she put away the foolish, maidenly longings she'd entertained through the night. There was no way her marriage to Ryan Montgomery could be anything more than a business arrangement.

"Lest you think otherwise, I want to assure you that your loan to the Montmac Ranch will be fully repaid in the autumn."

Emma jumped at the unexpected sound of Ryan's voice, for he hadn't said two words to her since they'd boarded the train in Denver. After a long pause, she answered his statement honestly. "I didn't think otherwise."

"Oh."

Emma wasn't sure, but she thought she may have heard a note of surprise in Ryan's curt reply. "Look," she said with a sigh, turning her head to face him. Her heart began to pound rapidly in her chest as her gaze swept upward over the strong male jaw and cheekbone. "I'm not proud of my part in this whole mess; in fact, I'm quite sorry. But let me assure you that nothing is going to have to change because of our . . ." She looked both ways before whispering, " . . . marriage. No one will ever have to know that we were married for these few months." Going on in a more normal tone of voice, she added, "I'm still your cook, your employee. That hasn't changed. What we have is a handshake deal . . . well, we did go a little beyond a handshake, though, didn't we?" she muttered aloud, not able to prevent a wry grin from flitting across her lips.

"Indeed we did." For just a second, Ryan's stern expression softened. "You'll be paid interest on your loan, too," he added, "in case Edward failed to make that point clear to you. He and I agreed upon the amount of one full percentage point above what the banks will pay during this period of time."

"One percentage point above the bank? You can't—"

"I can, and furthermore, I insist."

"That's too much money, Ryan." Emma used his name familiarly, without thinking. "I don't need that much."

"I don't give a . . ." With what appeared to be a great deal of effort, Ryan cut himself off. "You'll take it," he concluded in a tone that said the argument was closed. He rested his head against the back of the seat and closed his eyes. "I appreciate your consideration in regard to keeping the matter of our . . . business arrangement . . . confidential. I'll see to it that the annulment is handled in a discreet fashion, as well."

Though no more words passed between Ryan and Emma during the remainder of their journey to Cheyenne, Emma sensed that an uneasy truce, or perhaps, rather, an uneasy trust, now sat between them. Ryan appeared to doze at several short intervals, but with all the confusing thoughts that whirled in Emma's mind, she could not drift off to sleep. Not helping matters, either, was the fact that her eyes were repeatedly drawn by the strong planes and angles of Ryan's face while he slept.

You married this man, Emma Louise, her conscience spoke. *That means that you and he made a sacred covenant before the eyes of God—*

Your marriage to Ryan Montgomery doesn't have a thing to do with God! a shrill, righteous-sounding voice inside her spoke. *It has to do with business . . . and with helping each other out; nothing else.*

The thoughts and voices inside Emma's mind continued to war as the train neared Cheyenne. Her stomach, already quite unsettled, twisted into a tight knot when another thought, a thought she had tried to deny and suppress all the long night through, crashed its way through the others and shouted above the din to make itself known:

She wanted Ryan Montgomery—in the way a woman wanted a man.

"Chey-*enne*," the conductor called loudly as the train began to slow, his deep voice causing Emma to jump in her seat. Bending forward, she retrieved her leather satchel and set it firmly in her lap, while next to her, Ryan awoke and stretched his long legs as best he could.

As it had been in Denver, the sky was overcast in Cheyenne. There was no rain here, however, and a cool brisk breeze blew across the prairie and over the passengers on the Cheyenne Union Pacific depot. Emma welcomed the freshness of the wind against her face as she departed the train, anxious for any sort of tactile respite to free her from her troubling thoughts.

And from the realization that Ryan Montgomery walked only a few steps behind her.

The eastbound train to Pine Bluffs was scheduled to arrive in approximately twenty-five minutes, not leaving them enough time, really, to leave the depot and do anything in Cheyenne. Ryan wordlessly strode ahead of her, cutting a swath through the crowd of disembarking and waiting passengers, many of them soldiers, on the platform.

Was she supposed to follow him? Emma wondered, clutching her satchel tightly to her. Or was he seeking distance from her? Just then, loud male whooping broke out from a large knot of soldiers. "Hey, it's Captain Montgomery!... Good to see you, Captain!... Congratulations, sir!... I'll be a son of a... Montgomery, you sly dog, you! Now we know why you resigned!"

An expectant hush fell over all the passengers on the platform as one of the men stepped toward Ryan with a broad smile on his face. In his right hand he held up a newspaper. "Congratulations, sir!" he cried.

Congratulations? Emma thought with panic ... and horror. She wrapped her arms more tightly about her satchel. *No. There's no way. They can't possibly know....*

Ryan's voice was low and tight as he replied, "Would you kindly tell me what you are talking about, Sergeant Penlay?"

"Your wedding, sir," the sergeant replied loudly, shaking the hand in which he held the paper. "No kidding, it wasn't more than ten minutes ago that we spotted your marriage announcement in *The Cheyenne Daily Sun.*" He craned his neck to search among the passengers on the platform. "Do we get to meet the missus, sir?"

Emma's heart shriveled as Sergeant Penlay's eyes settled upon her. At the same time, a well-dressed businessman on the other side of the platform spoke. "I read the announcement in the Denver *Daily News* a couple days ago," he called. "They did quite a nice little write-up."

Their marriage announcement had appeared in not one newspaper, but *two*? Emma shriveled inside as she realized exactly what damage had been done . . . and the extent of the silent wrath that emanated from Ryan's smoldering eyes.

The remainder of their wait for the eastbound train was absolutely awful. Not only did she have to bear the introductions to and exuberant congratulations from each member of the group of soldiers until the southbound train arrived and cleared them from the platform, but she also knew that every other person on the platform was watching. Witnessing. Surely it wouldn't take long for Maureen to learn of her and Ryan's marriage . . . that is, if she hadn't already heard.

Ryan was perfectly silent during the ride from Cheyenne to Pine Bluffs, making no reply whatsoever to her nervous, stammering apologies about the whole affair. It was late afternoon by the time they'd arrived in Pine Bluffs, and Emma's last slim hope that the news of her and Ryan's marriage hadn't traveled past Cheyenne was dashed as the telegraph operator hung his head out the window of the depot building and hollered his congratulations.

"Your ma's pretty gol-durned excited about the two of you elopin', too," he added with a grin. "She looked like she was about bustin' for joy when she and the little ones passed through here earlier today."

Maureen knew.

Oh, dear God, now what? Emma silently prayed, dread zinging all through her body. Maureen knew she and Ryan had gotten married. The telegraph operator knew. The soldiers knew. In fact, everybody in the entire Territory of Wyoming knew, it seemed, of her joining to Ryan Montgomery.

Ryan looked mad enough to kill as he stalked off to where Zach Ferguson was waiting with the carriage.

"Howdy, Cap'n Montgomery, Miss Taylor . . . I mean Mrs. Montgomery," the chubby-faced cowhand greeted, further establishing the fact that the news of their marriage had, indeed, rippled far beyond the four walls of the Kesslers' parsonage. With a curious glance at tight-lipped Ryan, Zach rushed forward to relieve Emma of her satchel, chattering nonstop about what a shock everyone at the ranch had had to learn that their day trip to Pine Bluffs had turned into an elopement in Denver.

Tipping his hat to reveal a shock of bright red hair, he offered his congratulations and went on, "You know, come to think of it, Edward has been actin' real funny ever since he an' Miz Ginny got back. Nervous. Jumpy-like, an' all. I s'pose they was there with you an' the captain when you got married, huh?" Without waiting for an answer, he continued. "It ain't been no better since Miz Maureen got back this afternoon, neither, wantin' to know all the details of your weddin'. The place is in an uproar, all right, with them squealy little girls runnin' around, and what with all the plans for the—" Abruptly he cut himself off with a sheepish grin. "Oops, I'm talkin' too much. Come on, let me give you a hand up here." With that he assisted her into the carriage, following her in, a moment later, upon Ryan's curt orders.

"Guess I'm ridin' with you, Miz Montgomery," the lad said with a puzzled expression, ducking as he came through the doorway. "After all that train ridin', I guess the cap'n wants to take a turn drivin'. Boy, for gettin' married, he ain't in a much better mood. You two have a fight already, or somethin'?"

By the time the carriage pulled up in front of the two-story frame structure, Emma was almost insane from her fretting and worry—as well as from being a captive prisoner to Zach's friendly but garrulous tongue.

What were they going to say to Maureen? For that matter, what had Edward and Ginny already said? Had Edward told his mother the truth? She rejected that possibility almost as soon as she thought of it. Edward was a master of evasion and clever half truths. But then again, Maureen was no fool. . . .

"They're here! Ma, they're here!" shouted a tall girl about twelve or thirteen years of age, bursting through the front door and down the steps of the veranda even before Ryan had brought the carriage to a complete stop.

"See what I mean about them squealy little Montgomery girls?" As Zach shook his head and reached for the door handle, another girl exited the front door and stepped rapidly across the front porch, appearing to be only slightly more contained than her sister.

"Ryan, Ryan!" the first girl said excitedly, holding her skirt above her ankles and running over to the carriage in a most indecorous fashion. "Hi, Ryan!"

"Colleen," Ryan acknowledged with a noncommittal nod as he set the brake. Ever since Sergeant Penlay and the other soldiers had publicly acknowledged his marriage to Emma Taylor, white-hot anger and frustration had burned inside him. He wanted to throttle Edward and Ginny . . . and Emma, most of all. What he wouldn't give to be able to pick Miss Curly up by her scrawny little neck and shake her until the stuffing came out of her. For it was *Emma's* marvelous plan, *Emma's* incredibly brilliant plot, that had placed him in this disastrous situation.

And you think you're completely blameless, Montgomery? a voice inside him asked. *You didn't have to go along with any of this, you know.*

A wisp of tenderness flicked through him as he thought of the enmity Emma's only brother now held for her. He recalled, too, the fright in her melting brown eyes as she'd stood on the Cheyenne depot and endured the many introductions and ribald congratulations. Too, he'd hard-heartedly ignored each of her pleading, stammered apologies during their journey from Cheyenne to Pine Bluffs.

Serves her right, another voice inside his mind spoke. *She had no business trying to pull off such a scheme.*

During the ride to the ranch, he'd tried to come up with a plausible explanation to give his mother for this whole situation, but, grimly, he realized the only "solution" to this problem was to tell Ma the truth. It would hurt her, he knew, but there was clearly no other alternative.

"Oh, I can't believe you went off and got married, Ryan!" his youngest sister was squealing, pulling him from his unpleasant thoughts. "How romantic! It must be true love! Did you bring my new sister back with you?" she asked ecstatically, rushing over to the door of the carriage, where Zach was just clambering out.

"Come on, Zach," Colleen ordered impatiently, "hurry up and get out of there and let me meet my new sister."

With a muffled curse Ryan jumped down from the driver's seat, giving a brief acknowledging nod to his second-to-youngest sister, Ruthie, who hung back shyly. Just then, the screen door opened and a broadly smiling Maureen exited, followed closely by his other sisters Moira and Irene.

"Oh, you're not supposed to be here yet," Moira wailed to Ryan. "We aren't finished with the—"

"Quiet, Moira," Irene shushed, holding her index finger over her lips.

" 'Tis of no matter, girls," Maureen soothed, drying her hands on her apron. "They'll know soon enough." Walking down the steps toward Ryan, she opened her arms. "Welcome home, me precious, precious love."

Dumbly, before Ryan knew what was happening, his mother was in his arms, squeezing the daylights out of him and tearfully murmuring her happiness at him "goin' off an elopin' with me cook." Over her shoulder, he saw Moira and Irene standing arm in arm on the veranda, smiling widely at him.

How could it be, that these two full-grown, graceful-looking women had grown out of the two little sisters he remembered? When he thought of Moira and Irene, his mind's eye continued to picture them about the same age as . . . Ruthie and Colleen were right now. And Ruthie and Colleen, blossoming young women that they were, continued to live on in his mind as a pair of sticky-fingered little scamps barely out of toddlerhood.

With a bolt of melancholy, he realized that he knew his four sisters about as well as he did any four strangers. He hadn't attended Moira's wedding, nor Irene's, and he doubted he could recall either of their husbands' faces, much less their names. And the little ones . . . what did he know about them? Anything at all?

How was it, then, that their faces radiated such happiness for him? Such unconditional love?

A fresh burst of squealing ensued from Colleen as Emma was assisted out of the carriage by Zach. Just like that, with one last squeeze, Maureen released Ryan from her embrace and rushed over to greet her newest daughter-in-law. Moira and Irene, too, walked eagerly down the porch steps toward their frightened-looking new sister-in-law with glad, welcoming smiles on their faces.

Enough! Ryan's subconscious cried, while consciously he felt the cooling dampness of his mother's tears against his chest. Things had simply gone too far.

Ryan cursed to himself as he pulled the wet area of his shirt away from his chest and grimly stepped forward, determined to clear up this whole terrible misunderstanding. Painful as it was going to be to be informed otherwise, poor Ma couldn't be allowed to believe that he and Emma had gone off to Denver and married for reasons of love.

"Ma," Ryan called in his most commanding tone, a tone that his privates and sergeants and lieutenants knew meant business. "Ma, you need to know somethi—"

He trailed off with both outrage and dismay.

No one was listening to him. In fact, his delighted gaggle of kinswomen had surrounded his panic-stricken business partner bride and were ushering her up the veranda steps into the house.

"Come on, Ryan," Ruthie called shyly over her shoulder. "Come and see how pretty we've decorated the house for you and Emma."

They'd decorated the house? What the . . .

Ryan ordered a grinning Zach Ferguson to take care of the horses, then strode up the porch steps to where his mother and sisters stood with Emma in the foyer. The joyous chattering of the women was as painful to his ears as the whining of insects, and immediately his gaze was drawn to Emma's tearful, overwhelmed expression. *Please do something,* her brown eyes beseeched, making his stomach contract with purpose.

His gut further tightened as he looked past her and saw the gay bows and streamers decorating the staircase banister. A stepladder stood off to the side of the foyer, and a broad banner, crookedly hung and bearing the words WELCOME HOME NEWLYWEDS adorned the wall above the parlor doorway.

Ginny stood near the ladder with a clearly nervous expression on her face. Her gaze dropped to the floor—in shame?—when his eyes alit on her, further feeding the angry fire inside him. *How could she and Edward have let this go so far?* he wanted to bellow. What was the matter with them?

As Ryan visually dismissed Ginny and bore down on his mother, determined to lead her away by the arm and tell her everything, his arm was taken instead by that of his brother. "Come over here, Ryan," Edward pleaded in a quiet, urgent voice, pulling Ryan toward his office. "We need to talk, and fast."

"I don't have anything to say to you."

"Ryan, you've got to listen," Edward begged. "Ma came roaring home with Joey and the girls late this morning after she saw your wedding announcement in the paper. Before I knew which end was up, she went and gave me all kinds of hell because we tricked her, you know, because we ditched her in Cheyenne and didn't tell her about the wedding, and then, before I got a chance to say anything more, she started crying in my arms—I mean *really crying,* telling me how happy she was that you and Emma had found love." He sighed raggedly, helplessly. "What was I supposed to say?"

"For once in your life, have you ever considered the truth?"

Edward shook his head. "Look at her, Ryan. She's going to be devastated if we tell her the truth right now. She's already got a big party planned for tonight."

"Well, she'll just have to unplan it."

"Ryan, can't you please just play along with things, just for a little while?" Edward continued to plead. "Just until we figure out a way to tell Ma the truth without hurting her."

It was on the tip of Ryan's tongue to say, "Hell, no," but the words, "Oh, hell," came out of his mouth instead as he saw his mother weeping for joy and hugging Emma. Unable to contain their happiness, Ruthie and Colleen were dancing excitedly about the hallway, and then, from the rear of the house, burst Joey.

"Wyan! My Wyan!" he shouted, his voice carrying clearly over the female hubbub in the foyer. "My Wyan m-made Joey's best wish c-c-come true! My Wyan m-make Am-ma Joey's sister!"

Ryan looked toward the foyer, not being able to ever recall seeing a happier smile on Joey's face. Then, before he knew it, his youngest brother had pushed his way past the pack of women in the wide entryway and came at him, arms wide open.

"Oh, I wuv my Wyan s-so much," Joey said emotionally, hitting Ryan square in the chest. "An' my Am-ma, too. I wuv you all s-so m-m-m—" Choked up and not able to finish his sentence, Joey simply hugged Ryan more tightly, letting his body convey what he could not put into words.

Ryan's stiff resolution to get the truth out into the open was quickly crumbling away as Joey's chubby arms continued to squeeze him with all their might. Silence fell over the gathering, and quickly he glanced from Edward . . . to Ginny . . . to Emma . . . to his mother.

"Ryan, I truly cannot say I've ever been a happier woman," Maureen said gently from the foyer, her face beaming with radiance. "An' in you an' your sweet wife's honor, we've put together a little party for both of you."

With a heavy, heavy guilty heart, Emma watched the indecision flicker on Ryan's handsome face. She knew it wasn't fair that she'd left it to him to set matters straight, but she was simply overwhelmed by how all their elaborate plans had folded in upon themselves as easily as a house of cards would topple in a breeze.

Except for the sound of an occasional feminine sniffle, the Montgomery house was quiet; all eyes were focused on Ryan and Joey. Hesitantly one of Ryan's big hands came up to stroke Joey's dark head, and the inimical former army captain opened his mouth as if to speak.

What was he going to say? Emma wondered. What could he possibly say, except for the truth? As she made an attempt to swallow what little moisture was in her mouth, she asked herself what it was that she really wanted him to say.

Again she thought of the tender side of his personality she'd seen yesterday afternoon, of the strong yet gentle man who had picked her up from the floor and deposited her on the bed. And again as she remembered his touch, she felt the same flush of hot and cold and shakiness sweep through her entire body, and a small, secret part of her whispered, *Yes, you really do wish you could be part of this family: you really do wish you could have a marriage with this man.*

She had begun to think, that for all of Ryan's pretending that he didn't need anyone or anything, he really did. During the past difficult days she'd been allowed a few glimpses past the tough armor he wore, and she knew instinctively that there was something painful locked inside this man.

A long shiver of disbelief worked itself down Emma's spine as she saw Ryan's barely perceptible nod of acquiescence to Edward. She nearly collapsed to her knees, dumbfounded, when he took a deep breath and said, "Thanks for all you've done, Ma," gruffly, awkwardly.

"Emma, love," Maureen spoke, only barely penetrating Emma's astonishment. "Somethin' came in the mail for you an' Ryan. We picked it up on our way out here today."

Before she knew what was happening, one of Maureen's younger daughters—Colleen?—had thrust a sturdily wrapped brown-paper package into her hands.

"Go on, Emma, open it," the dark-haired girl hastened to add, a mischievous smile playing about her lips. "We're dying to know what's inside."

"Colleen!" Maureen exclaimed, confirming to Emma the girl's identity. "Such manners!"

"Sorry, Ma," Colleen apologized. Her merry hazel eyes did not look one bit sorry as they continued to plead with

Emma to hurry and open the package.

Emma turned the small package over in her hands, wondering who could have possibly mailed a parcel to Mr. and Mrs. Ryan Montgomery of Pine Bluffs. She glanced up at Ryan, who now stiffly stood, arm in arm, with Joey. Seeing Emma's gaze, Joey smiled even wider, and he joyfully waggled his fingers at her.

The expression in Ryan's dark eyes was impossible to read, but he had clearly allowed his wide-open window of opportunity to pass. He could have easily set the record straight—but he didn't. That must mean that he wanted her to go along with allowing Maureen to believe they were starry-eyed newlyweds.

Or was he expecting *her* to speak up?

Their eyes locked for a long moment, during which Emma felt a confusing rush of emotions. Not among the least was a strong sense of shame for continuing to deceive Maureen Montgomery . . . nor the strong pull of attraction she felt for Maureen's darkly magnetic eldest son.

"This package is addressed to both of us," she heard herself say to Ryan in a faint voice. "Wh-who do you think might have sent it?"

"Here, let me cut the string for you," Colleen said, miraculously producing a sharp pair of scissors.

Snip. The brown paper loosened as the string fell away, and several curious heads moved closer to see what had been wrapped inside the package. With shaking fingers, Emma withdrew a photograph from between two layers of cardboard. All the air seemed to leave her lungs as she gazed upon the images of her and Ryan, for instead of capturing the sullen, ill-tempered expression on Ryan's face, Mrs. Kessler's camera had somehow managed to record a stunningly handsome, kind-looking man seated in a pool of sunshine.

It was his eyes, mostly, that were different. Instead of the crisp blackness that normally emanated from his gaze, a certain softness shone in its place. A softness, as well, played around his full, shapely lips, giving him the countenance of a peacefully satisfied man. Her expression in the photograph was equally serene, without a trace of the gut-churning guilt and fear she had experienced throughout the wedding ceremony.

In fact, they looked every bit the very content, just-married couple. How on earth had Mrs. Kessler managed to take such a photograph? What kind of wizardry did the woman possess? Quickly Emma averted her gaze, feeling more disturbed than ever.

"Oh!" Colleen exclaimed reverently. "It's your wedding picture—it's so beautiful!"

"Aye, 'tis at that." Maureen sounded dangerously close to dissolving into tears once again as Emma handed her the photograph. "Oh, Ryan, you look so much like your da on our weddin' day. . . ."

As the Montgomery women crowded even closer, each trying to get a good look at the photograph, Emma silently read the enclosed note.

"Dear Mr. and Mrs. Montgomery," it began in a spidery hand, "I realize you were reluctant to be photographed, but I must insist that you accept this photograph as my wedding gift to you. Even the minister agrees that he has never seen such a perfect picture as this. Also, I hope you do not mind that my husband and I gave notice of your marriage to the paper. We were so honored to be a part of your special day, and we pray that God will bless you always. With much love and all best wishes for your new life together, Mary Kessler."

Now what, Emma Louise? her inner voice asked as she clutched the note to her chest and stepped to the side of the foyer. A strong feeling of unreality descended upon her as she leaned heavily against the wall, and she dumbly wondered if she could possibly be dreaming. A slight touch against her hand made her flinch, making her realize that she was, indeed, wide awake.

"Try not to worry, honey," Ginny nervously whispered, having sidled over to Emma while the other women *ooh*ed and *ah*ed over the photograph. "We're going to figure out some way to sort this whole mess out."

Sort this whole mess out? Emma could only utter a strangled sigh in response to her sister-in-law's encouraging words. The web of lies that had been spun had become too tangled, too snarled to simply "sort out." And woven into its very fabric, as well, were her strong and unsettling feelings for the man she had married.

How on earth she was going to find the strength to get through the party tonight, not to mention the days that lay ahead, she did not know.

Chapter Fourteen

"One more kiss, Montgomery!" Ferguson called above the din of the merrymakers. "An' not none of this little peckin' stuff like you been doin'. I want to see some *real* kissin'!"

A loud cheer arose from the persons assembled in the parlor, and McDermott's deep voice quickly joined Ferguson's in urging Ryan to "plant a good one" on the lips of his new wife. "C'mon, Captain," the rangy ranch foreman teased as Ryan remained motionless, "after all you done in the army, you surely ain't afraid of kissin' a little bitsy curly haired woman, are you?"

Emma felt Ryan's arm tighten around her shoulders, felt his tightly exhaled sigh against her frame. Throughout the evening they'd already been forced into several such demonstrations of their love for one another, and Emma didn't know how many more times she could paste a smile on her face and offer her lips to her unwilling husband's embrace without going stark raving mad.

News of the "love match" and subsequent marriage between Andrew Montgomery's eldest son and his widow's cook had, according to one local gossip, caused "jaws to drop and tongues to wag from one end of the Territory to the other all day long," for as far as most folks had been concerned, Captain Montgomery was a man destined for permanent bachelorhood, if they'd ever known one.

Despite the short notice, and despite the calving season being in full swing, a large number of friends, neighbors, and cowboys had responded to Maureen Montgomery's invitation and turned out this evening to bestow their congratulations and well wishes upon Ryan and Emma. The party had been going on nearly three hours now, and Emma was certain her nerves were truly about to snap. Dinner, a bath, and a few quiet moments alone had helped prepare her for the initial onslaught of curious and delighted folks who now filled the lower level of the Montgomery ranch house to bursting, but the energy it took to maintain the façade of a starry-eyed new bride had quickly drained her of what little reserves she possessed.

Or was it simply *Ryan* that unsettled her so?

With a deep silent sigh she forced her lips into what she hoped was some semblance of a smile and slowly tilted her face upward.

Reckless flustered feelings coursed through her afresh as Ryan's head bent toward hers. He was going to kiss her again. How many kisses was that now? Six? Seven? Possibly even eight, counting their kiss at the Kesslers' parsonage.

She swallowed, and then the circumstances . . . the people . . . the sounds . . . the room . . . *everything* faded away, everything except the downward sweeping motion of Ryan's lashes, the touch of his lips against hers.

So different than Jon Severson's.

And then the moment was over.

As Ryan abruptly released her and stepped away, the cheering calls of encouragement from the party-goers quickly turned to groans of disappointment. "You call that a kiss, Montgomery?" Ferguson wailed in mock outrage. "Now, git back over there, pucker up, an' do it right!"

"Ferguson, y' big troublemaker," Maureen scolded, pushing her way through the room to slip her arm around Emma's waist, "let the kids alone. I doubt me new daughter is accustomed to such public displays of affection. Now, you go on an' have yourself another slice of cake an' mind yer manners."

"Yes'm," Ferguson answered with grinning sheepishness, moving off toward the array of simple but delicious food and drink arranged on the dining room table.

Having been fetched from his chuck wagon this afternoon, the new cook, Mueller, had managed to produce an impressive amount of baked items for Maureen's party in a very short period of time. Several other tantalizing cakes, pies, cookies, and various other dishes had been added to the table throughout the evening, also, by thoughtful partygoers, making Emma realize that good, honest folks in the West weren't much different than good, honest folks in the Midwest.

"Come with me a minute, Emma, love," Maureen said with a gay smile, her eyes following the broad shoulders of her eldest son as he moved through the room. She nodded in satisfaction when he was hailed down and drawn into conversation by an elegantly suited elderly gentleman near the piano.

"Do you have someone else for me to meet?" Emma asked, allowing herself to be drawn along by her beaming mother-in-law. As much as she tried to appear interested about where Maureen was leading her, as much as she tried to smile pleasantly at the people they passed, Emma knew she must look terribly distracted. Ryan glanced at them as they walked from the parlor, his expression appearing relaxed but still inscrutable. A shiver of some unidentifiable emotion rippled through her torso as their glances briefly met.

Ryan Montgomery.

The man had thrown her so far off balance that she wasn't sure she would ever regain firm footing again in her life. Not only had he kept her wobbling this entire past month—especially these past four days, he'd nearly caused her to fall to her knees this afternoon when, for whatever reason or reasons, he'd failed to bring the truth about their marriage to the fore.

And this evening . . .

Each and every kiss he'd been obliged to give her continued to burn vividly on her lips in a way she was certain she would never forget. Each touch of his hand . . . his arm . . . the feel of his hard-muscled ribs and chest . . . the fleeting brush of a powerful thigh against her side . . . the freshly washed scent of him in her nostrils . . . each and every one of these things, too, had conspired to keep her off balance. Wobbling. Tipping. Falling.

As far as outward appearances were concerned, he was carrying out his role as bridegroom in a most believable manner.

"Come along upstairs with me, love," Maureen spoke. "I've been meanin' to seek a moment alone with you all evenin', an' it looks as if this is goin' to be my one an' only chance." Smiling and murmuring greetings to several guests as they passed through the foyer, Maureen determinedly guided Emma toward the staircase.

"We're going upstairs?"

"Aye, love, we are. Jus' bear me out."

"Am-ma! My Am-ma!" Joey joyfully cried, appearing at the top of the staircase. He descended carefully down the steps and enfolded her in his pudgy arms for at least the fiftieth time since she'd arrived back at the ranch. "My Am-ma! M-my crazy 'peshal friend . . . an' m-my sister!" He planted a wet kiss on her cheek, and his voice dropped to a husky whisper. "Oh, I w-wuv my Am-ma. An' God heared me! G-god heared my b-best wish."

"Have you been upstairs for a while, lamb?" Maureen asked, smiling tenderly at her son's obvious happiness while Emma died another hundred shameful deaths inside. "There's nothin' ailin' you, is there?"

Joey released Emma, shook his head, and put his hands over his ears. "Noisy, noisy, noisy p-peoples . . . tawk." Taking his hands away from his ears, he held them out before him, palms down, and brought his fingers down several times against his thumbs, in a manner reminiscent of lips loosely flapping. "Tawk, tawk, tawk, tawk."

"Why don't you come over here and talk, talk, talk to me, Joey?" Irene beckoned from farther down the hallway, having noticed that her little brother seemed to be at loose ends. She added a friendly wave to Emma. "Come on, Joseph Montgomery, I haven't had much of a chance to visit with you yet, and I'm starting to think you're so happy with your new sister that you've forgotten your old ones!"

Joey sighed and looked back and forth between his two "sisters." He sighed again, indecision apparent on his broad face. "I-ween sister n-need Joey now," he finally said, leveling a melting, apologetic gaze at Emma.

"Go ahead, Joey, by all means," Emma replied graciously, her love for this dear young man welling in her heart as she realized how carefully he considered her feelings. "I'll look forward to spending some time with you tomorrow."

"Ok-kay!"

Maureen shook her head as Joey hurried down the hall to join his sister, then motioned for Emma to join her in climbing the stairs. "I'm not sayin' I'm understandin' any of it, but I have all the proof I need that the Lord used you to work miracles with not one of my boys, but two," she said softly as she reached the top landing. Emotion was apparent in her lilting voice, and her hazel eyes shimmered with tears. "Though we're without Andrew now, rest his soul, we Montgomerys are truly beginnin' to come together again as a family. An' *you're* the one puttin' us back together, Emma Montgomery." Quickly she brushed at her eyes, one first, then the other, with a rough, chapped knuckle. "I knew you was a special one, Emma, I knew it in me heart the very first time I saw you shiverin' out on the front porch. There's such sweetness, such goodness in you that a person cannot help but be attracted to it."

Such sweetness in her? Such goodness? More like such wickedness, such weakness, Emma thought, feeling more ashamed than ever. As she once again recalled her mother's abhorrence for *any* kind of lying, she also wondered how, in a million years, a few simple little lies could have possibly turned into a tangled-up nightmare such as this.

For heaven's sake, her brother had disowned her. Worse still, Mr. Kessler had been led to believe she was expecting, and two newspapers had run stories of her marriage to Ryan Montgomery—a marriage that had deliberately been performed a hundred-and-fifty-some-odd miles away

from Pine Bluffs in order to ensure Ryan's anonymity—
yet now, tonight, it seemed as if every human being west
of the Mississippi knew Captain Montgomery had taken
a bride.

Oh, Lord, what else could possibly happen?

Don't even ask, a superstitious voice inside her cautioned. In fact, she decided, before things got any worse, she
was going to pin Ryan down this very night about just what
it was he had in mind to do about their situation—about
exactly *when* and *what* he was going to tell Maureen.

Also, she found it most disconcerting that, for all Ryan's
anger toward her and her "foolproof" idea of a secret
business arrangement marriage, he had made a conscious
decision this afternoon, in the eyes of his family and community, to continue to play the role of bridegroom.

Why?

"Come closer, Emma." Maureen had already moved down
the hallway and stood outside the second door on the right.
"I have a little somethin' to show you."

Feeling numb and sick all at once, Emma slowly walked
toward her temporary mother-in-law.

"Cover your eyes, now."

"Cover my eyes?"

"Jus' humor an' old woman, dear, will you?" Maureen
chuckled as she reached for Emma's hands and gently
guided them toward her face. "Mustn't peek."

What on earth? Emma wondered as she obediently placed
her hands over her eyes, at the same time having the sinking
feeling that one more awful thing was about to happen.
The soft squeaking of the door's hinges only intensified
the feeling.

"All right, love, you can open your eyes."

Slowly Emma brought her hands down from her face
and saw that she was standing in the open doorway of a
generous-sized, beautifully decorated bedchamber. Golden
lamplight bathed the room with its mellow glow, making
everything within the room appear soft, muted. Arrangements of fresh, fragrant wildflowers and grasses spilled
from vases, the bed was turned down invitingly, and, with
a shock, Emma's eyes lit on her trunk.

"Wha—" she started to say, certain that her eyes had nearly popped from their sockets. "You can't possibly mean—"

Maureen nodded, a happy yet melancholic smile playing about her lips. "I do indeed, an' I'll not hear a word to the contrary. All four o' me girls worked themselves like mules earlier this evenin' tryin' to get everyone's belongin's switched about without you or Ryan knowin' they was up to anythin'. We wanted to keep it a surprise, you see."

"But—"

"But nothin'. I've no longer a need for a room this size; I'll be takin' the one down the hall that Ryan's been usin' off an' on. This room used t' belong to me an' Andrew, daughter, but as of tonight I'm honored to say it's yours an' Ryan's."

Hers and Ryan's . . .

That meant . . . oh, Mother Mary and all the saints and angels preserve her soul . . . that meant that she was going to have to *sleep* with Ryan Montgomery. She hadn't even considered the possibility this afternoon when Ryan had allowed his opportunity to expose the truth to slip by.

"An' maybe, jus' maybe, God willin', I'll be bouncin' a wee one on my knee yet," Maureen shyly hinted, making Emma's heart freeze with panic. The Montgomery matriarch smiled and shook her head in mock disgust. "There's Moira an' her Texan husband, Billy . . . an' Irene an' her long-legged man, Jacob . . . an' me own Edward an' his dear, sweet Virginia . . . an' not a one of 'em seems to be in any kind o' hurry to make a grandmother of me. You'd think Edward an' Ginny would have gotten around to it by now . . . they've been married the longest, nigh on two years."

"W-well, I'm sure—"

"Aye, love, I know the wee ones will come in time. It's just me selfish yearnin's that rear themselves from time t' time. Now why don't you go on into your new room an' freshen up a bit? You're lookin' mighty peaked, daughter . . . an' I shouldn't wonder after the past several days you've had. I'll make your excuses below an' let your new husband know you've retired." Maureen turned to go back down the hallway, then paused, half turning back toward Emma. "An' may God bless you again an' again for your healin' touch on the Montgomery family," she added softly.

Emma felt lower than dirt as she watched Maureen gracefully move down the hall and disappear down the stairs. She heard a few words of her mother-in-law's lilting Irish brogue drift back to her as Maureen cheerily greeted a Mrs. Radel, but her voice was soon engulfed by the party's happy, noisy sounds. The celebration grew even more merry, a few moments later, as a skilled pair of hands began to play an animated tune on the piano.

Emma sighed and turned her head to look into her inviting new bedchamber, not quite daring to step inside. The room was lovely, no question about it, and the fluffy bed beckoned to her tired body. She looked back down the deserted hallway, then at the bed once more.

Perhaps it wouldn't hurt to lie down for just a couple minutes.

As she walked into the room and closed the door behind her, she realized that if this situation hadn't gotten so monstrously out of hand, or, specifically, if she weren't so directly involved, it would almost be laughable. Grandchildren, indeed. She walked to the bed and tested the mattress with her hand.

It felt divine; absolutely divine.

With her fingers caressing the soft linen bedclothes, Emma looked around the room and tried not to let the beguiling smell of sweet fresh grasses and flowers intrude upon her consciousness. It was no use; she yawned. The sounds of the party were muted in here; far away. A heavy wave of tiredness crashed over her, making her eyelids droop. As she gave in to her physical and emotional weariness and sank across the end of the bed, a wry smile flitted across her face.

So you wanted some time to talk to Ryan Montgomery alone tonight, did you, Emma Louise? she asked herself, wrapping her arms around a plump pillow and burying her face in its softness.

Looks like you've been granted the whole night.

The majority of the party-goers had disbursed by the time Ryan climbed the staircase and turned to the left. As he trudged heavily down the hall toward what had always been his parents' room, he realized that a wide spectrum of conflicting thoughts assailed him.

Exhaustion, anger, weariness, belligerence, fatigue, hostility . . . curious expectancy.

His jaw had nearly dropped from its hinges when Ma had informed him, an hour or so ago, that Emma had retired to "their" room and was waiting for him. In truth, he hadn't given any thought to his and Emma's sleeping arrangements this afternoon when, in a moment of weakness, he'd allowed Edward to manipulate him into this newest set of circumstances.

It's not Edward's fault that you've fallen into his lying ways, an inner voice criticized. *You could have easily set matters straight—but you didn't.*

It wasn't only the fact that Ma's party would have been ruined . . . nor was it because all his sisters had dropped what they were doing and rushed home: The truth had stuck in his craw this afternoon because he'd known how completely it would have crushed his mother's joy. And Joey's.

He just couldn't hurt either of them one more time.

Ryan realized he'd stopped outside the door of his new bedchamber and was blankly staring at the panels. Beyond this wooden barrier his bride awaited him. Sighing, he ran his hand through his hair and glanced down to make sure his shirt was neatly tucked in.

Why'd you do that, Montgomery?

I don't know, he answered himself, trying not to think about the sweetness of Emma's warm fragrance, the sweetness of Emma's soft lips, the sweetness of Emma's petite form against his side. He sighed again, thinking that things between him and Emma had simply gotten out of control. Besides that, he was now trapped in a predicament from which there was no graceful way to extricate himself. When Ma learned the truth—and, sooner or later, she *would* have to learn the truth—she was going to be sadly disappointed in all of them.

What's going to happen to Emma then? a voice inside him asked. *Where will she go? Her brother said he'd washed his hands of her. . . .*

Enough! Ryan turned the knob and opened the door, harshly telling himself that he'd thought quite enough of those kinds of thoughts. The glow of the lamp, burning softly on the dresser and illuminating the room with its golden glow, struck him first of all. His sharp eyes traveled around the room then, not failing to notice the vases of fresh flowers . . . nor the cunning way the covers were folded down from the top of the bed . . . nor the lovely young woman who lay sleeping on her side across the end of the bed.

Emma.

Her name silently hummed on his lips as he pushed the door closed. *Emma.* From where he stood he had an excellent view of a pair of stylish boots and trim ankles. His gaze traveled past them, taking in the shapely bestockinged calves that peeked out from beneath her skirts. *God knows you did enough kissing and discreet feeling tonight, Montgomery, but a gentleman wouldn't take advantage of a lady while she's sleeping,* a voice inside him admonished, dissuading him not at all from continuing to visually feast on the charming view she unwittingly presented.

Silently he walked to the foot of the bed, looking his fill of the petite woman. How could she be so dainty, so delicate . . . yet so womanly? His gaze followed the pleasing line of trim waist that flared gently into rounded hip, then, traveling in the opposite direction, his hungry eyes drank in the sight of a shadowy curve of breast just visible beneath the back of her upper arm.

Emma Taylor had a body that begged for a man's caress, if he'd ever seen one.

Emma Montgomery, he quickly amended, reminding himself that he and his temporary wife had some talking to do, and the sooner the better. He reached his hand out to shake her to wakefulness, but stopped his fingers just a fraction of an inch from her elbow, remembering the feelings that had flooded through him when he'd touched her yesterday.

Touched her—hell! his subconscious decried. He'd scooped her up off the hotel floor and carried her to bed, and he hadn't wanted to stop there. Even though she was crying as if she'd lost her best friend, all he could think about was whether or not her lips would taste the same as they had after the wedding ceremony . . . and whether or not they'd yield to him . . . whether or not *she'd* yield to him. . . .

Emma stirred and exhaled deeply, causing the errant brown curl that lay across her cheek to flutter. Carefully Ryan pulled himself upright and backed away from the bed. Best not to even lay a finger on her. Things would be clearer in the morning, anyhow, with a good night's sleep separating the insanity of the past several days and a rational, intelligent discussion of the best possible solutions to their very large problems.

As he cast his glance around the room, looking for a likely spot to settle himself on the floor for the night, it struck him that he'd just thought of his problem as "their" problems—as in *his* and *Emma's* problems. Silently he cursed to himself one more time.

He also realized, however, that he hadn't thought of Jim Hopper's suicide in . . . in how many days now?

Shaking his head, Ryan roughly untucked his shirt from his pants and glanced back at the bed. He'd just take a few pillows from the bed and find a blanket and . . . he froze with his hand on his belt buckle, a silent shock running through him as he realized Emma's lustrous brown eyes were open and fixed on him.

"We need to talk, Ryan," she finally said in a voice thick with sleep, breaking the long silence that had drawn out between them. Propping herself up on one elbow, she cradled her cheek in her hand, still keeping her eyes on his. "I don't know what you have in mind for the rest of the summer, but we can't go on living out this lie . . . *I* can't go on living out this lie."

Ryan didn't immediately answer, finding his attention quite captured by the rosy pink flush of Emma's cheeks. If he'd thought her a charming picture while she slept, the picture paled in comparison to how she looked at this moment. Sleepy. Sensuous. Artlessly seductive.

"Well, I don't know what we can do to change things tonight," he replied slowly, trying not to imagine what it would be like to take this woman in his arms and use the marriage bed exactly for what it was intended.

Making long slow love.

What's the matter with you, Montgomery? an inner voice castigated. Had the past nine years of hardness, sacrifice, and self-denial flown straight out the window? Had he forgotten his training at the Point? The meaning of discipline? He had to snap out of it—he and this woman needed to put their heads together and come up with a way to . . . His thoughts broke off when he realized Emma was speaking.

" . . . got to find some way to tell your mother the truth. I hope your family will find some way, someday, to forgive me for my terrible errors in judgment." In a graceful movement she pushed herself to an upright sitting position, hugging the pillow in her arms. When she spoke again, her voice was earnest, on the verge of tears. "I know I've apologized over and over to you, Ryan, but let me say again how sorry I am for involving you in all of this . . . this . . ." She closed her eyes for a moment, then began again, a deeper flush stealing across her cheeks. "And now here we are in this beautiful room . . ." She gestured at the flowers, the softly burning lamp, then finally at him.

The moment stretched out while something earthy and sensual sizzled in the air between them. Ryan nearly groaned aloud as she moistened her full lips with the tip of her tongue, and he watched her carefully, not knowing what she was going to say . . . in truth, not knowing what it was he wanted her to say.

"I'd be lying if I said your kisses did nothing to me," Emma admitted plainly, painfully, surprising him with her candor, "but nothing more than that can happen, Ryan. I can't sleep with you in this bed." She dropped her gaze to the pillow in her arms. "No matter that we spoke the words before a man of God," she continued in a low voice, "and no matter how married your mother thinks we are, I cannot sleep with any man until I am truly married."

"Why not?"

Was it really any of his business? Ryan knew the tone of his voice was sharp, petulant, but the coiled sexual tension inside him, buried too deeply for too long, had awakened to full life. It had also occurred to him—in the neighborhood of several hundred times during the past several days— that he could undoubtedly use Emma's guilt to gain her favors.

Sexual recompensation for his hardship.

Really, what could she do about it? Who could she complain to? She was his wife . . . he was her husband . . . and they *had* wed at her insistence. Legally.

"Because . . . because I'm still a . . ." She glanced up at him with an expression of extreme discomfiture.

"Still a what . . . still a virgin?"

Emma's shining nutmeg-colored curls bobbed in the golden lamplight as she dropped her head in shame and nodded.

A virgin. Ryan found himself nodding, also, as he wondered just what his reasons had been for pushing Emma to confirm her sexual purity. Had he really been hoping she would throw all caution to the wind and give in to the tugging flow of primitive desire between them? He took no pleasure in her present embarrassment; however, an inordinate amount of satisfaction surged through him at learning of her chasteness. Why that should please him so immensely, he did not understand; he only knew it pleased him more than anything he'd heard in a great long while.

"Your virginity is nothing to be ashamed of, Emma. On the contrary," he said gently, the drastic changes in his voice causing her to lift her heart-shaped face and stare warily at him. "I'll sleep on the floor until we get things . . . straightened out." He sighed deeply and took a step backward. Bringing his hands to his face, he blocked out the innocent, seductive sight of the sleepy-eyed woman who sat on the end of the bed. Willed away the prurient fire that raged within his loins and his mind.

"Th-thank you," came Emma's hesitant and quite obviously relieved reply. "You're so different than Jon, but I really didn't think you would . . . you know, use force . . ."

Her words trailed off uncomfortably.

Jon? A completely reasonable stirring of jealousy assailed Ryan as he brought his hands stiffly back down to his sides. Jon who? Completely ignoring Emma's unflattering implications as to his moral principles, Ryan fixed his gaze on her lovely face, trying to see, deep in her eyes, who this Jon man was . . . and what he meant to her.

"Jon Severson is the man my brother wants me to marry," Emma clarified just a moment later, sparing him from the indignity of having to ask. She blinked, then dropped her gaze in shyness . . . or was it a sudden fascination with the stray thread from the side seam of the pillowcase that she twisted round and round her finger?

"And?" he prompted, feeling his eyes narrow.

She sighed and continued to busily twist the thread around her finger. "And I'll probably end up marrying him some day," she said, speaking to the pillow in a small, resigned voice, "unless my extremely unbecoming opinions and actions, of late, have managed to destroy his overprotective, patronizing, but, alas, completely loyal feelings for me." At that quiet burst of mutiny, she fell silent.

What the hell did all that mean? Ryan wondered, continuing to stare at the headful of shining brown curls for several seconds longer. And furthermore, how the hell had this little bit of a woman managed to turn his life, his thoughts, and his emotions, in no particular order, into utter chaos? With the way things were going, in no time at all he'd end up like the thread from the pillowcase—wrapped completely around her finger.

Would that really be so bad?

Best to call it a night before anything else happened, he decided, stalking over to the chair near the window and grabbing the two decorative throw pillows from its seat. Emma remained silent as he tossed the pillows to the floor and blew out the lamp, and while he settled his frame on the carpeted hardwood floor, he heard the rustling of bedcovers—or, perhaps, of clothing?—then the sound of a body settling into a mattress.

If nothing else, at least Miss Curly could take a hint.

The room was quiet except for the sound of a few voices coming faintly through the floor. Ryan reached about for the pillows, finding them near one another, and, as he stacked the thin needlepoint cushions one upon the other and lay his head upon this pitiful excuse for a pillow, he realized his body throbbed with tiredness.

And more than tiredness.

"Ryan?" Emma whispered.

He couldn't help the deep sigh that preceded his exasperated, "What is it now?"

"If you . . . ah, want the bed, you can have it. I don't mind sleeping on the floor."

"Stay in the bed."

There. That seemed to shut her up. He sighed again and closed his eyes, pushing his head back firmly into the flimsy little pillows. He supposed he would want a blanket when it cooled off later in the night, but right now he was feeling plenty hot.

The indistinct sound of a woman's giggle drifted up through the floor to his ears, and he realized how much happiness had inhabited this home tonight, how much joy. He hated to admit it, even to himself, but he *had* enjoyed himself to a certain degree tonight. Enjoyed visiting with the neighbors, the friends . . . and with his sisters.

Moira and Irene were a pair of delightful, witty women, he had discovered. The younger girls, Ruthie and Colleen, were at those awkward, giggling, early adolescent ages, but they'd come up to talk to him several times through the course of the evening, and impulsive Colleen had even taken his hand in hers several times, he recalled with more than a little wonder. She had to have heard—for that matter, all his sisters had to have heard—the accounts of his foulness since he'd resigned his commission and come home. Yet, none of them seemed intimidated by him; in fact, they seemed determined to win him over with their love.

Edward was intelligent enough to have kept his distance during the party. Where he was concerned, however, something funny had happened inside Ryan during the relaxed, easy mood of the party. The barbed anger he'd been harboring toward his next eldest brother seemed to have dissipated, to a large degree, as people joked and talked and smiled and generally had a good time. It also occurred to him that it couldn't have been easy for a grieving Edward to immediately step into his father's large shoes, nor was it fair for Ryan or anyone else to expect that Edward might not make a misstep or two as he attempted to stride forward bravely.

Ryan realized he'd been awfully hard on Edward back in Denver, and to be perfectly truthful, he was indeed looking forward to the challenge of rebuilding the ranch to its former financial strength—with his brother's help.

As he thought of Joey, though, his newfound optimism slipped quite a few notches. After his youngest brother's uninhibited burst of emotion this afternoon, he had once again erected his armor of caution and wary watchfulness where Ryan was concerned. Ryan supposed he couldn't blame Joey for that, for he realized he'd done a great deal of damage, during the past several weeks, to the very special relationship they had shared over the years.

He knew he'd damaged his relationship with his mother, as well. Ryan couldn't help the small, sad smile that curved his lips as he wondered how long it had been since he'd seen his mother's eyes sparkle with as much delight as they had tonight. The entire afternoon and evening, her small person had radiated with a giant aura of lightheartedness and gaiety, such as he had not seen since his childhood days in Nebraska.

How could the news of his marriage have caused such rapture in her, especially after he'd been little more than a stranger to her for so many years? What kind of capacity for love and forgiveness did she hold? Particularly in light of the fact that he'd treated his father, the man his mother had loved with all her heart, in a truly unforgivable fashion for years.

"Really, Ryan," came Emma's whisper on the late-night air, interrupting his weighty reflections with an immediate picture of her winsome face in his mind's eye. "I'd be happy to sleep on the floor. In fact, it would make me feel better if you would allow me to—"

"Go to sleep, Emma." He cut her off, trying at the same time to erase the beguiling mental image that simply refused to be erased. He heard her change position in the bed, heard her long, nearly silent sigh.

He wondered, once again, what it would be like to know her in the most intimate way a man could know a woman.

"I can't sleep," she whispered in reply. "I keep thinking about . . . things."

Sweet Jesus, so did he.

"I don't know if you heard the real reasons behind my coming to your ranch," she began after a long pause, "but it all started with this idea I had for a collectibles shop. . . ."

There was going to be no sleep for either of them for a very long time, Ryan thought with irritation as he listened to Emma speak about her life back in St. Paul. He also found himself listening to her words with a certain degree of interest, however, wondering once again how much a part of her life this Jon Severson had been . . . or still was.

Chapter
Fifteen

Emma awoke early, before first light. For just a moment she was disoriented, not knowing where or even who she was, but the incredible events of the past days rapidly came pouring back into her mind . . . as did another startling realization.

She'd slept in the same room as Ryan Montgomery.

Or had she? For all she knew, he could have gotten up after she'd fallen asleep and . . . *And what?* her rapidly unfogging brain questioned with alarm. He could have done *anything* after she'd fallen asleep. Quickly she ran her hands over her clothing, finding everything securely in place.

She sighed in relief, wondering if Ryan still lay on the floor. With vivid clarity, she remembered the heated feelings that had stirred then sizzled between them last night, and she blushed with mortification to think that she and Ryan had actually discussed . . . *marital* activities. Good Lord, she'd even admitted her virginity to him, the most personal, private thing about her. What ever had possessed her to do that?

Michael had been correct—she was being corrupted— slowly, insidiously, but surely corrupted. She was certain to be consigned to perdition for all time for the bolt of pure excitement that had zinged through her as she'd

awakened from her brief nap last evening to see Ryan
standing before her, pulling his shirt from his pants. She
swallowed hard, remembering the flash of lean hard belly,
the careless stance, the powerful arms and shoulders . . .
and his hungry, burning eyes.

The opaque veil that had been drawn tightly over Ryan's
dark eyes during the seemingly endless evening had been
loosened—nay, incinerated—as his gaze had clearly com-
municated his physical want for her. As she sighed again
and toyed with the edge of the coverlet, Emma admitted
to herself that a physical want had arisen inside her last
evening. A desire . . . a wild, curious hunger to know more
of his kisses . . . and whatever may have followed.

Yet she'd been so uncomfortable with her traitorous
emotions, so nervous that something untoward might happen between herself and this man that caused her heart to
pound so wildly in her chest, that she'd chattered on and
on like an idiot after he'd blown out the lamp and settled
himself on the floor. She'd undoubtedly managed to bore
him senseless . . . or straight into slumber. How long—or
how briefly—he'd lain awake listening to her ramblings,
she couldn't say. The conversation had been markedly one-
sided, she recalled with chagrin, remembering how Ryan
had not offered any information in return about himself.

At least it had been better to bore him to sleep than to . . .
than to do the secret, sinful things his eyes had suggested.
A tingle shot downward from her breast to her navel as she
resolutely tried to push all thoughts of Ryan Montgomery's
bone-melting kisses from her mind.

If nothing else good had come of last night, though, at
least they had come to a sort of agreement, albeit short-
term, about what to do about Maureen and their marriage.
Ryan had pointed out that his mother had plans to take Joey
and the younger girls back to Cheyenne in a day or two and,
after a long pause, had tautly asked if Emma thought she
could continue the ruse just until then.

The thought of spending even one more night in the same
bedchamber with Ryan Montgomery had sent a thousand
feelings rushing through her in the space of a second, and
her riotous, reckless feelings had won out over the prim and

circumspect urgings of her conscience to separate herself from this man.

Emma sat upright in bed as she heard the sound of a body stirring, a deep breath being taken, then exhaled. Ryan *was* still on the floor, then. He couldn't have had a very comfortable night.

Pushing the covers aside, she quietly clambered out of the bed and felt her way to her trunk. From where she stood at the foot of the bed, she heard Ryan's slow rhythmic breathing. Good; he was still asleep. If she hurried, she could take a hairbrush and change of clothing downstairs and take care of her morning ablutions in the kitchen before anyone else was up.

Then it was back to work.

The new cook, Mueller, as well as the other Montgomery cowhands who had been able to attend the party last night, were already back out at the roundup camp. Right before Maureen had shooed Ferguson over to the dessert table, Emma had heard McDermott tell the outspoken cowboy that they couldn't stay too much longer, that they had to get back out on the range.

At the thought of not having to cook for all those hungry men any longer, Emma said a silent prayer of thanks. It wasn't that she didn't like them; on the contrary, she'd rather missed their jovial company during the past several days. It was surely providential, however, that Mueller had happened along when he did. A chill ran through her as she thought of how inadequately prepared she would have been to transfer her meager cookstove abilities to grueling open-range food preparation.

By feel, she managed, almost noiselessly, to locate the things she needed from her trunk and find her way to the door. The second-story hallway was every bit as dark as the bedchamber she had just exited, but the blackness about her melted to tones of gray as she carefully made her way down the stairs and walked to the kitchen.

The first faint rays of morning light were visible beyond the barn's large black silhouette, and Emma estimated the time to be somewhere in the neighborhood of five o'clock. Though the house was perfectly quiet, she completed her cleansing and changed her clothing with haste lest anyone awaken and find her in such an inappropriate state.

Three quarters of an hour later, an admirable fire was burning in the cookstove, the bread sponge had been finished and kneaded, and two large pans of sweet rolls were rising inside the warming oven. Emma began cleaning up the sticky, floury surface of the worktable with a sense of satisfaction, realizing she'd actually missed certain elements of her cooking duties. Though she would be loath to ever admit it aloud, there was something peaceful, something settling about kneading bread.

"What in heaven's name are you doin', love?"

The sound of Maureen's voice made Emma jump, for she hadn't heard her mother-in-law's footsteps overhead, nor had she heard her come into the kitchen. "Goodness!" she said involuntarily, bringing the wet dishrag up to her throat. "You startled me."

"Aye, an' I'm sorry for that, love," Maureen apologized. "But just what do you think you're doin'? You're not me cook any longer—you're me daughter."

"And your daughters can't cook?" Though Emma's quick reply was glibly good-natured, she mentally scrambled to find a way to convince Maureen that she *wanted* to continue cooking over the summer. "What would you have me do, then?" she asked with wide-eyed simplicity, bringing her hand—and the wet dishrag—down from her throat and gesturing about the room.

"You don't have to do anythin'. You've already done more than I could ever ask, Emma Montgomery."

"But if I don't cook, who will?" she asked logically. "*Ginny*? She's the first person to admit that she can't boil water without burning it. You're going back to Cheyenne in another day or two, and then—"

"Well, I been thinkin' about that, daughter . . ."

An uneasy feeling rose inside Emma's breast at her mother-in-law's contemplative expression. Maureen *was* going to take the younger girls back to Cheyenne to finish out the school term . . . *wasn't she?*

" . . . and I came to realize, last night, how truly painful it's been havin' me family split up an' livin' here, there, an' everywhere. I'm thinkin' I'll just be takin' Irene up on her offer of stayin' here an' tutorin' the little ones till the end of the term. She taught school the two years before she was married, you know, an' her Jacob is goin' to Santa Fe on business at the beginnin' o' next week, anyhow."

"S-so you're all going to stay . . . here?"

"Aye, daughter, all exceptin' Moira. Her Billy's probably already missin' her somethin' fierce. She's promised to come visit soon, though, an' bring her big Texan man along with her. He's quite a character, that Billy . . ."

Now what? Emma couldn't help herself from frantically thinking. Maureen had apparently taken the news of her and Ryan's marriage quite seriously, viewing their joining as a miracle . . . a catalyst for the rebirth and renewal of the Montgomery family.

Of course she took the news of your marriage seriously, Emma Louise, her conscience berated. *Why wouldn't she? Marriage is one of the most serious commitments of a lifetime. . . .*

" . . . and I'll be lookin' into hirin' a new cook for the summer," Maureen was saying. "I can hardly believe me good fortune that Mueller's been makin' noises like he wants to stay on here at the ranch, come fall. Says he's gettin' too old to keep chasin' around the countryside, driftin' from job to job. So we'll just find us a girl to cook over the summer, and—"

"No, no, you don't have to do that," Emma interrupted as feelings of shame threatened to overwhelm her. "Just because I m-married Ryan doesn't mean that I can't continue cooking. You all have your various duties around here . . . let this be mine. Please?"

"You actually *want* to keep cookin'?"

"Well, you just said Mueller was likely to stay on in the fall. Why don't I cook until then? It's only going to be . . ." Emma cleared her throat, finding it difficult to say the next word. " . . . family here at the house. Then you won't have to go to the trouble of hiring another cook. Surely you haven't forgotten all the trouble you had finding a cook this spring?" As she spoke, her mind raced with panic, wondering what she and Ryan were going to do about this newest change of events. Would it be for the best to admit the truth to Maureen right now, before things went any further, or to continue to live out the farce . . . *for the whole summer long*?

Maureen absently brushed at the small pile of flour before her on the worktable. "Aye, daughter, I haven't forgotten what a trial it was findin' a cook." A gentle smile graced her aging but still lovely features, and she nodded her head in assent. "If you're truly wantin' to cook for us, dear, I guess I cannot be tellin' you nay. We'll take turns at it, though, you an' I, an' if we can manage to teach Virginia a few things along the way, so much the better." Reaching across the worktable, she laid her hand across Emma's. "You're simply too good to be true, Emma Montgomery. Too good to be true."

Ryan awoke on the floor of his mother's bedchamber feeling stiff, sore, and cranky. His whole body ached, and his neck seemed to be frozen in a most uncomfortable position. A wide swath of sunshine poured from the window onto his legs and feet, making him feel unbearably overheated, and he judged that dawn had long since passed. How could he have slept so late? A sudden thought struck him and he quickly sat up, suppressing a groan at the resulting pain in his aching ribs and back.

So Emma was already up.

As he slowly stretched his muscles and pushed himself to his feet, he wondered how she'd managed to rise so quietly so as not to awaken him. *Maybe she wasn't quiet at all, Montgomery*, a part of his mind berated as he stared first at the rumpled bedclothes, then at the open trunk of female clothing in front of him, *maybe she danced around and made all kinds of noise and you didn't hear her because you've turned into such a weak and feeble slacker that* . . .

Something in the trunk caught his eye . . . a small strip of vivid blue fabric just barely visible alongside the serviceable gray skirt that sat, neatly folded but slightly askew, on top of the pile of Emma's things. Unbidden curiosity arose inside him as he stared at the fabric, wondering what it was.

He'd seen Emma in a navy-blue skirt or dress or some such in the past—he couldn't recall the garment for certain—but he was certain that he'd never seen her in anything quite this shade of blue.

Ignoring the voice inside him that told him to go downstairs, eat breakfast, and promptly begin his audit of the books, he bent over and reached into the trunk. His fingertips recognized the vivid blue fabric as silk, and a gentle tug allowed the lightweight garment to slide smoothly free of the trunk.

His mouth ran dry at the sight of the petite pair of blue silk knickerbocker drawers he held in his right hand. God in heaven, Emma wore undergarments such as this? As his left hand slowly came up and caressed the garment's richly embroidered waistband, the delicate fragrance of the trunk's sachet touched his nostrils.

His imagination ran wild.

Closing his eyes, Ryan briefly allowed himself the pleasure of fantasizing how Emma might look wearing such attire . . . and how she might look wearing nothing at all. The turbulent sexual thoughts and feelings he'd tried to push away last evening came crashing back over him, nearly felling him with their intensity, and desire, hot and sweet, coursed all through him as he tried to recall if he'd ever wanted a woman as badly as he did Emma Taylor . . . Montgomery.

The slamming of a door further down the hall and the not-so-distant sound of his younger sisters' laughter had the same effect as a bucket of cold water being thrown in Ryan's face. Blanching at the thought of anyone happening upon him as he fingered Emma's underthings like a lustful adolescent, he roughly shook his head and tucked the frilly knickerbockers back beneath the gray skirt, closing his mind to the possibility of how many more tantalizing silken delights might possibly be hidden below.

Still, he wondered with a growing sense of frustration, how was he going to be able to look at Emma the same way ever again without wondering what filmy feminine delicacies lay beneath her serviceable work clothing? Without imagining her slender hips and legs encased in . . .

Sighing as he tucked the tails of his badly wrinkled shirt into the waist of his badly wrinkled trousers, Ryan steeled himself for the long day of ledger work that lay ahead, a day that had no place for Emma and whatever undergarments she may—or may not—be wearing.

"G-good supper, Am-ma," Joey complimented as he carefully dried a plate. Turning himself nearly all the way around to look at her, he nodded in a definite manner. "Ch-chicken taste good." With a clatter, the clean dry plate joined its stack of mates on the worktable. "Too bad Wyan no taste. Ed-wer no taste."

"No taste?" Emma distractedly questioned as she stared at the large bowl containing the bread sponge she was making. How many quarts of flour had she already put in? Three? Four? She simply couldn't remember. Simply couldn't concentrate . . .

"No taste ch-chicken," Joey elucidated. "H-hurry . . . eat f-fast. G-gone. Go work m-more."

"Oh . . . yes, you're right. Ryan and Edward have been taking their meals so quickly that they probably haven't been tasting any of their food, have they?"

As Joey chattered on, so obviously pleased to be back into their evening routine, Emma's mind haphazardly bounded from subject to subject. Things seemed so unreal, so unbelievable, for despite the fact that Ryan was fully aware that his mother and three of his four sisters were not going back to Cheyenne, he still had not done anything to clarify his true relationship with her.

He didn't bring it up. She didn't bring it up. And that baffled and flustered her all at once, because they had been back at the ranch for a little more than two weeks now. Well, at least *she* had been here for a little more than two weeks, she amended, reminding herself that Ryan had been gone for several of those days.

And nights.

As she thought of the nights they had spent together, Emma sighed and gave the floury mixture a halfhearted stir. Too thin. She dumped another quart of flour on top of the gooey mass in the bowl and began to stir in earnest, realizing, at the same time, that no matter how many times she tried to deny it, a certain nameless something smoldered in the air between her and Ryan. Something warm; nay, something hot . . . and something she didn't fully understand.

As Joey had mentioned, both Ryan and Edward had been terribly occupied of late—or was it preoccupied?—with the business of running the ranch. First it was the in-depth accounting of the books that had consumed them, then, after a tersely worded announcement from Ryan, he and Edward had departed to the mountainside silver mine, located in the Medicine Bow range west of Laramie, to suspend operations.

They had been gone five days. Five long, painful days during which Emma grew to know and love the Montgomery family all the more, at the same time despairing the fact that she was living a life of shameful lies and deceit and was going to one day soon greatly disappoint each and every one of them. The Montgomerys were good, honest people—all of them so dear—while she was nothing better than a common liar, a despicable thief of their affections.

It was with great perplexity, also, that she had felt her heart quicken when Ryan and Edward had returned to the ranch three nights ago. *Quicken?* her inner voice scoffed. *The way your heart was pounding, it nearly burst right out of your chest.*

Why on earth had she felt that way? She couldn't think of any good reason for her pulse to thrum so vigorously at Ryan's return. Though she might possibly admit to having had more than a little worry for Edward and Ryan's safety as they closed down the mine and let the miners go—particularly since she had read a great many newspaper accounts over the years about what a rough breed of men miners often were—the gladness she'd experienced at knowing Ryan had safely returned to the ranch didn't have anything to do with the fact that she might have actually *missed* him. . . .

Did it?

Though he'd barely acknowledged her timid, "Hello," when he came up to the bedroom and settled himself on the floor the night he'd returned, she'd been unable to stop her whispering torrent of questions about how the termination of the mining operations had gone, how the miners had taken the news, if he and Edward had been in any danger, and so on.

Why she chattered in the dark like a nervous twit was beyond her comprehension. Well, maybe not beyond her comprehension. Though she was largely naive as to what, exactly, carnal relations between men and women consisted of, she had a very good idea that she kept up a running patter of conversation to forestall the pervasive, invisible, yet all-too-real stream of stimulating sensuality that wafted and whirled between Ryan and her on the warm spring night air.

Because of that, and because of the resulting reflexive looseness of her jaw, Ryan Montgomery now knew all manner of her reminiscences, ideas, hopes, and dreams . . . and in return she knew nearly none of his.

But knowing *nearly* nothing about Ryan was better than knowing absolutely nothing, Emma realized with a small particle of satisfaction, recalling how, during the past few nights, Ryan had begun to offer a few scraps of information about his past. With a curt casualness that belied the words he spoke, he'd told her a little of his dissatisfaction with the army and with the shabby way the United States government treated the red man.

That was only the tip of the iceberg, Emma was certain.

Her intuition told her that something painful and terrible was locked deep inside the man she had married, and for some curious reason she harbored a secret but rapidly growing determination to secure his trust, a desire to know and share his burdens. That in itself was odd and unexplainable, but what was more, she found that a good deal of her nervousness melted away when Ryan began to talk about himself . . . when Ryan cracked open the door to his heart just the tiniest bit.

Why was that? she asked herself. What was going on between them? Most specifically, why were they continuing to play the roles of man and wife some two full weeks after Ryan's asseveration that he was going to put a swift stop to all the lies and misunderstandings?

As Joey carefully carried the stack of plates over to the sideboard, Emma sighed and stirred the floury mixture a little more. Had Ryan not spoken to his mother about their . . . situation . . . because he was so deeply engaged in the business of running the ranch and had not yet found the time to do so? Or was it because he had not yet found the right words to use?

Or was there another reason entirely?

Emma contemplated that last possibility as she stirred the bread sponge, realizing that it almost seemed as if she and Ryan were engaged in some sort of nameless, dangerous game of avoidance . . . or was it a daring, silent sport of advance and evade?

Or were they playing with plain old fire?

Guard your heart, Emma Louise, a voice inside her cautioned as the wooden paddle with which she was stirring slipped from her fingers and clunked loudly against the side of the bowl. Guard her heart? What a strange notion. Why should she have to guard her heart? From what did she have to guard her heart?

She knew the answer to that full well. With every day that passed her feelings for this man become more powerful. She dreamed about his face, his hair, his smile; she wondered what it would be like to be his wife in every way. If she mistakenly thought her heart was in no danger, why did she lie in bed each night, trembling like a leaf in the wind, imagining what it would be like to have Ryan's lips on hers . . . wishing she could feel his big hands caressing her entire body? Did she really believe that it was for no reason that she burned to know Ryan Montgomery in the fullest, richest way a wife could know a husband?

"Am-ma look f-funny."

Joey's amused tone startled her from the staggering force of her thoughts. Giving him a sickly distracted smile, she picked up the paddle and began stirring the bread sponge with sudden renewed vigor.

"Am-ma quiet. Am-ma o-kay?" Joey persisted in a more concerned tone of voice, coming to stand next to her. "Am-ma think hard to-night?"

"Yes, Joey, I'm thinking hard tonight," she replied, feeling Joey's curious brown gaze searching her face.

" 'B-bout Wyan?"

"Yes," she answered honestly, finally looking up from the yeasty mixture and seeing her troubled face reflected in Joey's slanted soft brown eyes.

"Wyan make Am-ma sad, too?"

"Yes. No. I don't know," she whispered, feeling tears fill her eyes.

"Ohh, my sad Am-ma." Warm pudgy fingers closed over her own, causing a crest of tears to spill from her eyes. "Joey unnerstand sad. Joey wuv Wyan . . . b-but Wyan make Joey so sad. Wyan no smile. Wyan no time. 'Cept on party day, Wyan not tawk nice. He say, 'Go 'way, Joey. Busy, Joey. Not n-now, J-Joey.' "

Joey's voice broke just before he paused for breath, and Emma looked up to see fat tears tracing their way down his broad cheeks. Gathering the heartbroken youth into her arms, she laid her face on his shoulder and whispered, "Oh, Joey, I think your brother has so much hurting inside himself that he doesn't realize how much he hurts the people he lives with."

"B-but why?" Curiosity filled his voice, and he pulled back from her embrace to study her face.

Emma sniffed and tried to smile. "Well, I don't know, exactly, but I'm trying to find out."

Joey was silent a long moment before nodding slowly, at first, then vigorously. "Good. Am-ma find out. Very good. Help Wyan b-be nice 'gain."

"I would love to help Ryan be nice again," she replied in a low voice, feeling a shiver run through her as she thought of how very much she meant those words. Reaching for Joey's hand, she added, "And love is exactly what your brother needs, Joey, lots and lots of love. So, if you and I can continue being very kind, very compassionate, and very, very patient where Ryan is concerned, he just might

turn out . . ." She sighed, feeling a forlorn but faintly hopeful smile steal across her features. "Well, he might just turn
out as nice as you, Joey."

Instead of appearing comforted by her gently encouraging words, Joey dropped his gaze to the floor in obvious
emotional discomfort. "Oh, my 'peshal Am-ma s-so nice.
So curly. So good." He was silent for several seconds, his
brows drawing tightly together, then, finally, he burst forth
with what was troubling him. "Joey know Am-ma wuv
Joey. Mudder wuv Joey. Fadder in h-heaven wuv Joey.
Ed-wer wuv Joey. All s-sisters w-wuv J-Joey. . . ." He was
sobbing by this time.

"Yes, Joey," Emma responded sympathetically, "your
whole family loves—"

"No, no, no, no!" With agony, he interrupted her, looking
up from the floor to stare deeply into her eyes. "Not whole
f-fam'ly. N-not Wyan."

"You think Ryan doesn't love you? Oh, Joey, that's simply not true," she responded vehemently, for the first time
realizing how very deep the pit of pain and rejection inside
her brother-in-law must be. "I'm Ryan's wife," she boldly
spoke, at the same time praying she might be forgiven for
claiming such deceptive authority, "and I know how very
much Ryan loves you."

"An' Joey wuvs Wyan."

"He knows that, Joey, he really does, but right now his
spirit is troubled by things that seem stronger than he is."
Where this wisdom, this insight, was coming from, Emma
had no idea; she only knew that her words were precise
and accurate. A comforting warmth spread outward from
the center of her, and her voice gained even more strength
and surety as she spoke. "Like I said before, Joey," she
continued, "we need to be patient and compassionate with
Ryan. Although I sense he still has quite a battle to do within his heart, we can't let sadness or hopelessness overwhelm
us; we have to stand strong in our love for him. And in our
love for each other."

Stunned by the self-enlightening assertions that had just
come out of her mouth, Emma blinked and tried to shake off
the strange feelings gripping her. Heavens, in ten minutes

she'd gone from mixing bread sponge and trying to analyze her confusing fleshly feelings for Ryan Montgomery to offering comfort to his youngest brother . . . and gaining, in the process, a greater understanding of what she needed to do to change her artificial marriage into a true and loving union.

But did she truly want a genuine, lasting marriage with Ryan Montgomery . . . and, more importantly, did he with her?

Slowly, like the sun burning through thick fog, Emma gave silent voice to the desire living inside her to claim Ryan as more than a business partner and loan recipient.

"Am-ma smart sister," Joey spoke proudly, not allowing her to demur. With his fat fist he dashed away the tears from his cheeks. He smiled. "An' Joey strong brudder. We wuv Wyan to-togedder."

"Yes, Joey, we will," she whispered, still feeling shaken by the revelations of her soul. "We'll love him together . . . and we'll see what happens."

Chapter
Sixteen

Emma strolled near the bank of the little creek north of the ranch the following afternoon, a basket of just-picked buttercups hanging from one arm. The prairie had certainly changed since the last time she'd been out here. It looked just as she'd imagined it would in her mind's eye: lush and green and dotted with beautiful wildflowers.

Her feelings had also changed since the last time she'd been out near this creek, since the afternoon Ryan Montgomery had freed her foot . . . and captured her heart. Looking upward into the immense expanse of blue sky—this time being careful not to wander as she gazed—she realized how much a part of her this beautiful, rugged Wyoming land had become, just as the Montgomerys had become a part of her . . . and she of them.

The wind rustled crisply through the shiny green leaves of the cottonwoods, pulling her attention from the magnificence of the sky to the breathtaking, verdant landscape. The conversation she and Joey had had last evening continued to weigh heavily on her mind, however.

She loved Ryan Montgomery . . . and wanted a genuine marriage with him. But did Ryan love her in return? A long sigh escaped her at that thought, for though she was aware Ryan had some feelings for her, were those feelings the same thing as love? True love?

One thing she knew, those *feelings* between them, the ones that made her burn inside every single night, could not possibly be denied for too many more nights. The passion was undeniably there. Perhaps if she took the initiative, letting her love and her instincts guide her, the rest would follow. Devotion. Trust. Faith. Commitment. Enduring love.

But what if they didn't?

At this point, what have you got to lose, Emma Louise? she asked herself. She was hopelessly in love with the man. Marital love was only a deeper expression of that love . . . and she was married, after all.

Warmth, having nothing to do with the bright afternoon sunshine, curled through her at the thought of sharing a bed with her husband. Would he allow her to kiss him? Touch him? She swallowed hard at the thought of her fingers gliding over Ryan's powerful body. Then what?

"Emma!" Ginny called from farther down the creek bank, interrupting her heated musings. A basket dangled from her plump sister-in-law's lower arm, as well. "Come over here! I found some flax!"

It was impossible not to respond to the excitement in Ginny's voice. Emma smiled and began walking toward her, but the smile quickly turned into a wistful expression as she thought of Ginny's warm and loving relationship with Edward. If she and Ryan could know half as much peace and contentment in their marriage as Ginny and Edward knew in theirs, she prayed, she would be the happiest woman on earth.

"Late in the day as it is, I still cannot believe we're finally all sittin' down together for a meal," Maureen commented as the Montgomery family congregated in the back dining room. She smiled first at Ryan, then at Edward. "You two have been back from the mine more'n a week, an' yet I ain't seen but a glimpse of you here an' there. I hear tell you're spendin' your nights with us, but you could not prove it by me."

Edward shrugged and reached for a thick slice of bread. "We've been pretty busy, Ma. Between calving and round-up and branding, there isn't much time left over for anything else."

"Aye, son, the busy season stretches from snowmelt till snowfall, an' then some. I'm just so very thankful—" Maureen cleared her throat as she folded her hands together, arching a disapproving eyebrow at the outreached fingers that had nearly closed around a slice of bread.

What a guilty grin and a contrite "Sorry, Ma," Edward put his hands together and bowed his head.

. As Maureen gave thanks and asked a simple blessing upon her family, Ryan couldn't help lifting his head in surprise when his mother asked for God's help in healing Emma's pain. "What do you mean, 'Emma's pain'?" he asked in a brief, offhand manner as Maureen concluded her prayer and began passing the dishes around the table. "Where is she? Isn't she coming to supper?" He and Edward had just come in the back door after spending the day at the roundup camp, and until now he'd assumed that Emma was in the kitchen, putting the final touches on the meal.

"Emma put out her back this afternoon," Ginny said quietly, transferring a perfectly browned slice of roast beef to her plate, then passing the platter on. "She was carrying in an armload of wood and then she just bent wrong, or something."

"Yeah, she kind of like yelled, and then the wood fell all over the kitchen floor. We had to stop our lessons and go help her," Colleen added dramatically. "Poor Emma could hardly stand up straight, and I could tell she was almost crying."

"My Am-ma hurted bad," Joey concurred with sadness. "Cr-crash . . . boom. Am-ma hurted."

"Where is she now?" Edward asked in concern.

"She's upstairs restin', son. We put her in the tub to soak, then tucked her into bed." Maureen shook her head. "She's goin' to be mighty sore for a couple days."

Ryan was silent as the conversation at the dinner table continued to focus on Emma and how the bundle of firewood had slipped from her arms.

Emma.

As consumed as his days had been lately with the business of running and rebuilding the ranch, he still hadn't done anything about clarifying their true . . . relationship. He knew it was wrong, but it was just easier, for the present time, to avoid the whole issue.

Oh, and is that what you think you're doing, Montgomery? a voice inside him derisively questioned. *Avoiding the issue? Telling yourself you're so busy with work that you don't have time to deal with your predicament with Emma? Or could it be you're keeping any and all of your options open . . . just in case?*

Just in case what? he asked himself, spearing a chunk of potato with his fork. *Just in case she decided to yield herself to him?*

He couldn't say he hadn't thought of it.

As he chewed his potato, he realized that if he made love to Emma, a quick and easy handshake annulment would be out of the question. From that moment on they would be husband and wife in the way that Ginny and Edward, Irene and Jacob, and Moira and Billy were husband and wife. Permanently. For all time. Until death parted them.

Is that what he really wanted?

To be honest, he didn't know what he wanted anymore. Aside from the base part of him that burned to know Emma's body, Emma's womanly secrets, he was utterly confused. As much as he thought about her, and, conversely, as much as he tried *not* to think about her—tried, in fact, to push all thoughts of her from his mind—a part of him had secretly begun to look forward to their nights together, to their whispered conversations in the dark. To her companionship.

What did that mean?

The very thought of Emma being in so much pain that she'd had to be put to bed raised an unsettled feeling deep inside him, and he set down his fork, his ravenous appetite suddenly gone. What was the matter with him? *Come on, Montgomery, you're not going to actually go upstairs and check on her, are you? She just pulled a muscle in her back; she'll be fine.*

Ryan sighed, knowing he *was* going to have to go upstairs and check on her. Pretending not to see the knowing, compassionate expressions that both Ginny and Irene directed his way, he muttered his excuses and extricated his long legs from beneath the table.

"Tell her we're all thinkin' of her, love," Maureen said, nodding her approval at him. "I'll hold your plate in the warmer for you."

The scent of clean, perfumed female skin struck Ryan with subtle but potent force as he silently turned the knob and entered the second-story bedchamber where Emma rested. As he stood and breathed in the lingering fragrances of Emma's bath with something akin to pure physical pleasure, his muddled mind thought of all kinds of things.

Crazy things. Hot things. How was he supposed to . . .

"Ryan?" Emma's voice was thick with sleep. "Is that you?"

"It's me," he responded, trying to redirect his mind from its libidinous wanderings to his purpose—his one and only reason in coming up here—which was to dispassionately discover the extent of Emma's back injury.

It was as if the elements had joined forces to conspire against him, however. Not only did the room smell like heaven on earth, but also the curtains were drawn, casting the room into near-darkness. How was a man supposed to think for knowing that a beautiful woman lay all alone in a big bed in the dark?

Stop it, Montgomery. You're here to check her back, he reminded himself with great difficulty as he walked toward the bed, hearing Emma's deep intake of breath, the rustle of the sheets . . . then the smothered cry of pain.

He was at the bedside in an instant. "Where does it hurt?" he demanded, instinctively extending his arm toward her. His eyes hadn't yet fully adjusted to the room's dimness, so he was only able make out the general shape of her body. "Careful, now. Are you trying to turn over? Here, take hold of me."

"I-I'm trying to move onto my side." Hesitantly at first Emma's hands reached up and settled loosely around his wrist and forearm. "Thanks," she uttered in a strangled voice that ended in a hissing cry of pain as she pulled herself from her back to her side, squeezing his arm much more tightly than he would have imagined her capable of doing.

"You've got to let me look at your back," he insisted as her hands loosened, then fell away from his arm. Her breathing was rapid and shallow, and it was obvious she was in a great deal of pain. "You don't sound very . . . good," he finished awkwardly.

"I'll be . . . fine once I lie . . . still a . . . minute," she whispered. "It only hurts when I move."

Briskly Ryan walked over to the window and drew the curtains aside, allowing the evening twilight to lift a little of the room's somberness. Turning back to the bed, he swallowed hard at the sight of the curvy outline of shoulder, waist, and hip visible through the voluminous but sheer lawn nightdress. It appeared that she'd been struggling to change position for quite some time, for the bedclothes were in a frightful tangle about her knees. "I was a cavalry officer," he sternly spoke to Emma's backside, trying not to notice that the scent of the head-befuddling perfume was more intense the closer he came to her. "And I know quite a bit about anatomy and injuries."

"I'm no horse, Captain."

"I realize that," he replied to her insulted retort with an urgency that both filled and surprised him, "but you've got to let me examine your back. You may well have more than a simple strain, Emma, and one can't ever be too careful where the spine is concerned." The thought of sprightly Emma being a sufferer of never-ending back pain was aggrieving, and when he spoke again, he realized his voice was affected by his deep concern. "If you would just allow me to—"

"I . . . I don't know if . . ."

"All right, then," he conceded in a reasonable tone as, against his will, vision after vision of Emma's silky bare back filled his mind. "Just tell me where it hurts and let me feel the area through your nightdress." He took a deep breath and released it as silently as possible. Lord help him, he wanted to minister to her injury, but the idea of laying his hands on her flesh, even through the barrier of clothing, was unbearably stimulating.

He should just leave this room, leave this house, right now, before anything happened. He was deeply concerned about the physical condition of her back, he truly was, but mixed in with that was something raw and fleshly and earthy—something that didn't belong. Truly, he didn't even trust himself standing where he stood . . . seeing what he saw . . . smelling what he smelled.

"The affected area is down near the . . . ah, back of the hip, on the left side, if you must know." Emma's voice was so soft he had to strain to listen. "But I'm sure I don't need you to examine the . . . area. If I just rest and take it easy, I'm sure I'll be back to work in a few days."

"I'm not worried about you going back to work," he said roughly. Sighing once again, he dropped to his knees and hesitantly reached out a hand. "I don't care if you never cook another meal in your life. I'm worried about you making a full recovery."

"Oh . . . I see. You like my cooking that much, do you?"

"Like your cooking . . ." he muttered, at the same time pulling his hand back. "Are you trying to make a joke?"

It was Emma's turn to sigh. "I'm trying," she said, speaking toward the opposite wall.

"Why?" He could see the delicate movement of her back and ribs as she breathed in and out, could feel the feminine warmth of her body radiating out to him.

"B-because I'm frightened of what will happen if you touch me."

"But why?" Soft as a whisper, he reached out and touched the center of her spine through the delicate lawn of her nightdress. "Does this hurt you?"

"No." Her denial was breathless.

It was as if Ryan's hand had a will all its own. Slowly his fingers worked down her spine as his mind shouted for him to get up and walk—no, run!—in any direction. "Does it hurt here," he murmured, "or do I need to move down more?" His voice was low and caressing, with the seductive sort of quality that a doctor—or veterinarian—would most definitely *not* use while conducting an impartial assessment of an injury. He closed his eyes. *Just pretend you're running your hand over horseflesh, Montgomery,* he sternly commanded himself as his fingers skimmed over the filmy nightdress, discerning the waistband of her drawers . . . the delicate bony nubs of spine . . . firm warm muscle.

Horseflesh? God in heaven, there was no way he could pretend he was touching anything but prime womanflesh. Superior, choice, top grade, unparalleled . . .

He opened his eyes as he felt Emma's hand cover his own.

"Here," she said, guiding his hand out laterally from her backbone, her breath audibly catching as his hand settled over a slightly swollen area between her vertebrae and the full flare of her hip. "This is where it hurts."

"I can feel it," he said, gingerly exploring the area, momentarily forgetting his desire. His other hand came up to push cautiously over the corresponding area on the backside of her other hip. The right side was flat, not at all distended, and he nodded to himself in saisfaction. "It's not sore over here, is it?"

"No, it's just the . . . one side." Emma's breathing was rapid and shallow, and finally she lifted her head to look over her shoulder at him. "Ouch," she said under her breath, dropping her head, "I can't even do this."

"Don't twist yourself like that," he said, regretfully moving his hands away from her spine and taking his feet. "I'll come around to the other side of the bed and tell you what I think you did to yourself."

"Besides something stupid, what did I do to myself?" Though Emma tried to keep her tone light, Ryan could hear the note of suppressed anxiety in her voice.

He walked around the bed and knelt before her front side. "You strained your . . ." He trailed off, staring deeply into a pair of liquid brown eyes. How was he supposed to think when she was looking at him like that? He began again. "There are two joints that connect your lower spine to your . . ."

She moistened her lips and raised her eyebrows expectantly. "To my . . . what?"

At the sight of Emma's pink tongue, all of Ryan's remaining will was lost. Beaten. Vanquished. He reached out and settled his hand in the narrow curve of her waist and, with all the reverence of a man running his hand over a rare and priceless object, he delicately trailed his fingers downward, over her flank. "Your hips," he said hoarsely, acutely aware of the fact that she continued to stare at him with an unblinking, fathomless gaze. "Your lower back is connected to your hipbones."

"Oh."

That was all the permission he needed to continue his leisurely exploration of the slender, sinuous curves before him. Pure, unspoiled curves. Virgin curves. He swallowed, realizing how very much he wanted this woman but realizing, at the same time, what taking her would mean.

Why didn't she tell him to stop?

Indeed, where were the scandalized protestations of impropriety? The outraged demands that he immediately remove his hands from her person? Nothing of the sort was forthcoming as her eyes poured forth her wordless assent. Slowly she reached out to touch his face, her lips curving at the same time into a timid, tremulous smile.

Even if she wanted him only a tenth as much as he wanted her, that smile was all the permission Ryan needed to continue. Boldly he ran his hand back over the trail he had just traced, allowing his fingertips to wander up over her upper arm and shoulder, then down across the side of a small but pleasingly rounded breast.

"Emma," he groaned softly, feeling his desire for this woman consume him as he carefully eased himself onto the bed and watched her tentative, acquiescent smile give way to an expression of instinctive, matching readiness. "You strained your left sacro . . . iliac . . . joint," he whispered, bringing his hands up and cupping her face. "You just need to . . . you'll be right as rain in . . . your back needs to be rested for about a week . . . ahh, forget it. You'll be fine. Do you know how much I . . . what you do . . ."

At this close range, all coherent thought was out of the question. Even before his mind finished saying, *kiss her, you idiot,* his lips were on hers, urgently seeking the satiny,

secret recesses of her soft mouth. Her lips were open, inno-
cently parted, and with something like a lyrical moan she
yielded to the pressure of his lips and tongue, simply and
naturally.

It was almost too much to believe that Emma's arms
came up and wound themselves around his neck as the kiss
went on and on, but they did; it wasn't a dream. None of
this was a dream. Not only could he feel her fingers on
his neck and in his hair, he could taste her impatience, her
readiness, her eagerness. "I . . . don't want to hurt you," he
muttered against her mouth as he finally broke the kiss.
"Your back . . ."

"As long as I don't . . . move, my back is fine."

"I won't move you," he promised, delighting in the feel
of her words against his face. "I'll just . . ." The trust in
her limpid gaze unnerved him, sent a rush of culpability
spinning through him. "Are you sure you want to be . . .
doing this?"

"We're just . . ." She sighed and ran her fingers over the
edge of his ear. "Kissing. Surely that can't be harmful."

"It could be." *To your virginity,* he wanted to add, but
a split second later any and all vestiges of rational thought
were lost as her hands drew his head back to hers, his lips
to hers.

Emma.

He couldn't get enough, taste enough, feel enough of
her. The barrier of her nightdress both excited and frustrated him, for though its fabric was sheer enough to allow
his fingers to feel the warmth and substance of her form,
its fine texture was a poor substitute for the silky softness of the womanly curves and hollows that lay beneath.
Impatiently he fumbled with the ties on the bodice of
her nightdress and slipped his hand inside to caress her
neck, her collarbones . . . the upper swells of her breasts.
He groaned as his fingertips brushed over one turgid nipple,
then the other.

He needed more.

"Emma," he said urgently, pulling his hand from the
opening of her nightdress and cupping her chin. "I'm on
fire for you . . . I want to know every inch of your body . . .

inside and out." In the silence of the darkened bedchamber, his breathing was as rapid and ragged as his desire.

"I-I can't believe I'm saying this," Emma replied breathlessly, "but I want you to know every inch of my body, Ryan. I want to . . . know . . ." Her unfinished words hung in the air between them for the space of several heartbeats; then she spoke again. "But if we do . . . ah, this thing . . . it means that we . . ."

As if coming out of a trance, Ryan shook his head and allowed his fingers to drop away from Emma's chin. His racing heart seemed to lurch in his chest. "It would mean we're married—for good," he said woodenly, in that moment fully comprehending the momentous ramifications that the consummation of this physical act would bring. There would be no autumn annulment. No parting of the ways. Day after day, for the rest of his existence, Emma would be his wife.

Was one night of pleasure worth a lifetime of marriage?

Who says the pleasure is limited to one night? What makes you think you can't have this sort of pleasure each and every morning or night or afternoon of your married life?

Even as the controversy raged inside Ryan's brain, he was easing away from Emma's warm and willing body. "I'm sorry to have . . . disturbed you," he said stiffly as he rolled off the bed and stood up. Restiveness drove him over to the dresser to light the lamp.

"You need to rest your back," he said, needlessly fiddling with adjusting the size of the flame. "I've seen your type of injury before, and it only gets worse if you're up and about before you should be. You'll probably need some help getting out of bed tonight to use the . . . to answer nature's call. I'm sure Ginny would be quite happy to spend the night in here with you and assist you with anything you may need. I'll see to it that you get some supper, too, if you're hungry." There was simply no more adjusting to be done to the lamp. He fell silent.

Emma was silent as well; he had no idea what she was thinking. Or feeling.

He had a pretty good idea of what she was feeling just
a few minutes ago, though. He knew there was something
between them—he couldn't possibly deny the explosive
feelings that just occurred in this room. He should turn
around and tell her he couldn't go through with it. Tell
her he was just not ready to settle down and be married.

As he fingered the lacy doily beneath the lamp's base, he
became aware of one very significant truth: he *was* already
married.

"This is probably for the best, Ryan," Emma concurred,
interrupting his weighty thoughts. Her voice was small and
shaky. "I-I hope you're not angry with me."

"I'm not." Abruptly he turned and walked over to the
bed, trying to block all recall of what had just occurred
between them in this bed. "I think it's best, though, that
you and I not spend any more nights together." *Because I
don't trust myself alone with you for even two more minutes,*
he silently added.

Despite the fact that the movement caused her obvious
discomfort, Emma rolled from her side to her back to stare
at him. Slowly she nodded, whispering, "You're right."

"Well, I'll be going, then." Ryan nodded in return and
resolutely tore his gaze away from the one and only woman
who had ever raised such a plethora of feelings inside him.
"I'll send Ginny up."

Ryan bedded down all alone in the bunkhouse that night,
alternately overcome with feelings of relief at having made
such a narrow escape . . . and otherwise damning himself
for passing up an opportunity that had never before been
offered to him.

Quixotic imaginings aside, he knew he had read more
than simple sexual curiosity in Emma's gaze. Regard, caring,
respect, trust, affection . . . Good Lord, possibly even love
had shimmered in the melting brown depths of her eyes.
Not only had she offered her innocence to him, but she had
also been willing to pledge herself to him for a lifetime.

Why would she offer such a thing?

She doesn't love you, the dark part of himself whispered
morbidly, *no one could possibly love you.* What was there

to love? He'd walked out on his father nearly ten years ago, and because of his stubborn pride and inability to admit he ever made a mistake, his father went to his grave believing he hated him. Not only that, Ryan had shut his family out of his life, killed Indian men merely for the land they occupied, and right under his fatuous nose, his one and only true friend in this world suffered such melancholia that he believed the only answer to life was death. Emma would never love him if she knew all that.

Ryan sighed and roughly rearranged the pillow beneath his head. Even if—and it was a big if—Emma fancied herself in love with him, once she discovered the kind of man he really was, she would no doubt run screaming back to St. Paul, back to the safety of her secure little rich girl world . . . and straight back to the arms of the stuffy beau her brother wanted her to marry.

Jon Severson.

A bolt of jealous possessiveness gripped Ryan at the thought of Emma being held in any other man's arms. As a gust of wind caused the roof to creak overhead, he realized every muscle in his body was tensed for . . . for what? For action? For battle? Why should he care so much about whose arms Emma ultimately ended up in? If Jon Severson was her long-standing intended, which it sounded like he was, then who was he to come between them? Emma Taylor and Jon Severson were from the same world; the St. Paul man was undoubtedly better suited to her.

But Ryan was married to her. True, it all began as a backhanded financial deal, but now the rules had changed—and so had the stakes. He could have Emma if he wanted her; all he had to do was take her. Didn't he realize, that if not for her and her grand misguided schemes, he'd still be wallowing in his own melancholia? Emma had pulled him out of the black hole in which he had barely been existing, Emma had made him come alive, Emma had made him care about life again. . . .

A wave of tiredness—or was it mental exhaustion?—broke over him as he deliberated all possible courses of action open to him. Annul the marriage now. Annul the marriage later. Continue on with things . . . *Impossible!* his subconscious cried. *There's no more continuing on with things, Montgomery. You've got to make a decision. The one and only other option that remains open to you is to lay claim to the most luscious little curly haired woman you've ever laid eyes on. Make love to her. Make her yours in every way. . . .*

With great willpower, he tore his thoughts away from the sweet luscious kisses of Emma's mouth, the satiny texture of her fragrant skin, and far, far away from the soft breasts and erect nipples that had beckoned his touch. With sudden clarity, he knew his best course of action was to put as much distance as possible between himself and this woman who threatened the very substance of his being. He needed to clear his head of the confusing, chaotic thoughts that scurried and lunged about like so many wild cattle.

Tomorrow he'd ride out to the roundup camp and stay there for . . . a good week or so. Instead of accompanying Edward back to the ranch every night as he had been doing, he'd bed down under the stars with a blanket and a saddle, along with the hired help. No more sleeping like a hopeful dog at the foot of Emma's bed.

As he punched the pillow again and turned to his side, he thought that if a week of hard work, fresh air, and being in the company of several sensible bachelors didn't cure him of whatever ailed him . . . well, then, he didn't know what would.

"Mornin', Mr. Severson," the clean-shaven young clerk called, adding another newspaper to the nearly three-foot-high stack of newspapers on the chair in the corner of Jon Severson's downtown St. Paul law office. "Got the *Boston Herald* to add to your pile today."

"Thanks, Tom," Jon absently replied, not bothering to look up from the statement he was writing.

"Gosh, Mr. Severson, do you think you're ever going to catch up on all all your reading?" the clerk persisted. "If you don't get to these out-of-state newspapers pretty soon, I'm going to have to find a place to start another pile for you."

"Indeed." Jon looked up at the clerk and smiled thinly. "That'll be all for now, Mr. Applegate."

"Yes, sir." Tom nodded and backed out of the room. "Sorry, sir."

Sighing, Jon set the pen in its rest and studied the pile of newspapers that had grown to mammoth proportions in the past couple months. When *was* he ever going to get to reading all of them? His practice had been extremely busy during the past several months, with no sign that business would be letting up anytime soon.

More than missing his newspapers, though, he missed Emma. As the days she'd been gone had turned into weeks, then into months, he realized the magnitude of the mistake he and Michael had made in allowing her to traipse off to Wyoming Territory to prove whatever silly point she was trying to prove. Here it was nearly June, and she still hadn't returned. He should have pressed the issue of marriage while he had the opportunity, made her listen to reason.

It was just that he'd been so certain she would quickly fail at her . . . employment.

He'd been thinking of paying her a visit this summer—to talk some sense into her—but it didn't look as if his practice was going to allow him the time. He hadn't written her, either, he realized uncomfortably, even though he'd been intending to do so. It was just that he'd been certain she was going to be home . . . any day.

What on earth made a woman like Emma want to work? he wondered, rubbing his temples and rising from his comfortably padded chair. Not only did she want to work, but she also wanted to own her own business. There was no way he could allow his wife to do such a thing, simply no way. As he paced back and forth about the room, he realized that, except for Emma's willful streak of which he'd recently seen evidence, she was otherwise the perfect woman to stand at his side . . . the perfect woman to bear his children. Again, he thought with regret, he should have pushed the issue of marriage while he'd had the chance.

He knew Michael heartily approved of their joining. Funny, he hadn't seen much of his friend lately, he realized, pausing next to the large stack of newspapers. As was his own practice, he knew Michael's legal practice had been booming during the past months.

The last time he'd seen Michael, however, he'd noticed that his friend had seemed unusually unwilling to talk about Emma . . . curiously unwilling to even speak her name, it had seemed. In fact, it almost seemed as if Michael couldn't wait to depart from his presence. Jon sighed again as he fingered the eight-day-old *Boston Herald* the clerk had just delivered, supposing, at the same time, that much of Michael's cheerlessness and recently reclusive behavior stemmed from his continuing anger and frustration at his younger sister's reckless actions. He took his role as Emma's guardian and protector very seriously.

Glancing from the pile of newspapers back to his desk, to the dry statement he'd been working on, to the waiting piles of papers and briefs he had yet to begin, he realized he had never before allowed himself to lag so far behind in reading the many out-of-state newspapers he received, a peculiar but oftentimes beneficial and advantageous practice he had begun some years ago. What was the sense in even continuing to receive the papers if he never read them?

There was no sense in that at all, his soundly reasoning inner voice replied as he pulled the first ten or so papers off the stack and took them back to his desk. He might as well find out what was going on in New York . . . Philadelphia . . . Milwaukee . . . San Francisco. . . .

Two hours later he'd skimmed through the important sections of the first bunch of papers he'd grabbed. Looking at the clock and seeing that another hour remained until lunchtime, he decided to whittle down the unread pile even more. He'd resume work on the statement this afternoon.

A *Washington Chronicle* was on top of the next stack of papers he took, and he wondered how much longer the publication would be in print. Judging from what he'd read in several other papers, John Fornay's *Chronicle* was foundering. Too bad. Quickly he read through the columns of print and tossed the paper on top of the growing stack of papers he'd already read.

A fairly recent Denver *Daily News* was next. Nothing of relevance sprang out at him as he flipped through its pages, and he was just about to cast the journal to the floor when his eyes caught the subtitle, "Former Army Captain Marries St. Paul Woman," just beneath the bold black type that read THE SOCIAL WORLD.

Vaguely curious as to who this St. Paul woman might be, his gaze continued down the column of type. A moment later, he was certain he understood what it was like to suffer a heart attack. Or a stroke. Or a killing rage. Something painful stabbed him deep in his chest, clutched his lungs, made it impossible to take a full breath, and a burning, sweaty flush swept his body from head to toe.

Emma had married?

His eyes snapped through the short article once again, then up to the top of the page to reread the date. Emma's marriage had occurred nearly *three weeks* ago! Mindless of the mess he created, he angrily threw the other papers off his lap and, with shaking hands and a pounding heart, read through the article a third time. "Recently retired army captain Ryan Montgomery, of the Pine Bluffs area, and Miss Emma Taylor, of St. Paul, were united in marriage late yesterday afternoon at the parsonage of . . ."

There could be no mistake; there could be no other "Emma Taylor of St. Paul." She had been going to the Pine Bluffs, Wyoming Territory area . . . and the surname of the rancher who had hired her had been Montgomery.

Unbearable pain and fury oozed from every pore of his body as he stuffed the paper under his arm, grabbed his hat, and departed for Michael Taylor's office. Ignoring young Tom Applegate's questioning glance as he stormed through the outer office, he wondered if this was why his friend had been avoiding him lately. Did Michael know about Emma's marriage?

Indeed, he had to know, Jon reasoned, which suddenly shed a whole new light on why his friend had seemed only too eager to bolt from his presence the last time they'd seen one another.

He knew. Michael knew.

Well, Michael wasn't going to bolt anywhere today, he fulminated as he walked outdoors, giving no attention to the loveliness of the day, nor to the temperate late spring breeze against his face.

If Michael Taylor knew what was good for him, not only had he better be in his office this morning, he had better truthfully and satisfactorily answer each and every question put to him.

Chapter
Seventeen

"It sure is good to see you up and around again, Emma," Ginny commented as the two women peeled vegetables in the kitchen late one afternoon nearly two weeks after Emma's injury. "Even though Ryan told us your back would heal up just fine, I was still worried about you."

"I was a little worried myself," Emma said with a rueful grin, the memories of the past several painful days being still quite fresh in her head. "But thanks to all your help, I made it back to my feet. My goodness, during those first days, you and Maureen did practically everything—and I mean everything—for me." She made a show of shuddering in distaste. "I'd never want to be that dependent on anyone ever again. And if you don't mind, I don't think I'll be carrying any more wood for a while."

Ginny smiled and inclined her head toward the nearly overflowing woodbox. "Just look at that pile of logs there, Emma. I don't think you'll have to worry about bringing in wood for a year or so. Since you were injured, Joey's insisted upon keeping the woodbox filled. For you. He says it's his 'special job' now."

Emma smiled and nodded. "He told me about that on one of the many visits he made upstairs while I was recuperating. He painted me at least a hundred pictures, I swear, and brought me food and flowers and all kinds of special treasures . . ." Her grin faded to a pensive expression as her words trailed off. Sighing, she set down the potato she had peeled. "Oh, Ginny," she began again, "I don't know how I'm going to be able to leave Joey when it's time for me to go. All you Montgomerys have become quite dear to me, but Joey most of all."

Ginny was silent as she sliced a potato into quarters and tossed the slices into the water-filled cookpot on the center of the worktable, each slice making a musical plopping sound as it broke the water's surface. Reaching for another potato, she raised her eyebrows in an "Oh, really?" expression and casually asked, "Are you sure it's Joey you're going to miss the most?"

"I'm going to miss you too, Ginny," Emma hastened to reply. "I didn't mean to say—"

"I'm not talking about me, silly," Ginny interrupted gently, fixing her wide gray-green eyes on Emma's face. "I'm talking about Ryan."

"Oh." Emma felt a flush rise in her cheeks as she thought of the bold way he'd kissed her—and touched her body—that night nearly two weeks ago. If she'd had improperly immodest thoughts and imaginings about Ryan before the . . . incident . . . well, what had been going on in her head *since* then had to be purely indecent.

And it wasn't only her head that was affected—not by a long shot.

Ryan Montgomery had awakened something powerful inside her body, something she hadn't even known existed. Stars above, her whole body burned for him, longed for his touch, his breath against her face, his hot mouth against hers. Over and over she thought of their intimacy, of Ryan's whispered admissions of how much he wanted her, and each time, without fail, she felt a physical thrill of indescribable magnitude ripple outward from the core of her body. She swallowed hard, feeling her heart beat faster, wondering what it would be like to be Ryan's wife in every way . . . Ryan's lover.

"You have feelings for Ryan, don't you, Emma?"

"No . . . well . . . I mean . . ." she stammered.

"Oh, honey, I can see it all over your face. You look as miserable and confused as I felt when I first fell in love with Edward," Ginny said sympathetically. "For a while there, I didn't know what was happening to me." Her voice dropped to a confidential whisper. "Especially after he kissed me for the first time . . . I mean *really* kissed me." She cleared her throat and looked around the room as if to be certain they were alone. "Has something happened between you and Ryan, Emma? You know . . . something physical?"

"Well, he . . . kissed me and said he . . ." Emma felt her blush intensify, and she dropped her head forward in embarrassment. She could never admit the rest. Never.

"I wondered why Ryan's been avoiding the ranch house lately," Ginny said knowingly, though, curiously, in a pleased tone of voice. "I don't think I've seen him but once or twice since you hurt your back. He hasn't spent any more nights on the floor upstairs, either, has he?"

Miserably, Emma shook her head.

Ginny began peeling the potato she held, humming softly to herself as she worked. "If it's any consolation, Emma, Ryan's probably just as mixed up and rattled as you are. In fact, I'd bet on it."

"Ryan isn't . . . he couldn't be . . ." A flicker of hope lit deep inside her heart. "What makes you say that?" she finally whispered, raising her head to look at Ginny. "D-do you know something?"

"I know what I know," she said cryptically, gesturing toward her heart with the butt end of her knife. She offered Emma a beautiful smile of both encouragement and friendship. "Edward tells me Ryan's thrown himself into running this ranch with his whole heart, but I wonder if Ryan's not running *from* this ranch house for what he feels in his heart . . . for you, Emma. I notice he hasn't told Maureen the truth about your marriage yet, either. In fact, I wonder if the reason he hasn't—" Ginny's conjecturing was cut short by the sound of someone coming in the backdoor.

"Hello, daughters," came Maureen's voice just a second later. "I cannot believe we've already got some decent-sized radishes growin'," she said, holding up the basket in her arms. "But would you jus' look at them! An' the wee tender leaves o' lettuce, as well. We'll be dinin' in style tonight, to be sure."

"Fresh vegetables are the best part about summer," Ginny agreed, nodding as Maureen hung her broad-brimmed western hat on a hook by the door, then set the basket of vegetables near the pump. "I'd say we'll be eating new peas in another few weeks."

"Aye, we will at that. Have you an' Emma given any thought as to what kind o' dish we Montgomerys will be bringin' to the Gillands' big dance tomorrow night?" Maureen went on, changing the subject once, then once again. "It's too bad, for Irene's sake, that Jacob isn't back from Santa Fe yet, but Moira an' Billy are comin' out from Cheyenne." She cleared her throat and looked pointedly at Emma. "An' with the way you're gettin' better, young lady, I don't want to be hearin' any more about how you don't think you'll be up to goin' along to the party with the rest of us. Jus' look at you now! You'll be in even finer shape by tomorrow evenin'."

"Well, I really don't think I should—"

"Nonsense!" Maureen interrupted. "You'll have the time o' your life, daughter. Besides that, I have me own selfish reasons for wantin' to see you an' Ryan dancin' together. With him workin' the way he's been, you an' he ain't been spendin' near enough time in one another's company." She lifted an auburn eyebrow and cocked her head in Ginny's direction. "Not that spendin' your nights together necessarily guarantees a poor old woman a grandchild or two."

"Of course, Ma, I can't speak for Emma and Ryan," Ginny replied with a secretive grin, "but Edward and I have decided it's great fun to keep you guessing on the matter."

"Keep me guessin'!" Maureen exclaimed with a snort. "I'll soon be so feeble an' dodderin' that I'll be forgettin' even how to guess!"

"Feeble and doddering?" Ginny questioned dryly, shaking her head in denial. "I suppose that's why you can run circles around me?" Her expression turned mischievous just a moment later. "You know, Ma, there's something I've been meaning to tell you . . ."

"Aye?" Maureen's expression was one of comical wariness, and she folded her arms across her chest. "I'm listenin', daughter."

Ginny spoke in an ingenious tone of voice. "Well, if you hurried and found yourself a handsome widower, I'll bet you could still have a couple more babes of your own! We could all help you look for a nice sturdy fellow tomorrow night at the dance. . . ."

"Bite your tongue, Virginia Montgomery!" Maureen unfolded her arms and waved both hands at her daughter-in-law in a dismissing manner; however, she couldn't help the good-natured chuckle that escaped her. "God in heaven, what a thought! I suppose I was deservin' that, wasn't I?"

Virginia shrugged with mock solemnity. "It was just an idea."

The three of them burst into laughter as Maureen pulled a dreadful face. A long moment later, Ginny's expression became more serious as she leveled wide gray-green eyes at Emma. "And speaking of the dance, if either Edward or I has anything to say about it, both you and Ryan will be accompanying us tomorrow night."

"Really, Ginny," Emma protested uneasily, "I don't think—"

With seeming innocence, Ginny smoothly pretended she didn't hear her. "To answer your earlier question, Ma, a little while ago Emma was telling me about a dish from her childhood called 'dessert dumplings.' They sound absolutely delicious, and I think we should take a mess of them over to the Gillands'. I'll bet no one around here has ever tasted them."

"What on earth is a *dessert* dumplin'?" Maureen quizzically questioned. "I never heard of such a thing."

"Well, Emma described them as slightly sweet dumplings in caramel sauce, good hot or cold. Indeed, I bet you'll have all the area ladies lined up and asking for the recipe tomorrow night, Emma," Ginny said enthusiastically. "You'll have to tell them all it's an old St. Paul favorite."

Emma sighed helplessly as she looked from Maureen to Ginny, deciding that she may as well save her breath about the dance. She had no doubt she'd be going—*and* making several pans of Blanche Faraday's dessert dumplings to take along.

"It ought to be a good dance," Maureen said, nodding. "I heard they got Shorty Bissel to fiddle. I don't know how the Gillands managed such a feat; that kind o' fiddler don't come 'round often." As she stepped over toward the pantry door, she said, "Well, I'd best be off to find me Joey. I noticed this mornin' he's got a wee bit of a chest cold startin' up. With the way a cold goes in him . . ." She allowed her words to trail off as she stepped through the swinging door.

At Emma's questioning expression, Ginny soberly explained, "I don't know if you know this, Emma, but Joey's colds often settle into his lungs. As a matter of fact, we almost lost him to the pneumonia last fall." She lowered her voice to a whisper. "The doctor told us then that not many of Joey's kind make it to adulthood, and that we can't expect that he . . ." Tears shimmered in her gray-green eyes.

"Can't expect that he what?" Penetrating dread clutched at Emma's breast as she stared hard at her friend, willing her not to say the words she most feared she would speak.

"Joey's body just isn't as strong as yours or mine, Emma, and consequently he can't fight off ailments in the same way that you or I can," Ginny said as gently as she could. "The doctor told us Joey probably isn't going to live for too many more years, honey, if even that long."

"But that's not fair!" The idea of Joey lying still and lifeless was almost more than Emma could bear, and answering tears welled in her own eyes.

"No, it's not fair," Ginny agreed, awkwardly swiping at her cheeks with her elbow. She took a deep breath and released it, seeming to grow more calm with that simple action. "But instead of dwelling on how much time Joey may or may not have left here on earth, Emma, we need to look at each additional day the Lord gives us to spend with him as a special, precious gift."

Emma closed her eyes and nodded, hearing the wisdom in her sister-in-law's words, but feeling her heart rent asunder by the thought of life-loving Joey no longer being a part of this world.

Just what was the capacity of a woman's heart? she wondered with anguish. *Exactly how much room did it hold for loving, for healing . . . for hurting?* She sighed, a deep, shaky sound, and set down her potato. Not only did she have to try and find some way to reconcile her powerful feelings for Ryan, she was now faced with the additional anguish of having to seek balance and self-control in the face of Joey's looming mortality. It was too much, just too much. . . .

Her eyes fluttered open at a soft touch on her sleeve.

"You and I have done wrong, Emma." Ginny spoke in a low voice, her brows drawn together in seriousness. "Great wrong. And as silly as it sounds, I've been thinking that perhaps we were drawn down the path of lies and deceit to ultimately gain a greater understanding of virtue. Of truth. Because with truth and love, Emma, namely *your* truth and love, you have the opportunity to erase each and every one of our wrongs . . . to love, to heal, and to bind this family whole."

A long-ago learned verse jumped into her mind at Ginny's words. "'Let us not love in word, neither in tongue; but in deed and truth,'" she recited softly. "'And hereby we know that we are of the truth, and shall assure our hearts before Him.'"

"First Epistle of John," Ginny replied with a slow, gentle smile, "although I'm not certain of the chapter."

Despite her distress, Emma felt her lips curve into a crooked smile. "It's from the third. My mother made me pay particular attention to verses on truth." Like a rapidly withering flower, the smile faded. "And would you just look where that's gotten me."

Ginny gave her arm a reassuring squeeze. "I believe it's gotten you the chance at a kind of love and happiness you never could have known with that other man in St. Paul, Emma. Ryan's a little slow to come around, not to mention wary and distrustful and *hurt,* too, I think, but he's soon going to come to realize what he's got right under his nose—a wonderful wife who loves him with all her heart."

"I hope so," Emma whispered, meaning those three words as she had never before meant anything in her life.

The sun was setting in a sky of crystalline blue the following evening as the Montgomery carriage reached George Gilland's ranch on Muddy Creek, located just south of the town of Egbert. Ginny, Emma, and Irene had ridden inside the carriage, each woman holding a pan of dessert dumplings on her lap, while Edward and Ryan had opted for fresh air travel and had ridden up front. Ruthie and Colleen had been so anxious to get to the party that they'd departed an hour or so earlier with Owens and Lorenzo, riding in the flatbed wagon.

"So how was your ride, Eddie?" dark-eyed Irene asked as the carriage came to a stop and Edward pulled open the door. "It got more than a little hot back here." She handed Edward the towel-wrapped pan she held on her lap and moved herself forward on the seat. "Most of all, I'm dying to know how you managed to pry Ryan away from the roundup camp to come along tonight. I don't think I've seen him at all since Emma hurt her back."

Edward glanced over his shoulder. "Ma took a ride out to the camp to talk to him this afternoon," he said in a whisper, turning back. He shrugged his broad shoulders in a helpless motion. "I think we all know how hard it is to say no to Ma once she's made up her mind that one of us is going to do something."

"I remember only too well." Irene nodded, a brief smile flitting across her graceful features. "It's too bad she couldn't come along with us tonight. I know how much she was looking forward to this dance."

"We'll just all have to hope Joey's cold gets better quickly," Ginny said brightly. "It's probably for the best she's keeping him home and keeping him quiet. I can't imagine that the dust that's going to be raised tonight would be very good for his lungs."

A few minutes later the women had exited the carriage and walked into the barn, depositing their pans of dessert dumplings on a long wooden plank table along with dozens of other mouth-watering dishes. As Emma was ushered along through the crowd by Ginny and Irene to seek out Mrs. Gilland, she caught sight of Ryan's tall form. He appeared to be engrossed in conversation with several men over near the stables, a few of whom Emma recognized from the party Maureen had thrown.

Though Ryan's presence at this dance tonight was undoubtedly of Maureen's doing, Emma wondered if he was going to continue to pretend the whole night through that she didn't exist. The only acknowledgment he'd given her this evening was to nod politely at her when she'd boarded the carriage with his sisters, otherwise . . . nothing.

Perhaps that's just how men acted at these gatherings, she tried to rationalize, noticing how the men and women seemed to be segregated into groups of their own sex. She also took note that people of all ages had come to attend the Gillands' dance; a far different mix than the perfectly attired adults who attended the glittering society events of St. Paul. Here in this large Wyoming Territory barn, newborns nestled in their mothers' arms, toddlers and children of every imaginable shape and size ran and played and whooped through the crowd, quickly mussing their neatly pressed Sunday best; a few adolescents, a few elderly, and more than a few ranch husbands and wives were dotted here and there about the gathering, but by and large, the overwhelming majority of the party-goers were men. Bachelor cowboy men, if she had to guess. They stood around in their just-polished boots, stiff clean shirts, and slicked-back hair impatiently waiting for the music to begin.

Indeed, it seemed as if the band was about to strike up. Amid the sounds of people laughing and talking were sounds of the musicians as they warmed up. Emma was amazed at the agility with which the fiddler's bow capered over his instrument's strings, and she realized that Maureen hadn't exaggerated Shorty Bissel's talent one bit. Despite her worries for Joey and her trepidation at continuing to

play the role of Mrs. Ryan Montgomery, she found she was
very much looking forward to experiencing a Western barn
dance.

The mood of the party-goers was one of festive, restless excitement. Cora Belle Gilland smiled and waved at
Ginny's shouted hello, then came over to greet the three
of them in an effusive manner. Several other women also
crowded around, and Emma found herself nearly dizzy with
trying to remember the names of each and every person to
whom she was introduced.

Thank goodness the call came for the grand march. As
the fiddler drew his bow across his stings and the call-
er took his place among the musicians, the inside of the
barn erupted into a flurry of squeals and excitement and
people searching out their partners. So much for the men
and women staying separate, Emma thought fatalistically,
wondering if Ryan would seek her out or let her stand alone.
Too short to see over people's heads, she looked down and
busied herself with examining a hangnail.

A second later her heart was in her throat and her hands
were in Ryan's, and she was being pulled toward the long
line of couples on the other side of the barn.

He'd claimed her.

The music had begun, and couples were already being
announced. Old folks and young alike were clapping in
lively time to the march, raising an incredible din inside
the large wooden structure. Though Ryan had still not said
a word to her, a secret thrill riffled through Emma at the
thought that he'd sought her out. Dare she read anything
into that, or was he just doing his duty—his husbandly
grand march duty—in the eyes of his community?

Three quarters of an hour later Emma stood at the dessert
table, knowing the answer to that question: he had danced
with her only for appearances' sake. As soon as the grand
march was over and had led into a brisk polka, Ryan made
his curt excuses and went back over near the stables, where
the group of area ranchers reconvened.

He was still over there, deep in discussion with George
Gilland and Judge Tracy and Major Garland, and a few
other men she didn't recognize. From where she stood,

she could just make out the side of his face—a face that
sent her senses spinning out of control. That brief few
minutes spent in his arms had been a little piece of heaven. Greedily she drank in the bold lines of his jaw . . .
his profile.

"Dance, ma'am?"

Emma's preoccupation was interrupted by a hopeful-
faced cowboy of eighteen years, if that. She started to
politely decline his invitation, just as she'd turned down
each and every one of the several other invitations she'd
gotten to dance—even Edward's—but there was something
in this young man's appealing grin that made her hesi-
tate.

"Aw, come on, ma'am," he encouraged boyishly, the
barn's flickering lamplight not adding the age she supposed
he hoped it would, but instead emphasizing his youth. "Just
a quick spin around the floor? You wimmen is so outnum-
bered by us men that I ain't hardly got a chance to dance
at all yet tonight. Iffin you're tired, I can take it slow wit'
ya." He held out his hands and lifted his eyebrows. "Pretty
please, ma'am?"

"For heaven's sake, go on, dear," said the apple-cheeked,
elderly woman standing next to Emma. "You've been such
a gem to stand here and talk with me."

"Well, I . . ." For some reason, Emma found it impossible
to reject this nice young man outright. With an indecisive
glance at sweet old Mrs. Getwald and a last quick glimpse
of Ryan, who was still engrossed in his conversation, she
wordlessly nodded and allowed the young man to lead her
into the midst of a rousing polka.

True to his word, Kyle, as he'd introduced himself, was
a considerate partner, as well as a surprisingly good dancer.
They finished the polka and were just settling into the
slower rhythm of a popular waltz when Ryan's tall familiar
figure suddenly loomed over Kyle's shoulders.

"Excuse me," Ryan said in a clipped tone, tapping none-
too-gently on Kyle's shoulder. His dark eyes snapped with
fire.

"Aw, shucks." Kyle glanced up in good-natured acceptance of the cut-in. "Oh, well, mister, I din't figger I'd git to

go two whole dances with her, 'specially now that I got her out here." With a nod, he backed away and allowed Ryan to step into his position.

As Ryan's arms went around her, Emma's breath caught in her throat. He held her so close, so tight . . . so intimately. The hard length of his legs and torso pressed against the softness of her breasts, her belly, her pelvis, making her mind first go numb, then snap to confused attention, thinking all kinds of crazy, reckless thoughts.

Ryan pressed even closer, then loosed her slightly, signaling to her that it was time to begin moving to the music. After an ungraceful hesitation and slight stumble on her part, they were dancing. Waltzing. Gliding. With her face directly in front of his broad chest, Emma's wits were so befuddled that she actually had to count the steps in her head at first—one-two-three, one-two-three—but then, only a few moments later, moving in perfect time with Ryan became a rhythmic, instinctual thing. If Kyle had been an accomplished dancer, Ryan was even more so. His moves were graceful, courtly, and perfectly polished. *Where had he learned to dance like that?* she wondered. *Why hadn't he ever . . .*

"I didn't like that."

Ryan's words gusted into her jumbled thoughts like wind on a forest fire. Her face was level with the broadest part of his chest, and she watched, with growing weakness, as his crisp shirt stretched tautly over the muscular flesh beneath and his manly scent filled her nostrils. "Like wh-what?" she managed to reply, feeling some intense emotion coil low in her belly.

"You. With that other man."

The circle of their steps grew smaller, then nearly nonexistent, as slowly she lifted her chin and looked into his face. The desire and emotion that blazed there were impossible not to read.

"This time apart hasn't changed anything between us, has it?" he asked, bending his head down near hers. His deep voice vibrated through her, and his breath brushed the curly wisps of hair over her ear, sending a shuddering wave of . . . *of what?* . . . through her.

She shook her head in an inarticulate manner, feeling the atmosphere of the barn suddenly become sweltering. Heavy. Breathless.

"Let's walk outdoors," he murmured, drawing his arm more tightly about her and leading her away from the dancers toward the barn door. The crowd had swelled again at least by half since they'd arrived, making it difficult to get through the masses. Ginny and Edward, along with Moira and a man Emma assumed to be Moira's husband, Billy, were at the refreshment table having a glass of punch as she and Ryan passed. Edward raised his arm and started to call out to them, but Ginny's quick tug on his arm silenced him. At the same time she gave Emma a broad smile and an encouraging, barely perceptible nod.

Whether or not Ryan had seen them, Emma couldn't say; he continued to propel her toward the wide doorway in a determined manner. A few seconds later they were outdoors, enfolded by the beauty of a flawless velvet night. The sound of the lovely waltz music coming from inside the barn blended harmoniously with the nocturnal sounds of the outdoors, and Emma thought that she had never heard anything so beautiful.

The path from the barn to the house was lit by a single lantern on a pole. In its languid light Emma could discern far more horses and carriages and buggies and wagons than had been here when they'd first arrived. All of Laramie County must have turned out for the event, she thought dumbly, recalling how crowded the barn and the dance floor had been when they'd stepped outside.

"Where are we—"

Emma's words were cut off as they precipitously rounded the corner of the barn. A split-second later, in a swift, clean motion, she was lifted completely off the ground into Ryan's arms. His mouth claimed hers in a hard, possessive kiss that shattered any last remaining doubts about her feelings for him.

As the heat between them exploded, Emma found herself kissing him back with an urgency that surprised herself. She felt so wild, so reckless, so . . . passionately aroused. Even though Ryan's strong arms held her body tightly against his, Emma felt as if she couldn't get close enough to him. Her heart pounded with the strength and speed of a horse in full gallop, her breath came in frantic little gasps, and the coil of unexplainable emotion deep within her womanhood began to throb mercilessly.

"R-Ryan," she managed to say as his lips broke from hers and traveled down her throat. Fresh shivers broke out from head to toe as his hot mouth sought out the delicate, sensitive area just beneath the angle of her jaw.

"Don't talk," he muttered, delicately flicking his tongue over her chin, then capturing her mouth once more with his own. His breathing seemed to be as erratic as her own, she realized with a thrill of feminine triumph, and the sheer heat that emanated from him was no less than that from a red-hot stove.

The gentle night breeze caressed their hair and faces, while wild winds of desire between them buffeted their senses, all reasoning. Emma could no more think coherently than she could walk, so it was a good thing that Ryan was carrying her . . . where?

Where was he taking her?

His mouth had broken with hers, and he was walking, moving, carrying her in his arms as if she weighed no more than a mite. *How could she be so nervous and so eager at the same time?* she wondered in confusion, directing her gaze first at the strong lines of his jaw, then at the web of glittering stars above them.

The sounds of the dance grew fainter as Ryan moved farther away from the barn and the other ranch buildings. Emma closed her eyes as he continued to walk, almost in some sort of dream state. For some curious reason, the farther he walked, the more she thought she could hear the rustling of wind through leaves. How could that be? There weren't any trees around here . . . were there?

She opened her eyes as they entered a grove of trees. Somewhere, farther off, she could also hear the burbling sound of running water. Gently, beneath the privacy of a cottonwood tree, Ryan sank to the ground, still holding her in his arms.

"I want you, Emma," he said simply, cupping her face in his hands.

Here, under the tree, it was nearly pitch-black. A more romantic setting Emma could not imagine, and she nodded her acceptance, her complete surrender to this man she had married.

With a muffled groan, Ryan kissed her deeply. "Hold on," he whispered a long minute later, regretfully sliding his hands from her face. Reaching out before her, Emma realized Ryan was unbuttoning his shirt. Boldly her fingers reached out to give him assistance, at the same time delighting in the feel of his warm flesh.

In an impatient motion he brushed her fingers away, yanked his shirttails free of his pants, and pulled his shirt over his head, yet his movements were tender, so tender, just a moment later as he reached out and drew her to him, then eased them both to the ground.

"Emma," he muttered against her mouth, running his hand boldly over her breast and belly, seeking, searching. "How do you get into this . . . ah, never mind." His fingers had discovered the row of fastenings hidden deep within the center fold of her pleated bodice.

Emma thought she would die of pleasure as his fingers worked downward over her breastbone. The single thought—he wants me—echoed through her head, over and over, as his hands and lips wrought exquisite torture on her senses.

"What now . . . a corset? Oh, Emma . . ." Ryan's chafing sigh was almost comical as he tugged at the offending garment. "Be honest. Do you women wear these pieces of armor to enhance your figures, or is the intent solely to frustrate and thwart male advances?"

A fresh gust of wind rustled the trees overhead and caressed the exposed flesh of her neck and upper chest. "I should think a graduate of West Point would be able . . . to manage the simple engineering feat of unfastening . . . a corset," she said breathlessly, but also with poorly disguised humor. What was the matter with her? What was happening here beneath these trees was serious, sensual business. How could it also be humorous? Reaching up to trace the planes and angles of Ryan's face, Emma discovered a smile on his lips as well.

"Oh, Emma," he whispered once her corset was unfastened. His hands glided over the silk of her chemise, fully cupping her breasts in his hands, his thumbs toying with her nipples through the slippery fabric. Urgently his mouth captured hers, and as his fingers moved downward, toward the waistband of her skirt, something between them changed.

Gone was the lightheartedness, the playfulness. Beneath the stars and wind and sky, their passion grew into something earnest and intense and reaching. With a shuddering sigh, Emma abandoned herself to this man, her husband, and to the overwhelming feelings that had overtaken her, while overhead the wild scream of a night hawk seemed to symbolize all that was within her.

The sun had just set beyond the endless Wyoming Territory horizon as a very rumpled, very travel worn, and very cross Jon Severson climbed the steps of the Montgomery ranch house. *Ryan Montgomery.* The man's name kept going through his head, over and over, and he wondered at the morals and character of the undoubtedly weasel-faced man who had preyed on the sweet innocence of a well-bred young woman.

He had been shocked to the core to learn from Michael Taylor that Emma had indeed married and taken control of her trust fund—and, from further discreet investigation on Michael's part, that a large chunk of money had been deposited in a nearly empty Montgomery bank account. The most disturbing portion of this whole situation was, according to Michael, that Emma was a willing player in this vile drama—something Jon could just not let himself believe, not even for one minute.

No way; not his Emma.

She had to have been coerced, forced, or somehow seduced into such an arrangement. *Seduced?* his mind hissed, the most unpleasant thought of all slithering through his mind: Was Emma still as pure and unspoiled as she had been when she left for the ranch?

He pressed his knuckles hard into his forehead, trying to drive away the pain that unbearably hideous thought caused inside him. Emma . . . not a virgin? Her chaste innocence was perhaps her greatest appeal. How he longed for the day he could quicken her flesh with his touch . . . then her womb with his seed.

If living with all this appalling speculation throughout the past days hadn't been difficult enough, what was worse was having to endure these torturous thoughts while having to finish up his most pressing business concerns at the office; no small matter, to say the least. It had taken several long days and late nights to whittle his workload down to a manageable level so he could depart for the Montgomery ranch.

He had vowed to himself to extricate Emma from this mess by whatever means he could, fair or foul. The very thought of his Emma being in the grip of a pack of fortune hunters sent a fresh wave of wrath coursing through him. As he crossed the porch, then beat on the door with a heavy fist, he determined that the first thing he was going to do was have her marriage to this Montgomery swindler annulled and get every last cent of her money back for her. Next, he planned on shaking her until her teeth rattled, and then he was simply going to marry her himself, as he should have months ago.

"Coming," he heard a faint voice say from inside the house. "For the love of heaven, don't be breakin' down me door!" The door opened part way then, and an attractive, petite middle-aged woman peered through the screen at him. "If you'd be lookin' for the Gillands', you've missed by miles an' miles, mister," she said kindly. Mellow lamplight shone behind her, illuminating the golden highlights of her auburn hair.

"I'm looking for the Montgomerys," he said stiffly, pulling open the screen door in an insolent and intimidating fashion. "I suggest you get Ryan Montgomery for me right away."

"Oh? You would be suggestin' that, would you?" the woman questioned, not at all daunted by his threatening demeanor. Her small shoulders squared back as she pulled the heavy door wide open and stepped fully into the opening. Her Irish brogue was thicker, more pronounced when she spoke again. "An' jus' what would you be wantin' with me Ryan?"

"I'll not share my concerns with the help," he replied haughtily, not quite believing the effrontery of this pint-sized housekeeper.

"The help?" she sputtered, a dark flush suffusing her attractive features. "I'll repeat meself jus' once more, mister: Who are you, an' what be your business with me eldest *son*?"

"Ryan Montgomery is your son?" he asked, momentarily perplexed, the pieces of the mental puzzle he had put together suddenly not fitting well together at all. Doffing his hat, he began again in a more conciliatory tone. "My apologies for my ill temper, madam," he apologized. "My name is Jon Severson, Severson Law Offices, and I have traveled here from St. Paul on behalf of Miss Emma Taylor. I understand a very large portion of her trust fund has been transferred to a Mr. Ryan Montgomery."

"T-trust fund?"

He nodded grimly.

"Well, then, Mr. Severson," the woman answered slowly, stepping back, the dark flush draining from her face. "Perhaps you'd better come inside."

Chapter
Eighteen

"Come . . . inside," Ryan muttered, completely covering Emma's nakedness with his own. His flesh burned against hers as the wind soughed softly through the leaves of the cottonwood above them, and gently the heated tip of his hardness sought the slick portal of her femininity. At the same time, he rained fervent kisses on her mouth, her cheeks, her neck, causing her to become nearly delirious with desire, with wanting, and instinctively she opened her thighs to allow him access to the core of her sensual hunger.

"Oh, Emma," he groaned against her mouth, pushing his shaft forward another fraction of an inch into her softness. "I want to come inside you."

If Emma's senses had been set aflame by the feel of Ryan's hands and mouth, this newest instrument of pleasure that pressed boldly against her threatened to consume her completely. All of it, everything . . . the taste of him . . . the smell of him . . . the feel of her blood coursing powerfully through her body . . . the sound of his harsh breathing in her ears . . . everything fused to intensify the incredible sensations occurring at the central point between them, at the juncture they were only beginning to create.

Swept away by the wondrous feelings that caused every square inch of her body to pulsate with need, she could not articulate a reply. Instead, a soft, answering, pleading whimper was all that escaped her throat.

"Did you hear something, Alan?" A woman's voice, very near, spoke in alarm. "You don't suppose there's anyone out here, do you?"

With their lips touching, the most intimate parts of their bodies touching, Ryan's body went completely rigid over Emma's. Slowly his head lifted from hers, his breathing seeming to come to a standstill.

"Don't worry, Nancy," a man's voice, just as close, soothingly replied. "There's nothing out here except you and me . . . and this blanket." As if to verify his words, the sound of a large piece of fabric being unfurled carried to both Ryan and Emma. "You probably just heard a jack rabbit, or a ground squirrel, or . . ." The man's voice deepened suggestively. "Or maybe you heard the mating call of the redheaded Alanpecker."

"Oh, Alan! You're terrible!" A squeal and giggle drifted clearly on the soft night breeze, followed by a long silence.

Emma couldn't believe what was happening. Another pair of amorous party-goers had stolen away from the dance and, thinking themselves all alone, had thrown a blanket on the ground not more than fifteen feet from where she and Ryan lay beneath the spreading branches of the cottonwood. What to do? To move from their concealed spot would surely give away their presence, but, merciful heavens, they couldn't stay here and listen to the other couple make love . . . could they?

"Still think we shouldn't have come out here?" The man, Alan, spoke in a seductive tone.

"Well . . ." the woman's voice trailed off. "The children—"

"The children are fine. They won't even know we're gone."

"Well, they were playing pretty good, weren't they? . . . You know, maybe we could try a little of this . . . or a little of that . . ." Another long silence passed before she spoke again. "You *did* like that, didn't you?"

More silence, followed by soft murmuring and the man's voice once again, this time in an urgent tone. "Oh, Nancy, honey," he groaned, "you got me hotter'n a pistol. I don't know how you keep doin' it to me after nine years of marriage, but I just gotta have you. . . ."

"Oh . . . Alan . . . oh, yes. . . ."

Across the short distance, clothing rustled, voices sighed and moaned and murmured. "Shh," Ryan whispered unnecessarily in Emma's ear, silently easing himself off her. "We're just going to have to lie low until they're finished." Repositioning himself next to her, on his side, he allowed a thick arm to drape across her waist. A long, nearly silent frustrated sigh escaped him.

Emma nodded her understanding of their predicament, though she was dismayed to discover that the powerful passions Ryan's body had evoked in hers were not immediately extinguished by the interruption of their lovemaking. Nay, her newly awakened appetite only seemed to burn brighter and stronger inside her now that he had rolled from her. His arm tightened around her as a deep shudder rocked her body, and she nearly wept with the frustration of it all.

Perhaps if she wasn't still experiencing the magnificent sensations of Ryan's warmth against her quivering, wanting flesh . . . his torso against her side . . . the fleeting brushing of his hard shaft against her thigh . . . the unfamiliar texture of hair-roughened legs next to her smooth limbs . . . perhaps if she couldn't feel any of that, she wouldn't burn in this wanton craving for . . . for what? What was her body yearning for?

The same thing Nancy's body craved, she concluded, judging by the soft female moans and impelling whispers coming from the vicinity of the blanket. Emma took a deep breath, willing the couple to finish quickly and return to the party . . . and Ryan to resume where he left off.

If Emma was yearning for completion of the act they had only just begun, Ryan was ablaze with his need to bury himself deeply inside this exquisite woman who lay trembling next to him. He was excited beyond belief, and the rhythmic, passionate sounds coming from the other couple did nothing to calm his churning sexual equilibrium.

Emma's eagerness, her softness, the sensation of her velvety warmth against his hardness, had nearly taken him over the edge. He had been a mere heartbeat away from driving himself fully into her ready sheath, which would have . . .

He swallowed hard, having, for the first time in several minutes, some semblance of a logical thought. The act of piercing Emma's maidenhood would have made her his wife. In every way.

A tingle of . . . of what? . . . ricocheted through him at that thought. Excitement? Fear? Relief? Perhaps it was a good thing that the overheated Alan and his wife, Nancy, happened along when they did. Though there was an undeniable physical attraction between Emma and him, she had never once said anything to indicate that her feelings for him went beyond that of sexual curiosity.

She was nearly always good and kind and sweet to him, however, far more so than he deserved for the often abominable way he treated her. Could that possibly mean she had deeper feelings for him?

No, her benevolent nature wasn't a clear indicator of her feelings for him, he decided, thinking of the good and kind and sweet way Emma treated every other person in his family. She was just naturally a loving person, something he had never been.

You could change, a part of him whispered. Emma was probably afraid he'd reject her if she admitted any feelings for him deeper than those of basic human consideration. In fact he could be the one to take the lead. Take the first dare. Tell her how much he thought about her . . . how much he cared for her . . . tell her he wondered if he was falling in . . .

At the thought of declaring his burgeoning feelings for Emma, the name Jon Severson popped into his mind unbidden. Hadn't Emma named Jon Severson as the man her brother wanted her to marry? She hadn't sounded at all enthused when she'd mentioned his name; in fact, it had been in a resigned tone that she'd said she supposed she'd end up marrying the St. Paul man some day.

But she *had* said was that she supposed she'd end up marrying him.

Frustration coursed through Ryan as he realized what robbing Emma of her virginity might deny her in the future.

He closed his eyes, both suffering and delighting in the feel of her pliant, naked body next to his own, and at the same time knowing that making love to her tonight simply wasn't in her best interest.

He savagely quelled the inner voice that persisted in asking if making love to her would be in *his* best interest.

Across the short distance, Alan and Nancy sounded as if they were enjoying their romantic interlude with unrestrained relish. After nine years of marriage—and how many children?—they still went at it like that? It was certainly something to think about . . .

Ryan was startled from his thoughts as Emma's hands clamped around his forearm. Her breathing was shallow and erratic, and he realized that her skin had grown damp with perspiration.

"Ryan?" she whispered in a pleading tone. "Please . . . I need . . . something. I feel like . . ."

A silent groan went through him at her candid appeal, for he understood exactly how she felt. Knew exactly what she needed. Slowly he eased his fingers downward, across her flat belly, toward the moist, heated spot he had very nearly claimed for his own.

Emma's sharply indrawn breath and tightened grip on his forearm only confirmed what he already knew. Her arms were rigid on either side of her breasts, pushing them together and making them stand at splendid attention and, as he bent his head to suckle at their erect tips, his fingers slipped within her slick womanly folds.

The sound of the other couple's enthusiastic sex faded from his ears as, with great care and attention, Ryan brought Emma to what he knew was her first climax. Denying his own release was possibly the hardest thing he had ever done, but with his self-denial came a measure of pride and satisfaction such as he had never known. Emma's gasping breaths . . . her quaking flesh . . . the tight spasms around his fingers . . .

He had done that to her. He had been the first to present her with such an intimate gift.

As she lay panting in limp relief, Ryan pressed a tender kiss on her forehead and pushed himself to his feet. At some point, Alan and Nancy had concluded their business and departed from the grove of trees near the creek. Walking out from beneath the cottonwood where Emma lay, he stood, willing the cool night breeze to carry the heat and frustration from his body. Faint strains of music and laughter from the barn carried on the night air, and a feeling rose within him, one of melancholy, making him wish that things between he and Emma could be different.

From behind him, a pair of arms tentatively wound around his waist. "Thank you, Ryan," came Emma's soft voice against his back. "I-I don't know what else to say except that."

He nodded, then turned and enfolded her slight body in his arms. "Let's go home," he said, knowing there was no way they could go back to the dance, not now.

Not after this.

During their leisurely moonlit ride back to the ranch, Emma felt the fragile, tender bonds between her and Ryan grow stronger as he began talking—really talking—to her, telling her more about himself than he ever had. Curiously she felt no shame for what had just occurred between them, only contentment and rightness. Also, there now existed between them an easiness, an unspoken harmony, and she realized she loved this big man in a way she never would have believed possible. Soon, she told herself, she'd utter the words to him . . . tell him what she wanted most in this world was to be his wife.

In every way.

It was true, she thought with amazement, realizing that the dream of opening her collectibles shop had faded almost entirely from her mind. When had that happened? In fact, aside from someday going back to mend broken fences with her brother, she didn't care if she never returned to St. Paul.

She rejoiced in the fact that the caring, considerate Ryan she'd first seen evidence of on the springtime prairie was back. But the intuition she'd had about something terrible and painful being locked inside him began resonating within her, faintly at first, then clamorously, as he haltingly told her of his break with his father, then of his years in the military.

Some gruesome thing had happened to him while he was in the military, she knew it in her very bones.

"Joey told me you didn't like fighting the Indians," she hesitantly remarked, wondering if that was the source of his suffering. "And judging from what I heard about the Meeker Massacre, it must have been . . . awful . . . to have been there. . . ." She allowed her voice to trail off, hoping he would trust her enough to unburden himself, praying, at the same time, she would have the strength to hear whatever he might tell her.

"It was."

His succinct reply hung between them as the horses plodded along over the rough prairie ground. The night air had grown chillier since they'd gotten dressed and slipped away from the Gillands' dance, and Emma shivered. It was fortunate, indeed, she thought, that Ginny and Edward planned on staying at the Gillands' overnight so they could attend the worship service that was scheduled to take place in the barn the following morning, otherwise she and Ryan would not have had this precious, important time alone.

Sliding closer to Ryan's stalwart form, she hesitantly laid her hand on his arm. "Did you have any friends in the army who felt the same way?" she softly asked, knowing the general public's dim view of the red man.

Abruptly he pulled on the reins and stopped the horses. "How much do you know?" he asked harshly, turning toward her. In the moonlight, his expression was agonized.

"I-I don't know anything," she stammered fearfully, wondering what had even made her ask that question.

"What do you know about Jim Hopper?" he demanded in a terrible voice.

"Nothing," she whispered, realizing she'd unwittingly pierced the core of Ryan's inner agony.

"Nothing? Well, let me tell you *something*, little Emma, and let's see if you still want to be within a hundred miles of me once you know what I've done."

Night sounds filled the air around them as Emma searched for the right words to say. "Whatever you have to tell me,

Ryan," she said, **nearly** in tears at the guilt and anguish she heard in his deep **voice**, "I'm sure it's not as bad as you're making it out to—"

"You already know how I failed my father," he interrupted her, shaking his hand free of her arm. One of the horses startled at the inadvertent tug on the reins, causing the carriage to lurch and rock for a moment. With an explosive curse, he set the brake and wound the reins securely around the handle. "But do you know I also failed my one and only true friend in life?" he roared, turning fully toward her. "Jim Hopper is *dead* because of me . . . *he put a bullet through his head because of me!*"

Tears trickled down Emma's face as she listened to Ryan's outpouring of sadness and suffering, and she wished there was some way she could take his pain away. Finally, his stream of words wound down, and on an impulse that came from only God knew where, Emma clambered, rather ungracefully, into his lap and put her arms around his neck. To her surprise, he didn't push her away; in fact, he seemed to readjust his position to accommodate her.

"From what you've told me, Ryan," she said, staring up into the dark planes and angles of his face, "it sounds as if your friend suffered melancholia. You didn't cause that."

"But I—"

"Shh," she said, putting her forefinger across his lips. "Just listen. You were a good friend to Captain Hopper," she said soothingly, allowing her forehead to rest, for a moment, upon his broad chest. "A very good friend. But his decision to end his life was just that . . ."—once again she looked up into glittering dark eyes—*"his own decision. Not yours."*

Emma saw Ryan's eyes close, saw his expression of misery, and then his arms went around her so tightly that she wasn't sure she could breathe. What a burden he had been carrying around! What guilt! The horrible things she'd said about him—said to his face even—came back to haunt her, and it was with that much more love and tenderness that she hugged him back, trying to communicate to his heart what brimmed over in hers.

No further words were spoken, but the feelings between them ran deep and strong in the prairie night, and they sat there, arms wound tightly around one another, for a very long time.

Enfolded within the safety of Ryan's strong arms, Emma dozed on the way back to the ranch. The slow pace of the horses, the rocking motion of the carriage, the steady rhythm of Ryan's breathing against her ear all conspired to lull her into a state of delicious drowsiness.

She awakened to a kiss on her forehead as the carriage pulled up in front of the house. "Here we are," he said gently, allowing his head to rest a moment against hers. "Why don't you go on in while I unhitch the horses?" His hand cupped her chin then and guided the angle of her face upward. "Would you allow me to spend the rest of the night with you, Emma?" he asked simply, staring deep into her eyes. "I . . . I need you."

He needed her.

She nodded her assent, feeling her heart overflow with joy. Things were going to work out; they truly were. She felt as though she were floating on air as Ryan helped her dismount from the carriage and brushed another kiss against her cheek.

Her husband.

As she leisurely walked up the veranda steps, she became aware of the dim light burning from behind the first-story front window. *Did that mean Maureen was still up*? she wondered with alarm. Was Joey worse? Quickening her pace, she crossed the porch in a rush and let herself in.

"Maureen?" she called out in a hushed tone. "Maureen, are you—oh!" She broke off as the older woman suddenly appeared in the hallway. "You're up!" she commented unnecessarily. "And you're still dressed!" Dread ran through her at the Irishwoman's blunted expression. "It's not Joey, is it? Is he—"

Maureen shook her head and replied in a peculiar, flat voice. "Nay, Emma. Joey's sleepin' like a lamb. Doin' better, actually."

"Then what is it?" she asked with growing concern. "Are *you* ill? Something's the matter; I can see it all over your face." As she stepped forward to take Maureen's hands in her own, she stopped short at the sight of Jon Severson's stiff form in the doorway of the parlor.

Shock ran through her like a lance, lacerating her blissful heart, and she was certain her features had frozen in an expression of utter horror.

"Yes, Emma, I'd say something is the matter." Jon stepped forward, speaking in his customary formal tone. His ice blue eyes flicked disapprovingly over her disheveled appearance. "And I'm here to get to the bottom of it."

Chapter Nineteen

Ryan finished quickly with the horses and cut across the yard toward the back of the house, both his step and his mind lighter than they'd been in years. He was eager to get into bed with Emma, but not for reasons of the flesh. Not tonight. What he wanted most was just to lie next to her, to feel her support, her quiet strength.

It had been hard to say the things he had said tonight to her, to bare his soul and admit his greatest failings, but there was something about the way she listened to him that made him *want* to keep talking to her. Something pure, something sensitive . . . caring . . . nonjudgmental.

Something healing.

Did he also dare hope that the warmth that shone from her heart-shaped face contained just a little love for him?

As he entered the backdoor, he heard the sound of voices farther off in the house. Emma's voice was immediately recognizable, as was his mother's, but there was another voice, an unfamiliar male voice raised in anger, that set off an immediate alarm inside him.

Years of military training and seasoning had keenly honed his reactions and his senses, and he moved through the kitchen and pantry with rapid, silent stealth, his thoughts on the safety of the two women in life most dear to him.

Exiting the pantry, he stood undetected in the near-darkness of the formal dining room, trying to make sense of the scene he saw before him in the lamplit parlor. Emma sat stiff-backed on the bench of the piano, her expression appearing as lost and scared as it had the first day she'd arrived at the ranch. His mother sat, looking shocked and tired but equally stiff, on the edge of the sofa.

Standing before them was a tall, well-dressed blond man, appearing to be unarmed, his hands planted angrily on his hips. An unfamiliar hat sat on a nearby decorative table.

"What has happened to you, Emma?" the man demanded to know. "Have you lost every bit of the common sense God gave you? Can't you see these people for the charlatans they are?" He let out a long, exasperated sigh. "Though part of me wants to believe that this woman here"—he gestured toward Maureen with a sharp nod—"had no knowledge of the grand swindle that was taking place under her nose, her son—oh, excuse me, shall we say your *loving husband*—" he added sneeringly, "most certainly had a very good idea how much your trust fund was going to swell the Montgomery coffers."

"No—that's not true!" Emma cried. "Ryan didn't even want to marry me!"

"I find that extremely difficult to believe." The blond man's voice dripped with disbelief. "Wealthy young heiress comes to failing Wyoming Territory ranch on a lark . . ."

"Really, this whole marriage idea was mine, Jon." Emma sweet voice pleaded for understanding. "After I was here, I learned the Montgomerys were in a financial predicament," she said, flashing an apologetic look at Maureen. She sighed deeply and bowed her head. "I feared I was in danger of losing my job, so I came up with this marriage . . . arrangement . . . as a way to help them out, and at the same time preserve my employment." Her voice grew progressively weaker as she spoke.

The blond man folded his hands across his chest. "I'll thank you to look at me when you lie to me, Emma," he said condescendingly.

Jon . . . Jon Severson. This had to be the beau of whom Emma had spoken, Ryan correctly assumed, outraged that the dandified St. Paul man had dared to come here. How had he gotten here? He hadn't seen any conveyance out front, or in back, but, then again, he hadn't been looking for anything out of the ordinary tonight, not with his sweet-smelling wife snuggled tightly in his arms. Though he seethed at the supercilious manner in which the tall blond man spoke to Emma, he continued to hang back in the shadows.

Waiting.

Watching.

The riotous arrangement of nutmeg-colored curls shook as Emma's head popped up. "I'm not lying to you," she said with conviction. "And the money's just on loan. They're going to pay me back in the autumn when they sell their cattle."

"Oh, I'm sure they are," the blond man said sarcastically. "And may I see the written agreement that clearly spells out the terms of your 'arrangement'?" Arms still folded across his chest, he gestured in an impatient "give it here" motion with the fingers of his right hand.

"Th-there is no written agreement," Emma admitted after a long pause, dropping her gaze once again.

Ryan watched his mother look back and forth between Emma and Jon with an unreadable expression on her face as the blond man exploded in anger. "You grew up in the home of an attorney—you have been escorted, for how long? . . . by *me, another attorney*—and you see no importance in securing a written agreement regarding the transfer of such a large sum of money?"

"I-I trust them," she answered simply, shaking her head.

"Trust!" the attorney sputtered, momentarily speechless. "Your brother is absolutely one-hundred percent correct about you not having any concept of the value of money!" he finally spat. "Nor one whit of business sense, either! For God's sake, you entered into a legal and binding agreement when you wed this man, Emma."

"We made a deal and shook hands," Emma replied defensively. "And we agreed to a quiet annulment in the fall. Our marriage is nothing more than a simple business agreement."

Ryan stiffened at Emma's words.

"A deal, you say? A quiet annulment?" The attorney's tone of voice was unbelieving. "If there's nothing more to this abhorrent arrangement than a loan and a 'deal,' then will you please explain why you and your business-partner-only husband attended a dance together this evening?"

"Well . . . I . . ."

"Did you dance with him?" Jealousy was plainly written on the attorney's face.

Emma's head snapped up. "Y-yes, but I—"

The blond man took a menacing step forward. "Suppose you tell me, Emma, just how 'married' you are to this man."

"Ryan and I are married in name only," she whispered, with a quick nervous glance toward Maureen.

"I beg to differ with you," Ryan contradicted, stepping from the shadows into the light. "After what happened between us tonight, Emma, we're married in *every* way." Three stunned faces stared at him as he stepped over to within a few feet of the rapidly coloring Jon Severson. "I suggest you take your immediate leave of us," he advised in a tight voice.

Emma gasped, clasping her hands to her breast. "Ryan, we didn't—"

"Didn't we?" he persisted in an insinuating tone. "What would you say happened down by the creek, then?"

Ryan knew he was stretching the truth about how he and Emma had consummated their marriage, but he had taken an immediate dislike to this pompous and arrogant St. Paul attorney. Not only had being called a swindler infuriated him, but also seeing Severson disbelieve and talk down to Emma made him angry enough to want to beat the man to a pulp. At this moment the idea of being permanently married to Emma was every bit worth the satisfaction of preventing the blond man from ever laying claim to her.

He tried to put aside the deep, keening hurt that had slashed through him at the way Emma had tried to assuage her former beau. Just a few hours ago she had been willing to join her flesh with his . . . and now, before the eyes of his mother and this conceited, self-important attorney, she had just negated every wonderful thing that had happened between them this evening. *Didn't tonight mean anything to you?* he wanted to shout at her.

"As there seems to be a bit o' controversy on the matter," Maureen said, breaking the black silence that hovered over them, "I'm wonderin' if you'd mind explainin' exactly what you think it takes to seal a marriage, son."

"I believe I'd like to hear the answer to that question as well," said Severson, working hard to maintain a semblance of emotional control. A vein had popped out on his forehead, his color remained a dull shade of plum, and his jaws appeared to be clamped rigidly together.

Ryan was standing close enough to the attorney to feel the heat and desperate fury emanating from him, and he hoped, truly hoped, the St. Paul attorney would give him reason to forcibly show him to the door.

He'd enjoy that.

And if he didn't know better, he'd swear a bit of color had returned to his mother's pale countenance, a glimmer of vitality to the tired hazel eyes. One of her toes began to tap impatiently against the carpet, indicating that she expected an immediate answer to her question.

On Emma's lovely face sat protest, outrage, and mortification, however. Her accusing gaze bore into him, threatening him with every manner of feminine retribution if he should speak so much as one more word of their intimacy.

With an easy laziness he did not feel, Ryan walked over to the piano bench and placed his hand on Emma's stiff shoulder, in a gesture of husbandly familiarity. "We sealed our marriage in the usual way, Ma," he said bluntly, reaching into the mass of brown ringlets and extracting a piece of grass. Holding up the bit of vegetation as though it were an inestimable piece of evidence, he nodded and looked first at his mother, then into the glacial blue eyes of Jon Severson. "Need I say any more on the matter?"

Maureen nodded and came to her feet, answering before the attorney could speak. "Aye, son, it sounds as if the two o' you are married, indeed," she declared. "An' if you wouldn't be mindin', Mr. Severson," she said, bringing her hands briskly together, "I'll be showin' you the door. We have some family business t' be discussin'."

"I'm not leaving this house without Emma!"

"I'm afraid you will be," Ryan promised, flicking the piece of grass to the floor in challenge. "In the next ten seconds, if not before."

"Emma?" Jon thundered. "What have you got to say about this?"

Emma's heart caught in her throat as she finally ventured to fully lift her gaze to the rage-maddened expression of her former beau. She wanted to tell him . . . What *did* she want to say?

What *could* she say?

Her delay in replying had already damned her in Jon's eyes, she knew. Despite the curious bolt of elation that had zinged through her at Ryan's insistence that their marriage had been made genuine, she was furious with him, simply furious at his audacity to speak boldly of something so personal. She opened her mouth to apologize to Jon, to at least tell him she was sorry he had made the trip all the way out here, but Ryan spoke instead.

"Time's up, Severson," her tall dark husband snarled, taking a step toward the attorney. "It appears Emma has nothing more to say to you."

Merciful heavens, the men wouldn't actually come to blows . . . would they? Emma wondered with alarm, watching Ryan and Jon eye each other as if they were about to engage in mortal combat. A long tense silence hung in the air, and then, in a rough motion, Jon reached for his hat and jammed it on his head.

"I'll leave for now," the blond man spouted, "but you haven't seen the last of me, Montgomery. I promise you that. This whole deal smells to high heaven." He stalked toward the parlor doorway, then stopped and turned. "You haven't seen the last of me, either, Emma Taylor. I don't know what you've gotten yourself involved in, but you can bet I'll be getting you out of it. It's the least I can do for your brother." With that, he spun on his heel and let himself out. A few moments later came the sound of rapidly retreating hoofbeats.

"So that's how he got here," Maureen remarked, folding her arms across her chest and looking from Ryan to Emma, then back to Ryan again. "He must have tied the beast down t' the end o' the porch." She nodded her head a few times. "Well, I'm waitin' t' hear it, kids. What be the truth o' things?"

"He lied about the marriage being . . . sealed," Emma finally burst out, pointing at the broad-shouldered form of the man she'd wed. "You *lied*, Ryan! How could you do that?"

"How could I lie?" His mouth hung open in disbelief. "If you want to talk about lying, sweet wife, let's talk about *your* lying! Our marriage was built on nothing but lies and trickery—*your* lies and trickery, in case you've forgotten."

Emma endeavored to speak, to defend her actions, but for some reason she was unable to find anything suitable with which to counter Ryan's very accurate charges.

"And if you're suddenly so concerned with honesty," he stormed on, jabbing his index finger at her and taking a step forward, "I dare you to make this marriage legitimate before your lofty lawyer friend comes back for you." His eyes narrowed, becoming murky with molten, remembered fire. "You certainly seemed willing enough a mere few hours ago. In fact, you begged me—"

"Oh, you *dare* me now, do you?" Emma cried, outraged, forgetting Maureen's watchful presence. "Well, I *was* willing a few hours ago, for all the right reasons, I thought." By now, everything had narrowed down to a single locus—Ryan—and her indignation grew with the swiftness of fire licking at dry tinder. "But after this episode, I have some rather large reservations about spending the rest of my life with you, Ryan Montgomery. You haven't said anything to indicate your desire to make our marriage a lasting one; in fact, all you've told me is that you want me. Well, what the blue blazes does that mean? What *do* you want?" She paused a fraction of a second to pull in a deep breath of air, continuing on with barely a break. "Do you want to make love to me or do you want to be married to me? There's a big difference there—the difference between a few pleasurable minutes and a lifetime of ups and downs. You've got to *talk* to me, Ryan," she commanded, feeling this unfamiliar anger rage inside her. "I am not omniscient, nor am I any kind of mind reader. For a while tonight, you had me believing you wanted to be married to me, but now, after this episode with Jon, all I can conclude is that you don't care so much about a lasting union between us as you do with making certain Jon doesn't want to have anything to do with me. So just take your dares, temporary husband, and put them where the sun doesn't—" She broke off, horrified that she'd begun to lapse into vulgarity.

"If 'talk' is what you want, I'll talk to you," Ryan quickly replied, his features alive with vehemence and vigor. "I wanted you tonight in a way I've never before wanted a woman, but maybe it's a good thing we were interrupted when we were." He brought the heels of his hands up to his temples in a frustrated motion and shook his head. "I can't make any sense out of you, Emma!" he finally pronounced, squeezing his temples as though his thouhts were causing him great pain. "You flounced into our home and promptly turned it upside down with all your schemes and plans and fetching little smiles—"

"I beg your pardon—" Emma began tumultuously, but Ryan's voice plowed right over hers.

"—and then you befuddled our cowhands with your sweet talk and silly mistakes and your absolutely terrible cooking. I've never seen a bunch of decent men act more stupid than when you first started working here. And I suppose you don't think you misguided Edward by flaunting your inheritance in his face? . . . Never mind what havoc you've wreaked in my life! I didn't want to get married, dammit! The three of you shoved me into it!" He threw his hands outward in an incensed, frustrated motion. "And now, one thing after another keeps happening to keep us married. Newspaper notices, people saying 'congratulations' and shaking my hand, big parties in our honor, being forced to sleep together in the same room—would someone please tell me just how long a man is supposed to submit to such a ridiculous set of circumstances before he loses his mind?" Ryan's face was suffused with color, and he stabbed his right index finger toward her. "How do you think it feels to know that my own family likes *you* better than they do me? Can you even *imagine* what it feels like to see Joey gazing at you with those big brown eyes of his—knowing that he used to look at me in the same way? You're his favorite now, not me. He doesn't even—"

"Stop right there," Emma charged, coming to her feet and pointing her index finger back at Ryan. "If you were going to say Joey doesn't love you, you're dead wrong. He desperately loves you! For heaven's sake, when we're in the kitchen he talks about you all the time, tells me how wonderful you are." She took a step toward him, shaking her finger. "You know, Ryan Montgomery, in order to get something out of a relationship, you've got to put something into it. That means you've got to give Joey your time and your attention, and you've got to . . ."

Maureen smiled to herself as she slipped from the parlor and began to climb the stairs to the second story. Ryan and Emma were in love; she was sure of it. She only hoped they'd figure it out before they shouted the house down. How Joey had slept through all the ruckus was beyond her.

Rounding the corner toward Joey's room, she thought again of how shocked and hurt she'd been to learn—from a perfect stranger!—of the financial transactions and artifice that had taken place under her very nose. After all the talk of a nearly nonexistent cash flow, Edward had led her to believe he'd made a mistake in the books, that they hadn't needed a loan after all. And she'd been so overjoyed to learn that Ryan was stepping in to help run the ranch, so eager to relinquish the major portion of her responsibilities in order to spend time with her younger children, that she hadn't noticed anything amiss.

Then there was the news of Ryan and Emma eloping. . . .

Joey's door squeaked slightly as she pushed it open. Standing in the darkness of her youngest son's room, Maureen was satisfied to hear that his breathing was deep and even, with barely a hint of congestion. *Sleepin' like a lamb,* she thought, greatly relieved that he continued to show improvement. She stepped lightly toward his bed, her lips curved into a musing smile at the distant sound of the newlyweds' affray.

Aye, she recalled, she and Andrew used to have some good go-rounds like that—more than once in a blue moon. Bending over, she placed a featherlight kiss on Joey's brow, remembering how sweet it had been to make up with her big strong stubborn Englishman. So very sweet.

Some days, more than others, she missed Andrew so much she could hardly stand it.

Joey's forehead felt cool to the touch, she noted with relief. Praise God, he was on the mend. Each time he fell ill she wondered if his final sickness was upon him, the one that would take his precious life. Tonight she'd been granted a little more time to spend with her cherished son.

As she let herself out of Joey's room, she heard the sharp slam of a door from below. The soft sound of Emma's weeping carried up the staircase to her ears, and she felt great compassion for her newest daughter-in-law. Ryan was a good deal like Andrew: bullheaded, obstinate, and never the sort of man who liked to have his failings pointed out to him. Andrew *had*, however, been the type to walk away and think things over. . . .

Perhaps all Ryan needed was a little more time to realize how much his young bride loved him—and how much he loved her in return.

Silently she closed Joey's door and set off downstairs, prepared to offer her newest daughter all the understanding and compassion her Irish heart had to offer.

Going through the motions of life during the next few days, Emma thought frequently on the words of comfort Maureen had offered to her after Ryan had stormed from the house. If what Maureen had said was true—that Ryan did, indeed, love her, then why hadn't he returned to the ranch house since the night of the dance?

She considered, too, all he had confided to her during their moonlit ride home. His feelings of disappointing and failing his father . . . his remorse for never having said the things he wanted to say to his father before the older man's sudden death . . . his abhorrence for the declining military . . . his guilt and anguish over his friend's suicide.

She'd seen such need in him that night, such emptiness, that all she'd longed to do was fill the black and empty spaces of his heart with hope and love and tenderness, and any other good thing she could find. And for a brief period of time—she was certain of it—their spirits had meshed. Bonded. Connected. She'd felt it happen, and she'd known then, in her very soul, that Ryan Montgomery was the man God had intended for her.

How could it be, then, that a mere hour afterward she and Ryan were at each other's throats? How could it be that all the good feelings were gone, replaced by such disagreeable emotions as anger and uncertainty . . . and doubt?

Such doubt.

She sighed and wearily wiped the worktable with a luke-warm dishrag, not knowing *what* she wanted out of life anymore. She had always supposed she would marry Jon at some nameless point in the future, but entangled in her heart were incredibly strong feelings for Ryan. She wanted her business-partner husband . . . but did he want her anymore?

He said he needed you, Emma Louise, her inner voice whispered to her. *Maybe he's waiting for you to make the first move.*

"Ha-low, Am-ma," Joey greeted, walking into the kitch-en. "Wunch weady?"

"Yes, your lunch is all ready," she replied with a pon-derous smile, pointing toward the large picnic basket on the floor. "What a beautiful day it is for your mother and sisters to take you on a picnic."

"Am-ma not come? Am-ma sister."

"No, Joey," she said, sighing. "I'm just not feeling up to a picnic today." *I'm just not feeling up to anything today,* she added to herself, wondering if, perhaps, her best course of action would be to let Jon take her back to St. Paul.

He'd sent a wire to her yesterday, telling her he was staying at the Inter-Ocean Hotel in Cheyenne, and that he was coming for her in two days' time. Period. Emma had no doubt that in the meantime he was seeking any and all possible legal means to declare her marriage invalid.

Knowing Jon as she did, she was certain he'd be successful at finding a way to do just that.

Tomorrow. He'd be here tomorrow afternoon. . . .

"Am-ma sick?" Joey asked, peering into her face with concern. "Am-ma c-catch Joey's cold?" He sniffed loudly, demonstrating the clearness of his nasal passages, then coughed a few times for her benefit. "Joey all better now. F-Fast cold."

"You did have a fast cold, didn't you?" Emma replied, not able to prevent herself from smiling at Joey's presentation of simple evidence. "I don't think that's what I've got, though," she added more seriously. "I just need to spend a little time by myself this afternoon."

Joey screwed up his face and tilted his head quizzically to the side, as if he were trying to comprehend why anyone would want to stay inside on what was likely to be the most beautiful day of the whole summer. "Oh. Self," he finally said, relaxing his features and shrugging. "Oh-kay, cwazy Am-ma."

"Are we ready to go?" Ginny asked brightly, stepping into the kitchen and eyeing the expressions on Emma's and Joey's faces. "Are you sure you won't change your mind and come along, Emma?"

"No . . . thanks, Ginny," she replied. "I'd prefer to be alone this afternoon."

Ginny nodded, communicating her sympathy and understanding as she reached for the picnic basket. "Well, we're off, then. Do you want to give me a hand with this, Joey?"

"*Oh-kay!*" Joey's expression was one of pure excitement as he bent to help Ginny with the basket. "We g-go on pic-nic!"

Emma fought the rush of tears that burned in her eyes while Joey and Ginny left the kitchen, awkwardly carrying the picnic basket between them. *Could she really leave this place?* she wondered with great sadness. She looked around the familiar kitchen, thinking of how intimidating a place it had been when she'd first started here—and how comfortable and homey it was to her now.

A bigger question, though, was could she leave the Montgomerys? They'd become her family in the past few months. The thought of never again laying eyes on Joey—or looking into his jolly grinning face, or hearing his expressive, unique voice, or being enfolded in his chubby arms—was nearly as painful as the thought of never seeing Ryan again.

Go back to St. Paul and make up with your family, the voice inside her whispered. Ryan didn't want her, and Joey would get over her soon enough. Besides, she thought dispassionately, she knew Joey was going to die one day soon. His passing wouldn't hurt so bad if she were hundreds of miles away. She'd just go back to St. Paul with Jon tomorrow and leave the Montgomerys behind. That would be the best thing for everyone concerned.

As she walked back to the sink and rinsed out her rag, pausing to peer out the window at a faultless June day, she deliberately closed the door to her heart, stilling the small, quiet, dissenting voice inside her that whispered Ryan Montgomery was the best thing for her.

Chapter Twenty

Ryan was examining what appeared to be a sickened calf when he heard someone call his name. Looking up, he swore at the sight of his mother and Ginny approaching the roundup camp on horseback. The calf, perhaps not quite as ill as he seemed, sensed the intrusive human's momentary distraction and, with a loud bawl and a mighty kick, scrambled free and ran to the other side of the corral, to where his mother stood outside the rope rails, woefully bellowing for him.

The painful kick caught Ryan in the left leg, and it was with vehemence that a second vulgar curse slipped from his lips. Brushing the dirt and manure from his chaps, he eyed the calf rancorously, being of half a mind to go over there and . . .

In a harsh, angry motion he removed his gloves and tucked them between his legs while he readjusted his hat, telling himsclf to keep a grip on his temper. "You might as well let him out of here," he called to Lorenzo, who had just ridden up to the corral. "I can't find anything the matter with him."

"Whatever you say, Cap'n," Lorenzo cheerfully replied. "Say, there's your ma an' Miz Ginny," he added unnecessarily, pointing toward the two women, then lifting his arm in greeting. "Wonder what your ma's goin' to talk to you 'bout this time?" he called with poorly suppressed humor. "Last time she was out here, you was goin' to a dance two hours later."

Ryan sighed, knowing full well what—or, rather, who—his mother and sister-in-law had come to speak to him about.

Emma.

In fact, he was surprised Ma had let him stew this long without coming out here to give him her two cents' worth. He'd been expecting her for days. Edward had already tried talking to him about Emma, but he'd told his brother what he could do with his words of advice. He was ready for Ma, too, ready to tell her to . . .

To what? Butt out? Mind her own business? He could hardly do that after the double-dealing they'd pulled on her. He sighed again and put on his gloves, mentally preparing himself for what was certain to be a difficult confrontation.

Emma's winsome face appeared in his mind as he thought of the heated words the two of them had exchanged Saturday night. His thoughts traveled further backwards then, settling on their romantic interlude beneath the grove of trees . . . on her naked body . . . and on the heated love they'd nearly made.

He'd wanted her. In fact, he *still* wanted her. Saturday night he'd been a hairsbreadth away from throwing all caution to the wind and recklessly linking his body—and the rest of his life—with hers, and he still wasn't sure if Alan and Nancy had offered him the biggest escape of his life . . . or had only delayed the inevitable.

How could that pint-sized, curly haired little baggage have turned his life into such chaos? he wondered with utter frustration. Emma Taylor had turned his world absolutely upside down, making him more confused than ever he'd been in his entire life.

Was Emma confused as well?

Though he'd taken an immediate dislike to the pompous and arrogant Jon Severson, he couldn't help but wonder if perhaps Severson was the better man for Emma. He couldn't compete with the attorney's dandified appearance and polished words, nor could he boast a background of wealth and power and social standing. Jon and Emma came from the same world . . . perhaps it was for the best if Severson took her back to her pampered St. Paul existence.

But even as he considered Emma and Jon sharing the rest of their lives together, a sharp shaft of pain knifed upward from his vitals to his heart, and he knew he could never bear to think of his Emma belonging to anyone else.

"Come over here, son," Maureen called from the side of the makeshift corral. "We need to talk t' you."

Ryan nodded and started off toward his mother, not knowing what it was he was going to say to her.

"Emma's leaving this afternoon," Ginny burst out as he neared them. "Ryan, you've got to stop her from leaving with that Severson man." Tearstains were evident on her dusty cheeks, and beneath the grime her smooth complexion was both blotchy and windburned.

He shrugged, feeling the knife twist sharply inside him. "That's her choice."

"She's got another choice t' make, Ryan Montgomery." Maureen spoke earnestly, pulling back the brim of her hat so he could better feel the penetrating fire of her hazel eyes, he knew.

"Seems she made her choice the other night."

"Saints above, you're a big stubborn oaf, jus' like your father." Maureen dismounted her sleek gray mare and stepped up to the corral. "Emma wants *you*, Ryan," the widow cried in exasperation, startling both her and Ginny's mounts. "Not Severson. She loves you! I know this business o' love an' marriage is all new to you, son, but sometimes you've got t' fight for your love if you want it bad enough. You don't want that other . . . *man*"—she spat—"t' be takin' her off to St. Paul an' marryin' her, now, do you?"

No. He didn't want that at all.

"Oh, Ryan," Ginny spoke, awkwardly dismounting her roan. "Emma's so unhappy. We couldn't even get her to come on a picnic with us yesterday, and when we got back, she announced she was leaving with that Severson fellow Maureen told us about. She's all packed now, and he's coming to get her this afternoon." Reaching over the rope, she placed her hand beseechingly on his arm. "She doesn't think you want her in your life . . . in fact, she thinks you hate her."

After a long pause, he grudgingly admitted, "I don't hate her."

"Of course you don't hate her," Maureen averred, clearing her throat. "Now, what will it be, Ryan? Are you goin' to let Emma go off thinkin' all kinds of terrible things, or are you goin' to come back with us an' fight for your woman?"

Fight for your woman. The sun beat down hotly on the back of Ryan's neck as his emotions vacillated wildly. Did Emma *want* him to fight for her, or would she just as soon put this whole chapter of her life behind her? He remembered her challenging him that night as to whether he wanted to make love to her or whether he wanted to be married to her—yet he didn't recall as she'd made her preferences clear about what *she* wanted. Nor had she spoken any words of love.

True, but you felt her love that night, Montgomery; you know you did.

Love. The concept was so very foreign . . . and so very overwhelming.

"Your Emma's a rare treasure," Maureen added, emotion thickening her brogue, "an' I love her like one o' me own. Joey's so devastated she's leavin' that he won't come out of his room." She sighed and looked directly into his eyes. "Can't you at least come back an' talk with her, son? With a clear head an' a heartful o' love, you'd be surprised what miracles can be accomplished."

"I suppose I could come talk to her," he finally said, dropping his gaze. "But if she wants to go with Severson, there's not much I can do to stop her."

As Emma paced back and forth across the spacious second-story bedroom Maureen had bestowed upon her and Ryan, she wondered how much longer it would take for Jon to arrive. She'd informed the Montgomery matriarch yesterday afternoon of her decision to go back home, she'd packed all her things, and now there was nothing else to do but sit here and wait.

It was simply too uncomfortable to be out about the house with the family. Since she'd given her resignation to Maureen yesterday afternoon, it was as if a pall had fallen over the Montgomerys. Maureen and Edward and Ginny had tried their hardest to talk her into staying, telling her Ryan truly did love her, but after five days of hoping and praying Ryan would return to the ranch house, Emma's fervid hopes for making a true marriage with her husband had dwindled to ashes.

But if her decision had been difficult for the Montgomery women to accept, it had been doubly hard on Joey. He'd retreated to his room last evening after hearing her news, refusing, still, to come out. Emma sighed, fussed with straightening the wrinkle-free coverlet on the bed, and promptly sat down upon it. She knew she should go talk to Joey, try to explain the truth of things to him, but she just couldn't make herself go to his door. It would be much better, she told herself, to write him once she got back home and got settled. Take her time and carefully compose her thoughts, instead of putting her foot in her mouth and bungling things . . . or looking into his almond-shaped eyes and completely breaking down.

A knock at the door pulled her to her feet.

Was Jon finally here? She hadn't heard a carriage. . . .

"Am-ma?"

Emma's heart twisted at the plaintive sound of Joey's voice outside her door. "What is it, Joey?" she called weakly, hoping he might be content to blurt a brief message through the wood, or perhaps simply push one of his paintings under the door.

"C-come in, Am-ma. Tawk." Heaven above, he sounded so pitiful. He'd lain his head against the door, she could tell by the muffled difference in the sound of his voice. "Pwease, Am-ma," he appealed once again. "Joey tawk . . . Am-ma."

"Yes, of course." Slowly she arose from the bed and walked to the door, her footsteps and her spirit both unwilling. Afraid. Reaching the door, she took a deep, steadying breath before she turned the knob and pulled.

If her heart had twisted at the sound of Joey's voice, it turned completely over at his pathetic appearance. His normally neat clothing was wrinkled and rumpled, as if he had slept in the garments the entire night, and his face was pale, with bright blotches of crimson standing out on each cheek. Perhaps the most telling sign of his despondency, however, was the fact that after a period of several weeks of not carrying around anything, in his left hand he once again clutched her hair ribbon.

"Am-ma g-go 'way now?" he asked, looking past her to the trunk that sat near the foot of the bed. The hair ribbon in his hand shook furiously, and his breathing seemed abnormally rapid.

She nodded, not trusting her voice to speak.

"Why?"

"I-I have to, Joey," she said as gently as possible, feeling tears fill her eyes. "Things between your brother and me just haven't . . . worked out very well, and it's for the best that I go back to my home and family."

"Am-ma fam-ly here!" he insisted, anguish choking his voice. "B-best wish . . . Am-ma sister, 'ever an' ever. *Joey's* sister!"

Tears spilled from Emma's eyes as she realized what pain she was causing this young man. As she fumbled for her handkerchief, she noticed the moisture glistening on Joey's round red cheeks, as well. A sob broke from her chest, and she bent her head in misery.

A peculiar noise issued from Joey, then, something between a cry and a hack, and he began coughing as if he couldn't stop. Alarm spurted through Emma's body as she heard the wet, congested quality of the adolescent's cough, his inability to catch his breath.

"H-h-hurt," he managed to say, wrapping his arms across his chest.

"Joey!" she cried, reaching for him, intending to guide him over to the bed. She nearly recoiled in shock at the searing temperature of his skin. "Oh, dear Lord, you're burning up," she wailed, fearful he might expire before her very eyes. "Maureen!" she called at the top of her lungs.

"Ginny! Irene! Anyone—help! Please come!"

Joey stumbled and sank to his knees, still hacking and choking, his color a ghastly, ashen shade of blue. Emma fell on her knees beside him, relieved to hear the sound of footsteps on the stair. "Oh, Joey, you've got to hang on until we can get you some help," she whispered, flinging an arm across his shoulders to help support him.

He nodded, indicating he understood her words, just as Irene burst into the room, followed closely by Ruthie and Colleen. "What is it?" Irene exclaimed, taking in the scene before her, her beautiful dark eyes imbued with fear. "Oh, no! Ruthie, run and get Edward right away. He's out by the barn, I think. He'll have to ride into town and get the doctor."

Ruthie immediately left to do her sister's bidding, while Colleen ran and knelt at Joey's side, opposite Emma, offering her older brother words of encouragement and support. Finally the coughing spell passed, leaving Joey shaky, weak, and drenched with perspiration. Working together efficiently, the three women stripped Joey of his sweat-soaked clothing and settled him in the big bed, propping him nearly upright with several large pillows. Irene left to get fresh, cold water with which to bathe her brother's fever-ravaged body, while Emma and Colleen took turns sponging Joey's face with a cloth soaked in the tepid water from the pitcher.

"Where's your mother?" Emma whispered to Colleen, concerned that Maureen hadn't responded to her call.

"Um . . . she and Ginny went for a ride this morning," Colleen answered evasively, rising to rinse the rag which Joey's fevered skin quickly turned from warm to hot. "They ought to be back pretty soon."

A strong suspicion took root in Emma's mind as to just where Ginny and Maureen had gone riding, but Joey began to cough again, pulling her attention from her own worries to her concern for this dear young man.

She was thankful this coughing spell was nothing like the first, and was soon over. The pain in his chest when he coughed seemed severe, though, and Emma tried to help him splint his torso the best she could. Gradually the dusky color left Joey's face, leaving his complexion pale and waxy. His breathing remained rapid, too rapid, and his eyes shone with unnatural brightness. Emma's heart contracted painfully as she noticed that he still held her hair ribbon clutched tightly in his left hand.

"Are you feeling a little better now?" she whispered while Colleen once more rinsed the rag.

Joey closed his eyes and nodded, as if it cost him simply too much energy to hold his lids open any longer. As Colleen reapplied the cloth to his forehead, Emma watched the rapid, shallow manner in which his chest rose and fell. How many times did he breathe in a minute? Forty? Fifty? She and Colleen exchanged anxious glances at his ominous appearance.

The door slammed below, and heavy footsteps soon pounded on the stair. "Has he got the pneumonia again?" came Edward's deep voice, even before he came into view.

"I think so," Emma replied, "he's—"

"Try to bring down his fever if you can, and make sure he sits up so he can . . . oh, good, you've already got him propped up," Edward said, appearing in the doorway. Ruthie arrived just a moment later, squeezed past him, and ran over to the bed.

"I'm back, Joey," she said, taking his hand, "and I found Edward. We're going to get the doctor for you, so he can make you all better."

Weakly, eyes still closed, Joey nodded.

"I'm going for the doctor now," Edward reiterated, just as Irene appeared behind him, carrying two heavy buckets. He took them from her and carried them to the bed. "I don't know how long I'll be," he said, looking back and forth between Irene and Emma, "but just keep him comfortable till I get back." Pausing a moment, he gazed into his little brother's face with undisguised concern. "These four ladies are going to work on breaking your fever, Joseph," he said in a thick voice. "You probably remember how terrible that feels, but I know how brave and strong you are."

"I be . . . bwave," came Joey's barely perceptible reply.

Edward nodded, then turned and quickly left. A few minutes later, the sound of retreating hoofbeats carried in on the light June breeze.

The next hour and a half was a blur of worry and anxiety for Emma. True to his word, Joey was brave—probably braver than all of them combined—as the four of them tearfully sponged his body with the frigid water. He coughed frequently, terrible wet sounds that came deep from within his chest. Even though his teeth begin to chatter soon after they began trying to bring down his fever, not once did he resist them or even cry out. Irene had chipped several large pieces of ice into each bucket, so the temperature of the water with which they now bathed Joey's body was markedly cooler than the lukewarm liquid in the pitcher.

"Is Edward back?" Emma exclaimed as the sound of approaching hoofbeats carried in to them. "Has he got the doctor?" She was more frightened than she'd ever been in her entire life, and more than ready to relinquish the monumental responsibility they held for sustaining Joey's life.

"I pray it's them," Irene said softly, sighing as she bent to wring out her cloth. "I don't know that we're making much headway here, Emma."

Ruthie bounded over to the window. "It's Ma and Ginny . . . and Ryan!" Her eldest brother's name was added with undisguised delight. "Ryan came back!"

"My W-wyan," Joey muttered, his eyes fluttering open for a brief moment. "Wyan c-come." His words ended in a grimace of pain, and once again he began to cough.

"I'll go warn Ma about Joey," Ruthie said, racing from the room.

Butterflies of dread fluttered to life within Emma's stomach at the mere mention of Ryan's name, even at the same time she struggled to ease Joey's pain. She was hoping she might have left the ranch without seeing him again. She didn't *want* to see him again. Lord, how was she supposed to face him after all that had passed between them. . . ?

After his rejection of her.

"My Wyan . . . love," Joey said as if he could read her mind, "m-my Am-ma." He nodded in an affirmative manner as he labored to pull air into his lungs. "Yes. Wyan . . . love."

"I really don't think so," Emma demurred, dropping her gaze, mortified that Irene and Colleen were witness to this exchange.

"Well, we happen to think he does," Colleen replied in a cheeky, yet matter-of-fact fashion, "only he hasn't gotten around to figuring it out yet." She, too, stepped impatiently to the window and peered outside. "Irene!" she exclaimed, "here comes Edward with what looks like Doc Beecher!"

Just a scant minute later the sound of several concerned voices carried upstairs from below. Emma swore Maureen appeared in the bedroom even before the kitchen door banged shut.

"Me poor, poor lamb!" the auburn-haired woman cried, running over to the bed. "Oh, Joseph, love, I had no idea you were ailin', son. Edward's brought the doctor, though, an' we'll fix you up, jus' as right as rain." Tears spilled from her hazel eyes as she took in the piteous appearance of her youngest son.

A ghost of a smile curved Joey's lips as his mother pressed several anxious kisses upon his brow. A moment later the room seemed to be filled with people and commotion, and Emma edged away from the bed, feeling out of place, as Joey's siblings crowded around and listened to the brief, concise report Irene gave of Joey's condition.

Doc Beecher was wiry and middle-aged, the no-nonsense type of man who commanded respect by his very presence. He, too, however, listened carefully to Irene before making his examination of the febrile adolescent—a thorough examination that was carried out in a kind and compassionate manner.

"The boy's got pneumonia," he concurred gravely, nodding his head several times and rummaging in his bag. "I'm going to give him an injection of morphine to slow his breathing and suppress the cough. As you remember," he added, glancing up at Maureen, "it will also make him much more comfortable. I'd like to apply chest splints once he's resting a little easier, too."

Unwillingly, Emma's gaze happened upon Ryan's broad-shouldered form as the doctor spoke, and she was relieved to note that his attention was focused on Joey, not on her. *How much longer until Jon arrived?* she wondered, hoping she might be able to slip away unnoticed in all the hubbub. She edged even closer to the door.

She could wait for Jon downstairs. . . .

"Where . . . my Am-ma?" Joey rasped, his voice faint but clear. "D-don't go, Am-ma!" Immediately he began to cough in a frightful manner.

Emma froze, her heart tearing in two.

"No more talking, young man," Doc Beecher ordered. He turned, then, and stared directly at her; in his right hand was a glass syringe with a long hypodermic needle attached. "If you're Miss 'Amma,'" he said crisply, tapping the chamber of the syringe with his index and second fingers, "I suggest you get back over here. My patient wants you at his side."

"Yes, Doctor," she murmured, ashamed, feeling all eyes upon her.

"I'm going to inject you now," the physician said, turning back to Joey. "It's going to smart a bit, but you'll soon feel much better."

"Where . . . Am-ma? . . . Sister."

"I'm right here, Joey," she said, feeling tears once more rapidly gather and spill from her eyes. Was he going to die? She didn't think she'd ever seen anyone as ill as this young man.

"H-hold . . . Joey's . . . hand . . . please?"

"Of course I'll hold your hand," she somehow managed to say, feeling Ginny's gentle arms about her shoulder, guiding her to the bedside.

"How about the rest of us clear out of here and let Joey get his rest?" Ginny said, briskly clapping her hands together. "We'll wait downstairs, Maureen," she said, ushering everyone but Maureen, Emma, and Dr. Beecher from the room.

Emma held Joey's hand over the next half hour, watching his body relax by slow degrees. Finally he slept, his breathing much more restful than before. Dr. Beecher, who had been alternately pacing about the room and stopping at the bedside to peer closely at his patient, nodded in satisfaction, although his eyes held a troubled expression.

"I can't make you any promises this time, Maureen," he said quietly, candidly, laying his hand upon the widow's shoulder, "but I'll do all I can. I don't think you need me to tell you how ill your Joseph is."

Looking up into the physician's face, Maureen nodded, then dropped her gaze back to the bed.

How could Maureen be so calm and accepting of the fact that her youngest son might soon die? Emma wanted to shriek, feeling her emotions roil wildly inside her. The blue hair ribbon lay trapped between his palm and hers, and she studied the shape and form of Joey's pudgy brown hand, trying to conceive that the chubby fingers might also never move again.

Dear God, that meant that his warm brown eyes might never shine their merry light on anyone ever again . . . that she might not hear his unique voice ever again . . . that he might never rise ever again.

The doctor's unadorned words had penetrated to Emma's very soul, unlocking the painful, powerful emotions she had tried so hard to deny. She loved Joey Montgomery with all her heart, just as she loved his brother, Ryan Montgomery, with all the passion and emotion a woman's heart could hold. There was no way she could leave this place today, not now, not when she had only just realized what was really meaningful, really important in life. . . .

A soft rapping came at the door. "Emma?" came Ginny's quiet voice as she opened the door a crack and peered in. "Emma, Mr. Severson is here for you," she said somberly. "Is Joey better?" she asked, glancing anxiously at Dr. Beecher.

"I've done what I can do," the physician replied. "It's in the Lord's hands now."

"We'll keep praying." Ginny nodded and wiped her eyes with the handkerchief she held in her hand. "Emma?" she repeated. "Did you hear me?"

Emma nodded. "I'll be down shortly," she answered hollowly, feeling the weight of Maureen's perspicacious stare from across the bed. As the door clicked shut, the older woman released a long, nearly silent sigh.

"Will you be goin', then?"

"I-I don't know," she answered truthfully. "Ryan doesn't—"

"Just tell him o' your love for him, daughter," the older woman advised, nodding sagely. "Speak what's in your heart." A small, beautiful smile lit her sorrowful features for just a moment, as if she were reliving a joyous memory from long ago. "It'll be enough," she promised tenderly, fingering a lock of her son's damp hair.

It'll be enough.

The phrase echoed through Emma's mind as she descended the stairs. Her knees trembled beneath her skirt, and she wondered if she possessed enough courage to confess her love for Ryan. Even if she did, what would he say? Would he—

"It's about time," came Jon's impatient voice from the foot of the stairs. "These people have kept me waiting for more than a quarter of an hour."

"I'm sorry, Jon," she apologized distractedly, trying at the same time to mentally select just the right words to tell Ryan of her feelings for him. "I'm sure Ginny told you of Joey's . . . is Ryan still here?" she asked Ginny, who stood near the tall blond man, wearing an extremely uneasy expression on her round face.

Her sister-in-law inclined her head in the direction of the parlor.

"I won't permit you to speak another word to the swindler," Jon ordered, taking her arm. "Come along. We're leaving right this minute."

"Let go of me, Jon," she said, trying to pull free of his less-than-gentle grip. "You're hurting my arm."

His fingers only squeezed harder at her request, and he pulled her toward the front door.

"Jon . . . wait! I can't go . . . I have to—"

"I suggest you let go of the lady, Severson," came Ryan's menacing voice from behind them.

"You're not in a position to make suggestions, Montgomery," Jon replied nastily. "And when I get done with you, you won't be fit to—"

"Let go of her," Ryan repeated, taking a step closer to them.

Emma's eyes met the snapping dark gaze of her husband, pleading with him. . . .

"We're leaving this minute, Emma," Jon asserted, turning his back on Ryan and pulling her another few steps forward.

"No, Jon, stop!" she cried. With a great, wrenching motion, she managed to tear her arm free of his grip. "I'm not going with you. I can't!"

"Oh, yes, you can . . . and you are," Jon threatened, reaching for her.

In a flash, Ryan positioned himself between her and the rapidly angering attorney. "It seems the lady doesn't care to accompany you."

Emma heard Ginny suck in her breath at the open challenge that hung in the air between the two men. From the corner of her eye, she saw her sister-in-law back away toward the parlor doorway, to where her husband stood at rigid vigilance. The wide-eyed faces of Irene, Ruthie, and Colleen were visible a safe distance behind their brother.

"Get out of my way, Montgomery, or I'll be back out here with the law!" Jon shouted. "I've got *legal authority* to remove Emma from your corruptive presence. You've got no right to keep her here, and by the time I get done with you, you washed-up West Point beast, you'll wish you'd never tangled with me. In fact, I'll *own* this hovel—"

Jon's words ended in a strangled grunt as Ryan's fist connected with his jaw. "That's *Captain* to you," Ryan said harshly, delivering several more blows, seemingly in the blink of an eye. "And unless you want more of what you've just had a taste of, I suggest you shut your mouth and walk out of here while you still can."

"Why, you—" Jon roared, shaking his head in pain and disbelief. He lunged at Ryan, blood pouring from a cut on his lip. The two men hit the foyer wall with a loud crack that shook the very foundation of the ranch house.

"Do something, Edward!" Ginny screamed, wrapping her arms tightly around her husband and burying her face in his chest.

Emma stood dumbly, in disbelief, as the two men struggled savagely in the hallway. *This isn't really happening,* she told herself. *None of this is really happening. You're going to wake up, and it will be a . . .*

"What in heaven's name is goin' on down there?" came Maureen's distraught voice from the top of the stairs, snapping Emma from her stupefied fog. "Will someone please get that horrible man out o' me house? *Right now!*"

"Stop it," Emma cried, bursting forward and catching hold of the bunched muscle of Ryan's upper arm. "Stop it, right now!" she commanded, pulling on his arm with all her might. "Don't fight!"

Instead of her action giving Jon an opening to land a damaging blow, it provided the attorney the opportunity to slide heavily down the wall and strike the floor with his haunches. The blood from his lip, and now his nose, had spread over his shirt and coat, and he unsteadily withdrew a handkerchief from his pocket.

"Leave him alone," Emma insisted, her tugging force not moving his solid body one bit. "I don't want to go with him because . . ." She took a deep breath and blurted out the truth. "I don't want to go with him because I love you," she admitted sincerely, her voice cracking. "I want to stay here with you . . . if you'll have me."

Slowly Ryan's arm lowered, and he turned to face her with a grim but astonished expression on his lean, handsome face. "You actually love me?" he said with a tinge of wonderment in his deep voice.

She nodded, tears spilling from her eyes.

"Why didn't you ever say so?"

"You never said anything about love, either," she retorted, tears clouding her vision. "How was I supposed to know how you truly felt about me?"

"Well, I . . ." His voice trailed off. A split second later she was in Ryan's arms, her feet dangling nearly a foot from the ground. "I love you, Emma," he said emotionally, bending his face to hers, "and I want you to be my wife for all time."

"Oh, Ryan, yes," she whispered, feeling her heart soar. "Yes!"

"Oh, yes!" Emma heard Ginny's voice echo, just as Ryan's lips captured hers in a hesitant yet promising kiss, a kiss in which she felt the pledge of a lifetime commitment.

"Let me give you a hand up, Severson," Edward said cheerfully, brushing past the two of them. Emma heard a rustle of fabric, then an agonized groan.

"Here, take my handkerchief, too," Edward added in a cordial tone. "Yours looks a little . . . used. There; that's it. All right, Severson, time to go outside."

"Just a . . . minute," came Jon's slow, strained voice.

Ryan turned to face the attorney, allowing Emma to slip sensually down the length of his body. His arms remained wound possessively about her, and he hugged her tightly to his side.

Emma winced as she took in Jon's bloody, bruised appearance. The fire that had been present in his icy blue eyes was no longer ablaze, however. "Are you certain of the choice you've made, Emma Louise?" he grudgingly asked, his normally impeccable manners lapsing as he spat blood into Edward's handkerchief.

"I am," she replied, feeling Ryan's arms tighten around her.

Severson nodded, defeated, and turned to leave.

"Jon, I hope you might tell Michael of my love for my husband," she added humbly. "I am deeply grieved by the gulf that exists between him and me."

"I'll do what I can," he allowed, not turning around. "Goodbye, Emma." Edward turned the knob and pulled open the front door.

"Farewell, Jon," she said softly. "Thank you . . . for caring about me."

The tall blond man, followed by Edward, walked out into the afternoon sunshine without reply.

After a long silence the hallway burst into an explosion of joy and laughter and celebration. Ryan and Emma were mobbed by tearful, ecstatic Montgomery girls and women, each of them blurting out her happiness for the young couple.

Maureen descended the stairs slowly, a glad yet bittersweet expression on her face as she took in the scene below.

Across the distance, Emma's eyes met hers, and despite the widow's deep worry for her youngest son, Emma felt the love and approval in Maureen's hazel eyes shine upon her, as well as the unspoken message that said, "See, daughter? I told you it would be enough."

Wrapped securely in the cocoon of her husband's love, Emma silently mouthed "*Thank you*," to the older woman, as Ryan's head once more bent toward hers.

Chapter
Twenty-one

"Well, you've been a real wife for a week now," came Ryan's lazy voice from beside Emma. "Any regrets?"

Emma groaned and stretched, finally opening her eyes to the early morning light that painted the bedroom in hazy tones. A cool breeze ruffled the curtains, but she lay on her side, warm and cozy and securely snuggled within the curve of Ryan's arm. "Mmm," she murmured, closing her eyes once more, feeling perfectly at peace.

"I'll take that as a 'no,'" he said, chuckling, tracing the outline of her arm with his free hand. "You know, I've been thinking about something that you said." His hand wandered downward to stroke her jaw, then lower, caressing the prominence of her collarbone.

"What's that?" she murmured, struggling to overcome the blissful lassitude that threatened to pull her back into slumber. Warm fingers stroked her neck, her cheek, sending delicate waves of pleasure rippling through her body . . . making her think of the sensual pleasures those fingers had given her last night.

She sighed.

"When we came home from the dance last week, you asked if I wanted to make love to you or wanted to be

married to you—and you added something about there
being a difference between a few pleasurable minutes and
a lifetime of ups and downs."

"Yes?" she hesitantly asked, her sleepiness falling away
as she recalled her angry words. Shame and worry rose in
her, and she turned within Ryan's arm to face him. "Did
I . . . offend you?"

"Only with the part about the *few* pleasurable minutes,"
he said with a wolfish grin, pulling her on top of him in
a sudden motion. His hands traveled down the length of
her back to settle on her rounded buttocks. "Admit it, dear
wife," he said, pressing himself boldly against her, "I give
you *many* pleasurable minutes each day."

"Oh, Ryan," she said with a giggle, dropping a kiss on
his proud nose. "Yes, you do give me more than a few
pleasurable minutes each day." She sobered then, thinking
of Joey. "I wonder how your brother did last night?"

"Well, I'd take it as a good sign we didn't hear anything,"
he said, his expression showing concern, as well. "His
progress is slow, but seems to be getting a little better
every day."

"I was so worried about him," she confessed, allowing
her cheek to seek the comfort of Ryan's chest. "I don't
know what I would have done if he'd died."

"The thought of Joey dying scares me, too, Emma."
Ryan's voice was low and honest. "But when the time
comes, we'll face it together," he promised, his fingers
stroking her curls. "And somehow, with our love, we'll
get through it."

Emma lay quietly atop Ryan's powerful body for several
minutes, listening to the cadence of his breathing, to the
slow, deep thudding of his heart. "I've been thinking a lot
about Joey," she finally said, lifting her head to gaze into
his eyes. "And about children like him who aren't fortunate
enough to be born into such loving families. I . . . I knew
another boy like Joey once," she added, dropping her gaze
to study the muscular planes of her husband's chest. "He
suffered an appalling existence."

Ryan was quiet, providing an accepting silence for Emma
to say more—or not, whatever she might wish. He sensed

she had something weighty on her mind, something with which she'd been struggling.

"Do you remember why I came out here in the first place?"

Ryan quelled the urge to make an impudent remark. "To earn money so you could open your business," he replied cautiously, wondering where she was headed.

"Well, I've been thinking about my business . . ." she began, trailing off.

"Emma, I don't care if you want to run a business," he said sincerely, proud of the pluck his petite wife possessed. "But I've got to warn you, I don't think a collectibles shop is going to turn much of a profit in the middle of the prairie."

"No . . . I've changed my mind," she said with sudden firmness. "Establishing a collectibles shop was a rather frivolous way for me to spend a portion of my inheritance. I have a lot of money, Ryan, and if you have no objections, I've been thinking on how I might put my fortune to use to help those less fortunate souls in life. Those who aren't lucky enough to have anyone to love them."

"What do you mean?"

"Well, I don't know exactly . . . maybe building a sort of home, or something. I've read about a doctor in England who operates a very different kind of institution for the mentally subnormal. He believes in providing his children with a loving and nurturing environment, so that they can grow and thrive and learn. . . . After being around Joey," she added earnestly, "I know these things are possible. I just feel a need to do something, Ryan, to turn something bad into something good."

Ryan was quiet for a moment, digesting her words, realizing there was a whole lot more to Emma Montgomery than what met the eye. "I'll support you any way I can," he said, enfolding her in his arms, realizing how truly lucky he was to have this kind and charitable woman for his wife. "In fact, something you once said to me has given me much occasion to think about what I can do to turn something bad into something good."

"I'm almost afraid to ask what I said to you."

"Only something about being brooding and self-absorbed, as I recall," he said with a rueful chuckle. "And then you went on to define heroes and has-beens."

"Oh . . . In the carriage . . . after our wedding." Soft fingers came up to caress his cheek. "I'm sorry, Ryan. Those were terrible, hurtful words, and I've regretted saying them many times."

"Why? They were true."

"Well—"

"Well, nothing. You were right, Emma. I haven't said anything yet, but I've been toying with the idea of a future political career," he said slowly. "I know there's no way I can bring back Jim Hopper, and there's no way one man can change the army from the inside out, but maybe as an elected official, I can have some sort of say in the way our government is run." Even as Ryan said the words, the idea grew in appeal to him.

But even more appealing at the moment was the tantalizing sight of Emma's lovely smooth thigh, exposed by the rumpled, tangled sheets. Impatiently pushing away the linen, he groaned at the sight of her fully naked body atop his.

"Oh, Emma," he muttered, pulling her head toward his and giving her a long, deep kiss. Urgent passion flared between them, the kind of passion of which he knew he'd never tire. "I love you so much," he admitted, glorying in the feel of her silky flesh, her soft curly hair, her warm breath against his face. "I don't know what the future holds for us, sweet wife, but I'm looking forward to facing it with you, one day at a time."

AUTHOR'S NOTE

If you're ever traveling through southeastern Wyoming on I-80, present-day Pine Bluffs is a stop well worth your time. Also known as the "Frontier Crossroads," the Pine Bluffs area is rich in both history and prehistory. The Texas Trail Museum and the High Plains Museum are open from Memorial Day to Labor Day, but the Pine Bluffs rest stop—complete with hiking trails and in-progress archaeological digs—is open to travelers year round.

I'd also like to mention that *Buckeye Cookery and Practical Housekeeping* is indeed a real book. The 1880 version is currently in print, thanks to the efforts of the Minnesota Historical Society Press. For more information on obtaining a copy of this fascinating five-hundred-plus-page volume, please write to the order department of the Minnesota Historical Society Press, 345 Kellogg Boulevard West, St. Paul, Minnesota 55102-1906.

Although "dessert dumplings" are not to be found in *Buckeye Cookery,* they are an old (and absolutely heavenly!) family favorite. If you would like a copy of the recipe, please send a self-addressed, stamped envelope to P.O. Box 333, Circle Pines, Minnesota 55014.

I am also delighted to receive mail from my readers—please address any correspondence to the above post office box.

If you enjoyed this book, take advantage of this special offer. Subscribe now and...

Get a Historical

No Obligation

If you enjoy reading the very best in historical romantic fiction...romances that set back the hands of time to those bygone days with strong virile heros and passionate heroines ...then you'll want to subscribe to the True Value Historical Romance Home Subscription Service. Now that you have read one of the best historical romances around today, we're sure you'll want more of the same fiery passion, intimate romance and historical settings that set these books apart from all others.

Each month the editors of True Value select the four *very best* novels from America's leading publishers of romantic fiction. We have made arrangements for you to preview them in your home *Free* for 10 days. And with the first four books you

receive, we'll send you a FREE book as our introductory gift. No Obligation!

FREE HOME DELIVERY

We will send you the four best and newest historical romances as soon as they are published to preview FREE for 10 days (in many cases you may even get them before they arrive in the book stores). If for any reason you decide not to keep them, just return them and owe nothing. But if you like them as much as we think you will, you'll pay just $4.00 each and save at *least* $.50 each off the cover price. (Your savings are *guaranteed* to be at least $2.00 each month.) There is NO postage and handling—or other hidden charges. There are no minimum number of books to buy and you may cancel at any time.

FREE
Romance
(a $4.50 value)

Send in the Coupon Below

To get your FREE historical romance and start saving, fill out the coupon below and mail it today. As soon as we receive it we'll send you your FREE Book along with your first month's selections.

Mail To: **True Value Home Subscription Services, Inc. P.O. Box 5235 120 Brighton Road, Clifton, New Jersey 07015-5235**

YES! I want to start previewing the very best historical romances being published today. Send me my FREE book along with the first month's selections. I understand that I may look them over FREE for 10 days. If I'm not absolutely delighted I may return them and owe nothing. Otherwise I will pay the low price of just $4.00 each: a total $16.00 (at *least* an $18.00 value) and save at least $2.00. Then each month I will receive four brand new novels to preview as soon as they are published for the same low price: I can always return a shipment and I may cancel this subscription at any time with no obligation to buy even a single book. In any event the FREE book is mine to keep regardless.

Name _____

Street Address _____ Apt. No. _____

City _____ State _____ Zip Code _____

Telephone _____

Signature _____
(if under 18 parent or guardian must sign)

Terms and prices subject to change Orders subject
to acceptance by True Value Home Subscription
Services Inc

0012-3

Diamond Wildflower Romance

A breathtaking new line of spectacular novels set in the untamed frontier of the American West. Every month, Diamond Wildflower brings you new adventures where passionate men and women dare to embrace their boldest dreams. Finally, romances that capture the very spirit and passion of the wild frontier.

___RENEGADE FLAME by Catherine Palmer
  1-55773-952-8/$4.99

___SHOTGUN BRIDE by Ann Carberry
  1-55773-959-5/$4.99

___WILD WINDS by Peggy Stoks
  1-55773-965-X/$4.99

___HOSTAGE HEART by Lisa Hendrix
  1-55773-974-9/$4.99

___FORBIDDEN FIRE by Bonnie K. Winn
  1-55773-979-X/$4.99

___WARRIOR'S TOUCH by Deborah James
  1-55773-988-9/$4.99

___RUNAWAY BRIDE by Ann Carberry
  0-7865-0002-6/$4.99

___TEXAS ANGEL by Linda Francis Lee
  0-7865-0007-7/$4.99

___FRONTIER HEAT by Peggy Stoks
  0-7865-0012-3/$4.99

___RECKLESS RIVER by Teresa Southwick
  0-7865-0018-2/$4.99 (July)